MW00568414

PRAISE FOR
THE STARCHILD COMPACT

Hard sci-fi reminiscent of Arthur C. Clarke or James P. Hogan, with a geopolitical twist worthy of Tom Clancy or Clive Cussler.
— Alastair Mayer, Author of the *Tspace Series*

The Starchild Compact is a compelling read from the first page. Robert has written a fantastically engrossing space mystery that takes place in our own backyard. This book brought me moments of wonder that I had experienced when I originally read Clarke's *Rendezvous with Rama*. This does what science fiction is supposed to do: capture our attention, speculate about the wild possibilities, and take us just beyond our previous imaginings. But this book is not all spectacle. Robert tackles some of the more personal issues of space travel that often go overlooked, with a particular eye toward the role of religion in that exploration. It is a masterful hand that can manage the personal and cultural response to the wonders of space and still present those wonders as pure delight. Robert has done that in *The Starchild Compact*. From the beginning to the end, this is a must read.
— Jason D. Batt, *100 Year Starship*
Author of *The Tales of Dreamside* series

In *The Starchild Compact* Robert Williscroft has said in print what a lot of people (myself included) would like to do about present day threats to our democracy and way of life, but don't have the means or cojones to do it. He also courageously extrapolates tomorrow's mores and the religious direction our society is taking. Williscroft tackles these germane and "heavy" issues while crafting a fascinating novel that is hard to put down. I have to admit that I was moved to tears, because I could not be with the space travelers to come back and see Earth's future. I'm looking forward to both the prequel and sequel.
— Myron R. Lewis, Co-author with Ben Bova of several
SF stories including parts of *The Dueling Machine*

In the not-too-distant future, a spacecraft heads toward Saturn's moon Iapetus to investigate whether it is an artifact, while a terrorist stows away on board hoping to destroy the science that contravenes the tenets of his religion. All this builds up the tension and suspense in this fascinating science fiction novel. Each part of this book solves and

PRAISE FOR
THE STARCHILD COMPACT

unfolds another mystery, making the book incredibly hard to put down. The research and science are impeccable. I marveled at Williscroft's imagination in conjuring up this story. I highly recommend this book!

– Marc Weitz, Past President
The Adventurers' Club of Los Angeles

Intrigue and danger blended with today's societal problems carry the reader on an unexpected journey. An internationally diverse spaceship crew comes together to face their differences and potential dangers on a voyage to Saturn's moon Iapetus, which they suspect may be an artifact. Their individual quirks and cultural traditions come face-to-face with the reality of a new paradigm with global repercussions when the crew discovers irrefutable evidence that the builders of Iapetus still have a presence in the Solar System. Highly recommended!

– Matthew Severe, Author of *The Lariat Thief*

Robert Williscroft once again delivers. Readers unfamiliar with Williscroft will be amazed at the depth of his characters and his meticulous science and engineering. *The Starchild Compact* is a remarkable story of politics, intrigue, science, engineering, and daring-do, driven by imaginative speculation. Nine exceptional men and women from divergent backgrounds undertake a voyage of discovery. Against a backdrop extrapolated from today's headlines, they struggle to accommodate their differences, while meeting the challenges a hostile universe throws at them as they journey to Saturn's moon Iapetus, all-the-while dealing with a Jihadist stowaway from the Persian Caliphate, a nuclear-armed world-power in this near future. They determine that Iapetus is an artifact, and discover its origins. They meet the Founders – direct descendants of the Iapetus architects. Who and what the Founders are profoundly affect not just the voyagers and the Jihadist, but all the peoples of Earth.

The author's fans, as well as new readers who crave anthropological authenticity and honest-to-Heinlein Hard Science Fiction, will be thoroughly delighted with *The Starchild Compact*.

– Martin Bloom, President
The Adventurers' Club of Los Angeles

THE STARCHILD COMPACT

BY

Robert G. Williscroft

For Erika –
RGWilliscroft
Aug 2016

Starman Press, 2050 Russett Way, Carson City NV 89703
or email
rgw@argee.net

Library of Congress Control Number: 2014919993
Williscroft, Robert G.
The Starchild Compact / by Robert G. Williscroft
Illustrated by Gary McCluskey & Robert G. Williscroft
Cover design by Gary McCluskey
Internal photos courtesy NASA's Jet Propulsion Laboratory

Keywords: Australia, Caliph, Caliphate, Canada, China, Eber, France, Gas Core Reactor, Germany, Hard Science Fiction, Hard Sf, Houston, Iapetus, India, Islam, Israel, Jihad, Jupiter, L-4, Lagrangian, Launch Loop, Mars, Moon, NASA, Noah, Persia, Qur'an, Russia, Saturn, Science Fiction, Sf, Spacecraft, Spaceship, Starship, Tether, United States, VASIMR

The Starchild Compact is a work of fiction. It contains real science and engineering, but the author makes no claims for the authenticity or accuracy of these elements. Any reference to individuals, governments, corporations, or entities is purely the result of the author's imagination. Any resemblance to actual persons, living or dead, or governments, corporations, or entities, past or present, is entirely coincidental.

ISBN 978-0-9821662-9-1
1. Fiction – Science Fiction. 2. Fiction – Action/Adventure.
First Starman Hardbound edition
First printing, December 2014

TABLE OF CONTENTS

ACKNOWLEDGMENTS

Several people contributed to the creation of this book.

Most significantly, my wonderful wife, Jill, whom I first met when I returned from a year at the South Pole conducting atmospheric research, and who finally consented to marry me nearly thirty years later, pored over each chapter with her discerning engineer's eye. She kept my time-line honest, and made sure that regular readers could understand fully the arcane details of the VASIMR driven Cassini II, and the Founders reactionless space drive.

Jill's daughter, Selena, and twin sons, Arthur and Robert, also read the manuscript, and provided their insights.

Hard Science Fiction author Alastair Mayer reviewed the manuscript and offered his scientific, engineering, and editorial insight.

Marc Weitz identified a couple of problems that I had missed, to the betterment of the book.

Matthew Severe corrected my Russian and pointed out several typos.

A tip of the hat to Gary McCluskey for bringing Cassini II to life with understandable illustrations. He also turned the cover from a sketch and several ideas into the breath-taking scene that graces the front of this book.

It goes without saying that any remaining omissions, errors, and mistakes fall directly on my shoulders.

Robert G. Williscroft, PhD
Centennial, Colorado
December, 2014

FOREWORD

The idea for this novel came to me while I was examining NASA photos of the *Cassini-Huygens* September 10, 2007, flyby of Iapetus. I was struck by the equatorial ridge, which is twenty km high and as wide. I also was struck by what appeared to be regular hexagonal sections on the surface paralleling the equator, and that some of these sections appear to have collapsed. I researched Iapetus further, discovering that its density (1.09 gm/cm^3) is way too low for a solid moon consisting of rock. Street wisdom is that it consists mostly of ice, but Iapetus appears to be rocky, very rocky. *Could it be hollow?* I thought.

I found a website constructed by Richard C. Hoagland: *enterprise mission.com*. Hoagland conducted a whole series of intricate examinations of the surface of Iapetus. Like myself, he was struck by the oddities he found, including something that appears like a two km high spire. He saw regularity over the entire surface, and pronounces on his website that Iapetus must be an artifact. Hoagland is a *true believer*, but I couldn't put aside the thought that there might be a derelict starship orbiting Saturn.

As part of my research, I made the fascinating discovery that Homer mentioned Iapetus as the brother of Cronus who ruled the world in the Golden Age. His wife was Clymene, daughter of Oceanus and Tethys. One of his sons was Prometheus who brought fire to the people of Earth. And here is the clincher: According to Hesiod and Horace, the sons of Iapetus were the ancestors of mankind.

As far back as the 1980s, I have been writing about Islam. I studied the *Qur'an*, and learned about the doctrinaire differences between the Sunni and Shi'a. I became concerned that the nature of Islam was such that devout Muslims would be compelled to Jihad, in order to bring the entire World under Shari'ah law. I wrote about the potential danger of an Islamic state, a Caliphate bent upon World domination. Over the years, I have written many articles on this subject.

In *The Starchild Compact* I bring together these three ideas – Iapetus as an artifact, the sons of Iapetus as the ancestors of mankind, and a Caliphate as a super power – in a logical concatenation that

I will not pursue further here, so as not to give the entire plot away.

This is a hard science fiction novel. It contains a lot of meticulously researched science. The numbers are real, and all the elements that make up an interplanetary voyage are consistent and true to physics and engineering as we know it today. For the Earth-based technology, everything is either possible today, or will be possible in the near future, based upon a narrow extrapolation of current science and technology.

The Founders' technology is more speculative. It is extrapolated from the leading edge of modern physics, related to black holes, particle physics, and the frontiers of astrophysics and cosmology.

The *Cassini II* spacecraft is the unifying element of Part One. Its design is intricate and detailed, although I didn't dump all that detail into the body of the story. Several drawings and some descriptive text precede the second chapter. Those of you who wish to understand exactly how *Cassini II* is put together will find that information in this section. Referring to these illustrations will help you follow the crew's onboard actions, and should make Part One more enjoyable.

I included a Cast of Characters to help you sort out the thirty individuals with more than a passing role in the story.

Historical elements are accurate within the scope of literary license. I have characterized the behavior of various ethnic and social groups based upon their historical roles in recent Earth history. My intent was not to disparage any particular group, but to describe how these groups might actually behave when confronted with the events that unfold in *The Starchild Compact*.

In the final analysis, however, *The Starchild Compact* is a work of fiction, a story of how things might have been, and what could happen in the near future, especially should my speculations about Iapetus carry some validity. You be the judge!

Robert G. Williscroft, PhD
Centennial, Colorado
December, 2014

DEDICATION

This book is dedicated to my step kids – the twins, Arthur and Robert, and their older sister Selena, and to their dad who entrusted them to me. They have made me feel years younger, and I found a friend in their father.

CAST OF CHARACTERS

CASSINI II CREW

Jon Stock – Captain; 50; American veteran of the first manned Mars expedition; educated at U.S. Naval Academy (Navy Captain); Cal Tech PhD Systems Engineering. (Later, Captain of Starchild.)

Dmitri Gagarin – First Officer and Astrogator/Systems Engineer; 40; Russian with ties to the first human in space; educated at Peter the Great SRF Military Academy (Colonel in the Russian Air Corps); Moscow Institute of Physics and Technology. (Later, retired to private life as a Hero of the Russian Federation.)

Ginger Steele – Second Officer and Communications Officer/Astrogator; 31; Australia – Hobart, Tasmania. Zulu heritage, blue-black skin. Facial features are classically Arian with the striking dark overcast; educated at University of Melbourne – Electrical engineering and astronomy; Stanford – MSc Electrical engineering/communications technology; PhD Planetary astronomy. (Later, crew member of Starchild.)

Ari Rawlston – Mission Specialist and Chief VASIMR Engineer/Computer Engineer; 41; Israeli; educated at Technion Institute of Technology. (Later, crew member of Starchild.)

Noel Goddard – Mission Specialist and Space Structural Engineer/Backup VASIMR Engineer; 45; Family ties to the famed early 20th century rocket scientist, carrying on the family tradition as a rocket engineer – Canadian branch of the family; educated at Princeton Univ. MSc Engineering. (Later, retired to private research at his personal lab in Canada.)

Michele deBois – Mission Specialist and Biologist/Botanist; 35; French; Sorbonne graduate in biology; PhD fm Berkley in Biology. (Later, the First Lady of France.)

Chen Lee-Fong – Mission Specialist and Systems Engineer/Backup VASIMR Engineer; 40; Chinese; educated at University of Science and Technology of China in Beijing – engineering; MSc rocket design – MIT. (Later, retired to private life as a celebrated Chinese Peoples Hero.)

CAST OF CHARACTERS (CONT.)

Carmen Bhuta –Medical Officer and Language Specialist/ Botanist; 32; Indian from an old wealth family; educated at University of Delhi; Harvard Medical School. (Later, India's Minister of Health.)

Elke Gratz – Mission Specialist and Historian/Computer Engineer; 33; German; Technische Universität Darmstadt. (Later, crew member of Starchild.)

Saeed Esmail – Stowaway; 30; From the Persian Caliphate; Fanatical Shia.

MISSION CONTROL

Rod Zakes – Mission Director; later Iapetus Federation Ambassador to Earth; even later President of the Iapetus Federation; 47; Served on the 1st Mars mission with Jon Stock; educated at Duke University, Aerospace Engineering.

OTHER CHARACTERS

Marc Bowles – American President; later Director of the Starchild Institute; 55; Navy Seal; Medal of Honor recipient for heroic actions in the war on terror; educated at Ohio State (NROTC); Harvard Law school (following military service).

PERSIAN CALIPHATE

Ayatollah Khomeini – Caliph of the Persian Caliphate
Eskandar Ali Jinnah (Alex) – Ismaili sleeper, a Nizari Hashashiyyin
Ismail Suleiman – Senior Caliphate General

MOSSAD HQ

Daniel Ben-Gurion – Head of Mossad

THE FOUNDERS

Noah – Founder Patriarch (remained on Earth circa 11th Century BCE)

Vesta – Founder Matriarch; Physician/Surgeon (remained on Earth in the present time)

Shem (h) – Son of Noah (remained on Earth circa 11th Century BCE with Persia)
Persia (w) – Artist & Poet

Cast of Characters (cont.)

Sons of Shem:

Eber (h) –Founder Leader (later, crew member of Starchild).
Azurad (w) – Research Physician /Biologist (remained on Earth in the present time)

Asshur (h) –Physics/Communications (remained on Earth in the present time).
Ishtar (w) – Writer/Historian (later, crew member of Starchild).

Aram (h) –Electronics (remained on Earth in the present time).
Sarai (w) – Civil Engineer/Explorer (killed in an accident during 1st Earth sojourn).

Arpachshad (h) –Engineer/Warrior/Weapons specialist (later, crew member of Starchild).
Rasu'eja (w) – Warrior/Weapons specialist (later, crew member of Starchild).

Lud (h) – Physician/Surgeon/Biologist (remained on Earth in the present time).
Shakbah (w) – Biologist (remained on Earth in the present time).

THE STARCHILD COMPACT

BY

ROBERT G. WILLISCROFT

PART ONE

On the wings of eagles...

Cassini II *on extended tether*

Chapter one

Saeed Esmail prostrated himself toward Earth, nearly 400 million kilometers back in the direction of the Sun. He felt his stomach heave, and vomited blood on his prayer mat, and wondered aloud why Allah had abandoned him. At that moment he was hit with massive weight, several gees at least, and a twisting, wrenching, totally disorienting surge that made no mental or physical sense. In his weakened state, all Saeed could do was let his body be tossed from wall to wall inside his tent, and hope that he would not tear the airtight fabric. He heard somebody screaming, and then his stomach heaved again, and bloody vomit filled the space around him, flying this way and that, finally collecting on the tent walls. The lights went out, and someone still was screaming, but as the wild gyrations began to settle into a repeating pattern, Saeed realized that he was the one screaming...and he couldn't stop. He reached for his head, pulling out fistfuls of hair...and he screamed again. He retched, but his stomach was empty, and only a little bit of blood mixed with spittle left his mouth, flying at an odd angle to the tent wall...and he screamed, but quieter now, and screamed some more, but quieter still, until his screams morphed into a frightened whimper as he curled into a tight ball on his prayer mat.

#

A subdued bong captured Saeed's attention. A comforting female voice announced, "In five minutes we will pitch over and commence our arrival burn at El-four. Please make sure you are securely strapped into your seat, and that you have stowed any loose items you might have been using during the transit. Remain securely fastened in your seat until the arrival announcement tells you it is safe to unbuckle and move about."

Saeed checked his harness, and curiously looked out the port. He saw nothing but stars, more stars than he had ever seen, and off to the rear, the beautiful blue marble that the earth had become – *praise be to Allah.* Then the star field began to rotate, accompanied by a slightly higher pitch from the gyros that penetrated into Saeed's conscious perception. The blue marble moved with the star-studded sky until it was positioned above the capsule's port bow. While this happened, Saeed felt no movement. His only sense was that the sky had rotated, as if Allah had reached out and rotated the heavenly backdrop with His mighty hand. Weight returned with a popping hiss as the kick thruster ignited for a few seconds burn. As his weight vanished again, the gyros whined, and the sky began to move from right to left. In short order Saeed could see the Moon through the ports on the other side of the capsule. It appeared no larger than it did from the Earth, but the left side was one that Saeed had only seen before in holographs. He could not see the Mirs Complex, although he knew it had to lie off the starboard quarter. Weight returned again for about a minute as the restartable kick thruster slowed their velocity to match the orbital velocity of the Russian Federation built Mirs Complex as it circled the Earth in the Moon's orbit, 385,000 kilometers ahead of the Moon.

Several clanks and surges later, Saeed felt his normal weight gradually return as the capsule nestled into its berth in the capsule arrival bay of the main Mirs Ring, and picked up its rotational speed.

Bong. "Welcome to the Mirs Ring," a bright female voice announced. "It is now safe for you to unstrap and move about. You may disembark to the left side of the capsule. Lavatory facilities are located immediately to the left of the passageway. Your personal belongings will be available in fifteen minutes at the baggage handling dock down the passageway to the right. We know you have choices when traveling off-planet. We thank you for using Slingshot, and hope you had a pleasant trip, and that you will think of us the next time you leave Planet Earth."

Saeed stepped out of the capsule and hurried to the men's room. Although the passengers had been warned about not drinking before the flight, and all the passengers had been issued absorbent diapers an hour before leaving Baker just in case, Saeed, as a faithful Muslim, abhorred fouling himself, and had held off, *by the grace of Allah*, until arrival.

While awaiting the baggage, Saeed checked the construction schedule for *Cassini II*, and then perused the poster-size diagram of the spaceship. *Cassini II* was a sixty-six meter long twelve-meter wide cylinder, divided into three modules – a twenty meter long crew module, called the Pullman, a twenty-three meter long equipment module, called the Box, and the twenty-three meter long power module and engine cluster, called the Caboose. The large Iapetus-bound spaceship had been constructed entirely at Mirs, about a hundred kilometers away on the opposite side of the main L-4 complex. All three modules had been built in place.

#

Over the next several days, Saeed mingled with the *Cassini II* provisioning crew that verified the final loadout of the Box and the provisions stored in the Pullman. Another, more technical crew completed the final installation and testing of the gas core reactor and the advanced VASIMR engines that would drive *Cassini II* to Saturn in record time.

On the final day, prior to the flight crew arrival, the transport tug that ferried the provisioning crew to and from the massive spaceship experienced a catastrophic seal failure where the tug attached to the Box. The entire crew was suited up except, apparently, one Saeed Esmail, the newest provisioning crew member. Searchers found bloody pieces of his suit and a few helmet shards on a trajectory that would ultimately have taken them to the Moon. They never could quite figure out what had actually happened to Saeed, but it was obvious that he had somehow managed to shatter his nearly unbreakable helmet, and rip himself and his tough suit to shreds as he depressurized. The conclusion was that an untracked small meteor, two or three millimeters in size, had gotten him, and somehow maybe even caused the catastrophic depressurization of the tug. Saeed Esmail was not the first casualty on the project, although the consensus was that he might have been the last.

#

After ejecting the bloody suit pieces and helmet shards from a trash lock in the outer bulkhead of the Box, Saeed worked his way into the hiding place that he had created during the loadout wedged against the outer wall at right angles to both lower level accesses. It was an airtight polymer tent of just over five cubic meters, with its own oxygen supply and scrubber. It would keep him alive during the transit to Iapetus. He had the freeze-dried food, water from the emergency supply, and he could dump waste out the waste lock. His Link with its collection of holofilms, books, and the *Qur'an* would keep his mind occupied for the projected four-month trip. He examined the four burst transmitters that had been included in his life pack. About the size of a softball, each was designed to be ejected through the waste lock, orient itself with the ship to its rear, extend a gossamer parabolic antenna, and do a circular search for Earth, using a very limited supply of compressed gas. Then, using a high-density charge, the device would transmit a series of encrypted bursts until the charge was consumed. Saeed was to deploy the first at the tether extension, the second following the Jupiter boost, the third when they arrived near Saturn, and the fourth was for whatever circumstance warranted a special transmission.

In his hideaway, Saeed prostrated himself facing Earth, he hoped, and recited his prayers, adding a personal thanks to Allah for keeping him safe thus far, and on line to accomplish His holy mission.

#

Jon Stock stepped out of the launch loop capsule at Mirs Ring and made a beeline for the men's room. "Those capsules need a latrine," he muttered to himself as he splashed water on his face. Steely blue eyes stared out at him from the mirror. His hair was gray and cropped short above a craggy, clean shaven face that testified to his fifty years. A lean, muscled 183-centimeter frame belied those same years. He wore the uniform of a U.S. Navy Captain, his left chest bedecked with ribbons. One stood out top center, jet black, framed in silver, with a golden image of Mars attached to the center – the Mars Expeditionary Medal. Jon was the second in command on that first expedition to the Red Planet. When Commander Evans was killed in a freak accident on the surface, he assumed command, saved the mission, and brought the crew back. Now he commanded the international crew of *Cassini II* on an expedition to Iapetus. They would travel five times further than any human had ever gone before. And what awaited them at their destination might very well change human history forever.

Iapetus... Jon reviewed what he knew about Saturn's iconic moon. In 2004, the *Cassini-Huygens* spacecraft flew by Iapetus. Iapetus proved to be unlike any other moon. The surface seemed to display an intersecting grid of geodesic sections, something not normally found in nature. A narrow mountainous wall extended around Iapetus at the equator, so that the moon looked something like a walnut. Iapetus' density was far too low for a moon that appeared solid, but if Iapetus were substantially hollow, then the numbers worked out just about right. Several of the "geodesic sections" appeared to have collapsed inward, revealing what could be interpreted as complex structures underneath the surface layer. A tall, very narrow structure extended from the surface at one point, like a towering spike a kilometer high. Like the "geodesic structure," this spike had no "natural" explanation.

In September 2007, the *Cassini-Huygens* spacecraft made another relatively close transit of Iapetus following the equatorial wall, revealing that the wall consisted of a series of mountains up to twenty kilometers high, following each other in series, none side-by-side. It also supplied further details on a series of equally spaced craters on a line parallel to the equatorial wall and halfway between the wall and the North Pole.

Iapetus had remained a mystery. It was very difficult to imagine that all the things discovered by *Cassini-Huygens* were natural. The implications of the discoveries being artificial were staggering. As more and more information was gathered by space telescopes in orbit around Earth, on the Moon, and at the Mirs Complex at L-4, the possibility that Iapetus could have an artificial origin became quite real. The initial concept for a human investigation of Iapetus had been put forward by Launch Loop International (LLI), the consortium that had built Slingshot as an entirely civilian operation, followed by several other launch loops around the world. While there was lots of pushing and shoving by the governments of the territories where the launch loops were located, in the final analysis, most people considered a launch loop as something akin to an airline company, and in the end, most of the loops were left in civilian hands, although governments exercised whatever control they wished.

Iapetus, however, was seen by the world's major players as a potential prize like none other. If Iapetus turned out to be an artifact, eloquent spokespersons from various governments argued, then it belonged to all the people, not just to the greedy corporations that found it. This argument fell on sympathetic ears of a world population that had grown used to being told what to do by *benevolent* governments. When LLI partnered with their former rival, Galaxy Ventures, to form Iapetus Quest, they found themselves faced with an unusually consolidated array of governments united in their opposition to a privately funded and operated Iapetus operation. The United States, in its still dominant position on the world stage, muscled itself into the leadership slot in the newly recast government owned and operated Iapetus Quest. The international debate had raged on how to structure the crew of *Cassini II*. Many had argued for a civilian crew, structured however they wanted. Eventually, by negotiated treaty, arm twisting, back-room dealing, and even outright bribery and coercion, an international crew was assembled that represented the interests of the participating nations.

Because of the politics, the crew members not only had not trained together, but with a couple of exceptions, they had not even met. Jon had reviewed the material supplied by each crew member's respective government to the point where he felt he practically knew each individual. As he strolled toward the Great Room, Jon reviewed what he did know about several crew members.

He had met Canadian Noel Goddard at several conferences dealing with VASIMR engine technology. Goddard was his space structural engineer and one of the backup VASIMR engineers. He traced his roots back to the famed early 20th century rocket scientist, taking much pride from the connection. His immediate family was well-to-do, and he was tall, thin, and wiry. Jon respected him, but they had little in common, as exemplified by Jon's love of fast sports cars and Goddard's preference for luxury sedans – the larger, the better.

Jon had actually served on two occasions with Israeli Ari Rawlston, and considered him a friend. Ari was his Chief VASIMR Engineer and backup computer engineer. He stood 173 centimeters, with short curly dark hair and dark eyes – looking every bit the Semite he was. Jon was privately aware of Ari's Mossad connections, but the official papers did not mention it, and Jon kept this information to himself.

As Jon made his way to the Great Room where he expected to meet with his crew, Colonel Dmitri Gagarin, his Russian First Officer, caught up with him, resplendent in full uniform of the Russian Air Corps.

"It looks like both our governments made us dress up," the Russian said as he snapped a salute.

Jon instinctively returned the salute, and then smiled and held out his hand.

"Please, Colonel, let's drop the military protocol." They shook hands.

"That works for me, Captain." The Russian's English was nearly perfectly enunciated, with only the slightest trace of a guttural accent that betrayed his Russian origin. "Please call me Dmitri." He removed his peaked hat to reveal a shaved pate. He was a bit shorter than Jon at 178 centimeters, but was more stocky, and gave the impression of a tough guy who could handle himself in any situation, despite his forty years.

Although Jon needed to establish his authority from the outset, he was keenly aware that they were all strangers thrown together to satisfy the whims of a political world that had no concept of what it took to cross a 1.5 billion kilometer void, a distance so vast that a radio signal took nearly one and a half hours to get there from Earth. Such a trek would be difficult enough with a crew that knew each other, that had trained together, that was used to military structure and discipline. Only he and the Russian came from a military background, which Jon suspected might be more hindrance than advantage, especially with his First Officer. Jon was well aware that the only reason he was Captain, and not Dmitri, was the American muscle within the controlling government consortium.

Jon and Dmitri stood before the expansive window looking out into the star-studded backdrop of the Mirs Complex. The view moved slowly from right to left as the great multiple wheel station revolved to create one gravity at the rim where they stood.

"Magnificent view, isn't it?" Dmitri said with a sense of home-grown pride. The Mirs Complex was a private operation built and run by a consortium of firms led by a Russian based company, the Mirs Corporation that started out building deep submersibles for the old Soviet Academy of Sciences back in the late twentieth century.

"Gentlemen," a pleasant female voice with a soft Australian lilt penetrated their thoughts. The two men turned to see a very tall slender woman with blue-black skin and startlingly green eyes. She carried her Zulu heritage with obvious pride. "I'm Second Officer Ginger Steele," she said, extending her hand first to Jon and then to Dmitri. Her skin was smooth and her grip was firm. Ginger's close-cropped kinky black hair emphasized her long neck. By any measure, she was a beauty, and well aware of her impact on those around her. She wore a simple, elegant pale blue pantsuit and white silk blouse, with jacket draped over her shoulders, and white pumps with just a hint of a heel.

This one could be trouble, Jon thought, as he took in her unfettered small breasts and the almost laconic way she carried her 185-centi-meter willowy frame. Ginger was his thirty-one-year-old Commu-nications Officer and backup Astrogator under Dmitri.

"I'm delighted to meet you, Dr. Steele," Jon said, locking eyes with her.

Without flinching, she looked straight back. "Likewise, but please call me Ginger."

As if by mutual agreement, they both turned their attention to the Russian.

"*Ya rad stretits'ya stoboi, tozhe* (I'm glad to meet you, too.)," Ginger said to the Russian with a slightly accented turn of phrase.

"*Spasibo* (Thank you.)," Dmitri answered back. "And the lady speaks Russian on top of everything else," Dmitri added with a wide grin. "That's good, because I don't speak a word of IsiZulu."

"Neither do I," Ginger said, "but both my grandparents did."

"Since English is the official language of the expedition," Jon said, "that won't be a problem anyway."

"But it should be French," a slightly husky female voice toned in from behind them.

They all turned to take in a 165-centimeter, well-toned woman with shoulder length blond hair and green eyes. She wore a one-piece green jumpsuit with a neckline designed to display her ample assets to their best advantage. On her feet she wore the latest fashion in women's off-earth foot wear, slightly clunky appearing boots that actually were made of a soft artificial chamois. Her pose somehow broadcast a covert sensuality that Jon could not quite pin down. Had he not been aware from her record of her thirty-five years, he would have placed her in her late twenties.

"Dr. deBois, I presume," Jon said, squeezing the hand that she proffered in a slightly palm-down position, as if expecting it to be kissed.

"Michele deBois," she said with a coy smile, "Mission Specialist, biology and botany." She turned to Dmitri and brought her lips to both Dmitri's cheeks in the traditional French fashion, and then lifted herself on tiptoe to do the same with Ginger, pausing momentarily to brush her lips. Jon was certain that they had exchanged a few quiet words.

"*Mon Capitaine,*" Michele said, brushing her lips against his cheeks. "I save the best for last, *non?*" she said, with the slightest of French lilts.

"I would have to take issue with that," Jon said, glancing at the tall Australian.

"*Oui*...You're right," Michele said, moving next to Ginger and taking her hand. "The *Capitaine* must be right, *non?*" Her eyes twinkled and a husky chuckle escaped her lips.

And I thought Ginger would be trouble, Jon said to himself, and turned to greet the next arrival. "Folks, please say hello to Noel Goddard."

Handshakes all around with another tiptoe French welcome from Michele. Jon thought it interesting that Noel and Ginger stood eye-to-eye when they shook hands. Noel wore plain shirt and trousers, although a trained eye would have distinguished that they were absolute top-of-the-line. His shoes, likewise, were the best money could buy.

The next arrival was Chen Lee-Fong, the Chinese systems engineer and second backup VASIMR engineer. He seemed shy, and like the rest of the crew, did not show his forty years. Chen shyly shook each proffered hand, and flushed crimson to his short cropped dark hairline when Michele greeted him in the traditional French fashion.

"I am happy to meet you all," he said in flawless, unaccented English, but with an overtone that said he was not a native speaker. His smile remained tentative as he brushed his hands against his dark trousers in what appeared an unconscious effort to remove the foreign touch. He wore traditional business attire, and seemed unaware that with its normalcy, he appeared somewhat out of place in this crowd.

At that moment they were joined by a woman dressed in a peculiarly mannish pin-striped suit, but that on her, nevertheless, appeared distinctly feminine. She was a couple of centimeters taller than Michele, and wore her medium blond hair in a pixie cut that made her look younger than her thirty-three years. Although she was not the ravishing beauty of a Ginger, nor the sensual figure of a Michele, Jon decided that she was every bit as pretty – just different, and then he chided himself at making these comparisons in the first place. *I am, after all, the Captain*, he sub-vocalized as the newcomer introduced herself.

"I am Elke Gratz," she announced, adding a bit of German burr to her pronouncing her surname. While introducing herself, she stood at what Jon instantly recognized as attention, and bowed slightly from the waist, as she shook each hand in turn – a single, definite pump. Jon noticed that Elke responded in kind to Michele's French greeting, and this time it was Elke who initiated lips brushing lips.

"Elke is our historian and computer engineer," Jon announced to no one in particular. "Welcome to the *Cassini II* crew, Elke."

The crew members chatted among themselves, getting to know one another, at least on some superficial level. Several minutes later a petite, beautiful woman dressed in an Indian Sari approached them. Her long black hair hung straight down her back, and she sported a scarlet bindi on her forehead. Jon stepped up to her and took her hand, drawing her to the group.

"Please meet Dr. Carmen Bhuta, our ship's physician," Jon said with an expansive smile.

"I am so pleased to meet you all," Dr. Bhuta said, her words flowing smoothly from her beautiful face, carrying a hint of the language as spoken by the upper echelon of Indian society. "What an adventure this will be!"

Jon added, "Dr. Bhuta is also our language specialist." Responding to a couple of lifted eyebrows, he said, "I know that all of you are multi-lingual, and so could also qualify as a language specialist, but this talented woman has specialized in the creation of language, in how to bring an unknown written language to life. We all hope, I am sure, that her special skills will find some use before the end of this expedition."

"Now," Jon announced into the light conversation his comment had launched, "we only await our Chief VASIMR Engineer."

As if on cue, Ari Rawlston approached the group with a purposeful stride. "Sorry I'm late, folks," he said in absolutely native, born-in-the-USA English. "Some last minute matters regarding the VASIMR drive test tomorrow." Ari made the hand shake rounds, accepted Michele's kisses, and paused to punch Jon in the arm. "How's it hanging, Old Buddy?" Then he launched into a technical description of the next day's engine test.

The Cassini II Spacecraft

Cassini II: A sixty-six meter long cylinder, divided into three modules – the Pullman, a twenty meter long crew module, The Box, a twenty-three meter long equipment module, and the Caboose, a twenty-three meter long power module and engine cluster. The Pullman, Box, and Caboose are constructed of an aramid-based, radiation tolerant polymer that is stronger than steel, but far lighter. The cylinder walls consist of two layers a half meter apart, filled with a rigid foam polymer. This foam absorbs a significant part of incoming radiation, while slowing down the rest, without breaking down in the process. An additional layer between the foam and the outer walls consists of a viscous transparent polymer that cures to a hardness approaching that of the aramid-based polymer when exposed to hard vacuum. Should the cylinder skin be pierced by anything, the polymer would flow to the opening, sealing it, and then cure to a hard patch.

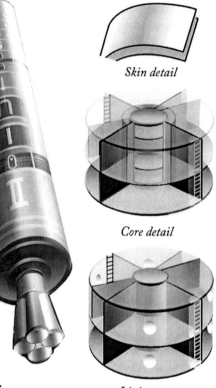

Skin detail

Core detail

Living spaces around Core

The Pullman: Twelve meters wide. Six three meter thick levels, one atop the other like a stack of poker chips or a roll of coins. Nestled

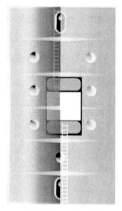

Pullman detail showing Core

inside the twenty meter cylinder at its center is an inner core cylinder six meters long by four meters wide. The six levels are separated by material similar to the cylinder walls, a quarter meter thick, reinforced by vertical stabilizers radiating out from a center strength member that extends the entire twenty-meter length of the Pullman. Viewports penetrate the outer walls in each living space, the Captain's quarters, the common area, and twice in the recreation level. They are meter wide circular ports made from a radiation absorbing crystalline sapphire matrix that has two polarizing layers whose alignment is governed by the intensity of incoming visible radiation – the brighter the light, the more polarized the ports. The space between the sapphire layers is filled with the same transparent viscous polymer that forms the filler in the outer walls.

The Core: (in the center of the Pullman) Surrounded by a meter thick water-gel jacket, so that it doubles as the radiation safety zone. The water can be extracted as an emergency water supply, or even a source of oxygen. The upper one-and-a-half-meter space is devoted to liquid oxygen storage. Next is the two-meter high Command Center – often referred to as the Core. The bottom two-and-a-half meters contain the module stabilizing gyro. The Command Center is accessible along the axis from Levels 2 & 5 by offset ladders that maintain the integrity of the radiation shields.

The Box: Twelve meters wide, twenty-three meters long. Two three-meter levels above two six-meter levels with a one-and-a-half-meter end cap at each end. A meter wide reinforced cylinder containing a ladder runs through the length of the three-meter levels into the upper six-meter level. The three levels can be accessed from this core cylinder.

The Caboose: Four sections – (1) a three meter high, twelve meter wide local control module; (2) a ten meter long, twelve meter wide fuel module; (3) a four meter long, three meter wide cylindrical gas core nuclear reactor; (4) a six meter long, four meter wide engine cluster.

DETAILED DESCRIPTION OF CASSINI II
CONSTRUCTION AND LAYOUT

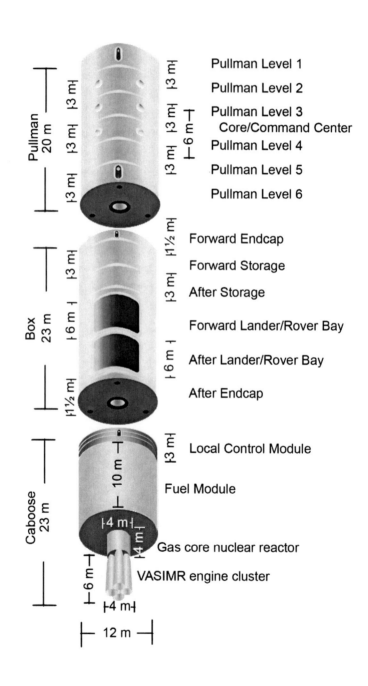

The Pullman:

Pullman Level 1: Water recycling machinery and pumps; storage for consumables and spare parts; airlock to space.

Pullman Level 2: Captain's personal quarters occupies one-half; the other half houses electronics and a common area for the crew that includes the Canteen.

Pullman Level 3: Two pairs of individual living quarters (outboard of the Command Center) that share a common lavatory between each pair; accessible by two ladders from Level 2 and two from Level 4, offset ninety degrees from the lavatories.

Pullman Level 4: Two pairs of individual living quarters (outboard of the Command Center) that share a common lavatory between each pair; accessible by two ladders from Level 3 and two from Level 5, offset ninety degrees from the lavatories.

Pullman Level 5: Recreation/exercise area to maintain fitness during freefall; a small sickbay.

Pullman Level 6: Electronics, bio-lab space, engineering shop, a botanical area designed to supply a bit of fresh vegetable variation to the crew's diet, and atmosphere equipment – additional stored oxygen at ultra-high pressure, carbon dioxide and noxious gas scrubbing machinery with oxygen recovery, circulation blowers, and electrolysis equipment for emergency generation of oxygen from any source of water. Airlock center of deck connecting to the Box; airlock to space.

The Box:

Forward Endcap: Tether reel and associated equipment; top air lock connects to Pullman; bottom air lock connects to Storage levels.

Forward & After Storage: Virtually everything the expedition would need for an extended stay on or near Iapetus, including freeze-dried foods and an emergency supply of water for use in the event of a catastrophic failure of the recycling system in the Pullman. The module stabilizing gyro (between After Storage & Forward Lander bay).

Forward Lander Bay: Lander/Rover One; fuel; spare tether; spare VASIMR engine. Has a large door, called the Barn Door, that opens to space.

After Lander Bay: Lander/Rover Two; fuel; spare tether; spare VASIMR engine. Has a large door, called the Barn Door, that opens to space.

After Endcap: Tether reel and associated equipment; top air lock connects to After Landing Bay; bottom air lock connects to Caboose.

The Caboose:

Local Control Module: Local Reactor Control Panel; Local VASIMR Console; storage for critical reactor and VASIMR spares.

Fuel Module: Insulated storage tanks for liquid hydrogen; the module stabilizing gyro.

VASIMR Engine Cluster: Four Variable Specific Impulse Magnetoplasma Rocket engines (VASIMR for short).

Chapter two

The next day found all nine crew members in the Pullman, settling into their respective quarters. Jon had decided to designate the third deck as female country. Ginger and Michele were directly below him, sharing a lavatory, and Dr. Bhuta and Elke shared a lavatory below the common area. Below them, Dmitri and Ari, who were directly beneath Ginger and Michele, split the deck with Chen and Noel. Gender distinctions rarely were an issue in the modern world, and Jon had no thought of so-called male-female issues. He was only concerned with the physical comfort of his female crew members, since sharing lavatory facilities was the only remaining recognized area of gender differentiation. It was a no-brainer, therefore, to pair up the women. The only remaining question was whether to keep all four on the same deck, or to split them up. Given the interactions he had observed surrounding Michele's meeting the other women, the question probably would turn out to be moot anyway.

The big deal for the day was, as Ari had outlined the day before, the VASIMR test. The reactor had been activated during the early morning hours, so that by the time the Skipper and his three VA-SIMR engineers – Ari, Noel, and Chen – were ready to conduct the test, the reactor was up to full power.

The reactor was a new variable output gas core design wherein gaseous uranium-hexafluoride fissile material was injected into a fused silica vessel where it produced extremely high-energy ultraviolet light. The variable fissile density of the gas controlled the reactor's output. The VASIMR hydrogen propellant flowed around the transparent vessel, absorbing the high-energy ultraviolet, and then was directed into the four VASIMR engines. Furthermore, the outer wall of the hydrogen chamber was lined with photovoltaics that converted the high-energy ultraviolet directly into electricity. Part of this power was diverted for ship functions, and the rest drove the VASIMR engines. These engines generated high frequency radio waves to ionize the super-hot hydrogen propellant into extremely hot plasma. Magnetic fields accelerated the plasma to generate thrust. Because every part of the VASIMR engines was magnetically shielded, they did not come into direct contact with the ionized plasma. This gave the engines very long life, and enabled them to be virtually maintenance free.

The test really was very simple. Once the reactor had reached full power, it was throttled through its power range to ensure that the magnetic valves functioned properly. Then, with the reactor throttled to its lowest setting, hydrogen propellant was circulated into the VASIMR engines to be ionized to plasma and ejected through the nozzles. Remotely operated robots measured the specific impulse of the engines and any leaking neutron flux from the reactor.

In actual practice, it was a bit more complicated. With Jon hovering in the background, Ari positioned himself in the Pullman Core at the Remote VASIMR Console, the RVC, that doubled as the Remote Reactor Control panel, the RCP. Although the RVC was functionally identical to the other three consoles in the Core, it was dedicated to VASIMR and reactor control except in an emergency. He put Noel and Chen in the Caboose at the local Reactor Control Panel, the local RCP, and the Local VASIMR Console, the LVC, respectively. Radiation and magnetic field levels were constantly monitored at each station during the test. First, Ari had Noel run the reactor through its dynamic range using the local controls. It was a step-by-step process following specific protocols with a series of automatic measurements taken at each step. Then he ran through the same set of tests again from the RVC. Any significant difference in a locally versus remotely controlled step would have been cause to stop the test and determine the problem. The results of the two runs coincided to three decimal places, which was a remarkable display of engineering precision.

The VASIMR tests were run in a similar fashion, except that first each individual engine went through its paces, then they were paired for six configurations, and finally run as triplets for four configurations. Because there were so many more variables, the results between the local and remote tests were a little less precise, but still well within specs.

At the end of a long eight hours, Ari turned to Jon. "That does it, Skipper. You've got a functioning ship."

#

Saeed tensed when he heard Noel and Chen enter his level from the core cylinder on their way to the Caboose. When they continued to the lower level access, he permitted himself to relax, *praise be to Allah*. The hours passed slowly, but he filled his time with memorizing long portions of the *Qur'an*, a worthy task for a holy warrior.

Some eight hours later, when the two engineers passed through the Box a second time, Saeed barely noted their transit. He was puzzling over a turn of phrase he had discovered in the *Qur'an* that seemed to speak directly to Jihad and his own fated assignment.

Saeed read in the Qur'an at 4:74: Let those fight in the way of Allah who sell the life of this world for the other. Whoso fighteth in the way of Allah, be he slain or be he victorious, on him we shall bestow a vast reward.

Was the *Qur'an* speaking of his trip to Iapetus – the other world, or was it just referring to the afterlife? Saeed puzzled this question for the entire day, with a growing conviction that he had discovered a new truth, a truth that put him in a special status before Allah.

The Other World Warrior. He liked that phrase, hardly noticing that he had capitalized the words in his own perception.

#

Captain Jon Stock floated comfortably in his seat at the Command Console in the Pullman Core. Unlike the control console on his Mars expedition that sported flat panel displays and traditional readouts and switches, the *Cassini II* Command Console consisted of a slightly recessed holographic display tank and a Link pad. The holodisplay contained pertinent readouts that could be set to whatever display preference Jon wished. It also displayed a computer enhanced view from any one of the several dozen monoview and holocams inside and outside the ship. When Jon wasn't at the console, he could call up whatever display he wished on his personal Link. His holodisplay currently showed the launch status readouts. On his right sat his second in command, Dmitri Gagarin. His console was designated the Astrogation Console, although it was functionally identical to the Command Console. It displayed the immediate Astrogation parameters that controlled their launch. At the moment both console displays were more form than function, as the onboard computer would control the actual launch. Strategically placed throughout the Core, several holocams recorded their activities and broadcast them to an eager worldwide audience. The console displays were more for that audience than for any immediate use to Jon and Dmitri. Both officers had opted to wear their uniforms for the occasion, and had even exchanged salutes for their audience when Dmitri entered the Core a few moments following Jon's arrival.

To Jon's left, Ginger Steele occupied the Communications Console. It, too, was functionally identical to the Command Console, but Ginger was actually performing a required function as she coordinated the communication link between *Cassini II* and the waiting world. At L-4, a one-way signal was delayed by just under one and a half seconds. With appropriate manipulation and insertion of micro-delays between words and phrases, it was possible to make the delay seem to disappear. Ginger's computer controlled all this, but it still took a human touch at the "controls" to make it appear completely normal. Ginger had taken her doctorate in planetary astronomy at Stanford, which more than qualified her as the assistant Astrogator. But it was her undergraduate work at the University of Melbourne and her graduate work at Stanford in electrical engineering and communications technology that developed her skills in this area. She wore a dark blue jumpsuit that emphasized her height and unrestrained subtle curves, so that in the looks department she completely eclipsed both military officers.

Ari Rawlston was the fourth person in the Core, occupying the RVC, opposite the Command Console. Like Ginger, he wore a dark blue jumpsuit, but by common agreement, it did not do for him what hers did for her. And like Ginger, he actually had something to do when the time came – throttle up the reactor, and then energize and throttle up the four VASIMR engines. This could have been accomplished by the command computer, but both Jon and Ari were more comfortable controlling this step directly. For the launch, Ari put Noel and Chen in the Caboose at the RCP and the LVC, respectively. A local holocam flashed their jumpsuit clad images through Ginger to the waiting world to satisfy their respective governments and keep their legions of fans happy.

Doc Bhuta took station in sickbay, clad in a traditional white smock covering her jumpsuit. Her long black hair was attractively wrapped around her crown to keep it from floating freely in the zero-g. Her image, too, passed through Ginger to the world. Michele stationed herself in the botanical garden, more for her public than for any other reason. Her shoulder length blond hair was caught up in a ponytail that was flipped up over her head to form a floating golden crown, and her green jumpsuit made it abundantly clear that she was female. Jon placed Elke on the second level in the electronics section, not because she was needed there, but to satisfy her need to be useful, and to give the watching world a sense that all bases were covered. Her dark jumpsuit was professional, and was virtually indistinguishable from those worn by Noel and Chen.

Representatives of the world press interviewed each crew member. The protocol for the interviews, and even the interview order, had been worked out weeks before by government negotiators for each participant. Jon had attempted to take control of the process, but was ordered in no uncertain terms by the U.S. government liaison to back off. He was the last individual to be interviewed.

"We are embarking on an historic voyage," Jon told a worldwide audience at the end of his interview, "a voyage with immense implications. The entire world knows why we are undertaking a one and a half billion kilometer journey to a remote moon of the planet Saturn. The entire world knows what Iapetus represents – potentially. We will turn that potential into a certainty. My crew and I represent all of you. We carry with us your hopes and dreams, and for some of you, I am certain, your fears and worst nightmares. But know that we are seeking truth. We intend to follow that path, no matter where it leads. So far as it is humanly possible, we will take you with us. You will see what we see, hear what we hear, and discover with us what we discover. Thank you for letting us represent you on this epic quest. Wish us Godspeed!"

#

Jon turned to the Command Console and keyed the Link All-Call to reach everybody. "Report status," he ordered.

One-by-one, each of the crew members reported "Go" or some version thereof. This, too, was for public consumption. They had actually rehearsed it several times to get the rhythm down pat. An indicator in the bottom left of Jon's holodisplay had been green for several minutes, indicating that *Cassini II* was ready for launch. A half hour earlier, space tugs hired by the various wire services had pulled back several hundred meters. Several dozen long-range cameras in those tugs remained locked on the sixty-six meter long cylinder. At L-4, one of the deep-space astronomical telescopes turned to focus on the spaceship. Everything and everyone was ready. There was absolutely no more reason to delay.

"Throttle up the reactor," Jon ordered quietly, his words flashing around the world.

"Throttle up the reactor, aye Sir," Ari responded, and manipulated his pad, causing an indicator bar in his holodisplay to move from one end to the other, watched by eyes around the world.

Some fifty meters behind them, magnetic valves dilated to enable pressurized gaseous uranium-hexafluoride to flow into the fused silica chamber in the reactor's core. The fissile density of the radioactive gas increased rapidly, so that within just a few seconds the mixture began to produce prodigious quantities of high-energy ultraviolet light that passed through the silica walls to impact on the array of photovoltaic receptors. These cells immediately began to generate large amounts of electric current.

"At full power, Skipper," Ari announced.

"Roger that," Jon said. "Power up the engines. Set thrust to point one."

"Power up the engines, aye Sir. Setting thrust to zero point one gees." Ari used the term "gee," which was the generally accepted terminology for earth normal gravity. He set the VASIMR engine thrust for the four engines to produce a ship's thrust equivalent to one tenth the gravity on Earth.

Almost instantly, everything in the Core, and all over the ship, took on a weight equivalent of one tenth that of the Earth's gravity.

"We are underway," Jon announced.

"This is CapCom, Houston. We read you underway at eight-oh-three Zulu. All systems nominal."

"Roger, CapCom," Jon responded. "We're fine here, other than a couple of items that found their way to the deck." Jon passed a silent signal to Ginger who did something to her pad. "Terminated general broadcast," Jon announced. "CapCom, Cassini," indicating he, the Captain, was speaking, "all comms through you now."

"Roger that, Cassini. Give me a two level comms check."

"CapCom, Cassini One," Dmitri said into the circuit.

"Roger that, Cassini One."

"CapCom, Cassini Two," Ginger said.

"Roger that, Cassini Two." There was a pause of several minutes. "This is CapCom. Your systems remain nominal. Shifting to continuous standby monitoring. CapCom shifting to standby. Bon voyage, guys. We've got your back!"

#

Saeed noted the passage of the two engineers on their way to the Caboose. Not long thereafter, he felt the gentle one-tenth-g thrust, and recognized they finally were underway. He paused in his memorizing the current *Qur'an* passage to give silent thanks to Allah. He was underway to the *other world* as promised in the *Qur'an*. His holy mission, now more important than ever since his epiphany, was a reality. He barely heard the engineers returning to the Pullman, as he was fully engulfed in a spiritual rapture that overcame him as he pondered his Islamic good fortune.

#

"We're private," Jon announced to the crew members in the Core. "Ari, bring Noel and Chen up. We're on a four-hour Core watch routine with the engineer types. The Doc, Michele, and Elke will set their own hours. Dmitri, you have the first watch, then Ginger, Ari, Noel, Chen, and myself. If you're going to switch with someone, let me know please.

"Let me get out of this uniform, Skipper, then I'll take over," Dmitri said.

After Dmitri returned to the Core wearing a jumpsuit, Jon went to his quarters and removed his uniform. He glanced out the port, but could see no change. Earth was nearly centered in the round port, and as he looked at the partially cloud-covered mottled blue globe, he felt a sense of awe. Jon carried his Mars experience with an easy accommodation that surprised most people, and even caught him off guard sometimes. As one of only four people to have been there and done that, he knew that in the world's eyes, he was unique. As he looked at his home world through the meter wide port, he felt unique. They were going five times as far, and the destination was not a dead, empty world, but one that held the promise of...well, the promise of something else, something unknown in the most extravagant meaning of that word. He reveled in the feeling as he donned his jumpsuit and opened the connecting door to the common area.

Ginger stood before the port, tall, regal, and beautiful. She turned as Jon entered. "Captain...," she said, letting the word hang in the space between them.

He joined her at the port, and together they silently contemplated the unchanging stars. "Have you looked at the Moon from your quarters?" Jon asked her.

"Not yet," she answered. "I came up here instead, because...well, I'm not really certain why, but I came up here."

Elke joined them from the electronics bay. "Finally," she said.

After five minutes or so of quiet contemplation, Elke moved to one of the food lockers that lined the common area wall. "I'm hungry," she said. "Anyone want to join me?"

"I'll have a bite," Ginger said.

"Me, too," Noel said as he joined them from the central ladder way, followed shortly by Chen.

"Join us too, Chen," Elke told him, waving him over.

"Where're the other girls?" Ginger asked no one in particular.

"Right here, *ma Chérie*," Michele said poking her head out of the

ladder way, followed by Doc Bhuta, Michele passed out perfunctory
kisses all the way around, except for Jon, to whom she said, with a
twinkle in her eye, "*Mon Capitaine.*" Or were they that perfunctory?
Jon wasn't sure.

As the crew members sat in the common area, eating together
for the first time on their ship, underway, Jon noticed that Carmen
bowed her head briefly, before taking her first bite. He wasn't sure
that anyone else noticed.

Ari showed up a moment later, and Jon caught his eye, indicating
for Ari to join him in his cabin. With the door closed, Jon asked his
friend, "Is your Mossad antenna deployed? Does your gut tell you
anything?"

"Why's that, Jon?"

"Can't put my finger on it, Ari. Something I saw...something I
heard...something on holovision...something..."

"Did you hear the Persian Caliph's proclamation this morning?"

"Khomeini?" Jon asked.

"Yeh...that asshole."

"I did, but for the life of me, I couldn't tell you what he said." Jon
researched his memory. "Something about you, indirectly, I think."

"He condemned Israeli participation in this expedition – again,
like he's done a thousand times already," Ari said.

"But there was something about Jihad will continue, or Jihad
continues..."

Ari called the broadcast up on his link. They still were in range,
although the upload was patchy. When he received it, he displayed
it on his link. A quick search brought up this excerpt:

"You are stepping in Allah's preserve, may He be praised. The
Almighty will turn a cold shoulder to your efforts. He will bring Holy
Jihad to your stoop. Holy Jihad will follow you into the heavens and
cast you down, as surely as Allah is master of Heaven and Earth."
There was much more, but this caught Jon's attention.

"That's it, I think," he said. "What do you make of it?"

"It's just more same-o same-o, Jon. These idiots never give up,
do they?"

"Just the same," Jon said quietly, "I'll be glad when we are genuinely out of their reach."

Chapter three

The following morning toward the end of his four hour watch, Jon received Flash Cassini traffic on his display, designated *eyes only*. He acknowledged reception, and the display indicator vanished. A few minutes later, just before eight, Jon turned over the watch to Dmitri, and went to his quarters. The Earth had shifted from the center of his port toward the rear, and was only a small fraction of its former apparent size. They were now nearly four million kilometers from Earth, ten times the distance of the Moon. They were eating up distance at over eighty-six kilometers a second, going faster by about a meter per second for every second that passed. Roundtrip comms took nearly a half minute at this distance.

Jon called up the Flash Cassini communication on his Link, and entered his private decryption code. The duty CapCom appeared, and said cryptically, "The following message is for Jon Stock only." His image vanished, and was replaced by words floating in the display.

"At oh-two-hundred Zulu, we confirmed a velocity discrepancy for *Cassini II*. Based on the precise acceleration parameters transmitted from *Cassini II*, and the exact payload as determined from the engine test conducted after loadout, but before the crew arrived, and factoring in the measured mass of the entire crew and its effects, we have an excess of 80.93 kg of mass unaccounted for. Sometime between engine test and launch, 80.93 kg of mass was added to the *Cassini II* loadout. We are reviewing everything that occurred between those times to ascertain what we can from this end. We have recalculated the start-stop parameters based upon this new information. It will be uploaded into your astrogation computer when you give your specific authorization. We will send further Flash Cassini traffic when we have concluded our investigation. A final cautionary note. We ran exhaustive background checks on all the crew, but since governments were involved, we cannot know for certain that there is not some collusion taking place. Be cautious and watch your back."

Jon closed his Link and drew a cup of coffee from his personal spigot. He sat at his desk looking out the port beyond it at the dwindling Earth, and contemplated the startling news. Eighty-one kilograms – it could be almost anything, a missed container of supplies, an oxygen bottle, a missed piece of equipment, even a human. He thought about that for a moment – a stowaway on an interplanetary voyage. *Not likely – more the stuff of a holovision drama.*

Using his Link, Jon called Ari. "Ari, can you come to my cabin, please?"

Five minutes later Ari settled into a chair facing Jon's desk. "How long have we known each other?" Jon asked.

"'Bout twenty-five years, give or take."

"And how long have we been friends?"

"'Bout twenty-five years, give or take." Ari grinned at him. "What gives, Buddy?"

"Is there anything you need to tell me?"

"What do you mean, Jon?"

"I mean, is there anything you need to tell me...something I need to know, but you haven't told me yet?"

"Your comments yesterday, your feeling of unease...I didn't tell you that we picked up some chatter about the Caliphate trying to do something to this expedition. Nothing specific, and it disappeared almost as soon as it appeared. We heard nothing at all during the final week. Didn't seem important, so I didn't mention it to you."

"That's it...nothing else?" Jon locked eyes with his friend. "Absolutely nothing else?"

"Nothing, Jon...on our friendship, nothing..."

"Fair enough." Jon broke eye contact and tapped his Link. When the flash Cassini traffic appeared, without comment he rotated the holodisplay so Ari could read it.

A minute later Ari looked at Jon. "That's fucking crazy, Jon. They're saying we've got something or somebody onboard. It's insane!" Ari stood up abruptly, the sudden momentum change lifting him off the deck momentarily. "I should check their numbers. Maybe they got bore sighted on something, and missed it." He strode toward the stateroom door. "I should have an answer by the end of my watch."

#

During the remainder of Dmitri's watch, Ari worked on the problem. Rather than simply duplicate Houston's calculations, he opted to take another tack. He worked from the loadout manifest, verifying the mass of each item brought onboard. It was a tedious task that took him through Dmitri's watch, and well into Ginger's. Once he had derived the total mass of the onload, he combined it with the known mass of the ship itself, and compared this number to the total mass Houston had derived from the engine test. It matched to one decimal place – more than close enough.

Ari then examined the crew manifest, looking for anything un- usual. Two items stood out. Michele deBois' personal effects massed in a normal range, but the volume was about half again as much as would have been normal. Elke Gratz brought aboard a normal volume of personal effects, but they massed about fifty percent more than normal. Although neither discrepancy could have accounted for the apparently extra mass, Ari decided to visit each woman personally. He located Michele in her lab on the bottom level.

He opened the door to the space, only to find his way barred by a fine net stretched completely across a light weight polymer passage- way sealed to the door. He passed through a self-closing opening in the net, and two paces beyond passed through a second net into the lab. Michele was puttering with a tray of plants. Out of the corner of his eye, Ari saw something swooping toward him, and ducked.

"What the hell was that?" He quipped.

"Emmanuelle," she answered, "and there's Phillip." She pointed to a yellow canary – male, judging from its name. "I know, *Chéri*, no one knows yet. I suppose sooner or later..." Her voice trailed off. "You think it's a problem?"

Ari shook his head in amazement. "No, Michele, no problem, but you probably should have told someone." He gave her a warm smile.

"*Merci*, you beautiful man," Michele said, lifting herself on her toes, taking both his cheeks in her hands, and kissing him soundly and thoroughly.

Ari was slightly flustered by her unexpected response, but pleased in a way that excited him. Michele winked at him as he turned to leave.

Ari poked his head into the fifth level on his way forward, and found Elke pumping iron on the other side of the space. She was using a set of free weights that he knew were not on the manifest list. "Hey, Elke..."

"Hey, yourself."

"Never saw those before," Ari said in passing.

"Nope...brought them in my hand baggage." She grinned at him. "They work totally different in low-g." She handed him a dumbbell. "Try it."

He did...it was...and he handed it back. "Weird," he said. "Gotta go. My watch is coming up."

With the two discrepancies resolved, Ari found himself facing the same calculations using the same numbers as Houston a few hours earlier. He grabbed a quick bite in the Canteen, and then assumed the watch from Ginger. He was still tingling from Michele's kiss, and found himself comparing the two women – Ginger and Michele. In appearance they could not have been more different. Ginger's skin was blue-black, with her kinky hair cropped close to her head. Her small-breasted body was long and lithe. Her physical beauty was striking. Michele, on the other hand, was fair skinned and blond with a small tight curvaceous body that screamed sensuality. Her physical beauty was, if anything, even more striking – at least to Ari.

He thrust these thoughts from his mind as he concentrated on the calculations. He was dealing with third order derived numbers, and their derivation was tricky. Since the ship flew itself, he had nothing else to do, but follow the calculations to their inevitable resolution. Near the end of his watch he called Jon. "The numbers match," he said. "They're real."

#

Meanwhile, Elke had continued to work out in the rec room. After completing her free weight sets, she spent the next half hour on the treadmill, facing one of the ports with a view of the shrinking Earth. As she neared the end of the half hour feeling exhilarated from the exercise, she heard a sound behind her, and stepped off the treadmill, turning around. Michele had just entered the space, and caught her breath at the sight of Elke, perspiration flowing freely from her face, soaking her tank top, wetly outlining her nipples.

"*Ma Chérie!*" Michele exclaimed. "How beautiful you are!" She stepped up to Elke, stroked her finger across Elke's cheek, and put it into her own mouth. "Mmmm..."

Elke's entire body reacted to the sight of this beautiful petite woman taking pleasure from her physical exertions. She felt her nipples swell in response, and she reached out to touch Michele's lips with her finger. Michele opened her lips to accept the proffered finger.

Shyly, the two women walked hand in hand to the ladder-way and descended to Michele's lab on the deck below.

#

Jon sat with Ari in his quarters quietly discussing the situation. They had a good chuckle about the canaries, and exchanged a couple of wry comments about Elke's personal free weights. "I gotta tell you," Ari had concluded, "she certainly makes a tank top look good."

"What about our crew?" Jon asked. "I'm certain we can eliminate Noel. He's way too much part of the system – even if he is Canadian."

"I agree." Ari got to his feet and paced around the cabin. "Could the Russian have an issue with not being in command?"

"He has an issue, but I think he's a good officer. He certainly knows the command structure is not my doing."

"But could he have an agenda?" Ari stopped pacing and stared out the port. "What about Lee-Fong? He's a very good VASIMR engineer. He seems to accept his role totally."

"Yeh...but that's partly cultural. I'm not playing a cliché here, but there is no way an Israeli Semite can second guess a Mandarin Chinese. You see the world through a totally different set of filters – even if he did graduate from MIT."

Ari laughed. "You certainly have a turn of phrase, Jon, I'll give you that much." He sat back down. "That leaves the girls. Whatever it is, Ginger is not involved...I'd lay money on that."

"How about your life?" Jon asked quietly.

Ari appeared to think about it and then said, "Yeh, I think so. Ginger is clean. So's deBois, but for a totally different reason."

"And that is..." Jon was especially interested to hear what Ari had to say about the sensuous French scientist.

"Simple...Michele is totally self-absorbed. If it isn't good for Michele, she leaves it alone. Mark my words, before this trip is over, she will have gotten into each of our shorts – you included." Ari laughed. "As they say in Tel Aviv, if it's inevitable, you might as well lie back and enjoy it!"

"The Doc's a devout Christian," Jon said. "That could make her totally reliable, or a danger to the expedition, if she has come with a religion driven agenda."

"I haven't really interacted with her," Ari said. "She's a bit of a mystery to me."

"Same here. We need to keep an eye on her until we know how tolerant or intolerant she is." Jon paused, picturing her bowed head the previous day. "My guess, she's okay."

"So...what about iron pumping Elke Gratz?" Ari pulled the "l" to just behind his teeth, and rolled the "r" off the tip of his tongue.

"Elke follows the rules," Jon said. "If the German government gave her an agenda, she will take it all the way."

"But what are the odds? What could Germany possibly gain by setting us up somehow?" Ari sounded genuinely puzzled.

"Let's shelve it until we cut the engines and set the tether." Jon got to his feet. "Just keep your eyes and ears open."

#

Dmitri had spent several hours working up the exact time for engine shutdown. This never was exactly as originally calculated, even for as short an acceleration period as their two days. The reason it took so long was that he found his original time was less than what he currently calculated – sufficiently less that he was concerned. When he found that the problem would not resolve itself, when he found himself chasing his tail through a looped equation, he brought Ginger into the problem. He walked her through his calculations, and brought her to his dilemma.

"Have I missed something?" he asked her. "Did I bore sight myself into a stupid mistake?"

"I concur with every step you've taken," Ginger told him. "Can we work the problem backward to see what is causing the difference?"

Dmitri looked at her with astonishment and respect. "That's a great idea! Did that come from Melbourne or Stanford?"

Ginger's eyes twinkled. "Zulu, actually," she said. "My granddad made sure my thinking exceeded the box."

"You've got my Russian attention, Girl! Let's do it!"

In hindsight, Dmitri could see how simple the approach was. In practice, it turned out to be more involved than either of them had realized at first. But, a couple of hours later they both found themselves staring at a number floating in the Astrogation display: 81.73 kg.

"*Bud' ya proklyat!* (I'll be damned!)" Dmitri exclaimed.

"*Navernoe* (Probably)," Ginger said with a wink that caused the Russian's heart to flutter.

"We'd better bring the Captain in on this," Dmitri said.

#

They did, and Jon brought them up to speed about the flash communiqué, while simultaneously removing them from his list.

"Great job of independent confirmation," Jon told them. "We'll shut down the VASIMRs on schedule, get stabilized on the tether, and then address this."

They left his cabin to carry out their responsibilities, and Jon briefed Ari on the new development. Ten minutes before the scheduled shutdown, Jon took his position at the Command Console.

"Houston, it's *Cassini*. We calculate shutdown at eight-fifty-four-point-two Zulu."

The transmission was just under a minute getting to Earth, and another slightly longer transit back. "It's CapCom...Houston concurs."

"Set it in for automatic shutdown, Ari."

"Roger that."

"Give me a mark for the log, Dmitri."

"Three...two...one...Mark...engine shutdown."

"Engine has shut down," Ari said needlessly, as the ship went to zero-g at the moment of shutdown.

#

The shift to zero-g pulled Saeed from his meditations as he floated away from the deck along with some of the personal articles he had scattered around him. He knew that the ship would shift from acceleration to tethered status, and since he was at the center of rotation, that he would be virtually in free-fall until the deceleration leg some hundred days hence. He was prepared for the change, and once it was in effect, he would have the freedom to wander throughout the Box, since the Pullman would be a full two kilometers away.

The Box would be revolving at a bit over a half revolution per minute, producing a slight gravitational effect at the ends – five one-thousands of the force of gravity on Earth, or about one-quarter the gravity on Iapetus. It was not enough to matter, but it would move things away from the center.

Saeed settled back to await the unfolding of events. By the grace of Allah, he would remain undetected until it was time for him to act decisively in the defense of everything that was holy.

Chapter four

The next deep-space trip would be done under acceleration all the way, Jon was sure of it. The next generation VASIMR would be capable of at least one half-g thrust. That would make the trip to Saturn last just under thirteen days. And eventually, the acceleration would be at one-g. That would make the one and a half billion kilometer trip take just a bit over nine days. For now, though, the best they could do was two days at one tenth-g. That left a two day braking leg at the end, and about 114 days of coasting. This particular trip was special, because Jupiter lay sixty-nine days ahead of them, and they intended to use its gravity to gain extra momentum and shorten their total coast time by about two weeks.

For now, however, the task at hand was the separation of the three modules, and their extension to the ends of a four kilometer tether. Jon had gathered the crew to the Canteen where they "sat" watching the holodisplay shimmering in the space around which they were hovering.

"With apologies to those of you who thoroughly understand this maneuver," Jon said, "I'm going to walk you all through it." *Cassini II* appeared in the center of the display. "As I am sure you have figured out, if we simply extend a two kilometer tether from the Box to the Pullman and start revolving about the Box, we will be upside down here in the Pullman. So here is how we solve this."

As Jon narrated, the Pullman in the holodisplay separated, and pulled back a few meters. This was accomplished with a compressed gas powered ram that gave the Pullman a small amount of independent momentum, and four arresting cables that stopped the motion after two meters. Then the arresting cables detached so that the Pullman was entirely disconnected from the rest of the spaceship. Using internal gyros, the Pullman rotated in a yaw or pitch mode for 180 degrees – Jon explained that the name was simply a way to distinguish one from the other, since their only difference was that each motion was at right angles to the other. Once the Pullman's nose was pointing directly at the Box, the end of the tether snaked across the two meter gap, and attached firmly to the Pullman nose socket. The tether mechanism then pulled the module back into tight contact with the Box, where clamps secured the connection. With the Pullman now oriented properly, gyros in all three modules coordinated their efforts to cause the entire spaceship to rotate about the center axis of the Box, until it was rotating at five and a third revolutions a minute, producing one-g at both ends of the ship. As soon as this was attained and stabilized, both the Pullman and Caboose disconnected from the Box, and the tether mechanisms slowly extended the tether in both directions, slowing the rotation in the same manner as a pirouetting ice skater extending her arms to slow her spin, until each length was two kilometers, and the rotation had reduced to two-thirds of a revolution per minute.

"This," Jon said, "would give the Pullman one-g, and keep the moving starscape sufficiently slow to prevent disorientation."

In the holodisplay, the tethered four kilometer long structure rotated slowly clockwise, like a magnificent bolo, against the star studded backdrop. "Any questions?"

"What keeps it like that, all stretched out?" Elke asked.

"Physics," Jon answered. "So long as nothing affects it from the outside, it will continue in exactly this configuration forever."

"Well..." Dmitri lifted his eyebrows at Jon. Jon nodded a go-ahead. "Not quite forever," Dmitri said. "The ship is still subject to the pull of the Sun's gravity, and increasingly that of Jupiter and then Saturn. It will need adjustment from time to time."

"What about Mars, *Chéri*?" Michele asked.

"Too far away," Dmitri said. "Technically, it still has an effect, as does Earth, but we don't need to worry about that."

"Any more questions?" Jon looked around the group. "Okay... make sure nothing is loose in your quarters, because we'll be at full gravity in a while."

#

In actual practice, the Pullman flip maneuver was an intricate operation that carried enormous potential risk. The untethered Pullman had no motive power. If it were to break loose, if it were to become disconnected from the Box, it would follow its own path to Jupiter, where it would crash into the massive planet's atmosphere. Jon and Ari occupied the Command Console and RVC, respectively; Dmitri and Ginger were at their Astrogation and Comms consoles. Noel was suited up in the upper level of the Box, ready to perform an immediate EVA should something go wrong. Chen was suited up in the lower Pullman level ready to assist Noel if necessary.

With everyone positioned and everything ready, Jon gave the order to commence the decoupling. Clamps between the hulls released, and pressurized air charged the ram cylinder in the upper Box level. Under Ari's watchful eye through holocams positioned between the hulls, the ram slowly extended. Jon carefully examined each of the four arresting cables, since if they were uneven or one got disconnected, the Pullman would end up not plumb to the ship axis, and would require additional gyro maneuvering to correct. To Jon's relief, the four cables extended in unison, exactly as designed. When the ram reached its two meter extension, each of the arresting cables went taut, and Ari's display indicated equilibrium. A tap on his pad caused the ram to begin retracting as the pressurized air in the cylinder vented into the Box.

With the ram fully retracted and the tension on all four arresting cables at zero, Jon indicated for Ari to commence the flip. Ari released the four cables. The Pullman now floated free in its own independent orbit around the Sun. He had about an hour to complete his task before the tidal forces caused sufficient misalignment to require an

EVA correction by Noel and Chen.

"Chen, it's Ginger. Shift your station."

"On my way," Chen said as he commenced moving from the lower level to Level One at the other end of the Pullman. He remained suited with his helmet on since the trip was short and in free-fall.

Five minutes later, Chen announced, "It's Chen. I'm standing by in Level One."

"Commencing flip," Ari announced, as he spun up the pitch gyro.

With no perceptible difference to the occupants, the Pullman began a slow pitch about its center. Doc Bhuta, Michele and Elke were in the Canteen, and were able to watch the stars sweep past the port. Neither Noel nor Chen had an outside view, nor did the four occupants of the Core. Seventeen minutes after commencing the flip, Ari brought the pitch gyro to a standstill. Jon's indicators showed the Pullman in perfect alignment with the Box. Jon nodded to Ginger.

"Release the cone," Ginger transmitted to Noel.

A moment later, the cone moved straight away from the center of the Box upper level trailing the tether, and attached itself to the socket on the waiting Pullman, where clamps securely anchored it. With the tether firmly attached, and hard-wire module-to-module communications reestablished, Ari issued an electronic order for the tether mechanism to draw the Pullman tightly against the Box. A minute later, clamps firmly secured the two modules together. With a seal established between the modules, Noel doffed his suit, and returned forward to meet Chen and the rest of the off duty crew in the Canteen.

"This is the Captain," Jon said on All-Call. "Stand by for commencement of rotation...on my mark...five...four...three...two...one... mark...commence spin-up.

#

Saeed followed the uncoupling, flip, and recoupling by listening to the sounds that penetrated his refuge. He had a general understanding of what had happened, and he had been warned to remain hidden during the entire procedure, since a crew member would be within several meters of his refuge. He remained undetected, *praise be to Allah*.

Because Saeed was located nearly at the center of rotation, he would experience virtually nothing during the spin-up. He decided to use the time to set himself up with more comfortable living quarters, always paying attention to holocam location.

#

With Jon's order, gyros in all three modules commenced a co-ordinated spin-up. Jon's intent, guided by Houston, was to set the spin in the plane of their orbit, so that the tethered spaceship would appear to an outside observer to be following its track like a spinning bola, spinning flatly along the path.

Slowly, over the next hour or so, the sixty-three meter long, twelve meter wide cylinder commenced revolving around the center of the Box, gradually building up to an equivalent gravitation at both ends of one-g, rotating five and a third times each minute. By an hour and fifteen minutes into the event, the off-duty crew members sat or stood firmly planted, watching the stars sweep past the Canteen port.

"*Ou*," Michele wailed, "it makes me dizzy."

"Better not to look, then," Dr. Bhuta advised her. "Just sit quietly and wait for the tether to extend."

"Has anybody here been through this before?" Noel asked.

The three women shook their heads. "I had a day of centrifuge training last year," Chen volunteered.

"Me too, several months ago," Noel added. "Doesn't prepare you for this, though, It's pretty amazing."

A deck below them in the Core, Jon looked at Ari as his revolution indicator reached five and a third. "You ready to do this?" he asked. They were about to do something that had only been accomplished in simulations thus far. "Houston, are you with us?" The signal took a minute to get there and another to get back.

"We're looking over your shoulder, Jon. Everything looks nominal from here."

Over the All-Call Jon announced, "Commencing tether extension," and nodded to Ari. At both ends of the Box clamps released, and Pullman and Caboose inched away from the Box. "Let's keep it at ten meters a minute for the first hour, Ari." Jon said as he examined his display. "We know the physics, but there is no way a simulation can account for every element in a live system. Besides, we've got an unknown factor somewhere in this rig."

"I think I can begin to pin down that mass, Jon," Ari said. "I can measure the exact tension on the two tethers. We know to within a fraction the exact mass that should be in each module. The actual measured tensions should tell us if there is any extra mass in either the Pullman or Caboose."

#

"*Cassini II*, this is CapCom. Stand by for Flash Traffic! Please acknowledge."

"This is Jon Stock...Roger. Send your traffic."

"This is CapCom. We just measured a massive charged particle flux. It is thirty minutes deep, and traveling at 600 kilometers per second. It will reach you in eight and three-quarter hours. This is a big one, Jon. We recommend your crew occupy the Core from a half-hour before until one half-hour after the flux packet. We'll give you a heads-up when you should enter the Core."

Jon assembled the crew in the Canteen to explain the coming problem. "You'll be perfectly safe in the Core," he told them. Then he looked directly at Michele. "You had better cage and bring Emmanuelle and Phillip to the Core with you," he said to her with a smile.

"You know...*mais oui, mon Capitaine!*" she said, and kissed him on his cheek.

Eight hours passed more quickly than anybody had expected. After the first hour, Jon had given Ari free hand in extending the tether. By the eighth hour they were at just under two kilometers. At eight hours and fifteen minutes, Jon told Ari to put a hold on the extension, and all the crew members crowded into the Core.

"*Cassini II*, this is CapCom. Stand by for Flash Traffic."

"This is Ginger. Transmit your traffic."

"This is CapCom. Charged particle arrival in twenty-five minutes. Is everyone in the Core?"

"We're all in the Core, Houston; thank you for your concern."

Jon let his mind wander to future flights, journeys without the benefit of a CapCom and an Earthside monitoring of radiation events. It was a problem that needed solving, and as he pondered it, nothing obvious came to mind. How do you get advance notification of a deadly event? How much time do you need to get from anywhere into the Core? As he thought about it, the only solution that came to mind was to shield the entire ship as the Core was shielded. But was that practical? Could a vessel deploy a trailing drone that would detect and warn? Was there a way to use radar or some other electromagnetic detector to give a warning? He made a mental note to engage Dmitri and Ari in a discussion – perhaps everyone except the three non-technical women, perhaps everybody.

The alarm pulled him out of his reverie. "The external detectors have picked up the first wave," Ari informed him. "It's pretty intense. This won't kill you outright, but you'll wish it had."

"You got medicine for this kind of exposure?" Elke asked Dr. Bhuta. "I mean, if we were not in here?"

Dr. Bhuta glanced at the radiation monitor on the RVC. "Somewhat, yes. I can keep you alive, but it won't be pretty."

In their cage, the two canaries twittered their disgust at being caged. "Don't you worry, my little ones," Michele cooed to them. "Soon enough you will be free again to fly about your beautiful world."

#

Still hidden in the Box, Saeed had no way of knowing about the incoming charged particles. He prepared his first burst message that reported his successful boarding of *Cassini II*, and the uneventful powered passage. He decided not to inform the Caliph of his epiphany. That would come in due course, as Allah unfolded His path before him. Saeed ejected the burst transmitter through the waste lock, and went back to his tent.

Outside, the little ball sensed the magnetic presence of the ship, and using a bit of its small supply of compressed gas, oriented itself so the magnetic presence was at its rear. Then it split around its circumference, and ejected the front half with a small burst of air. Slowly, over the next few minutes, a gossamer circular film emerged from the cramped exposed section of the ball, impelled by minute quantities of air filling nearly microscopic capillaries in the film, so that eventually it took on a parabolic shape. Following a programmed search algorithm, the ball commenced a slight up and down, left to right rocking motion, until it detected the cacophony of transmissions that indicated the location of Earth. It steadied itself on that vector, and then commenced a series of millisecond burst transmissions, sending Saeed's report several thousand times before running out of power. Because Saeed ejected the transmitter from the rotating Box, it continued on an independent vector, following its own orbit, and soon disappeared into the depths of space.

Saeed wiled away the time memorizing the *Qur'an* and deepening his spiritual connection to Allah. He kept coming back to his incredible epiphany: *Let those fight in the way of Allah who sell the life of this world for the other.* The more he pondered, the clearer it became. Muhammad, *peace and blessings be upon him,* had written these words inspired by Allah. He had miraculously foreseen this momentous journey, and had placed these inspired words where he, Saeed, could find and understand them.

At the eight and three-quarter hour mark, Saeed had just lifted himself to vertical from a prostration toward Earth – toward Mecca. As the charged particles streamed through the Box, Saeed presented the largest possible profile. He felt a slight sense of dizziness, nothing to worry about, just a slight disorientation of his inner ear in the weightlessness of his abode. Three more times he prostrated himself; three more times he presented a full profile to the radiation stream. Then he lay down to rest for a while. He felt a bit weak, but it would pass.

Chapter five

It was good to have normal weight. Other than the magical effect on her breasts, Michele could live without zero-g. But weightlessness and boobs – now that was a good thing from time to time. Michele smiled in sweet memory of her weightless tryst with Elke. While Elke clearly didn't need weightlessness, Michele's own sense of zero-g youthfulness, and the freedom weightlessness gave intertwined bodies made it more than worthwhile, in her opinion. And when Ari had joined them – well it gave a whole new meaning to what three people could do together.

For the past hour, Michele had been checking her plants. So far as she could tell, they liked reduced gravity. While she knew this from the literature, it was interesting to see it first-hand. Emmanuelle and Phillip had taken to both low and zero-g without any noticeable downside. Although Michele was not expert in bird-flight physiology, she thought she could see some adjustment to the loss of downward pull. It had to be there, she thought, but the flight instinct was so ingrained that adjustment was transparently automatic. She had taken care to make holographic recordings of their zero-g and low-g flight for later analysis.

With lunchtime approaching, Michele doffed her smock and adjusted her green jumpsuit neckline. As she set her décolletage to its best visual advantage, she reflected for a moment on zero-g freedom, and then headed for the central ladder.

#

Ginger stood before the full length mirror in her compartment admiring her nude body. To her private satisfaction, she could see no perceptible difference in how her lithe body looked in zero-g, and now in the full pull of Earth gravity. She was amused by Michele's antics, but had to admit that she was a fine looking woman. Ginger liked the company of men – usually. When Michele kissed her at their meeting in the Great Room of the Mirs Complex, however, she had made a mental note to do some follow up – perhaps with the help of Ari or Dmitri, she added as an afterthought.

She slipped on a thong and then stepped into a one-piece pale blue jumpsuit. One last glance in the mirror to be sure she looked as good as she felt, and she made her way to the Canteen.

#

Elke sat before a small desk in her stateroom, working on her voyage history. She had been feeling a bit like a fifth wheel since *Cassini II* got underway – except for Michele. Elke smiled inwardly. Now that was a pleasant surprise. It obviously was not a permanent arrangement, but it certainly helped keep things in perspective.

Elke felt a stomach rumble. *Time to join the rest of the crew for lunch in the Canteen.* Following a quick pause in the lavatory she shared with Dr. Bhuta, she checked her image in the mirror – she cut a fine figure in her light gray jumpsuit. She stepped back into the lavatory and knocked on Dr. Bhuta's door.

"Let's grab some lunch, girl," Elke told the pretty Indian Doctor, who was dressed conventionally in a dark blue jumpsuit, her long black hair flowing loosely down her back.

They exited from Dr. Bhuta's room, Elke following the smaller woman up the ladder. The excellent view of Carmen Bhuta's petite trim body on the ladder ahead of her inspired Elke. During lunch, Elke joined the rest of the crew, but part of her mind kept replaying the climb from the doctor's quarters.

#

Carmen Bhuta sat before her mirror in her compact quarters applying lip color with a fine brush. With the return of normal gravity, she had let her hair loose. Almost, she could sit on it. She shook her head, and a dark wave cascaded down her back. Carmen smiled at her image, proud of her exotic beauty combined with her skill as a physician – the physician chosen for this history-making quest. She turned as she heard Elke in their shared lavatory. Now, there was an interesting girl – woman. She had to be the most physically fit female Carmen had even seen. There was something about her that Carmen could not quite identify, something that set her aside from the other women onboard. The lavatory went quiet. Carmen considered her situation. From her short time aboard, it was perfectly clear that she was the only person who was actively religious. She was put off by Michele's shenanigans, although the woman was hard not to like. As with everyone else onboard, she was a little in awe of Ginger – so striking in physique and so intellectually accomplished. For Carmen it was a bit intimidating, so that she sometimes failed to see her own unique position. Now when she considered Ari, she could not decide if he was Jewish by faith, or just a man with a long, proud heritage. Despite herself, she thought she and Ari had a bond of common heritage (at least in one sense). Noel – tall, educated, aloof, with a family heritage similar to hers. Money and privilege certainly rose to the occasion at times. Dmitri – now there was an interesting man. He was exciting in a masculine way, incredibly sure of himself, and so foreign in virtually every way Carmen could conceive. She looked forward to exploring his mind during the extended days that lay ahead of them. Chen came from a culture more distant from the West than hers, so that she looked upon him as foreign. In him she sensed a difference similar to Elke. It could have been no more than the difference from being Chinese, but she thought not. There was something else, and she intended to get to the bottom of it. Finally, there was Captain Jon Stock. Here was the real enigma – the man chosen to lead a talented team into the absolute unknown. He was distant, but friendly, commanded respect and – she suspected – even obedience when required, without being a master. She greatly admired the man she barely knew, but whom she intended to know better before the voyage was done.

She heard Elke in the lavatory again, but this time with a knock on her door, inviting her to lunch. She stood and beckoned the German into her room, shook her head to flow her hair down her back, and departed the room ahead of Elke, to climb the ladder to the Canteen.

#

Ari went back to his measurements following the radiation storm. The nearly eighty-one kilograms really bothered him. One part of him understood that his Mossad background probably was more the cause of his anxiety than the actual extra mass, but that same background made him think outside the box, and he didn't like the answers he was getting.

Working with Noel and Chen, he checked and rechecked the tension meters on the two tethers. The only thing they couldn't do was physically read the tension meters at their source, except for the one where the tether attached to the Pullman nose. The problem was, all the readings were normal, and normal meant only one thing. The excess mass was in the Box.

After checking and rechecking, Ari finally met with Jon in his cabin. "Skipper," he said more formally than he would normally address his friend, "I've looked as much as possible without an EVA. The excess mass has to be in the Box."

"Whatever it is can wait for our gravity assist maneuver around Jupiter," Jon said. "I got the drift of your thinking, but the likelihood of a stowaway is so remote as to be unthinkable...a motive...it always comes back to a motive. I think it more likely that somebody reversed a couple of numbers on a manifest." Jon punched up a spreadsheet. "Look," he said, entering 190 in a cell. In the next cell he entered 109. "I've reversed the nine and zero. What's the difference?" He let the spreadsheet do the calculation, but Ari had done a quick mental one.

"Eighty-one! Shit, Jon, could it be as simple as that?"

"Could be," Jon answered, "but remember, the actual number was eighty-point-nine-three, not eighty-one."

"I guess we just don't know," Ari said, "at least, not until we examine the Box."

"And that, my friend, is no mean task. I think we may want to wait till we're in orbit around Iapetus, doing the actual unloading for surface transfer. Realistically, what can happen between now and then?"

#

The next major milestone would be crossing into the asteroid belt. Unlike a planet's orbit, a specifically defined, exact track around the Sun, the asteroid belt is a loosely defined region lying between Mars and Jupiter, extending about the same distance as from the Sun to Mars. Most of the asteroids are concentrated within a half a million kilometers from the ecliptic. Although the asteroids cluster near the ecliptic, and extend up and down for a total thickness of about a million kilometers, asteroids are regularly found as far up and down as seventy-five million kilometers.

The crew members were in the Canteen discussing a holodisplay of the asteroid belt Jon had projected at one end of the compartment, with their track indicated by a red line passing directly through the belt.

"It looks like we will have a lot of company," Elke said, with widened eyes.

"*Oui*...I agree," Michele piped in. "We will need lots of care, *non?*"

"The scale is fooling you," Jon said with a smile, winking at Ginger. "Dmitri, you and Ginger want to take it from here?"

"Tell 'em like it is, Girl," Dmitri said to Ginger with perfect idiom as always.

"For more than a century we have identified and tracked individual asteroids, but we still have no idea how many there are." Ginger's striking pose actually competed with the holodisplay. "At the turn of the century, we thought there were about one-point-seven asteroids with a radius of at least one hundred meters in a cube of one-hundred-thousand kilometers on a side. The best current estimates are based on rocks about half that size. When you run the numbers, you get just under two asteroids in each cube of space one-thousand kilometers on a side. That's still a lot of space, guys...a billion cubic kilometers."

Each of the men was running numbers on his Link, but Ginger continued. "We're doing about one-hundred-seventy kilometers every second, so we cross a thousand kilometers roughly every six seconds. Somewhere during that six seconds, there should be an asteroid within five-hundred kilometers of us, one that is at least a hundred meters across. All the asteroids will be moving from our right to our left in the ecliptic." The dots in the holodisplay belt began a perceptible movement. "Here's the clincher," Ginger added, "and it's a double whammy. In the real world, asteroids tend to cluster together, which means that parts of the belt are virtually empty, whereas other parts are relatively crowded. Then, we have no idea about the distribution of rocks smaller than a hundred meters." She paused and looked at her fellow crew mates, one-by-one. "There most certainly are millions upon millions of smaller rocks, typically clumped with the larger rocks. These guys have an orbital speed of nineteen to twenty kilometers per second. That may be only a tenth of our velocity, but it's still pretty damn fast! We'll be moving through the belt somewhat like a bolo in a flat trajectory, as I said, at a hundred-seventy kilometers per second, presenting a vertical cross-section of twenty meters at the three modules, and virtually nothing at the tether. So vertically, the odds of a collision are virtually zero. Our horizontal cross-section, however, ranges from four kilometers to twenty meters as we rotate. Furthermore, we are clumped into three small packages, connected by a virtually nonexistent tether – from a cross-section point of view."

By this time, the men with their calculations had gotten the point, but Elke still awaited the bottom line, and both the Doctor and Biologist saw where it was going, but wanted the final numbers. "Bottom line is," Ginger continued, "we will encounter several asteroids in the sense that we will pick them up on our laser scanner or radar, but we're not likely to see one visually, as they will be moving far too quickly for the eye to resolve an image."

"Stealth company," Dmitri said with a chuckle.

"The real key here is," Jon said, "that we will be passing through the asteroid belt commencing in about twenty days or so, and lasting for about ten days, and then we have seventeen days of open skies to Jupiter." The path in the holodisplay swung around Jupiter and traced on to Saturn. "Two days before arrival we will retract the tethers and get ready for maneuvering. We'll be sufficiently close to Jupiter at least twice to require our remaining in the Core to avoid the high radiation of one of her belts."

"A question from a dumb engineer," Noel piped up, hand politely raised.

"We're not in school, Noel, you dumb bastard," Ari said in a manner that could only be taken humorously. Everybody chuckled, and Noel shrugged sheepishly, holding his hands out in front of him, palms up.

"Anyway...Dmitri, I presume you and Ginger have a fix on all the known asteroids we will pass?"

"That's a fact," Dmitri answered, "but that is only about seventy-eight-thousand of the two-hundred-twenty-five-thousand we expect to be there – that are larger than a hundred meters. As you have guessed, we really don't have a clue what we will find as we pass through the belt."

"We'll run a loose watch routine like we did before," Jon added. "Remember, none of the smaller rocks are totally determined. Even where we have good numbers, they are subject to so many forces, that we will not really know their exact position and orbital parameters until a couple of hours before we encounter them."

"What I get from all this," Elke said, "is that the odds are hugely in our favor. Do you think we'll see even one of these guys?"

"It's possible," Ginger said. "I'll let you know in a few days – once we're closer so I can find the bigger ones and determine their parameters."

"Find them, *Chérie*. I thought you know where they are." Michele sounded a bit perturbed.

"Generally, sure we do," Ginger said, "enough to point the radar and laser. Once we specifically locate one, then we can tell exactly where it will be for all the time it will matter to us."

"I knew that, *Chérie*...I think."

The questions stopped, so Jon collapsed the holodisplay, and motioned for Dmitri and Ari to join him in his cabin.

They settled down, and Jon said, "I want to play devil's advocate. What's our angle to the average orbital tangent of the rocks?"

"About forty-five degrees in the starboard quarter," Dmitri said.

"So here's the scenario." Jon activated his Link showing two lines crossing at a forty-five degree angle. A bar on one line indicated *Cassini II* traveling on its path, and a dot on the other represented an asteroid traveling on its orbital vector. "For sake of argument, we're in the same plane, and this guy catches a piece of the Caboose tether."

Jon held up his hand. "I don't want to discuss the probability – I know how low it is...but it's NOT zero, so I want to discuss it."

Dmitri and Ari grinned. "Sure, Boss," Ari said. Dmitri nodded.

"Will the asteroid snap the tether, slip over or under it, deflect it...what do you guys think?"

"Off the cuff, or do you want a real answer?" Ari asked, while Dmitri chuckled beside him.

"I think he wants both," Dmitri said. "How about two hours for off-the-cuff?"

Jon nodded his assent, and the two men left to put their heads together in private.

#

As Saeed passed the hours, he became increasingly uneasy. His upset stomach refused to go away. He actually felt like throwing up. He had a continuous headache, one that sometimes completely overwhelmed him. His concentration was down. He had not memorized a single *Qur'an* passage for over two hours. He prayed with more fervor than normal, relying upon the grace of Allah to return his strength. But he sensed that he was growing weaker instead of stronger. Obviously, he needed to muster greater faith, a greater unfettered connection to Allah.

It was a test...it had to be a test. Allah had tested Job, and now he was testing Saeed, *praise be to Allah*. Saeed reached deep into his reserves, and found a bit of untapped strength. He called up the *Qur'an* on his Link and concentrated on memorizing another passage, and then another, and then another...

Chapter six

Over the next twenty days they had smooth sailing – no problems with the ship's systems and no signs of asteroids. That meant, of course, that there was time for crew members to get to know each other more completely.

For Michele, the process was simple and direct, and simply told: Chen declined politely, and she decided not to approach the Captain. The rest...

Elke worked a smaller set that excluded the men, but her German practicality brought her together with Ari and Ginger on at least one occasion. Try as she might, however, Dr. Bhuta remained professional and pleasant. For the first time in her life, Elke was unable to elicit a response from another woman.

Ginger was a product of the modern world, and was happy to share intimate personal time as the situation dictated. Her remarkable physical looks made her the object of attention for virtually every crew member, except Carmen who remained coolly professional and seemed a bit in awe of her, and Chen, who quietly avoided her.

Jon and Ari honed their Hyperchess skills with a daily game that often brought Dmitri to the scene. The Russian had learned this space age variation of chess, but had never taken time to develop his skills. He knew the moves, but had no real sense of strategy. Dmitri spent most of his waking time with Ginger working out the Asteroid belt implications. They met from time to time with Ari, who added his structural engineering insights into the equation. Ari, in turn, worked through the various scenarios with Noel and Chen.

It turned out that Chen had special insight into the character-istics of the tether itself. Far from being a simple cable, the tether was a complex combination of strength, power, and communication elements. In a way, it resembled the SPCC developed during the mid-twentieth century for tethered deep submergence operations at sea. The SPCC (Strength-Power-Communications-Cable) con-sisted of a twisted bundle of power, communication, and strength elements about the thickness of a human thumb, wrapped in high tensile strength stainless steel wire. In the tether, the stainless steel was replaced by polyaramid fiber with ten times the tensile strength of steel at a fraction of its mass. Otherwise, the cable was quite similar.

The question that Jon had posed, whose answer had turned out to be way more complex that even he had envisioned, was simple enough. What would happen if an asteroid struck the tether – either in front of or behind the Box? Two days into the coasting leg, Jon had put the question to Houston. They were now approaching the outskirts of the Belt, and Houston still had not supplied an answer. So the question had turned out to be complex, and apparently was not very high on Houston's priority list. On day nine Jon called Dmitri and Ari to his stateroom.

"Tell me what you know about the asteroid question," he asked them. "Houston has come up blank thus far, so I'd like to hear your thoughts."

"Simple answer," Ari said, "we don't know. There are way too many variables, and a good percentage of them seem to have signif-icant impact."

"Best guess, then," Jon said. "What does your gut say?"

"One of three things: The tether slips over or under the asteroid; or two, the tether acts like a solid bar; or three the tether acts like an infinitely strong string. In the over-under, depending on which tether is touched, the Pullman or Caboose will experience a surging shock similar to the end of a snapping whip. We can't begin to estimate level of damage, but we think it may be moderate.

"For the bar, the cable will instantly sever, and either the Pullman or Caboose will head off on a tangent directly dependent on its position to the complex at the instant of severing. If it is the Pullman, we're screwed, since we have no way to get to the Box to get a landing unit to try and reconnect the tether. If it's the Caboose, and if we act fast, we might be able to launch a landing unit to retrieve the runaway Caboose – maybe.

"The string is the most complex. Momentum gets transferred to the tether and mostly to either the Pullman or Caboose, although everything gets a piece of the action. Depending entirely upon the moment vectors, which are totally unpredictable, Pullman, Caboose, and Box will be moving in a wild, mutually dependent set of motions. If individual units don't collide, we should eventually be able to sort things out with the gyros, and by retracting the tethers."

"That's the best we can do, Jon," Dmitri added. "The variable dependent scenarios branch so quickly, that we get lost in minutia before we get underway. We actually froze the computer at one point. I can't recall ever doing that before."

"Okay, thanks, guys. Don't spend a lot more time on this, but present it to Elke. Let her have a pass from a computer engineering aspect. She may know a way to find the more significant branches in your chaotic tree."

#

Saeed had been certain that he would begin to feel better, but it was three weeks later, and he finally had to admit that he was in serious trouble. Between prostrations, he brushed his hand through his full head of dark hair, and returned a handful of hair to his mat. What was happening? Why was Allah letting this happen? Saeed absolutely knew that he was Allah's chosen instrument. In his mind, the *Qur'an* left no question: *Let those fight in the way of Allah who sell the life of this world for the other. Whoso fighteth in the way of Allah, be he slain or be he victorious, on him we shall bestow a vast reward.*

He prostrated again, felt his stomach heave, and vomited blood on his prayer mat. At that moment he was hit with massive weight, several gees at least, and a twisting, wrenching, totally disorienting

surge that made no mental or physical sense. In his weakened state, all
Saeed could do was let his body be tossed from wall to wall inside his
tent, and hope that he would not tear the fabric. He heard somebody
screaming, and then his stomach heaved again, and bloody vomit filled
the space around him, flying this way and that, finally collecting on
the tent walls. The lights went out, and someone still was screaming,
but as the wild gyrations began to settle into a repeating pattern,
Saeed realized that *he* was the one screaming...and he couldn't stop.
He reached for his head, pulling out fistfuls of hair...and he screamed
again. He retched, but his stomach was empty, and only a little bit of
blood mixed with spittle left his mouth, flying at an odd angle to the
tent wall...and he screamed, but quieter now, and screamed some more,
but quieter still, until his screams morphed into a frightened whimper
as he curled into a tight ball on his prayer mat, waiting for the end.

#

It wasn't supposed to happen this way. Ginger had the watch
in the Core. They had given up on their calculations, for all practical purposes. Elke had had some interesting ideas for resolving the
infinite branching, but in the end, all she was able to show was that
they had found another of Nature's fractals. Bottom line – there was
no meaningful solution. Their best guess was that the odds of an
asteroid intersection were so small as to be negligible.

It took Ginger less than a second to grasp how wrong their
assessment was.

One moment she was in her chair, working away at one small
aspect of the problem, sort of like worrying a hangnail, the next she
was on the overhead, left arm bent at an unnatural angle. And then,
with a sickening, twisting surge, she was on the opposite deck...and
then on the bulkhead...back to the overhead...

It continued for several minutes, before her world took on a chaotic kind of repeating order – bewildering, but somewhat predictable.
Ginger hauled herself into the Command Console seat using her
good arm, and strapped in. Then she ripped her jumpsuit open, and
pulled the left shoulder down around her left elbow to stabilize her
broken humerus, and tucked her left hand into her jumpsuit against
her stomach to keep the ship's erratic motion from moving her arm.
Using her right hand to control the holodisplay, she began to conduct

a survey of the ship. Jon stumbled into the Core, glanced briefly at Ginger's exposed breast and wrapped arm, and strapped himself into the Comm seat, apparently getting into synch with the erratic motion.

"How bad is the arm?" he asked.

"Simple fracture. I'll live." She smiled briefly at him. *Hell of a way to get his attention,* she thought. "I'm checking the ship right now."

"Okay...good. You check inside, I'll survey outside." On the All-Call Jon said, "Doc, if you're okay, I need you in the Core – NOW!" He tore a piece from the front of his jumpsuit and leaned over to tuck it around Ginger's bare breast. "Hang in there, Girl!" he said to her.

Although Ginger had no body shame, and normally was comfortable exposing her body to people she knew, somehow it felt different with the Captain. Had her features been capable of blushing, when he covered her breast she would have been crimson. As it was, she dropped her eyes and said softly, "Thank you Jon. I really appreciate that."

Dmitri came stumbling into the Core, favoring his left leg. "Are you hurt?" Jon demanded.

"Twisted my left knee. I should be okay in a couple of days." He gave Jon and Ginger a broad grin as he adjusted to the lurching motion. "Your arm?" he asked Ginger.

"Broken humerus – I'm okay for now."

"Ari – to the Core," Jon said on the All-Call. "Ginger...anything inside I need to know about?"

"Not right now, Skipper. Stuff tossed around – no major damage I can see on first survey."

"Outside shows we're whipping around like a cart on a carnival ride whip," Jon told them. "Everything's moving relative to everything..."

Ari stuck his head into the Core. It was wrapped with a white bandage that already was taking on a red stain behind his right temple. Before anyone could ask, he said, "Knocked off my feet and hit something – not sure what. Doc fixed me up, is why I didn't get here right away. Sheeze, Ginger, what happened?" She told him.

"You okay to work?" Jon asked Ari.

"Yeh..." He grabbed a chair arm for support as the Pullman whipped-lashed again.

"Ginger, see If you can raise Houston. They're going to want to know about this. Nothing they can do, but they'll want to know."

Ari eased himself in front of the RVC. "Let's see what I can do with the gyros," he said with a grimace.

Ginger took that to be an expression of pain.

Jon announced on the All-Call, "Everyone stay put, unless you're injured and need help. Talk to me if you have to. Doc, we're standing by..."

Ginger had composed a message and sent it on its fourteen minute trip to Houston. Her message was concise, yet sufficiently detailed to inform Houston that *Cassini II* had a problem, but that they were getting a handle on the situation. To Ari's delighted surprise, whatever had happened, the tethers were still intact. He furiously manipulated the gyros in all three modules. While Ari struggled with the gyros, Dmitri turned his attention to reeling in both tethers. He had to work closely with Ari, so that he took up slack as Ari was able to develop it. All the while, the Pullman was whipping along its chaotic path, reversing its direction in the most unpredictable way every time it reached the end of the tether. Simultaneously, the Caboose whipped along its own path, at times passing perilously close to the Pullman. And the Box was pulled first one way as the Pullman reached the end of its tether, and then the other as the Caboose pulled it back.

Over the next hour, with Jon orchestrating their actions, Ari and Dmitri slowly brought the monster under control. Ginger kept up a running commentary to Houston, and CapCom wisely remained silent, except to provide an occasional aside to a fascinated world that was following the events out beyond the orbit of Mars.

#

Carmen Bhuta was in her room when all hell broke loose. She was flung to the deck, thrown across the deck to come up hard against a table leg. The moment it happened, she knew she would carry a nasty bruise for the next couple of weeks. As her room whipped this way and that, her first thought was primitive terror, the fear of dying out in space, far from home. But when that didn't happen, even though her world was acting like a crazy carnival ride, the Doctor assumed control. She dragged herself into a sitting position, grabbed a belt, and secured herself against the table leg. Then she began checking each of the crew members using her specially modified Link that gave her immediate access to any crew member's vitals.

Jon was what Jon always seemed to be, cool and collected – unaffected by whatever it was that was happening. Dmitri appeared to be injured, but he was coping, and didn't need her services at that moment. Ginger – now there was an enigma. The girl obviously had been physically hurt. From the readings, she clearly was in pain, but like Dmitri, she was coping. She tried to reach Ginger, but Ginger's Link was set to reject incoming calls.

Ari burst into her cabin, bleeding profusely from behind his right temple. "Can you stop the bleeding, Doc? Then I got to get to the Core."

In between the wild surges, Carmen patched Ari's laceration, which – he told her – came from the edge of a table. As he lurched out of her cabin, Carmen shook her head in amazement. *These guys are something special*, she said quietly to herself as she gripped the table leg to keep from being thrown to the deck again, despite the belt. She continued checking the rest of the crew. Noel seemed okay, but Chen was unconscious. Carmen called Jon using her executive override to tell him about Chen, and to find out how long the problem was likely to last.

"Chen will have to take care of himself until we get this under control," Jon told her. "I need you to examine Ginger's arm. It's broke, and she's in a lot of pain. Don't go do anything heroic. Stay put until you can safely get here. I mean that – you are a vital part of this mission. We need you!"

Elke was also okay, but she seemed to be undergoing physical stress. Carmen called her. "What are you doing, Elke?"

"I was in the gym. I'm okay. I presume you need my help, so I'm on my way to you." At that moment the Pullman took a particularly strong lurch. "Oof! That will become a bruise," Elke said.

"Be careful!"

"Don't worry, Doc. I can take care of myself, and you need me!"

Carmen checked on Michele. Apparently unconscious. "Elke... Michele is non-responsive. Can you check on her? I think she's in her lab."

"On my way, Doc. I'll call you."

#

It took everything Elke had to keep hold of the rail. It was time to focus, and not get distracted by anything. As the room twisted and whipped in unpredictable ways, Elke tried to find a rhythm. She moved in fits and starts, always having at least one firm hand-hold. She sprinted across the gym during a moment of quiet, reaching the central ladder just as the room twisted wildly again, lifting her off her feet entirely. Within a few minutes, Elke found a rhythm of sorts, and using her athlete's prowess, moved down the ladder, across the lower room, and into the bio lab.

Michele lay on the deck in a pool of blood, obviously unconscious. Plants were strewn everywhere, and with each lurch, tumbled around some more. As Elke entered the lab, Michele groaned, and pitched against a sample table as the Pullman lurched again. Elke hooked one leg around the table leg, grabbed the barely conscious blonde, and held her close as the next round of whipping jerked them around. At a pause, Elke wrapped her legs around the French woman, keeping her foot still hooked around the table leg, and began to probe Michele's bloody scalp with her strong fingers. She touched a wet spot near the back of her scalp, and Michele groaned.

"I got you, Baby, I got you!" Elke ripped off her left jumper sleeve, and folded it into a pressure dressing. Then she reached inside her own jumpsuit, tore at her thong, and pulled it off her body. With deft, sure fingers, she used the thong as a strap to hold the pressure dressing to Michele's head. "I got Michele, Doc. She's got a scalp laceration, but I dressed it with a pressure pad. She'll be okay until this shit stops." Michele groaned again and opened her eyes.

"*Ma Chérie,* you're here..." Her eyes rolled up again as she slipped back into unconsciousness.

"I can't leave her, Doc," Elke said. "She's still in trouble. She needs you as soon as you can make it."

#

"Jon, I need someone to check on Chen," Carmen said. "He's unconscious. Noel seems to be okay. Maybe he can do it."

On the All-Call, Jon said, "Chen, if you can hear me, call the Core. Noel, find Chen. Be careful, but find him!"

#

Noel was in the lavatory when everything went crazy. The narrow confines of the small room allowed him to brace himself so that he suffered no trauma from the wild whipping about. Under the circumstances, it seemed prudent to him to remain where he was until things settled down. With nothing to do but stare at the wall and tighten his muscles every time the Pullman wheeled off in a different direction, Noel reflected on what might have happened. The only thing that made any sense at all made no sense whatsoever. They had to have been struck a glancing blow by a small asteroid on one of the tethers. Nothing else he could imagine would result in such chaotic tumbling. Even as he sat there, he could hear the gyros screaming in protest as someone – probably Ari – was working the blend of engineering sense and art that would eventually bring everything under control. Although he was tempted to call the Core, he knew better. They didn't need his interference at that moment.

Then he heard the All-Call, and knew that Chen was in trouble. A few minutes before the strike, Noel had been in Chen's stateroom discussing a matter with him. That was the natural place to start. Timing his movement to the pauses between wild swings, Noel opened the door to Chen's room, to a chaotic jumble of everything not tied down, including Chen. Chen was being flung around like a dishrag. Noel managed to grab a leg and stop his tumbling, but it was clear that Chen was fully unconscious. Noel checked his breathing and pulse – they seemed okay.

Noel had no executive override like the Captain and Doctor, so he called Carmen using his normal Link. Carmen answered immediately. "His vitals are strong, Noel. Can you find any injury?"

Between surges, Noel carefully felt Chen's entire body. "Some bruising from being tossed around, but nothing major that I can tell."

"Okay...see if you can stabilize his head and neck. I want his head, neck, and shoulders NOT to move relative to each other. Can you do that?"

Noel looked around him for something that could act as a back-board. Another lurch caused him to grip Chen firmly to hold him to the deck, minimizing movement. While waiting for the surge to pass, Noel noticed a roll of common duct tape rolling across the deck, and had an inspiration. He grabbed the roll of tape and secured

Chen to the deck with strip after strip of tape. He carefully ran two strips across his forehead out to both sides, and several across his shoulders. He secured his legs, and then passed several long strips down the length of Chen's body to prevent longitudinal movement. It took about ten minutes, but when he was done, Chen could not have moved if he had wanted to.

"He's secured, Doc." Noel examined his friend. "You'd better get here pretty soon, though. I think he's in serious trouble."

#

"What's the situation, Doc?" Jon asked Carmen, as Ari and Dmitri started to make real progress in containing the wild gyrations.

"Two potentially serious injuries – Michele and Chen. We could lose them if I can't get to them. You have to get this thing under control!" The Doctor's voice was as firm and commanding as Jon had ever heard.

"We're working on it. Another ten minutes, and you can move about – carefully!" Jon glanced at Dmitri and Ari for confirmation. "I'll let you know – about ten minutes."

Eight minutes later the wild gyrations nearly ceased. "Got you, you miserable bastard!" Ari shouted at no one in particular.

"Come to Papa," Dmitri said with equal enthusiasm as he switched the tether retrieval to high speed. "We got it, Skipper," he said to Jon, as he wiped perspiration from his pate.

"Cool," Ginger said. "Anyone have an aspirin?" And she fainted away.

Chapter seven

The terrible pitching and yawing finally stopped. Saeed felt close to death's door. Had Allah abandoned him, or was this a test like Job's, a test of his faith in Allah's goodness and mercy? *Praise be to Allah*. Obviously, Allah had caused a serious disruption of *Cassini II's* voyage. Saeed could not begin to understand Allah's reasons, *praise be to Allah*, but obviously, He had done a mighty thing to the spaceship. Perhaps in demonstration of His omnipotence, He had reached down from on high to touch the vessel with His finger – sufficient to demonstrate His power, *praise be to Allah*, but not enough to destroy the spaceship. The Caliph would need to be informed.

Weak though he was, and through the blur of his radiation disrupted thought process, Saeed recorded his message. It consisted of a rambling, nearly incoherent recitation of his epiphany, the tether extension, his suddenly becoming ill, and Allah's intervention resulting in the near destruction of *Cassini II*. The burst transmitter had survived the solar storm and the asteroid impact. It deployed normally, found its target, and transmitted its message before disappearing into the depths of space.

In Teheran, Caliph Ayatollah Khomeini and his two closest

advisors reviewed the latest message from their Saturn bound warrior. The recording showed a haggard image of a mentally distraught Saeed going on at length about a near disaster, Allah's Prophet Warrior, the Other World, the new Jihad…. Clearly, something had happened. When they learned in the following days of the near destruction of *Cassini II* and its crew, part of the puzzle fell into place, but that still left the mystery of Saeed's mental state. The Caliph extended his international feelers for clues to the mystery.

One of these was Eskandar Ali Jinnah, a never-before-activated Isma'ili sleeper, a Nizari Hashashiyyin, who worked as Alex Jinnah, an engineer for *Cassini II* Mission Control.

#

All three modules were finally locked into a single unit. The resulting zero-g was shortening the recovery time for Dmitri's knee. Using onboard sensors, he calculated their new orbital parameters while Houston ran the calculations with their remote data input from Earth. The numbers were different, but not enough to matter. Ari and Noel intended on spending the first several hours after the hook-up checking and rechecking the reactor and VASIMR engines. From the Pullman, the control electronics seemed to have sustained no damage, but they wanted to check the actual circuits, and Ari actually wanted to do an EVA for a visual inspection of the engines themselves.

"Let's find out now, before we commit to the Jupiter boost," Ari said. "If we've got a problem, we can use the Jupiter transit to get back home." Jon was not about to argue with that logic. So Ari – who still sported a small bandage taped to his temple – and Noel prepared to move through the Box into the Caboose for their internal inspections, followed by the first EVA since getting underway.

Michele was recovering nicely. Other than a headache from her mild concussion, she was in good shape, although she complained about the patch of hair Carmen had to shave in order to close the wound to the back of her scalp. Carmen allowed her to putter around in her lab so long as she didn't exert herself. Zero-g made that unlikely, but Elke stayed with her just in case.

Ginger's arm, now firmly encased in a rigid cast, was healing. Her only complaint was that she itched inside the cast, and Noel came up with a piece of flexible wire that solved that problem.

Chen still was a problem. Carmen had found no broken bones, but something had put him into a coma, where he still remained. She finally determined that he had flexed his neck in such a way as to severely pinch his spinal cord, causing his brain to put him into the coma. His vitals had fully recovered, but his brain wave patterns completely befuddled her diagnostic computer. Houston was equally bewildered, and offered no useful suggestions.

They were about twenty days away from the Jupiter Boost. Jon was convinced that it was in their best interest to get a complete handle on their situation before they committed to the boost. As Ari had said, it could be their ticket home, if they needed it.

Both the Box and Caboose indicated normal pressure and atmosphere content, so Jon authorized Ari and Noel to transit through the Box to the Caboose. "Just keep me in the loop," he told them as they opened the hatch to enter the Box.

#

Ari floated through the connection hatch into the tunnel, followed by Noel. When they both were inside the tunnel, someone in the Pullman shut the hatch. When it had sealed, Ari opened the Box hatch.

"What the fuck is that awful smell?" he shouted, and slammed the hatch shut. "Skipper, we got some kind of a problem in the Box."

"That was puke, pure and simple...human vomit," Noel said.

"Can't be," Ari said. "Not possible. You getting this, Skipper?"

"We are," Jon said. "Hold on. We're going to lock in a couple of the Doc's breathing masks."

A few minutes later, the hatch to the Pullman opened briefly, and two packages sailed into the tunnel. "Put them on, and stuff the bags into your pockets," Jon told them. "Now, be careful!"

This time, Ari eased the hatch open, moving very slowly. When it had opened about a centimeter, suddenly the hatch jerked out of his hand, opening wide. A crazed, creature screaming *"Allahu Akbar!"* lunged at him with some kind of pole, but without momentum or leverage, the pole just bounced harmlessly off him. Using moves that were second nature to him, although not practiced in zero-g, Ari grabbed the arm of the creature, spun him around, and wrapped his legs around the creature's legs.

Almost immediately, whatever fight had remained in the creature left. "We just found part of our eighty-one kilos," Ari said to Jon on his open Link. "You better get the Doc in here right away."

He took a closer look at the stowaway, for that surely was what they had. The facial hair – what remained, that is – indicated his gender. He couldn't have massed more than fifty-five kilos at full weight, but he looked to be around forty-five at the most right now. He was no more than 162 centimeters, with curly dark hair – what remained of it, and dark eyes set into a sharply featured Semitic face.

Ari addressed him in Arabic: "Your name, Warrior."

Saeed looked at Ari in astonishment. "You speak Arabic!" His demeanor assumed a formal nature, insofar as that was possible in zero-g in his emaciated condition. Ari loosed his leg hold on the little man. "I am Saeed Esmail of the Caliphate, Prophet of Allah, all praises to Him, and the Ayatollah's warrior." Despite his condition, his face seemed to shine for a moment, and then he collapsed into unconsciousness.

Ari and Noel looked at each other in complete astonishment. "What was that all about?" Noel asked. Ari translated for him.

"You've got to be shitting me. We're four-hundred million kilometers from Earth, and we've got a stowaway spouting medieval religious crap!"

Before Ari could muster a sufficient response, Carmen floated through the lock, black bag in hand. Ari steadied her and said, "He just went unconscious, Doc. He's a Caliphate Jihadist. He's unpredictable, so be careful."

Carmen quickly took his vitals and examined his eyes and scalp. "Radiation," she said, "radiation sickness...has to be." She looked at Ari. "The solar storm a while back...I think he was exposed to its full intensity. Without immediate medical attention he will die." She stowed her instruments in her bag. "Help me get him to Sickbay, both of you." She indicated that Noel and Ari were to take him by head and foot to guide him through the lock. "Captain," she said on her Link executive override, "please meet me in Sickbay." It sounded more like an order than a request.

"This is crazy," Noel muttered to Ari. "This guy was sent here to kill us!"

"You don't know that," Ari said. "Let's at least give him a chance to explain himself."

Ari examined the stowaway as they moved him through the lock and into level six. *He could be my brother. Saeed Esmail – Happy, prosperous son of Abraham...what is this deluded young fool doing out here? What does the Caliphate intend? Where does this lead?*

The Captain arrived and took in the stowaway with reserved astonishment. "Prognosis, Doc?"

"I say pitch the little terrorist through the main lock," Noel said through clenched teeth.

Jon gave him an intense look, one that Ari had seen from time to time in his relationship with his American Navy friend. "Stow it!" Jon said curtly.

"Give me an hour, and I can be more specific, Captain. This man is near death from radiation exposure."

"Ari, stay with her. If he poses an immediate threat, do what you must, but try to keep him alive."

"He's too weak to be a threat, Jon," Carmen said.

"Not necessarily," Ari commented. "This guy is driven by a fanaticism no one onboard can ever really understand. I'll stay with you."

#

Jon returned to the Core and strapped himself into the Control Console chair. He set up a Flash transmission to Houston. The message: "Set up an *Eyes Only* reception for Mission Director Zakes. Acknowledge by return Flash Message. Include my Zulu time to transmit." Since the one-way transmission time was now fifteen minutes, Jon wanted to ensure the privacy of his communication to his old friend and shipmate on the Mars Expedition, Rod Zakes. He sent the transmission, and then unstrapped and floated across the Core and up the ladder well to the Canteen for a cup of coffee. *Cup,* he smiled to himself, *we drink from a bulb, but still call it a cup. Creatures of habit we are. Even that poor wretch down in Sickbay – a creature of his own habits and beliefs.*

Jon glided into his cabin with the bulb of black coffee, settled onto his easy chair, grinning to himself again, as he noted the habitual behavior. *Why do I like the feel of the chair when I can float in perfect comfort anywhere in the room?* He lifted himself from the chair and rolled over so he was looking at the deck. *So why does this fool less comfortable?* He asked himself, as he rolled back and settled against the chair fabric.

Jon couldn't get over the utter strangeness of a stowaway on his expedition. The Caliphate had not participated in the process nor competed for a place in the crew. The Ayatollah had been noticeably quiet about the entire expedition. The Islamic mindset was one Jon simply could not understand. Christians and the Jews, and most of their derivatives, had adapted to the modern world. They had allowed their faiths to evolve with the progress of knowledge, so that being a Jew or being a Christian still had meaning within the framework of a modern world. Islam seemed to reject the modern, except for weapons technology. When the Iranians had established their nuclear arsenal, they quickly swallowed up the entire Arab world, establishing an Islamic Caliphate that stretched from Pakistan in the East, to Uzbekistan in the North, Turkey in the Northwest, and across the entirety of North Africa from Somalia in the East to Mauritania in the West. The only holdout was the tiny nation of Israel.

The entire Caliphate was ruled by the current Ayatollah Khomeini, the Nizari Aga Khan of the Isma'ili Shi'i, who derived his power in a "strict" succession from 'Ali, the cousin and son-in-law of the Prophet Mohamed. The Ayatollah, with his council of twelve Imams, ruled the Caliphate under strict Shari'ah law as interpreted by the Shi'i branch of Islam.

And now, Jon thought, *one of their guys – one of their Jihadist Warriors – is on my ship halfway to Saturn. And I really can't let him die. The Caliphate certainly knows he's here. If he disappears, the Caliphate could launch a nuclear attack on Israel, or even Europe, Asia, or the U.S.* Jon shook his head in dismay as his Flash Traffic indicator roused him from his reverie. He took the call on his Link. CapCom wanted him to commence his *Eyes Only* transmission in five minutes. Obviously, they had hustled to get Rod to Mission Control.

Jon wrote out a general description of the stowaway and what they had found. He explained Saeed's serious medical condition, and indicated that they would do what they could to keep him alive.

A half-hour later he received a cryptic response, informing him that Houston would get back to him, and not to transmit anything else about the matter until then.

#

"Captain, I need to speak with you," Carmen said to Jon on her executive override. "Saeed is sedated and restrained in Sickbay. Ari is with him. May I come to your cabin?"

"Of course. I'll have a Latté waiting."

When Carmen arrived in the Canteen, she could still smell the pungent coffee aroma from the Captain's activities. Apparently, while he waited for her to arrive, Jon busied himself in the Canteen, operating the complicated gadget that enabled a person to make a Latté in zero-g. It was an ingenious device that mixed coffee, a special powder, and air resulting in a Latté that was close to the real thing. Jon handed her the bulb when she floated through his door shortly thereafter.

He commands our lives, but he makes me coffee, she thought, remembering how Jesus had washed his disciples' feet. She noticed that he seemed to be sitting in his easy chair, although it was obviously for effect, since one place was as good as another in zero-g. "Thank you, Captain." She put as much warmth into her voice as possible. He nodded expectantly. "Saeed apparently was exposed to the full brunt of the solar storm we experienced. He is suffering from a serious case of radiation sickness, and will die unless he receives a bone marrow transplant." She paused to let that information sink in. Jon waited quietly for her to go on. "Back on Earth, a bone marrow transplant is no big deal. But out here, under these circumstances...well, it's never been done in zero-g, and I've never done it." Jon raised his eyebrows and looked intently at her, making her feel a pressing need to say more. "I know what to do, and certainly am capable of performing the procedure, but you have to know that it is a huge risk. It might be a death sentence instead of a cure."

Jon smiled encouragingly, and said' "What happens if you don't do a marrow transplant?"

"He dies...in two or three days maximum. He dies."

"What about a donor?" Jon's question surprised Carmen, because of its obvious implied insight into the problem.

"I ran his DNA against the crew. Ginger is a surprisingly close match given the obvious physical differences between her and Saeed, but Ari is as close as a person can be without being an identical twin." Jon looked at her, his face expressing surprise. "They could be brothers," Carmen told him.

"I'll be damned! Does Ari know?"

"Not yet. I wanted to discuss the matter with you first. We could use Ginger, but the odds of success would be less than fifty percent. If we use Ari, we're up above ninety percent – basically as good as it gets if you don't have a twin."

"Okay, set it up, but let me inform Ari. How are my injured crew?'

"Ginger will be out of her cast in a couple of days, Dmitri's knee is virtually healed, Ari's bandage comes off tomorrow, and Michele is more bothered by the shaved patch of hair than anything else – she's doing fine. Chen hasn't changed, and I'm worried about him. What bothers me is that his brain wave pattern is normal, yet he remains in a coma. I don't understand why, and Houston hasn't come up with anything useful, either."

#

Ari's initial reaction to Jon's request that he donate bone marrow for Saeed's transplant was incredulity. As he thought about it, however, it began to make sense. His entire family came from Semitic stock that had Palestinian roots going back centuries. The Persian Caliphate had eliminated borders throughout its empire, even forcefully resettled entire villages to compensate for perceived differences or requirements that fell out of its interpretation of the *Qur'an* and *Sunnah*. It was not unreasonable, therefore, to find a Shi'ite of Palestinian heritage closely linked to the Persian Caliphate out of Teheran. Assuming Saeed survived, it would be interesting to see how he handled having Jewish bone marrow.

Ari presented himself to Carmen for the procedure. "I'm going to put you under," she told him, "and remove bone marrow from your iliac crest with this." She showed him a rather large syringe. "I'll remove about two-hundred milliliters, and slowly infuse it into Saeed's blood stream. You'll be done in about an hour, but I'll keep you under observation for another hour, so I'll have you for just under three hours." She smiled at him with a professional demeanor that almost seemed a bit cold to Ari. "You'll be sore for a couple of days, as if you had smacked your upper hip during the tumble. That's it, really. Your body will replenish the missing marrow in about a week."

"You understand the irony, don't you Doc?"

"I do," she answered with a smile that felt much warmer. "Here, let me strap you down."

Just under three hours later, Ari peered through bleary eyes at the Doctor's pretty face. "How are you feeling, Ari?" she asked.

"I've felt better," he said, with a nonchalance he didn't feel. "It feels like you whacked my hip with a sledge hammer."

"Just be happy we are in zero-g," she answered. "I thought you were the tough guy in the crew."

Ari tossed her a wry grin as his world came into focus again. "Let's keep it a secret," he said, winking at her. "I got work to do." He sailed out the Sickbay door.

Chapter eight

This time Ari and Noel stopped briefly in the forward Box end cap to examine the huge horizontal tether reel. The tether was tightly wound on the horizontal reel, layer upon layer, each winding tightly set against the previous one, exactly as it was supposed to be. They continued through the Box to the lower end cap.

Noel got there first, and when Ari arrived, he found Noel staring at the take-up reel. Instead of being tightly wound on the horizontal reel, as it was in the forward end cap, what Ari saw was a jumble of winding over winding, sort of a rat's nest that is every fly fisherman's nightmare, but on a gigantic scale.

"Jon," Ari said on his Link, "You're going to want to look at this in person."

Jon showed up a few minutes later, followed by Dmitri not long after that.

The four men took some time to examine the reel and rat's nest from every angle, occasionally probing between loose windings.

"The way I see it," Jon said at last, "is that we have only two options." He floated down over the part of the reel where the end passed through a guide and then to the exit point in the center of the end cap. "We can take a chance that the aramid cable wrapping is undamaged. After all, the conductivity appears intact. That means we return to tether using this one. And while we do it, you, Ari, remain right here physically monitoring the unreeling. Assuming it goes well, when we are on extended tether, you can EVA your way back to the Pullman. If you find a damaged area, then we retract it back, and go to Plan B. The other option, Plan B, is to change out the reel now." He paused for a bit. "Give me some feedback."

"No need to EVA back," Ari said. "We just retract the tether long enough for me to return to the Pullman. Then extend the tether again."

"If it's damaged," Dmitri said, "then we obviously save time by changing the reel now."

"But," Ari interrupted, "if it's in good shape, we waste the good tether. If we need it in the future, we're screwed."

"I agree," Noel said.

"I guess I do, too," Dmitri said. "I'd rather use up some extra time now, and have a spare available, if we ever need it."

"Okay," Jon said. "I think I want to hear from Houston on this one." He headed back.

"I'll follow up with Jon," Dmitri told the other two, and headed forward after Jon.

Ari and Noel went through the lock into the Caboose, and proceeded to check out the circuits locally. They split up the task, with Noel checking the reactor circuitry and Ari checking the VASIMR circuitry. To Ari's great relief, there appeared to be no damage. With that, they wrapped it up, and returned to the Pullman to eat and rest up before their EVA.

#

Jon put a call through to Houston. Since the signal would take seventeen minutes to reach Houston, he put everything into his message "It's like this," he told them, after explaining the problem with the rat's nest of tangled windings. "The after tether has electrical integrity, but until we let it out, we simply don't know about the aramid wrapping. I thought about having a couple of guys go EVA and pull it out, but the tether is designed to be pulled out by the Caboose at one gravity. No two guys on this vessel are going to make that happen. We can extend the tether with someone watching at the reel. Probably, he will detect any degradation of the outside of the tether. If it's good, we extend it fully, and the observer makes his way back to the Pullman in an individual flyer, since there is no way he can descend two clicks in a gravity field. If it's damaged, then we replace the reel – that's a two-day operation. We're seventeen days away from the Jupiter boost, and fifteen days away from retracting the tether before the boost.

"Now, here's the problem. If the tether is damaged, we need to make a command decision whether to continue the mission, or return home. If the decision is to return home, we should be thinking about using Jupiter to give us the homeward momentum. This means we need to examine the tether in the next ten days or so. I'm sure you see the ramifications. I don't want scrubbing the mission to be my decision. My take – our take – is to go, no matter what. We're happy staying in free fall until after the boost, and then extending the tether and determining any damage.

"I'll be standing by for your analysis and recommendations."

What Jon got back from Houston thirty-four minutes later was a curt: "Roger...stand by."

The full answer took several hours. When it came, it was from Rod Zakes, *Eyes Only*, double encrypted.

"I don't need to tell you that the implications of your stowaway have potentially staggering repercussions here on Earth. You need to ensure absolutely whether Esmail transmitted anything back to Earth. We are assuming he was trained, and left to his own resources, once he got to El-four. We traced him to the provisioning crew, where apparently he staged an accident that "killed" him, using the surrounding activity to set up his surreptitious presence. Did he have a transmitter with him? We presume from the sophistication of the enterprise that he very likely had a burst transmitter – possibly more than one. If he didn't transmit, our task is easier, but if he did, we will have to prepare for the inevitable onslaught of propaganda. The answer to this question has the highest priority.

"You need to consider that if he transmitted, and should he succumb for any reason at all, the Caliphate will be all over it. No matter what happened, we will be blamed for his death. With Ari on board, it will be twisted into a Zionist plot, and two billion Muslims will rise in protest. The Europeans will appease, the Asians will delay, the Russians will stir the pot, and we alone will be holding back the tide. It might even give the Caliphate the reason it has been seeking to nuke Israel.

"I'm NOT being melodramatic – this is our best assessment, fully vetted by State and the White House. So, assuming he's transmitted, we NEED to find a way out of this! Deal only with me about this, always *Eyes Only*.

"As to the tether situation, we will not order you to continue if you believe – in your best judgment – that the mission is fatally compromised by the asteroid impact on the tether. Assuming, however, that you will do what I would do, we recommend you remain coupled until after the boost. Then solve your problem. You have a good spare. Remember, the likelihood of this happening in the first place was infinitesimal. The odds of it happening again are equally small. One caveat – keep the old tether. You never know when it might come in handy.

"Good luck, and God's speed, my old friend. With all your troubles, I still envy you. We picked the best man for the job, and I guess you now have the opportunity to show us just how right we were."

#

Jon brought the entire crew together in the Canteen. Carmen had assured him that Saeed was sedated and would remain out for several more hours. Chen remained in his coma with virtually no change in his condition. His vitals were strong and his brain wave pattern continued to be normal. Carmen had transmitted to Houston the entire store of data she had taken on him since the accident. The best medical minds on Earth were working on a solution, but in the meantime, Chen remained in Sickbay, apparently sleeping peacefully. Chen's condition bothered Jon, but he left its solution to his ship's doctor and her Earthside support team. Ginger sported her cast with a certain air of pride – hinted at, but not expressed, and Jon thought she winked at him as she glided into the Canteen. Ari was fully recovered, having discarded the adhesive bandage after returning from the Caboose. Jon was grateful for his friend's dedication, and gave him a warm smile when he and Noel floated in. Michele found a way to cover her shaved spot, sporting two ponytails that fanned out around the back of her head in zero-g like a halo. They made her look younger – a fact that she discovered almost immediately. Jon thought she was pretty as a picture, and said so when she and Elke arrived, knowing how much it mattered to her. Elke continued to be solicitous toward Michele, which was fine with Jon, because this gave Carmen more time to handle Chen and now Saeed. Dmitri was the last to arrive. In zero-g, Jon couldn't tell about his knee, but Dmitri was not one to complain, and Jon respected his decision not to make an issue of his injury.

"We've heard back from Houston," Jon said without preamble, "on both matters." The group formed in interesting picture. Jon and Noel tended to respect the visual up and down, orienting themselves as if they were under gravity. The rest of the crew placed themselves in whatever position gave them a good vantage. In addition, Jon couldn't help but notice that Michele ensured he had a good view of the physical effect that zero-g had on her breasts. He gave her the satisfaction of noticing, and then tried his best to keep from noticing any further. "Houston is concerned that our guest may have brought burst transmitters with him – even that he might already have used one. Because we don't know, we have to assume that the Caliphate knows he made it onboard successfully. Houston wants heroic efforts to keep him alive."

"That goes without saying," Carmen said. "We're already doing that."

"I know, Dr. Bhuta. We all are cheering your efforts." He returned his focus to the group. "So, as of now, all Earthside communications go through me – no exceptions." He looked at Carmen. "That includes you, too, Doctor." Jon tried to remain dignified during his discourse, but in zero-g, dignity is difficult to maintain. As he indicated Carmen, he raised his hand, and the next thing he knew, he was floating above the chair he had been "occupying," rotating slowly. Ari reached out and steadied him. "The thing is, there can be no slipups with communications, no accidental mentions of the problem...nothing at all." He smiled grimly. "Houston suggests that we remain coupled until after the boost, and that we solve our tether problem on the Saturn leg. I think we pretty much agree with that." He glanced around the group for feedback. "Ari, you and Noel perform your EVA inspection so we can address any problems you find ASAP. Dmitri, you and Ginger join me in my quarters to go over the Jupiter boost." He allowed himself to float away from the chair toward the coffee urn. "One more thing," he said softly. "You all know what happened to Saeed. Don't take a solar storm announcement lightly. Make sure – absolutely sure – that you are in the Core when the storm passes. We cannot afford to lose any of you!" He filled three bulbs with the steaming aromatic liquid. "Besides," he added as an afterthought, "Doc Bhuta has her hands full now. We don't want her to be the only one working around here."

#

In his stateroom, Jon tossed a bulb to Dmitri and the second to Ginger. Ginger touched the tube to her lips and squeezed.

"Aiee!" Ginger's face screwed into mock horror. "What's this sweet syrup?"

Dmitri sipped his own bulb. "How can you drink this piss?" He exchanged bulbs with Ginger.

"It's simple, really," she said. "It's blond because I'm not, and not sweet because I am."

"Give it up, Dmitri," Jon interjected with a wry grin. "You can't win this one." He called up a holodisplay and coupled their Links so they could fully interact. "Let's get to work."

They watched as the astrogation computer turned their current parameters into a visible blue track in the display. Dmitri made an adjustment, and the display shifted so they were looking at it from above. Superimposed in the display, their old track appeared in red. "As you can see," Dmitri said, "our track has been vectored toward Jupiter."

Ginger picked up. "The closer we get to Jupiter, the more energy we must expend to return to the ideal track." As she spoke, a series of yellow vectors sprang from their current blue track that curved toward, and finally merged with the red track. At each departure from the blue track, a series of numbers appeared, listing the required energy expenditure, the thrust vector at one-g, and the time under thrust.

"What we're saying," Dmitri added, "is that sooner is better than later."

"Ari and Noel are prepping their EVA right now," Jon said. "If they find nothing amiss, we'll do the burn."

\#

"How many EVAs have you done?" Ari asked Noel as he grabbed an inner garment and handed another to Noel.

"One, actually," Noel answered, "while at the International Space Station during training."

"That's it?"

"Yep...that's it, just one time."

"So..."

"Well...I also had several underwater sessions to practice RL work. Enjoyed it, actually. Seems I have a knack for it."

"Yeh...reaction-less work." Ari looked incredulous. "Who thinks up these terms?" Ari pulled an outer suit from its Velcro bulkhead attachment and pushed it toward Noel. "Ever used one of these?"

"Not this model," Noel answered, but I've used an earlier light weight model."

These suits were a radical departure from the bulky suits that had been part of space exploration for so long. Lightweight and flexible, even in hard vacuum, they worked on a technologically advanced application of earlier high-altitude suits. An inner garment formed a flexible, skin tight membrane that substituted for atmospheric pressure, and contained several physiological sensors. A slightly less tightly fitting outer garment retained a minimal atmospheric environment inside the suit, and provided temperature and wear resistance. Ari and Noel entered the outer suits feet first through an airtight zipper-like opening in the suit's back.

It took Noel a bit of getting used to the suit, since initially it felt like his chest was being squeezed. When he breathed deeply as Ari instructed, the pressure seemed to relax, although it came back as he exhaled. He found that with a bit of effort, it almost seemed like the suit was helping him breathe. The gloves were comfortably flexible, although Noel decided he would be glad to remove them when he returned to normal atmospheric pressure. He pitied the guys who had to flex their fingers for eight hours. They each wore a close-fitting skullcap that contained various additional sensors that would transmit their physiological condition back to the ship, and Doc Bhuta.

They were floating in the lower bay of the Box, their clear helmets still attached to the holding platforms. "So you're not an EVA virgin, and RL is part of your skill set?" Ari's voice was friendly, without any sting of sarcasm. "There is a major difference here. You were tethered at the ISS, right?" Noel nodded. "And you didn't have any propulsion..." Noel nodded again. "Well..." Ari pushed himself across the space, what little there was, to a rack containing several pairs of boots. "TBH Propulsion Boots – these are the latest and greatest." He pulled a pair from its Velcro holder, and showed Noel the small nozzle recessed into the sole of each boot at the ball of the foot. The nozzles angled forward about thirty degrees.

"TBH?" Noel asked.

"Stands for Thomas, Bird, and Hellbaum, three NASA guys who invented the first jet shoes back in nineteen-sixty-seven. NASA tested the jet shoes Earthside back then, but so far as I know, they were not introduced into current use until just a few years ago. Once you get used to them, they're better than any of the old back-pack rigs." Ari handed Noel a pair and proceeded to put another pair on his own suited feet. They fit like riding boots, but with completely flexible ankles. The boot uppers consisted of two stiff, shaped polymer bags that contained pressurized hypergolic fuel components – UDMH and nitrogen tetroxide, innocuous by themselves, but bring them together, and they spontaneously combust, producing a significant thrust. The fuel valves were controlled by a microswitch under each big toe. "Press down your big toe," Ari explained, "and ten newtons of force push the ball of your foot. Just bend your knees for the appropriate thrust vector, including torque. You'll get the hang of it in no time, and be tap-tapping yourself all over the place."

Noel slipped his head into the transparent, spherical helmet Ari handed him, and pressed it to the sealing collar around his neck, just like in training. The collar sealed to the clear globe with a faint click; from inside, the helmet was completely invisible. Noel felt a faint movement of cool air as his breathing system cut in. Simultaneously, Noel's suit Link activated. A holodisplay appeared in front of him exactly as it would under normal conditions using a regular Link.

"Com check, Noel." It took Noel a moment to react. "Noel, com check!" Ari's voice was insistent.

Noel reached up to adjust his skullcap, forgetting about the helmet, and struck it with his gloved hand. "This is Noel...roger."

"Ari, Noel, it's Jon...com check." They both responded.

Noel conducted a safety inspection of Ari's backpack. It consisted of three relatively thin cylinders. Two were specially insulated bottles that held liquid oxygen. The middle slightly larger one contained a breathing bag that used an electronic-molecular trick to scrub carbon dioxide. The gas fed through a flexible tube attached to the suit's right shoulder into the suit just below the collar ring under the chin, and back out through a similar tube over the left shoulder. The electronics pack nestled below the cylinders at the small of the back. After Noel finished his examination of Ari's backpack, he attached a lightweight flush fairing. The fairing served to eliminate possible snag points on the backpack. It displayed in bright florescent letters: RAWLSTON. Following Noel's indication that his unit was okay, Ari inspected Noel's backpack and installed his fairing with its fluorescent label: GODDARD.

Ari reached for a coil of light line. "Just in case," he said over the circuit, grinning at Noel. "I don't want to end up chasing you all the way to Jupiter."

Chapter nine

They floated through the lock, and Ari secured the hatch behind them. Noel turned to face the ship, brought his legs together bent slightly at the knee, and experimentally tapped his big toes. Although he barely felt the momentary thrust against his soles, the effect was to make the ship and Ari seem to shrink slightly. His intellect told him he was moving directly away from the hatch at a nominal velocity, but his senses preferred the shrinking explanation. Noel was tempted to haul in on his safety line, but instead, he straightened his legs so the nozzles pointed slightly forward, and tapped again. This put him into a slow tumble forward that he stopped by bending his knees and tapping when his feet pointed away from the ship. Another tap with slightly bent knees, and the shrinking stopped.

"Pretty good for a newbie," Ari said on the circuit. "My first time, I was tumbling in three dimensions." He laughed. "Try a couple of maneuvers...I'll keep the line on you."

Noel found he was adept at maneuvering with the TBH boots. In no time he found himself pirouetting, pitching, rolling, yawing, and even recovering quickly from a full-fledged uncontrolled tumble.

"You guys gonna play all day, or get some work done," Jon

growled from the Core.

"You got a holocam on this guy, right?" Ari asked. "It's his first time, you know."

"He's done a lot of ice skating, Ari, up in Canada. I know they don't have a lot of ice where you come from, but Noel cuts a pretty figure on the ice."

"No shit, Noel, you never told me."

"The subject never came up," Noel said. "The skills are similar." Noel found that he could replace a push-off with a toe tap, and his instincts took care of the rest. It was rather surprising, and he enjoyed the hell out of it.

"Jon's right, Noel...let's get to work."

As Noel jetted the hundred meters he had drifted, he looked about at the star filled universe surrounding him. The sky was so jammed with stars that it was virtually impossible to pick out the familiar constellations. The Sun was easy to find, but unlike from the Earth where it was about the size of a silver dollar, it was about the size of a dime, perhaps a bit smaller, but still too bright to look at directly. Jupiter showed a noticeable disk, as did Saturn, although it was much smaller. Mars, behind them was just a glowing red dot off to the side of the Sun. And the Earth was just a blue "star" on the Sun's other side. The Milky Way was a spectacular band of mottled white that filled a section of sky arching above and below their apparent orientation. Since Noel knew that the Galactic ecliptic intersected the Solar ecliptic at about sixty degrees, he was able to orient himself with respect to their current position – something that gave him a real sense of security and genuine satisfaction. Noel rejoined Ari, and they did a careful inspection of the external cable feed from the forward end cap of the Box. Other than some superficial marking where the major strain by the tether against the nozzle had occurred, everything looked fine.

They made their way along the Box to the after end cap. Like the forward end cap, it also showed some wear marks, but there appeared to be no actual damage. "Okay," Ari said, "let's do the Caboose. We'll split up, but keep in visual range of each other. Remember to stay clear of the checkered stripes."

"Yeh, I know, neutron flux from the reactor."

With a light line loosely connecting them, Ari and Noel moved around the fuel tanks at the forward end of the Caboose. They found no damage. The reactor segment was also damage free. The forward portion was easy to examine, because of the smooth exterior. A simple visual check did it. Any damage would have been obvious. The four VASIMR engines, however, were not faired, so that the two men had to move in and about each engine as they conducted their inspection. The process was slow and tedious, and they had to untether themselves in order to avoid entangling the line. The process took a good four hours, but finally they met, floating free at the business end of the Caboose, and exchanged high fives. The systems were undamaged.

In high spirits, they jetted back to the after end of the Box, activated the air lock, and entered the space they had left several hours earlier. Noel placed gloved hands on both sides of his helmet and rotated it to the left one half turn. With a soft hiss, the seal released, and he removed the clear globe. Ari did likewise. "Let's get cleaned up and grab a bite to eat," he said, slipping through the back of his suit.

#

Elke was upset – more than upset, she was pissed off. Order and clarity were important, but order had left her world when the asteroid struck the tether. And the Saeed matter just made things worse, and far more complicated. Her immediate instinct was to toss him out the lock without the benefit of a suit. But it wasn't her call, and the man in charge had his orders...and order mattered above all else. As the one crew member without an immediate task, and only one of two uninjured, Jon had assigned her to scour the Box, looking for anything that might be a communicator.

Once Elke got used to the smell, the task was tedious and boring. If anyone could find the proverbial needle in the haystack, Elke knew she was the person. She started at Saeed's encampment, searching thoroughly one meter out in all directions. If it wasn't sealed, she opened it – she examined literally everything...and found nothing. This meant one of only two things – there were no communicators, or Saeed had hidden them somewhere other than his encampment. Since she could not assume there were no communicators, she now had two choices. She likened her choice to how computer chess programs developed. The initial approach had been to use brute power, analyzing as many moves as possible within the available timeframe. Obviously speed helped, and a so-called super computer played a fantastic chess game. The more elegant approach, and one that languished for decades as computers became more sophisticated, was to analyze the game the way a human player does, and pick the most effective strategy. Only in the last twenty years or so did this approach begin to show real results. She could use brute force in her search, continuing around the encampment compartment, item by item, and on to the next compartment, until she either found something, or finally determined that there were no communicators. Or, she could use finesse, and that is what she chose. She floated inside Saeed's tent, and let her mind wander in a focused way, trying to think like Saeed, something that did not come naturally to Elke.

Saeed had to know that sooner or later he would be found out – it was inevitable. He couldn't be left in the ship when the crew descended to Iapetus, and he couldn't just take unidentified items with him to the surface. So, anything he wanted on the surface would have to be hidden inside something that would necessarily be moved to the surface. There were two combination lander/rovers, so logically, if Saeed had hidden any communicators, they would be inside one of the lander/rovers.

Elke dropped down one level – she still thought of it as down even though *back* was probably more appropriate in their current zero-g configuration – and made her way into the strange looking combination lander/rover stored in the six-meter-high chamber. Like *Cassini II*, the lander/rover was constructed of aramid polymer, lightweight and strong. The machine was a four-and-a-quarter-meter long, three-meter wide cylinder sitting horizontally atop three sets of large foam filled rubber tires that rested against the back deck. The front end was a tough radiation resistant transparent polymer, and the cylinder contained three sapphire matrix ports down each side and three along the top. A medium size nozzle surrounded by hypergolic fuel tanks extended three-quarters of a meter from the back. Three extendible pads spaced around the back of the cylinder were designed to absorb the landing forces – such as they were on Iapetus, where the gravity was only 0.02g, some forty times less than on Earth. The lander's three-and-a-half-meter interior configuration was split by a deck running the length of the cylinder with a two-meter space above the deck, and storage below the deck, accessible from both inside and outside. The main deck consisted of a front section that sat six passengers three across with storage behind them. A three-quarter-meter chamber behind the rear bulkhead contained a compact variable output gas core reactor. Like *Cassini II's* main reactor, this smaller compact version was fueled by gaseous uranium-hexafluoride fissile material. The gas was injected into a small fused silica vessel where it produced extremely high-energy ultraviolet light that generated prodigious amounts of electricity with photovoltaics that surrounded the outer wall. This electricity was directed to the electric motors on the six wheels, and to the vehicle interior. The lander/rover landed vertically on the pads. When it stabilized, a fourth pad extended from beneath the nose in the rover configuration, and the rear pad aligned with the top of the rover configuration extended until the lander tipped onto the nose pad and the six wheels to become the rover. It had a one-atmosphere interior, accessed through a lock on the vehicle's left side. In addition, there were emergency exits in the overhead and undercarriage that opened directly to the outside without benefit of a lock.

Elke conducted a systematic examination of the interior, commencing with the control panel that crossed in front of the clear polymer front end. Since the lander/rover was designed to operate in both zero-g and very-slight-g, every usable surface was covered with compartments, some with elastic net covers, and some with doors. Virtually all the compartments were filled with things that the planners determined would be necessary on Iapetus' surface. Elke systematically emptied each compartment, examined each item, and restowed them in their original configuration. It was slow, tedious work, but Elke didn't complain – she just opened one compartment after the other, searching. In the bottom-most rearward locker on the starboard side, behind a relatively massive storage capacitor that was a spare for their surface burst transmitter, she discovered two spheres about the size of a softball, although she didn't characterize them as such because she wasn't familiar with the game. She didn't recognize what they were, but after a bit of experimentation, she opened one, and immediately deduced that it was a combination miniature holocamcorder and a transmitter of some kind.

"Captain, it's Elke," she said on her Link, "I found them!"

#

Carmen had spent most of her waking and sleeping hours with her two patients. Chen remained unchanged, vitals well within normal range, and brain electrical patterns nominal. Yet he remained in a coma. She had attached both electrical and mechanical stimulators to his extremities to maintain his muscle tone, and she fed him intravenously. The crew's regular diet contained carefully designed levels of mega vitamins, and Carmen ensured that Chen's feed line was similarly fortified. She was convinced that sooner or later he would come out of it.

Carmen's other patient was well on the path to recovery, so much so, in fact, that she reduced his sedation, and allowed him to become aware of his surroundings. When he first awakened, he seemed confused, bewildered even at his circumstances. He muttered something that Carmen could not really understand, even though she was fluent in eight languages, and conversant in a dozen more. She placed herself in his line of vision and said to him in Arabic, "I am Dr. Bhuta, Medical Officer on *Space Ship Cassini II*. Do you understand me?"

Saeed looked at her through eyes that appeared still a bit out of focus. "How do you know my language?" he asked, followed immediately by, "What happened to me?" He tried to move his arms and legs, but discovered that they were restrained. He began to struggle.

"If you do not settle down," Carmen told him in Arabic, "I will sedate you again." He stopped struggling immediately, which she took as a sign that he was more lucid than he appeared. "You were seriously injured by radiation," she told him. "A crew member gave you a bone marrow transplant, and that saved your life." She left his field of vision to let him think about that for a bit.

"Captain," she said on her Link, "you asked to be informed when Saeed awakened. He is awake."

"Roger that, I'll be right down."

Jon showed up several minutes later with Ari in tow. He was carrying the two communicators.

"He's still a bit bore sighted," Carmen told him. "It helps to place yourself in his line of vision."

Jon floated so that Saeed could see him and what he held in his hands. "I am Captain Jon Stock, Commander of *Space Ship Cassini II.*"

Saeed looked at him with stoic eyes.

"Do you recognize these?" Jon asked, indicating the communicators. Saeed remained silent. "I asked you a question." Jon's voice took on a demanding tone. "I know you speak English – Answer me!" Saeed continued to remain silent.

Jon turned to Carmen. "Unhook him from everything, Doc." He turned to Ari. "Ari, cuff him!"

Carmen started to protest, but Jon raised his hand with a look that instantly silenced her. A minute later, Saeed floated between Jon and Ari, his hands cuffed behind his back. He wore a loose fitting white jumpsuit and no shoes. They crossed the compartment to the airlock opposite Sickbay. Unceremoniously, Jon shoved him into the lock and closed the inner door.

Carmen was horrified. "Captain...Jon...you can't do that!"

"Silence, Dr. Bhuta! Not another word!" From his tone, Carmen was convinced that if she spoke again, she would follow Saeed into the airlock. She watched in sickening horror as Ari began to cycle the air pump, sucking the air out of the lock. Jon activated the intercom. "You have fifteen seconds to start talking or I'll open the outer door. Do you understand?" Jon turned to Ari. "Tell him in Arabic!"

Ari did, as he continued to pump air out of the lock. "Ldyk khmsh ashr thanyh lbad'a almhadthat aw swf yfth albaaba alkharji-alkharjy. Hl tfhm?" Ari continued, "...ashrh thanyh..."

Ten seconds, Carmen whispered to herself. Speak you little fool! "...khmsh thanyh..."

Five seconds, Carmen held her breath.

Saeed began to scream...high pitched and terrified. Ari stopped the air evacuation, but kept the pump running. "*Wswf tjyba ala aseelty?*" Ari demanded, asking if Saeed would answer his questions. Saeed continued to scream. "*Hl ant?*" Ari demanded again.

Will you? Carmen whispered.

"Nam, aqsm baallh, nam, wsajyba!" Saeed screamed

Yes, I swear to Allah, I will answer! Carmen continued to translate under her breath, simultaneously fascinated and horrified by what was transpiring before her.

"IIe swears he will answer," Ari said. Jon nodded, and Ari commenced repressurizing the lock. Halfway to full pressurization, he stopped and said through the intercom: "*Hl ant mtakd?*"

Are you sure? Carmen whispered. *Say yes!*

"Wana wathq... wana wathq... wana wathq! Aqsm baallh, wana wathq!" Saeed was screaming hysterically again.

I am sure...I am sure...I am sure! I swear by Allah, I am sure! Carmen continued to translate under her breath, terribly afraid for what might happen next.

"He says he'll talk – he swears he will," Ari said with a grin. "Just like old times, huh?" He turned to Carmen. "Did you really think we were going to jettison him?" He slipped an arm around her tiny shoulders. "You know better than that, Doc. We're the good guys!"

Chapter ten

Carmen hovered in a lotus position next to Chen, looking at him, and thinking about the half hour past. Her long black hair was wrapped around her head and piled so that she appeared to be wearing a dark crown. Her pale blue jumpsuit showed her svelte form without advertising as Michele did. She was deep in thought. What would have happened had Saeed not agreed to talk? He certainly believed he was moments from an agonizing death. She had thought so as well. She simply couldn't wrap her mind around what had happened. Two powerful men had bullied a sick little human into agreeing to betray his own beliefs...but what about their safety? What about the mission? What about her own beliefs? Carmen kept stumbling on the simple fact that Jon's and Ari's threats violated every tenant of her Christian faith and her solemn Hippocratic Oath. And yet, without the information they would have obtained by now, they all were threatened. It was confusing and complicated – somewhat like what she experienced when she first began to study biology.

Her childhood faith required that God put his finger into the mix and bring things about in a way that simply didn't agree with what she was learning about what science had discovered. With time, however, she came to understand that her faith had plenty of room to incorporate anything science had to offer. Just as the Church had once believed that the Earth was the center of everything, as human knowledge grew, so – eventually – did the Church's understanding. Not only was it okay for the Sun to rule the Solar System, in the long run, the Solar System's real magnificence totally dwarfed what the Church had earlier believed, and this – in turn – had led to a deeper understanding of God's magnificence. The question of how life came about brought Carmen another quandary, but ultimately, she was able to see the hand of God in the spectacular machinery of life, and in the intricate detail of her own specialty.

Here and now, however, Carmen was faced with another kind of challenge. How do you juxtapose the safety of all against the safety of one – especially when that one has transgressed so grievously against the rest? Where does expedience trump principle?

At that point, Elke drifted into Sickbay, bearing two bulbs of coffee. "A Latté for my favorite Doc," Elke said with a warm, inviting smile.

This was not the first time Elke had come, bearing gifts, and not the first time Carmen had been taken aback by the gesture. "Thank you, Elke. What brings you down here?"

"I heard about the interrogation, and thought you might want some company." Elke reached out and touched Carmen's cheek.

Inwardly, Carmen withdrew, suppressing a sense of revulsion. Instead of responding, she sipped her Latté and busied herself with Chen's feeding tube.

"How's our patient?" Elke asked.

"It's a mystery," Carmen answered, glad to be on another subject. "I've really never seen anything like it." Elke floated to her side, and Carmen allowed herself to drift away from the close proximity of the woman on the make. "Elke...can we talk?"

"Sure...what's up?"

"I know things are pretty loose and randy around here. I also know that you are a confirmed lesbian," Carmen winced a bit at the word, "and I get it that you are attracted to me." She paused and took a long breath. "I'm not wired that way, and my religious faith prohibits what you are asking me to do. Can you understand that? I don't want to hurt your feelings, and I don't want to insult you, but I don't want you to insult me either." Carmen allowed herself to display a little smile. "Can I be your doctor? Can we be friends...without that other intruding into the friendship?"

Elke's face dropped, and Carmen thought she might begin to cry. Then Elke sighed and gave Carmen a sheepish smile. "I think I really knew that, Doc. I'm sorry...you <u>are</u> my doctor, and you <u>are</u> my friend. We'll keep it that way."

#

"*Cassini II* is near the Jupiter boost, Sahib." The gray bearded man in flowing robe and turban bowed low before the seated Caliph. "Your Houston Hashashiyyin reports that the ship suffered a near disaster when the after tether was struck by a small asteroid."

"Such things are possible?"

"Yes, Sahib...there is more." He placed his forehead on the glistening floor tiles, fully expecting the Caliph's wrath. "Your Jihad Warrior Saeed Esmail was discovered by the crew – he is seriously ill caused by radiation from a solar storm."

"And the rest of the crew?"

"They were protected by a shielded compartment, Sahib."

"And Esmail...?"

"He was undiscovered at the time, Sahib. He was unaware..."

"So the crew was not at fault?"

"No, Sahib. In fact, the crew saved his life...an Indian doctor, Carmen Bhuta – a Christian, Sahib."

"And Esmail's last transmission?"

"Just before the asteroid hit. He was already seriously ill, Sahib. His mind was affected."

The Caliph stroked his beard in contemplation.

"There's more, Sahib." He rolled his shoulders forward, pressing his face against the cool tiles. "The Israeli Ari Rawlins donated the bone marrow that saved Esmail's life."

The Ayatollah Khomeini rose to his feet, his 190-centimeter stature towering over the terrified messenger. "A Jew...a damnable Jew! A Jew saved my warrior?" He lifted his hands into the air just above his face. "Damnation!"

#

Jon informed Houston of the two burst transmissions from Saeed. He told them that he was confident there were no other transmissions. With one-way time at about half-an-hour, two-way conversations were tedious, complicated by the eyes-only restriction Houston had placed on all communications. Rod Zakes especially wanted to know if there had been any transmissions from *Cassini II* besides Jon's and Saeed's. When Jon told him no, he even asked if Jon knew for sure. Once Jon had satisfied him, Zakes explained.

"NSA has picked up some chatter apparently emanating from the Caliphate that contains current information that only you, I, and a half-dozen other persons know about. I was hoping it came from your end. If so, you could fix that with no Earthside complications. It seems I've got a leak here, Jon, from the inner circle. Do you remember that code you and I created when we attended Crypto school together? The one that nobody could crack? Computerize it at your end. Use an off-line unit, and never put that unit online...ever. We'll use that from now on."

Jon remembered the code well. They each owned original editions of Robert Heinlein's *Stranger in a Strange Land* and James P. Hogan's *Code of the Lifemaker*. Their code was a simple double encrypted word substitution. They started with the last word on the last Heinlein page, creating a substitution cipher with those letters followed by the remaining alphabet in order – that for the first word of the message. The next substitution cipher was the second-to-last word on the next-to-last page, then the third-to-last on the third-to-last page, and so forth. If a message actually went through all the book's pages, they would start the cycle again with the second-to-last word on the last page. The encrypted message was then run through exactly the same procedure using the Hogan book. Each successive message in a thread would commence with the next word on the last Heinlein page. The resulting double encrypted messages were virtually impossible to crack without knowing which specific books were used.

Ever since then, Jon had carried page images of those books on his personal digital stash, as he knew Zakes did. He programmed his offline unit to create two word lists following their old algorithm, and then set it up to produce a final double encrypted message copy. He tested the encoder by encrypting a short poem by Edna St. Vincent

Millay that both he and Zakes loved:
    I burn my candle at both ends,
    It will not last the night.
    But oh my foes, and oh my friends,
    It gives a lovely light.
    He sent it off, and about an hour later received an encrypted reply. It broke out to: *Yes it does, doesn't it?*
    They were in business.

#

    Saeed's life had always been filled with certainty. He was a devout Shi'i, devoted to the Caliph. He was a Jihadist, a warrior assigned to the noblest task in history. His purpose had always been clear and his focus sharp. This was even more so after his epiphany in the Box, with his new understanding of Allah's purpose in his life (*may Allah be blessed*).
    But then everything changed. Allah seemed to have abandoned him in the middle of his journey, his task unaccomplished. Allah had stricken him with a terrible disease that the Christian doctor had cured with the generous, life-saving donation of a crew member he had tried to kill. To make matters worse, under questioning, he had failed his faith and his training. The Captain and the one they called Ari had broken him in less than a minute. He hung his head in abject shame. He was unworthy of the name *warrior*. His Jihad was an ignominious failure.

#

    With Ari's report that *Cassini II's* exterior was undamaged, Jon had the crew set up for a burn that would place them for an optimum boost from Jupiter's gravity. Jupiter's disk was visibly growing by the hour, like the hour hand of a clock. You couldn't see it move, but when you looked back, its movement was evident. So, with Jupiter. Jon assembled his astrogation crew in the Core. The first step was to flip the Pullman back to its burn orientation. Once Jon initiated it, the ship's computer was entirely in charge of the operation. Nevertheless, Ginger, Dmitri, and Ari took their accustomed places in the Core, strapped in, ready to take over should something go amiss. With the experience they had gained during the first flip, they were able to accomplish this one in a bit less than fifteen minutes. With the Pullman's base firmly locked to the Box, they were ready for the correction burn. Dmitri did a final astrogation check, Ginger opened her communication channel and verified that the holocams were receiving, but recording only, since Jon's transmitting prohibition order still was in effect. Ari conducted a final systems check, and all three gave Jon a thumbs-up.

"Let's do it," Jon said, and Ari activated the VASIMR master control. Gyros whined as *Cassini II* changed her aspect, guided by the computer. Then a slight sense of weight settled over everything, as the VASIMR engines commenced their thrust.

"One tenth gee," Ari announced unnecessarily. "About four times the gravity on Iapetus," he added.

The burn lasted for nearly an hour before it shut down. They now were on the ideal orbit for the Jupiter boost.

"We're doing about one-hundred-seventy kilometers a second," Dmitri said as they unbuckled, and headed for the Canteen. "That's going to increase dramatically in the next couple of days.

Jon floated to the port in the crew area, from which he could see Jupiter clearly, its bands appearing angry and alive. "It's beautiful," Ginger said, gliding up beside him, handing him a globe of coffee straight from the urn. They floated in silence, side by side, sipping their coffees, sharing the moment.

Jon was keenly aware of Ginger's closeness, and felt a powerful attraction that was difficult to shake. Over the weeks, he had come to understand that Ginger was signaling, without actually doing so. He remained aloof, not because he wanted to, but because his job demanded that he be. Ginger seemed to respect that, but he often found her nearby when he was not doing anything.

"*Mon Capitaine ...ma Chérie Ginger!*" Michele floated into the space between them, her bubbly presence totally altering the mood. "It's sooo beeeutifool," she said expansively. "I could look at this all day."

Jon had to agree. As they watched, the Great Spot crept past the western edge to begin its transit of the planet's face. Jupiter was noticeably larger as Jon retreated to his cabin. He was expecting traffic from Zakes any time now. As he shut the door, Ginger poked in her head to announce incoming traffic, including a personal from Zakes.

Jon took the message off the Link and passed it to his offline unit where his program quickly made it readable.

"I found the leak. It was Alex Jinnah, one of my Mission Control engineers. His full name is Eskandar Ali Jinnah. It turns out this guy was a somewhat reluctant participant. Once I identified him, he spilled his guts. He was an Isma'ili sleeper, a Nizari Hashashiyyin, put in place while he still was in grade school. He was recently activated and forced to report to the Caliphate, by threats of violence against several distant family members in Iran. That's the bad news. The good news is that he will work for us as a counter-agent. I'm his control. With his assistance, I think we can get to the bottom of this."

There was more, but this covered the essence of their problem. Jon had to decide what to do with his unwelcome guest. It would have been much easier had he not survived the transplant, but now Jon had to deal with the problem. He called Ari by Link, asking him to bring Saeed to his cabin.

#

Saeed was back in Sickbay, restrained to the bed he had occupied before his interrogation. Carmen was in the general area, but spending more time with Chen. Saeed had access to the ship's vast entertainment system, but anything related to the Caliphate or to Islam had been blocked. Although the restriction disturbed him, he found that he actually enjoyed watching some of the modern sitcoms. When he tired of them, he would shut his eyes and review the portions of the *Qur'an* he had already memorized. He found that by concentrating, he could recall many pages, as if he were reading from the screen.

Saeed was in the midst of one such internal recitation when Ari glided into Sickbay and shook him into awareness of his immediate surroundings. "Come with me," Ari addressed him in Arabic. "The Captain wishes to speak with you." Ari detached him from his restraints, cuffed his hands behind his back, and unceremoniously pulled Saeed like a sack of flour forward to Deck Two. As they moved through the ship, fear arose in Saeed once more. He had cooperated, hadn't he? Remembering his shame, he girded himself for the inevitable. They would ask him questions. He would refuse to answer. They would threaten him again, and this time he would become a martyr. But as they moved through the ship, and as he observed so many things he had never before seen, things for which he had no names, and whose functions he could only imagine, he changed his tack. If he would redeem himself from his former shame, simple martyrdom would not do. He would have to take them with him. He was meant to survive until that moment presented itself.

Ari pushed Saeed through the door into the Captain's private quarters, and brought him to an awkward stance, floating vertically off the deck before the seated man who had nearly ended his life so recently. He was a big, powerful man, perhaps 183 or 184 centimeters, powerfully built, with a face that hid a cruelty that caused Saeed to wilt behind his stoic mask.

"You will address the Captain in English," Ari said to him in Arabic.

"*Aqa* Captain Stock." Saeed bent at the waist in what would have been a bow in gravity, but what became an awkward tumble in their zero-g environment. "I meant no disrespect *Aqa* Captain." Saeed managed to straighten himself out and regain a bit of personal dignity. "I offer you my service. My life is in your hands, as Allah wishes, may He be praised."

Saeed fully expected to be battered around by this powerful man, and was prepared to accept whatever happened as if it came from Allah himself. Instead, he heard the Captain say in a quiet, almost gentle voice, "We have a problem, Mr. Esmail, a problem that you can solve for us."

This took Saeed by complete surprise. A man of power in his world acted powerfully, spoke with power, punished with power. But this powerful man, this man with the power of life and death spoke evenly, without rancor. Saeed listened carefully.

"You were sent here to destroy us and our mission. I cannot allow that. But I am not now willing to end your life. This vessel has no brig. I have no way to confine you, except as I have already done, by tying you to a bed. You are a human being, and I am reluctant to do this to you for the remaining months of this mission. So now you understand my problem. To guarantee the safety of this mission, I must kill you...but I don't want to do that. My only alternative is to confine you to a bunk for the duration." The Captain stopped talking, and Saeed waited for him to continue. The pause grew longer...thirty seconds...a full minute...a minute and a half, and still the Captain said nothing.

Finally, Saeed felt the words escape his lips, almost as if they had done so on their own accord. "But I can give you my word to do no harm."

"You're a Jihadist Warrior...you swore an oath before Allah to carry out your mission. How can I believe you, or trust that you will keep your word?"

"I can swear another, greater oath to Allah," Saeed heard himself saying, almost as if something or someone else were causing him to speak. And then, at that exact moment, he understood. Allah had opened another door into his future. His destiny, his mission was not here on this space ship, it was out there on Iapetus. The words of his epiphany rose unbidden into his mind: *Let those fight in the way of Allah who sell the life of this world for the other. Whoso fighteth in the way of Allah, be he slain or be he victorious, on him we shall bestow a vast reward.*

It was crystal clear now. Saeed knew what to do. He straightened as well as possible, came to attention, and said formally in Arabic, "Before Allah, may He be blessed, and all that is holy, I swear a mighty oath to abide by my word, to renounce my Jihad, to serve the Captain and crew of *Cassini II*, to give my life in their defense if necessary. I bind myself to this oath under penalty of eternal damnation. All praises to Allah."

#

Ari translated Saeed's words to Jon, and said, "You can trust him."

"That's it, then," Jon said. "Remove his cuffs and find him a place to bunk."

Chapter eleven

Jon had briefed Rod Zakes in detail about Saeed's truce. The message commenced its nearly forty minute journey before Jon retired for the night. The next morning, Jon ran Rod's lengthy response through his decoder, and then read his remarks with considerable interest. The first part of the message concerned logistics. Their nominal time to Jupiter was 57.7 days. Their nominal time from Jupiter to the braking burn without the boost was 56.5 days, but with the boost was about 49 days. Houston said they would know with more accuracy after the boost. Their Jupiter approach and departure paths took them through several radiation belts, but Houston assured Jon that the hull would stop the radiation – except at perijove, where they would have to remain in the Core for several hours.

Rod then informed Jon that Houston had picked up considerable chatter from the Caliphate about a forthcoming announcement of great importance. Jinnah had received no communications from the Caliphate, and had no idea what the chatter was about. Without further information, Rod's best guess was that the Caliph intended to announce the presence of Saeed on *Cassini II*. With the current state of tensions between the Caliphate and the West, Rod said

Houston's best take was that such an announcement could trigger demonstrations and riots across the non-Caliphate Muslim world.

Jon could see it coming before he read it. Houston had decided to preempt the announcement. The American ambassador to the Caliphate had already requested an audience with the Caliph, and his staff had managed to set the meeting for 1530 Tehran time, which was 0600 Houston time. At that time, or as soon thereafter as the ambassador's staff informed Houston that the meeting was taking place, Houston would announce to the world that a Persian lad working at L-4 had managed to sequester himself aboard the *Cassini II*, and that he was just discovered. The announcement would include the information that the Caliph had been informed about the stowaway, and that the Cassini Coalition would ensure the safety of the Caliphate's wayward citizen. The announcement would also inform the world that the crew had accommodated the young man, and that they were confident he would become a contributing member of the crew. Privately, the Caliph would be told about Saeed's radiation dose, and informed that he was sequestered under guard, and would be dealt with appropriately upon the ship's return to Earth. Rod explained that Houston would be feeding information through Jinnah to the Caliphate that Saeed had found a sympathetic crew member, and using this guise, Houston would feed misinformation to the Caliph in an effort to discover his underlying motive – if there was one beyond sheer Jihad destruction.

Jon summoned the crew on All-Call to meet in the Canteen. Dmitri and Ginger floated in together followed by Noel who was rubbing sleep from his eyes. Ari arrived with a wide-eyed Saeed in tow. Michele and Elke arrived next, appearing slightly disheveled and a bit flustered. Carmen showed up a minute later with a holodisplay of the still unconscious Chen floating beside her. Jon acknowledged their arrivals, tossing an apologetic grin at Michele and Elke. As usual, the crew assumed their now customary positions in the Canteen. They each "owned" a spot by some unspoken agreement. As they arrived, Jon marveled again at the crew's wide diversity in physical size and life-style perspective coupled to a remarkable degree of competence. He smiled as he recalled their initial meeting in the L-4 lounge – their verbal jostling and posturing. They were a well-honed team now, with – he reminded himself – some interesting internal dynamics.

"By now, you will all have met our newest crew member, Saeed Esmail. While I am deeply disturbed at how Saeed got here, he has convinced me that he no longer poses a threat. He has vowed to become a productive member of the crew, and I intend to give him that chance – with one absolute proviso. Saeed must have a crew member near him at all times, except when he is sleeping. Saeed, you bear the ultimate responsibility for ensuring someone is always near you. You gave me your word, and I have accepted it, but I would be failing in my job as Captain if I did not take this precaution. We all are on this venture together. Our lives are completely interdependent – yours too, Saeed.

"We are in the final stages of the Jupiter boost, plunging toward the gas giant at one-hundred-eighty kilometers a second, and accelerating as we approach. We will be traveling well over two-hundred kilometers per second at perijove, and once we depart the immediate vicinity of Jupiter, we will recalculate our orbit and conduct a corrective burn to put us on our final leg to Iapetus. We will be passing through several radiation belts in the next few days. All but the one at perijove are virtually harmless to us inside our hull. Be prepared to assemble inside the Core at fifteen-hundred hours three days from now." Jon looked at each crew member. "Including Chen, Doc," he said directly to Carmen.

"We'll continue the watch rotation in the Core," Jon said. "The likelihood of something happening that our actions might ameliorate is pretty small. But since we are otherwise just passengers until we arrive at Iapetus, we might as well be prepared for even remote possibility events."

"Like an asteroid hit," Dmitri commented. Nobody laughed.

#

Ari was confident that Saeed would keep his word for the time being. His worry, however, was that as time passed, Saeed's thoughts would turn back to his original mission. Saeed's oath bound him as well as anything could, but the moment he perceived that Allah had released him from that oath, all bets were off. Ari determined to be present when that happened – and he was certain it would.

There was no way to know what lay ahead on Iapetus. In the

meantime, however, Ari had a major potential problem on his hands – the tether. And he felt the need to babysit Saeed, which further complicated things. From what he could tell, Saeed had no practical skills. He had virtually no knowledge of how the universe actually functioned. He had no science background, knew nothing of history, except a distorted version seen through a Qur'anic lens. He didn't understand economics, except in its simplest sense, couched in terms of wages for work accomplished. The one area in which Saeed excelled was his knowledge of the *Qur'an*. Ari was astonished to learn that Saeed had memorized long sections of Qur'anic scripture, although his understanding of what those passages meant often bore little resemblance to what they seemed to mean to Ari when he read them. Saeed appeared to be the product of a madrasa that had prepared him for the sole task of martyrdom.

In his new role as a crew member, Saeed appeared eager to learn. Because of his lack of a technical background, he could do little more than memorize sequences of actions for any of the ships' systems. To Ari's surprise, however, Saeed had a knack for manipulating the gyros. Once Ari showed him what to do, Saeed seemed to go by instinct. Within a few hours he was nearly as good as Ari at moving the ship from one orientation to another. Ari suspected that with more practice, Saeed would exceed his own ability.

#

Saeed took great pleasure in assisting Carmen. He was genuinely concerned about Chen's condition, and spent hours watching over him, exercising his limbs, and caring for him. He also enjoyed talking with Carmen about their respective religions, frequently in Arabic. Saeed sensed quickly that the Doctor was the only crew member with a deep-seated faith, and although he considered her to be an infidel, her Christian faith was preferable to no faith at all, which is what he observed in the rest of the crew.

Ari was an enigma for Saeed, who had never personally known a Jew. When he brought this up to Ari, Ari had told him in no uncertain terms that he was Israeli, and that aboard *Cassini II*, one's background and religious belief were unimportant. Ari took the trouble to explain things in detail to Saeed, in Arabic if that was what it took for Saeed to understand. Saeed quickly discovered that his education was sorely

lacking, and he absorbed information like a sponge. He was particularly pleased that he could reorient the ship at least as well as Ari
could, although he had no idea how his manipulations actually caused
the ship to twist and turn. He suspected there was very much to learn
before he would understand such things. In the meantime, however,
Saeed memorized everything the crew members showed him.

Saeed never forgot his oath before Allah. His cooperation, his
willingness to learn, to participate was genuine. Nevertheless, he also
never forgot his original purpose and his epiphany in his hideout.
The wonderful words of his Qur'anic calling formed the backdrop
for his every action: *Let those fight in the way of Allah who sell the life of
this world for the other. Whoso fighteth in the way of Allah, be he slain or
be he victorious, on him we shall bestow a vast reward.* He had, indeed
traded his life on Earth for that out here – on Iapetus, even. And
thus, he was commanded to fight in the way of Allah. Having done
so, win or lose, he would receive his ultimate reward. For the time
being, his fighting mode was to hunker down, and to await Allah's
message releasing him from his oath.

#

Jupiter loomed large, and then very large, as *Cassini II* raced
toward perijove. Ginger found herself spending more time than usual
gazing through the port at the churning inferno that was Jupiter's
atmosphere. As a child, she had watched Jupiter's moons through
her twenty centimeter reflector, tracking their progress around the
gas giant, thrilled that she could reach out with her extended eyes
to a dynamic universe. Then she discovered the historical records of
the fly-bys and the deep-space photography of the Hubble and its
successor. As she progressed with her education, her interests became
more specific, so that during her Stanford PhD days, she actually was
allotted time slots with the L-4 Deep-space Telescope. First it was
Jupiter, but when she reviewed the *Cassini* fly-by of Saturn and the
close-ups of Iapetus, she was hooked. Ginger was fascinated by the
narrow equatorial mountain range that ringed the moon – twenty
kilometers high and twenty kilometers wide, like a wall that had lost
its geometric definition to the ravages of time and an incoming hail
of meteorites drawn in by Saturn's mass. Then there was the tower in
the southern hemisphere, rising like a pencil a kilometer-and-a-half

above the surrounding plain. Ginger had mapped the satellite's surface, confirming that it consisted of an underlying hexagonal/pentagonal geometric pattern. Hexagons occupied the poles themselves, surrounded by a band of hexagons. The triangular openings between the hexagons were filled with pentagons, and the remaining equatorial band was sinusoidal and filled with hexagons. Here and there on the Iapetus surface, the surface of several large sections appeared to have collapsed, as if the underlying structure had given way.

In heated college dorm discussions at Stanford, Ginger had insisted on applying Occam's razor to explain what everyone could see. Applied here, that meant – for better or worse – intelligent design. In the simplest possible terms, someone or something had built the damn thing! Ginger smiled as she recalled those discussions, and gazed out the port at a close-up of Jupiter's swirling atmosphere that was like nothing she had ever seen, completely filling the sky in all directions, looming massively with an ominous foreboding.

Ginger gracefully turned her lithe body away from the port as a soft chime signaled the call to assemble in the Core for the final perijove approach. She joined the rest of the crew in the now somewhat crowded space. Saeed arrived with Chen in tow, having taken for himself the responsibility for the unconscious man's safety.

Ginger strapped herself into the seat before the Astrogation Console, her mind still filled with reminiscences of her bygone college years as her fingers roamed the console controls. The next thing she knew, her holodisplay filled with the atmospheric turmoil flashing by at over 200 kilometers a second a few thousand kilometers beneath them. Although Ginger could easily interpret what her eyes beheld in the display, she was not so sure of some of the others could, especially Michele, Elke, and the Doc, and, she reminded herself with a grimace, the little terrorist Saeed. She worked the controls for a few moments, and then announced to the assembled crew in her clear contralto voice with its slight Australian lilt, "Please turn your attention to the large holodisplay. The computer has taken the perspective of a distant observer looking at our perijove passage across Jupiter's face. The image you see is a construct, but the cloud surface of Jupiter is real time for where we actually are, and extrapolated to the rest of the visible surface. Our ship's image, of course, is also a construct."

The image was a dot against the swirling cloud surface of Jupiter. Ginger moved the display closer until *Cassini II* took shape. Then she rotated the view to a polar perspective, and superimposed a track line indicating their parabolic orbit. "Now you can see where we are and where we are going," she said. "Jupiter has a circumference of about four-hundred-fifty thousand kilometers at the equator, so at our present speed, it will take us just under nineteen hours to cover half that. That's how long we need to stay in here."

#

Saeed was awestruck by the wonders he saw. In his wildest imaginings, he never envisioned that he would be part of something like this. He bowed his head silently and reached out to Allah, groveling before the Almighty, prostrating his mental self to Allah in thankfulness for this gift. *Let those fight in the way of Allah who sell the life of this world for the other...* came unbidden into his mind, and again he knew the peace and tranquility brought about by his certainty of purpose.

I await your command, he mouthed silently in Arabic. He did not notice the holocam focused on his face.

#

Ari had split his attention between Ginger and Saeed for the entire nineteen hours in the Core. Ginger, who towered over him by a full twelve centimeters, was a wonder to behold as she captured the crew with her engaging displays and explanations. *That is a female*, he thought, *who could change a man's mind about bachelorhood.* As distracting as Ginger was, however, Ari saw his primary job in the Core as keeping a close eye on Saeed. The entire crew was in one tight location. If Saeed were going to break his word, this would be the obvious time. Ari set up the holocams to keep track of Saeed's position, with at least one focused on his face at all times. Ari kept his attention on the multiple holodisplay at the RVC, with its multiple view of Saeed.

At one point shortly after Ginger had brought up the polar display of their track around Jupiter, Saeed seemed to bow his head, and Ari paid close attention to his face. Saeed's lips moved, but Ari couldn't make out what he was saying. As quickly as he could without drawing attention to his actions, Ari called up a facial recognition program, and coupled it to a language program. He set the parameters to lip reading and Arabic, and a few moments later the words appeared in his display in flowing Arabic script: صاخلا رماوألا راظتنا يف انأو, which he translated as *I await your command*.

Chapter twelve

Jupiter was fast shrinking behind them since they passed perijove a day and a half ago. From his personal quarters Jon could almost watch it diminish through his port. The crew was in high spirits as they prepared for the correction burn followed by the tether extension. Jon knew he was looking forward to feeling weight again, and he was pretty certain that the rest of the crew agreed with him.

"Enter," Jon responded to a knock on his door. Dmitri entered and made himself comfortable.

"I have the burn calculations here, Captain," Dmitri said, activating his Link.

Jon activated his Link and compared the numbers to what he had received from Houston in the morning message from Rod. "Looks like your numbers differ from Houston's by about five percent," Jon said. "Would you mind running a new set from fresh observations?"

"Would have done it anyway, Jon." Dmitri grinned at him. "Be back in about an hour." The well-muscled Russian left in good humor, his pate catching a gleam of light as he passed through the door. "Looking forward to getting my feet back on the deck," he said in parting.

They could have gone with either set of numbers, but Jon wanted to give himself the greatest possible margin for maneuvering once they arrived in the vicinity of Iapetus. The interplay of gravitation fields would be so much more complicated there. He called up his latest Hyperchess game with Ari. It was his move, and Ari had really pulled a good one during their last session, caging his remaining Rook while threatening his Queen. Jon suspected he was in trouble. He tried to concentrate on his next move, but his mind insisted on reviewing for the hundredth time the complications Saeed had brought into his life. Jon trusted Ari's judgment, but he couldn't shake the feeling that Saeed was a fused powder keg.

Sooner than Jon expected, Dmitri returned with new calculations based on fresh observations. The numbers had changed a bit, but not enough to concern Jon. "Let's go with your numbers," he told Dmitri, "but run another set just before the burn."

"You got it, Captain."

Jon checked the time. "In an hour and twenty minutes, right?"

"I'll assemble the maneuvering team in the Core," Dmitri said. "Might as well do a dry run before the real thing."

#

The burn was anti-climactic, although it lasted for several hours. *One-tenth-g actually feels pretty good*, Dmitri decided, sipping his black, very sweet coffee out of a real cup for a change. He lounged comfortably in the Astrogator's chair.

"How can you drink that stuff?" Ginger asked him from the next seat. Her coffee was blond and unsweetened.

"I prefer black and sweet – like my women."

"That's a worn out phrase, and besides, you take it any way you can get it!"

"Aussies one – Ruskies zero," Ari said from the RVC, sipping from his own cup of black and very sweet coffee, as close as he could get to his favorite Turkish brew.

Dmitri knew better than to take on both of them, especially the Israeli, whose sharp humor came clad in the idiom of half a dozen languages. Dmitri had no self-esteem problems. He knew he was the best Mother Russia had to offer for this historic voyage. But he had no illusions either. The accomplishments of the young woman beside him were astonishing, especially considering her tender age. And the tough little Jew – granted he had a year on Dmitri, but he had crammed several lifetimes into his forty-one years. He raised his coffee cup in a toast. "Вот для наших безнадежное дело!" (*Vot dlya nashih beznadezhnoe delo!* – Here's for our hopeless cause!)

To which Ari responded, "для всех красивых женщин!" (*Dlya vseh krasivyh zhenshchin!* – For all the beautiful women!)

To which Ginger muttered half aloud, "Guys…"

#

In preparation for extending the tether, Ari and Noel rigged several extra holocams around the tether reel in the Box lower end cap. There was no realistic way to observe the letting out of the tether in person, since there really was no practical way to return to the Pullman with the tether extended its full two kilometer length. Before setting to the task, Ari had turned Saeed over to Carmen so he and Noel could concentrate on the job. The idea was to observe closely while the tether extended, and then to keep close tabs on the reel during the remainder of the trip, since it was the anchor point for the extended cable, carrying the mass of the Caboose two kilometers away.

It took the better part of two hours before the extra holocams were installed and tested. Finally, Ari informed the Captain that they were ready, and the maneuvering team assembled in the Core. To simplify matters when they got closer to Saturn, Jon had decided to set their rotational plane perpendicular to their direction of travel, so that the same side of *Cassini II* would present itself continuously to their destination. Ari explained to Saeed what was needed, and then allowed him to manipulate the gyros. Saeed actually seemed to take pride in accomplishing the maneuver. When he was done, the ship was perpendicular to the ecliptic with the port in the crew lounge area above them facing their direction of travel. Saeed accomplished this with one smooth motion, so that when he was done, the ship was in position with no need for jockeying.

"Excellent job," Ari told him.

"I agree," Jon added, and commenced their third Pullman flip maneuver. The process was a practiced routine by now. The Pullman uncoupled from the Box, the ram pushed it away to the limit of the anchor cables, and then the anchor cables uncoupled, leaving the

Pullman completely disconnected from the rest of the ship. Under Ari's close supervision, Jon allowed Saeed to flip the Pullman on the gyros. Saeed performed the maneuver with the skill of an old hand. With the Pullman's nose lined up to the Box, Jon released the tether cone, and moments later the Pullman was securely anchored to a two-meter length of tether.

"Okay," Jon said. "Lock her to the Box, and commence the spin-up."

While Ari latched the Pullman securely to the Box, Jon announced on All-Call, "This is the Captain...Stand by for commencement of rotation." He glanced at Ari, who nodded assent. "On my mark...five...four...three...two...one...mark...commence spin-up."

With a high-pitched whine audible throughout the ship, the gyros in all three modules commenced a coordinated spin-up.

#

Slowly, over the next hour or so, the sixty-three meter long, twelve meter wide cylinder commenced revolving around the center of the Box like a propeller in flight, gradually building up to an equivalent gravitation at both ends of one-g – as before, rotating five and a third times each minute. By an hour and fifteen minutes into the event, the off-duty crew members sat or stood firmly planted, watching the stars sweep past the Canteen port. As gravity took over, the special place that each crew member had unconsciously acquired disappeared as their senses reoriented themselves to a room with a designated top and bottom. An occasional clatter here and there throughout the vessel gave witness to items still not in their proper place.

"*Ou*," Michele wailed, "it still makes me dizzy...even more so."

"Better not to look, then," Carmen told her, feeling a distinct sense of *déjà vu*. "Just sit quietly like you did the last time and wait for the tether to extend."

"It seems like just another routine operation this time," Noel noted.

"Not routine for me," Michele moaned. Elke stroked her hair.

"If you're not feeling better by the end of tether extension," Carmen said to her, "come to sick bay for something to settle your inner ear."

"Thanks, Doc."

Carmen checked on Chen in her holodisplay. He appeared comfortable, and his vitals were still normal. If anything, the weight would contribute to his recovery. She watched the bright disk that was Saturn rotate past the port, once every eleven seconds. Iapetus was not yet visible. She mused about their destination and the ultimate role she might play. *Language skills...* She smiled inwardly. *It's a good thing I have my medical skills to offer.* The idea that Iapetus could be an artifact seemed preposterous to her. An alien civilization didn't exactly conflict with her faith, but it did not really jibe with it either. She came up against the problem once again that she had dealt with so many times in her career. Carmen had carefully partitioned her mind – this side faith, that science. She had no need to balance one against the other. She simply slipped into whichever mode was appropriate to the situation, and moved forward.

Carmen was fascinated by the early twentieth century interest in Martian canals, pushed by Percival Lowell. By midcentury, of course, the issue had largely been settled, and in 1965 *Mariner 4* put the final nail in the canal coffin. She smiled as she thought of Jon Stock on the deck beneath her, hero of the first Mars expedition. He brought a special dimension to the Iapetus expedition. What would they find, she wondered. The best close-up observations remained inconclusive – sufficiently convincing to cause the nations of Earth to launch this expedition, but would they end up being the *Mariner 4* of the twenty-first century?

#

A deck below them in the Core, as Ari's revolution indicator reached five and a third, Jon said, "You ready to do this?"

"Piece of cake," Ari answered in perfect idiom.

Over the All-Call Jon announced, "Commencing tether extension," and nodded to Ari. "Ten meters a minute for the first hour."

At both ends of the Box clamps released. Pullman and Caboose slowly moved away from the box, driven by the centripetal force of their rotation. The Pullman and Caboose continued their measured pace for the rest of the hour, until they were 1,200 meters apart.

"Ease it up to ten meters a second, Ari, and hold it there for two minutes. Then bring it down to zero over the next thirty seconds."

Ari entered the parameters into the system, but kept his fingers near the controls in case something went wrong.

"Do you really believe you can make any difference if the computer doesn't do its job?" Dmitri asked. "If that robot doesn't perform, we have much larger problems, and your doing a manual override will make no difference at all."

"My instincts have gotten me out of more than one jam," Ari retorted.

"No offense, my friend. I was thinking about the last jet fighter I piloted. Impossible to fly without the fly-by-wire computer. I told her where to go, and set the flight parameters, but she flew the plane."

"Nevertheless," Ari muttered, and kept his fingers poised.

Two and a half minutes later both the Pullman and Caboose settled into their two-kilometer extensions from the Box, and Jon shifted the maneuvering watch to standby. The crew went into normal cruising routine that they expected to maintain for the next 48 days.

#

Fifteen days into the Saturn leg, Ginger cornered Dmitri in the Canteen and asked him to join her in the Core.

"I've been doing some planetary observations," she told him. "I set up my deep-space camera to compensate for our rotation, and it had worked with total precision...until an hour ago. Now I am experiencing a slight precession, a precession that is unpredictably variable." She brought up a holodisplay, and flicked from one view to the other, views that she said should have been identical. Each successive image jumped ever so slightly. "Since it has to be the platform – us," she grinned at Dmitri, "I took some exact measurements of our relative positions between Pullman, Box, and Caboose. The Box and Pullman are totally stable. But look at this." She pulled up successive images of the Caboose. Although it was barely noticeable, the centerline formed by the Caboose and tether was ever so slightly angled to the centerline formed by the Pullman and its tether. "What do you think?"

Dmitri did a quick check on her calculations – they were correct. "We'd better inform Jon right away," he said.

Shortly thereafter, Jon arrived in the Core, and Ginger walked him through the same explanation she had just given Dmitri.

"How long has this been going on?" Jon asked.

"A bit over an hour," Ginger answered, "but it's accelerating."

Jon stood in quiet thought for a few moments. "The only thing I can think of," he said finally, "is that the tether anchor is somehow lifting off the deck. Apparently we missed a weakened seam during our inspection following the asteroid hit." He examined the holoimages from Ari's extra holocams. "Nothing jumps out at me," he remarked. "We need to fix whatever it is."

Although Dmitri deferred to Jon's expertise, he felt compelled to add his own comments. "The devil is in the details," he said, adding, "It's an old Russian proverb."

Jon wasted no time. On the All-Call he summoned the crew to the Canteen. Ten minutes later he told the assembled crew, "We have a tether anchoring problem in the Box. It may be mission critical, so we have to address it." He explained what Ginger had discovered, and his take that the reel anchor for the Caboose tether was lifting, even though they couldn't see anything on the holocams. He turned to Ari. "Retract the tethers, Ari. Get us to a neutral stance as quickly as you can. And do it gently. We don't want any sudden strain on the reel anchor."

Ari set a fifteen-minute rate that reeled in the tether at about two meters a second. Sixteen minutes later both the Pullman and Caboose were firmly clamped to the Box.

"Saeed, bring the rotation to zero," Jon ordered.

Under Ari's watchful eyes, Saeed accomplished the task over the next fifteen minutes. Once *Cassini II* was stable, Jon said, "Okay, Dmitri, Ari, Noel...you come with me. Saeed, you stay with Ginger. Ginger, you have the conn 'till I get back." With that, he led the way through the Pullman into the Box, and through the Box to the lower end cap.

Ari brought along an aerosol can containing a florescent fine powder. He sprayed small amounts along the seam between the reel base and the deck, and around the bolts that reinforced the reel's deck connection. Then Noel rubbed the area with a silicon-saturated cloth that removed all the surface powder. A fine bright line remained running half way around the reel base, indicating a thin crack. Two of the anchor bolts indicated slight loosening.

"This is remarkable" Noel said. "I've never seen one of these seams tear."

"It's very much like a cracked weld," Jon said. "It takes a pretty good shock to bring it about."

"Like an asteroid hit," Dmitri added.

"How do we repair it, Ari?" Jon asked.

Ari floated silently, apparently in thought. Dmitri had been in a lot of tough situations in his life, but nothing like this. He was glad to have Ari's expertise and experience in handling these new synthetics. Give him two pieces of steel and a welding torch, and he was at home. But he really knew very little about the special adhesives and curing required for these polyaramid derivatives. Stronger and lighter than steel or even titanium, and the welds were equally strong – but what they had here said differently. Dmitri stretched himself out to get a close-up look at the crack. "How far under the base do you think the crack goes?"

"I'm working on that," Ari said, and Dmitri looked up to see him working his Link. "Based on the maximum angle Ginger saw, the extent of the crack – I'd say about a third of the way under the base."

"If the entire mass of the Caboose lifted it only that far," Dmitri said, "there is no way we can duplicate that without extending the tether again, and I don't think we should do that until we have repaired this."

"There's another way," Ari said. He pulled up a holodisplay of a schematic of the Box. We drill through the deck to the anchor plate here," his pointer indicated a spot under the deck, "and here and here. Then we evacuate the Box, fill the holes with adhesive, and then repressurize the Box. This will force the adhesive throughout the loosened underside of the plate. Then we drill holes all the way through the deck and the plate here, here and here, and insert additional anchoring bolts that we reinforce with more adhesive. Finally, we evacuate the Box a second time to let the adhesive vacuum cure for two days."

"We can do this," Jon said. "I'm going to check with Houston, but we can do this."

"It would help if we could get ultraviolet under the plate – it cures better with UV, but lacking that, at least we can flood the outside with UV.

"Дьявол кроется в деталях (*D'yavol kroet·sya v detalYeh*)," Dmitri said half to himself.

"What's that?" Jon asked.

"An old Russian proverb," Dmitri said, "like I said before. The devil is in the details."

Chapter thirteen

Jon sent Rod Zakes an encrypted message detailing the problem with the reel anchor, and sent it on its fifty-minute trip to Earth. He assumed that Houston would give the matter due consideration – at least several hours, and then get back to him; and that is what happened. Ten hours after his original message left *Cassini II*, Rod's response formed in Jon's local decryption machine. Reduced to its essence, Rod's message confirmed Jon's judgment: do the repair as Ari had outlined.

#

An hour later, Ari and Noel made their way through the Pullman, into the Box, and down to the bottom end cap. They carried with them a simple hand drill, several extended bits especially designed to cut through cured polyaramid synthetic, and two syringes containing the adhesive they would inject between the base and deck.

"With no gravity assist," Ari said to Noel, "we need to get leverage from something else."

"And how do we do that?"

"How tall are you?"

"One-eighty-five centimeters...Why?"

"I'm one-seventy-three and the space between decks is three meters. Do the math." Ari grinned at Noel. "Your feet on the deck, me on your shoulders, the drill bit on the overhead..."

From his Link Ari set up a holodisplay showing the Box schematic. The four drilling points were clearly indicated. He tapped his link and four spots appeared on the overhead. "Let's do it," he said to Noel.

It took them the better part of an hour to drill the four holes. Ari reported to Jon, "We're ready to evacuate the Box and then inject the adhesive."

"Let me know when you guys are ready."

#

Ari and Noel returned to the Pullman to suit up, while Jon evacuated the Box from the remote controls in the Core. Although he could have just cracked the doors and explosively released all the air, out of an abundance of caution, he pumped most of the Box atmosphere into storage bottles. In the back of Jon's mind at all times was the thought that you can never have too much air, but if you have too little, you're screwed. So he took the time to pump down the Box – to scavenge it.

About a half hour later, he told Ari over his Link, "That's as good a vacuum as I can get without opening the hatches." He had displays from each of their holocams before him. He followed their movement as sensors followed their motion into the Box, automatically switching his third view to one that displayed the two men.

Ari inserted a sniffer nozzle into one of the holes. "We still have a lot of gas molecules floating around here," he told Jon. "I think we need to open the hatch to give it a shot of hard vacuum."

Jon had made it a habit of leadership to evaluate but never second-guess his people. Now certainly was not time to change that habit. "You got it, Ari. Stand by..." He shifted one view to a holocam pointed at the Box garage door – the name they had given the large hatch through which the lander/rover would exit. Then he cracked the hatch, and was rewarded with a puff of crystalline vapor, as the remaining moisture laden air escaped.

"Let's give it an hour to evacuate between the plates," Ari said. "Noel and I will examine the landers in the meantime.

#

Noel was fascinated by the combination lander/rover. He had pored over the schematics, so that, in a sense, he felt he actually knew the machines, but other than a cursory look when passing through the Box, he really had had no chance to examine one closely.

He floated in front of the machine, taking in its five-meter length resting against the back deck on three pair of large rubber tires. At three meters wide, it was a squat ungainly cylinder sporting a slightly bulbous front end of tough radiation resistant transparent polymer. The upper length of the cylinder, viewed horizontally, had three sapphire matrix ports down each side and three along the top. As ungainly as it appeared, Noel had calculated that in rover mode, its mass was distributed below the horizontal median, so it actually was quite stable. The hypergolic nozzle appeared to his eye to be somewhat off the cylinder centerline, but Noel knew that this was to compensate for the mass distribution. He couldn't see the nose pad folded against the vehicle hull between the wheels, but he closely examined the three landing pads spaced around the nozzle at the back of the cylinder, folded against the hull into three recessed slots. They were designed to extend out and down in a scissor-like fashion. Their lower sections and the main hinges against the hull were hydraulically dampened to cushion the landing. He found their robustness interesting, given Iapetus' low gravity, some forty times less than on Earth. The landing pad on top of the nozzle carried a telescoping shaft that, when extended after landing, tilted the lander, pivoting it on the remaining two landing pads until the nose pad contacted the surface. Noel examined the upper escape hatch. The recessed mechanism for popping the hatch from the outside in an emergency was easy to grasp with a gloved hand, but designed so that it would not snag on anything brushing the opening. The internal pressure indicator by the recessed handle glowed bright red, indicating that a pressure differential existed between the outside and inside of the rover. He pulled himself around to the air lock on the left side. Its pressure indicator showed green and red, indicating the lock was evacuated, but the interior was pressurized.

Ari floated up alongside him. "We probably don't want to go inside," he said. "That will just put more gas molecules inside the Box."

"Yep."

They pulled themselves to the transparent bulbous nose. Noel activated a beam attached to his wrist, and flashed it into the rover. Noel could not bring himself to call it by its convoluted official name – lander/rover, and in his mind it was a rover that could fly when necessary.

"That's not necessary, you know," Ari said to him with a broad grin. He tapped his Link, and the rover interior lights came on. "All the comforts of home," Ari said, "but not quite so luxurious as that Town Car you like to drive. More like my beat up old Land Rover."

"I gotta tell ya," Noel answered, "I can't wait to put this thing through its paces." He moved down to one of the large front wheels. "This motor," he said, tapping the wheel's hub, "puts out more power than both our car engines combined."

"That's a fact."

Noel pressed himself against the deck. There was more than sufficient clearance for him to slide under the rover. He pulled himself hand-over-hand until he reached the centerline. Illuminated by his shoulder torch, the nose pad was clearly visible in its recessed slot. There was sufficient clearance between the hull edge and the pad leg to prevent any damage to the pad should the rover bottom out against the surface. All moving parts were protected with flexible seals to keep out the clinging dust they expected to find on the surface. Past experience was the Moon and Mars. While the Moon dust was both invasive and abrasive, Mars dust was, in addition, corrosive. In both cases, if the stuff got into a bearing race, you might as well forget it. Consequently a lot of design went into seals. It wasn't his specialty, but Noel knew a lot about it. As the space structural engineer on the crew, he was expected to be the expert in these things – and he figured he probably was, although he had come to realize that Ari was one of those special people who seemed to know as much or more about everything than even the acknowledged experts knew. They were so different in so many ways, but Ari was a good guy to have at your back, whether in a dark alley or facing a daunting engineering challenge. Clearly one of the good guys, in Noel's opinion.

"Hour's up," Ari announced. "I'll go check the holes."

Noel pulled himself out from under the rover, and floated to the partly open hatch. "Opening the garage door completely," he announced generally.

"Roger that," Jon answered.

Noel activated the hatch opening mechanism, and the large garage door pushed out a half meter, and then swung out and back against the hull. The view was magnificent. Noel rolled on his back and let his eyes take in the band of light that filled part of the sky like a brilliant white rainbow. As he let his eyes adjust, here and there the band of white began to resolve into individual points of light, not just white, but colors spanning the entire human range of vision. It was hypnotizing, and Noel could have stayed there for hours enjoying the sight. He felt a hand grab his leg.

"Hey, Buddy, you're drifting out the hatch, and you don't have a safety line or your TBH boots." Ari pulled him inside the Box. "Just how were you going to get back?"

"I guess I got carried away. Sorry..." Noel felt embarrassed, but Ari didn't give him any time to think about it.

"We're ready to do the adhesive," Ari told him.

#

Jon monitored the process from the Core. He was concerned about Noel's lapse in safety, and resolved to make a point to the entire crew. He recalled reading about an undersea rescue attempt off the east coast of Florida back in the twentieth century. The Jonson *Sea Link*, a mini-sub, had gotten tangled in cable on the bottom. The pilot was the son of the owner, Jonson. The *Sea Link* had no escape mechanism, and Jonson was unable to free himself. After several hours, as his air supply was running low, Navy divers from a submarine rescue ship attempted a rescue. The ASR established a four-point moor near the location of the entangled submersible. Their intent had been to moor directly over it, but precise navigation was still several decades away at that time. The divers went down, and eventually located the craft, about fifteen meters beyond the maximum extension of their umbilicals. They could signal to Jonson, but could do nothing to get him out. By the time the ASR repositioned itself in a new four-point moor, Jonson was dead.

Jon could see a situation where an untethered crew member could find himself in a similar situation – where safety was just out of reach. Unlikely...sure, but possible, so he resolved to make sure it didn't happen.

On the holodisplays in front of him, Jon watched Ari and Noel inject the adhesive into half the holes, cover the holes with a net-like fabric, and then move back to examine their work.

"Okay, Jon, let's close the hatch and repressurize before this stuff cures as is."

Jon activated the hatch closing mechanism, and then flooded the space with air. Ari and Noel removed their helmets and examined the adhesive. Ari pointed to the holes he had left empty, and moved a portable holocam right up to the opening, shining a light into the hole. Jon observed adhesive oozing into the hole, a sure sign that it was spreading throughout the loose underside of the reel.

"Looks like you got it," Jon said to the team in the Box. "Get your asses back into the Pullman, and we'll go back to vacuum to cure it."

"You got it, Skipper," Ari said as the two men glided back to the Pullman.

#

The following morning Michele joined the rest of the off-duty crew in the Canteen while Jon and the maneuvering watch extended the tethers in what now was a routine operation. To her surprise, the close-in rotation had less effect on her stomach than before. Dr. Bhuta spent most of her time chatting with Saeed in what appeared to Michele to be a friendly, respectful relationship. She could not abide the little terrorist, as she referred to him privately. He made her skin crawl, and she tried to avoid him whenever possible. She agreed with Elke that they should have pitched the little terrorist out the lock the moment they discovered him. Of course, doctors were different. They had to be in order to treat everybody. Michele knew that Carmen had no discretion when it came to whom she would treat. Her Hippocratic Oath underpinned everything she did. Michele respected that, but she knew she never could be a doctor, precisely because she was not capable of that kind of compassion. Plants were better patients, and she could prune and eliminate as she felt necessary without reference to anything higher that her own intellect.

Michele glanced around the Canteen. Carmen – the ship's physician – the Doc. Michele did not really know her, either as a woman, lover, or friend. They were so different that she had not been able to touch her inner person, so that their relationship remained cordial, but somewhat formal. Elke – she smiled remembering the many intimacies they had shared, her beautiful body, her delicious taste – just remembering caused warmth to spread from her core. She looked at Noel, tall and handsome, and almost yearning in his lovemaking, and smiled inwardly remembering his quaint shyness in the presence of both her and Elke. Her thoughts turned to the crew members in the Core, especially to Ginger, long and lithe, and initially very willing, but lately, apparently caught up with the Russian Dmitri. And speaking of Dmitri, Michele chuckled inwardly at his feigned roughness that hid a very tender intimate partner, one that blossomed when Ginger joined them. Ari was awesome, like a machine that wouldn't quit, especially when Elke decided to join them, despite her proclivities. Her regret, however, was *le Capitaine* – he seemed immune to her charms, and so far as she could tell, he maintained a professional relationship with Ginger as well. Carmen seemed out of the question, and Elke only did guys when she was there as well. Michele smiled at her vision of an enthusiastic Elke sandwiched between herself and Ari.

The memories of this voyage would last well into her declining years, as she continued to think of anything past forty. With the return of weight, the delicious freedom her breasts experienced in free fall had vanished under the downward pull of the ship's artificial gravity. Michele saw her thirty-five years as the beginning of a slide to the awful truth of forty. When the two year younger Elke or the four year younger Ginger admired the tone of her naked body, Michele continued to hear a silent "...for someone approaching forty." The men's opinions didn't count, because men were always uncritical when women made themselves available. Michele had to admit that she took pleasure in the uncritical admiration of Elke and Ginger, but she still harbored reservations about their underlying perspective.

Jon announced full tether extension, and Carmen asked Michele how she felt. Michele smiled at her. "Fine, Doctor. It wasn't nearly so bad this time."

"Good...you look more relaxed, too." Carmen paused, looking quietly at Michele. "So beautiful and so accomplished," she said. "You are a lucky woman."

#

Ari carefully examined his holodisplays from the Core. To his relief, the repair seemed to be holding. Despite their careful preparation, and the extra time at full vacuum to ensure even distribution of the adhesive, he remained a bit skeptical. Such a repair had never before been attempted – not that they had any real choice. Doing the trip under free fall was not a realistic option, except for absolute necessity. Rotating the joined ship at five and a third revolutions per minute was also not realistic. He knew about Michele's vertigo, and suspected the rest of them would suffer ill effects from prolonged rapid rotation as well.

As he concentrated on a close examination of the repair, he felt a soft female touch on his neck and shoulders. He turned to find himself gazing at the swell of Michele's breasts as she managed to display herself artfully in her pale blue jumpsuit.

"What's up, Plant Lady?" he asked with a chuckle. "Is the gravity making you horny?"

She just smiled back and leaned against him.

"Can't now," he said. "I got the watch for another two hours." He ginned at her. "Afterwards?"

She kissed him and left.

#

The days continued without further major incident. The maneuvering team rotated the Core watch, but there really was little to do on watch, except to be there in the event something did go wrong. Jon took his turn, not so much because he had to, but to make sure the others understood that he was not just the Captain, but also a crew member. Jon made it a habit to visit Doc Bhuta at least once a day in sickbay, just to let her know that he was interested in what she was doing, and to check on the status of Chen. More often than not, when Jon visited Sickbay he found Saeed ministrating to Chen. Otherwise, Saeed was normally near Ari, who had taken on the task of ensuring that Saeed kept his promise.

Jon also stopped by Michele's lab. She was always circumspect, but made it clear that he was at the top of her list. He marveled at how she could make an ordinary jumpsuit seem like a harem pajama, and occasionally regretted his early-on decision to remain above any crew involvement. Frequently, he found Elke in Michele's lab, puttering around and otherwise making herself useful. He had become aware of her sexual orientation shortly after the voyage began, and initially was concerned that it might pose a problem. Michele solved that, however, since she seemed not to care what gender her partner of the moment was, and Elke appeared not to be the jealous type. He suspected that Michele had even pulled Elke into an occasional threesome where she had to interact intimately with a man. He chuckled as he thought about Michele's shenanigans. She was a unique female, if only for that; but then add her scientific competence, and you had an unmatched package – at least so far as his experience went.

Initially, Jon tried to keep track of the couplings, but as the voyage lengthened, and as ways to keep busy became limited, the one eternal human activity had virtually taken over. Jon was a product of modern western culture that viewed casual sexual coupling as a simple part of living, but at fifty, he had established his values when casual coupling was still less casual. With the eradication of sexually transmitted diseases, and the virtual elimination of unwanted pregnancies, the historical Roman Orgy had become a routine part of modern life. Nevertheless, Jon still was somewhat uncomfortable with the idea, and tended to refrain from full-scale participation in the ebb and flow of casual sexual encounters, even when he was not constrained by his leadership position.

So he dreamed, and in his dreams Michele or Ginger and sometimes Michele and Ginger took center stage. Jon knew that Michele would always be focused on her own needs, and suspected that when she made love, she voraciously pursued her own satisfaction. Ginger was another story. She had clearly signaled her availability to Jon, but did not flaunt herself, and that had an even stronger effect on him than Michele's flirting. Whereas he was entirely comfortable with Michele's many liaisons, he found himself strangely jealous when he became aware that Ginger had been with one of the other male crew members. He chided himself when this happened, but he could not rid himself of his reaction.

Jon stood before his port watching Saturn slowly rotate around his field of view – two full revolutions every three minutes. The ringed planet had grown very large, filling nearly half the view. They were on the verge of possibly the most momentous event in human history, and Jon experienced a sense of awe that exceeded even his feeling when he first stepped out on the arid surface of Mars. In less than a day now, they would reel in the tether, reorient the Pullman, and commence the braking burn that would last for about two days. Then they would vector toward their rendezvous with Iapetus, and destiny.

#

It was time. The maneuvering watch was in place, and Ari had once again assigned Saeed to stop the rotation once he had retracted the tether. Despite his status as a prisoner at large, Saeed had come to think of himself as a member of the crew. The Jew, Ari, had become as close a thing to a friend as he had ever had. Saeed took a special interest in this fact, and researched the *Qur'an* for corroboration. To his total surprise, he found several passages where it was clear that Allah (*praise His name*) held the Jewish people in high esteem, second only to Islam. He made a mental note to bring this information to the attention of the Ayatollah when he finally returned. With his new insights into Allah's will (*may He be praised*), Saeed was certain that he would obtain much higher stature than he presently held.

The moment Ari linked the Pullman and Caboose to the Box, he permitted Saeed to bring their rotation to a stop. Then he performed the delicate reversal maneuver on the Pullman, and clamped it back into the configuration *Cassini II* had when she departed L-4. Saeed anticipated every move, and decided that he could have performed the operation, had he been given the chance.

It was good to be part of something, Saeed thought, but he also reminded himself that his was a higher purpose, and the moment of fulfillment was drawing closer.

#

"Have you verified the braking burn parameters?" Jon asked Dmitri.

"Yes, Captain, twice, and the numbers conform with Houston's to three decimal places." Dmitri glanced at Ginger who gave him an answering nod. "We're ready to orient the ship for the burn."

"Okay, then, lock in the parameters, and make it happen."

Although the reorientation was automatic, Dmitri kept his fingers on the controls to override any problem that might happen.

"It's do as I say, not as I do," Ari kidded Dmitri, reminding him of his own comments about Ari's cautious finger hovering during their first major maneuver. For reasons he didn't quite understand, Dmitri felt a bit irritated.

"Ready to commence braking burn in thirty seconds," Dmitri said.

After a painfully long wait during which Dmitri had to resist a powerful urge to commence the burn manually, Ginger announced: "Five...four...three...two...fire!" Dmitri felt the slight push of the one-tenth-g, watched several items settle to the deck, and observed somewhat surreptitiously the way Ginger's lithe body adjusted to the slight gravitational pull.

Ginger caught his look and said with a wink, "The effect is much more pronounced on Michele, you know."

Dmitri blushed without comment, and focused on his holo-display, miffed at himself for being so obvious. *It's a wonderful new world*, he told himself, *but some things never change.*

He sat back and stretched, letting the slight g-force soothe his muscles. Jon secured the Maneuvering Watch, so that Dmitri remained alone in the Core for this watch cycle. He didn't mind, and spent the time first exploring the face of Saturn through the stern-pointing sensors, and then focusing on Iapetus. He clearly saw the equatorial ridge, and he thought he could see the geodesic pattern, but the moon was in the wrong position with respect to the Sun and reflected Saturn light for him to be sure. He spent the rest of his watch thinking about how they would approach their task – assuming, of course, that Iapetus really was artificial. One part of his mind was convinced, but another had real trouble with the entire idea – it seemed so preposterous.

After watch, Dmitri continued his Hyperchess game with Jon, but he found his mind wandering, so that he and Jon ended up talking about Iapetus instead of continuing their game. "How do you propose to attack the problem?" he asked.

"Don't know yet," Jon answered. "A lot of people will be wanting to help us decide once we have a series of clear photos of potential landing sites."

"You're going to listen to them?" Dmitri asked a bit incredulous.

"Have to. They're footing the bill," Jon said with a smile. "But don't worry. They are there. We are here."

"That about sums it up," Dmitri said with a grin.

#

Orbital insertion was almost an anti-climax. Jon ordered a short corrective burn about an hour before insertion. The insertion burn placed them in a circular orbit, tilted about five degrees from the moon's ecliptic, and about fifty kilometers above the pockmarked equatorial surface. Since Iapetus had a synchronized rotation and orbital period of 79.33 days, a polar orbit would have accomplished very little, except to expose them to a swath of moon north and south of a slice of equator, leaving the rest of the moon unobservable. This way, they could see the entire equatorial region, which was of special interest, and, because of their height, a significant amount of landscape to either side of the equatorial ridge.

"We're here, boys and girls," Jon announced on All-Call. "Now the fun really starts!"

Chapter fourteen

Jon assembled the crew in the Canteen. Outwardly he appeared calm and in control, but inside he felt like a little boy on Christmas morning. He didn't know whether to shout, run around in circles, or turn summersaults. But since they were in free fall, and since he was the Captain, he opted to float quietly in his traditional position, and let the crew bubble off a bit of steam. As he watched his crew, a line from an old TV series came unbidden into his mind: *...to go where no one has gone before...* He sucked in his breath slowly and let it back out. He smiled at Michele's antics as she made the rounds, soundly kissing everybody – even Saeed, who blushed and wiped his mouth. He was surprised that Carmen had brought Chen to the meeting, even though he still gave no indication that he was part of anything. Carmen had reminded him only two days earlier that Chen was not in a vegetative state, but that his mind was fully functional. For reasons nobody understood, he simply was not yet ready to rejoin the crew. Carmen had shared with him her belief that Chen was aware of his surroundings at some level, and that allowing his vicarious participation would enhance his eventual return. Jon certainly had no objections.

"We made it," Jon said simply. "We're here." He paused to let the crew settle down.

Michele had kissed everyone but him, and she chose this moment to plant one on his lips. "*Mon Capitaine*," she said sweetly. Everybody laughed and applauded while Jon regained his composure. Even Saeed seemed to enjoy the moment.

"No long speeches, I promise!" This, too, was greeted with laughter. "We had a couple of moments, but you guys held on, and we made it through the potential disasters, and that includes you, Saeed," Jon said pointedly, but with a smile, to the stowaway. Now we must decide the next step in our journey – where do we land?" Jon paused, and everybody commenced talking at once. He held up his hand. "I sent Houston an arrival notification. We're a long way from home, guys, over nine times as far from the Sun as is the Earth. That's over one-billion-three-hundred-sixty-five-million clicks. It took my signal nearly one and a half hours to get to Houston." Jon paused to let the significance of that number sink in.

"If the Sun goes nova right now," Ari said, "we won't know about it for an hour-and-a-half."

"That's right, Ari. We're a long way from home." Jon then told them what he thought about the mission ahead. He wanted each of them to spend as much time as possible during the next several days, studying the surface from their particular perspectives. He asked each of them to imagine what they would do if the project were entirely theirs. "Where would you land?" he asked, "And what would you do to prove that it's artificial, or not, and if it is, how would you determine the best way to find out more about the builders?"

He retired to his quarters to await Houston's response.

#

In Mission Control, Rod Zakes held up his hand for silence. Virtually everybody who had anything to do with the project had crowded into the room. Members of the press were there as well, their bright lights and holocams adding an unfamiliar veneer to the proceedings. There was virtually no standing room left. Several younger people had actually squatted on the floor between the rows of consoles. You could hear a pin drop.

"They're orbiting Iapetus!" Rod announced. A shout went up

from the assembled people – clapping, high fives all around, hand-shakes and hugs, even a few tears. "Now the fun starts. Jon has asked us for input on selecting a landing spot. You know what that means." Groans from the crowd. "We might as well get inputs from you guys too," Rod added. "Who knows; Jon might even take the advice."

The news of *Cassini II's* arrival in orbit around Iapetus flashed across the planet. Holocasts everywhere were interrupted with the news flash. In minutes, with a few exceptions, everyone on the planet knew the news. Pundits droned on about the possible artifacts on the surface of Iapetus, and pontificated on possible landing sites. The ambassadors from Australia, Canada, China, France, Germany, India, Israel, and Russia, all called the State Department at about the same time, requesting an immediate audience with the President. Each was politely referred to the President's Science Advisor who explained to each in turn patiently that they had several days to weeks to make the decision. He asked the ambassadors to consult with their governments to assign a specific person to study the incoming transmissions, in order to make any possible suggestions. He reminded them that the Mission Commander, Captain Jon Stock, had the ultimate respon-sibility for making the decision.

The French and the Russians immediately announced by news conference that their crew members would plant their respective national flags on the surface of Iapetus. German newspapers were outraged – at France, not at Russia. The Indians sent a nasty diplo-matic note to Pakistan, now a Caliphate territory, and received back a formal meeting request, ambassador to ambassador. The Chinese put their navy on a war games exercise in the Yellow Sea. And the Israelis quietly discovered another secret Caliphate missile site, and sent a surreptitious commando team to reprogram its targeting software, so that should it ever be launched, it would land on Teheran instead of somewhere in Israel.

Quietly, almost without fanfare, teams of scientists in each spon-soring country began to study the holographic transmissions as they arrived, applying every bit of skill they could muster to determining the best landing site.

\#

Caliph Ayatollah Khomeini, sat in his elevated chair looking down at his two trusted advisors. "Eskandar Ali Jinnah, our Mission Control mole," he told the robed attendants, "informs me that Saeed Esmail remains a prisoner under strict confinement." Both men nodded with obedient attention to his words. "A sympathetic crew member, probably the Indian Doctor, is assisting him in getting information back to Jinnah. Esmail is requesting specific instructions regarding his Jihad." The old Imam waved his advisors closer. "We are in touch with India at the ambassadorial level to determine our common interests." He paused meaningfully and folded his hands together tent-like. "Let us devise an answer and communicate it to our warrior in the sky."

#

The Mission Control engineers in Houston were of three minds about equally divided regarding a potential landing spot. The equatorial wall was an obvious target, even though at high magnification it resolved to a narrow string of towering twenty-kilometer high mountains. The argument was simple enough: Why couldn't a twenty-kilometer high, twenty-kilometer wide wall become a string of mountains over many eons? A second object of interest in the southern hemisphere was a 1.6-kilometer high spire or narrow tower. The argument here was also simple: What natural thing could produce such an object? The third potential landing spot was a bit more subtle. The entire surface of Iapetus appeared to consist of interlocking six- or five-sided geodesic sections. Some of these sections in a band just north of the equator were lower than the rest of the moon's surface, as if they had collapsed inward, almost as though supporting structures had given way. The accompanying argument was also more complex: If Iapetus were artificial, and if these artifacts represented geodesic sections, and if they really were collapsed, then they might present a convenient way to access the moon's interior.

Rod favored the third approach, and he favored giving Jon the largest possible latitude to make on-the-scene decisions. From the inputs he was receiving from the press and the President's Science Advisor, general opinions were all over the map, with a substantial number focusing on the three options his own people had come up with. Less than a week into the process, Alex Jinnah approached him. Rod motioned him to his private office.

"I got a message from the Caliphate," he told Rod in his private office. "They cut a deal with the Indian government, and they want me to establish a link to Dr. Bhuta."

"Did they give you a message for her?"

Jinnah nodded, and handed him a printout. Rod read it with a knot in his stomach:

"Greetings, Dr. Bhuta:
    Your mother and father have been placed in protective custody at a secure location to ensure your receptivity to this communication. In your response, to ensure that we are talking with you, please supply the type of gemstone in your mother's favorite ornamentation, and the name she has given this jewel. You are to communicate with Saeed Esmail, obtain his password, and communicate it back to us."

"How were you to get this message to Dr. Bhuta?" Rod asked him.

"As you know, personal messages to crew members from immediate family members were to be transmitted uncensored. Dr. Bhuta has traditionally conducted written communications with her parents in Sanskrit. In her younger years, she enjoyed a hobby of encrypting and decrypting coded messages; her father participated in these exercises. The Sanskrit message I am to send contains a lead-off word that indicates to the initiated receiver that the message contains an encrypted second message. The message I handed you is to be that second, encrypted message."

"Do you have any idea where they're headed with this?"

"None at all."

Rod dismissed Jinnah with thanks, and commenced composing his own encrypted message to Jon.

#

Several hours later, after absorbing the disturbing news from Houston, Jon called Ari to his stateroom. Ari entered, shut the door behind him, and floated at relaxed attention while Jon explained the problem.

"Do they suspect?" Jon speculated. "Or are they just being careful?"

Ari just grinned at him. "Your guess is as good as mine." He floated over and read the message in the holodisplay himself. "Does it matter? We get the secret word from Carmen, and carry on. Until we discover their motive, speculation will do us no good."

"You're right, of course," Jon answered.

"I'm worried about her parents," Ari said. "I think we need to get some of my guys in place to whisk them out when the time comes." Ari floated in thought. "Remember my old friend, Dan Ben-Gurion?"

"He must be getting on by now."

"Not really," Ari said with a smile. "He's about your age."

Jon just rolled his eyes.

"He heads up Mossad now, you know." Jon nodded. "Have Rod contact him with the details, and Dan will put an extraction team into place. Give him an hour's notice, and he can have them out."

"Sounds like a plan," Jon said, and dismissed his friend.

He sat for a while in quiet contemplation, and then he asked Carmen to join him in his stateroom for a cup of coffee. Several minutes later, Carmen arrived, accompanied by a holodisplay of her patient. Jon handed her a steaming bulb of latté.

Carmen thanked him and said, "This isn't about coffee, is it?"

Jon smiled at her, and handed her the communication from the Caliphate. Carmen read it twice, carefully, and then looked up at Jon with fear in her eyes. Her bottom lip trembled, and Jon found himself aching to hold her and comfort her.

"Obviously," she commented, "this has been intercepted." She paused to control her composure. "I have to believe that they think they are communicating with someone onboard – apparently me."

Jon noted to himself that once again a crew member had quickly and accurately assessed entirely unexpected information. "Essentially, Dr. Bhuta," Jon said, shifting to a more formal basis, "you are correct, but I will not confirm anything else, and you are ordered not to reveal any of this to the other crew members."

Carmen looked at him gravely. "I understand, Captain, and accept the restriction." She sipped thoughtfully from her bulb. "Emerald and Carmen," she added, almost as an afterthought.

Jon looked at her with raised eyebrow.

"The gemstone," she said. "Please let me know when my parents are safe." She slipped through the door under a cloud of worry. Jon plucked the still warm latté bulb from midair where she had left it.

Jon composed a detailed communication to Rod, giving him the code words and supplying him what he knew about Ben-Gurion. He ended with, "Let me know as soon as Carmen's parents are ready for rescue. Perhaps you should consider security for all immediate family members of the crew. I don't think anyone anticipated any of this. We're really kind of helpless out here. More than anything right now, we need to know their motive."

#

Carmen approached Saeed with a certain degree of trepidation. She was about to ask him for information that would immediately imply that she was operating against the best interests of the crew. This made her uncomfortable in a way she found it difficult to put into words. She confronted him in sickbay.

"You have a verification password that you received before taking on this mission. I need that password. I also know that you received a duress password that you are to give when you are under duress. The lives of my parents depend upon my transmitting the correct password back. Please remember that I saved your life. You live because of me.

#

Saeed listened to the doctor's words. She seemed sincere, and there was no question that he owed his life to her. But his mission was paramount, and no one, especially not a woman, could stand in the way of his success. Dr. Bhuta had acted as the instrument of Allah, *praise be to Him*, when she saved his life. It was, therefore, not her doing, but a holy purpose that guided her actions. Consequently, he did not owe anything to her, but only praise to Allah for His miraculous intervention. His instructions had been quite clear. If he was captured or under duress in some fashion, and found the opportunity to communicate, or even to broadcast, be interviewed, or in any other way to get word to the Caliphate, he was to work the word "David" into his comments. If he was unencumbered, and free to come and go, then he was to work the word "Solomon" into his comments.

You have been good to me, Dr. Bhuta," Saeed told her. I will not endanger your parents. The password you seek is "David." He gave her his warmest smile while reminding himself that lying to an infidel was not a sin.

#

The four men had been waiting patiently for several hours outside a converted warehouse in the industrial area about a kilometer south of the Zahedan International Airport runway near Iran's southeastern border where it met the borders of the former countries of Afghanistan and Pakistan. They looked every bit the part of ordinary industrial workers of the Caliphate. They spoke fluent Baluchi, the most common language of the region, and also Farsi and Arabic, and they carried papers that proved their citizenship and loyalty to the Ayatollah. They were short, swarthy, with dark curly hair, and their Baluchi accents indicated to an astute observer that they originated in the Afghani mountains to the immediate northeast. They wore dark glasses that served as efficient, high-resolution night vision devices. Under their traditional, loose-fitting garments, they each carried a modern pulse weapon with a lethal charge, equivalent to a thousand rounds of old-fashioned lead bullets – each weapon about the size of an old .45 caliber semi-automatic. They also carried concealed on their persons a half-dozen or so knives, some for stabbing, some for cutting, and some for throwing, and each man carried a small poly-aramid garrote. Between them, they also carried two harness slings, a collapsed balloon shaped like a dirigible, and an unmarked cylinder of helium, manufactured in pre-Caliphate Iran – all part of a renovated Fulton surface-to-air recovery system.

It was well past midnight. Stars twinkled through a layer of scattered clouds. The airport had long since shut down, and the city of nearly a million inhabitants centered several kilometers to the northwest slept quietly under the heavy hand of Sharia Law. Even the students at the Islamic Azad University were settled for the night, their studies of the esoteric concepts of Islamic jurisprudence set aside until after the first morning prayer.

The warehouse was guarded, but not in force. Four guards oversaw the one-story building that was located southeast across an empty green space from a poorly maintained formal garden with intersecting pathways and a central fountain. At any given time, two guards walked around the building, and two relaxed near the main entrance located on the northern end of the building. The only sound at this late hour was the splashing of the fountain. A soft hot breeze blew from the west off the Kavir-e Lut desert, bearing the distinct smell of salt, reminding the four watchers that they were near one of the hottest, driest spots on the planet.

One of the men held up his hand and motioned with two fingers for two to approach a small door in the southwest corner of the warehouse. Then he pointed to the other, signaling for him to keep an eye out for the walking guard. He indicated that he would watch for the other. The two men approached the door soundlessly, fiddled with the door handle for a moment, and quietly opened it, and slipped inside. One of the men activated a small infrared torch that fully illuminated the interior of the small room they had entered, as viewed through their night-vision glasses. They crossed the room to a door on the other side, opened it quietly, and found themselves in a jerry-rigged sleeping quarters, occupied by Carmen Bhuta's father and mother, sleeping in a bed just sufficiently large to accommodate both of them.

The two men approached the sleeping prisoners, and firmly clamped a hand over each mouth. Whispering in English, the man holding Dr. Bhuta whispered, "Quiet! We're here to get you out!" And to Dr. Bhuta's unasked question, "We're Israeli Mossad...put on trousers, both of you. Yes, Ma'am, wear your husband's pants...quickly, we are on a tight schedule." He glanced as his tritium illuminated watch, and motioned to his companion to hurry.

They slipped through the back room, glanced through the cracked door, and quietly closed it to wait for the patrolling guard to pass. "Quickly now," he said. "You must run, but soundlessly. Follow me!" He exited the door, holding the frightened woman's hand, who, in turn, held her husband's hand. They were followed by the second Israeli, who broke the woman's handhold, and grasped Dr. Bhuta's hand to guide him separately toward the garden. In the dark as they ran, they were joined by the other two Israelis. One ran out ahead of them carrying the helium cylinder and the balloon while the other covered them from behind. By the time they reached the garden, the black balloon had been inflated and was straining skyward at the end of a thin aramid cable.

The leader explained softly, "Put on these two harnesses," which they did with the others' help. "A low-flying aircraft will intercept the cable being held aloft by the balloon. You will be lifted off the ground together and drawn into the aircraft. Try to spread your arms and feet to minimize twisting. Don't worry if it happens, however, you'll be fine."

"But...but," Dr. Bhuta protested, squeezing his wife's hand.

"Don't talk!" the leader demanded in a whisper. "The only cover we have is the fountain." He looked at his watch. "Thirty seconds," he said, and counted down softly.

At zero nothing happened, but he kept his attention raptly on the cable. Suddenly, with a quiet whoosh, the couple was swept into the sky and disappeared against the star sprinkled backdrop, accompanied by a faint squeal.

The four men disposed of the empty cylinder in a pile of other empty cylinders at the back of the warehouse, and quietly faded into the dark alleys. An hour later they were making their way eastward at a fast trot toward a plateau just over the mountains east of the airport where they expected to be extracted before morning light.

Chapter fifteen

"What did you just tell me?" The Ayatollah Khomeini rose to his feet as he bellowed the question, shaking his fist.

The terrified messenger dropped to the tiled floor, prostrating himself. "Dr. and Mrs. Bhuta have disappeared, Sahib. They were there, and then they were gone." He tried to melt into the ornate tiles.

"And the guards?" The Caliph continued to bellow. "What about the guards?"

"They saw nothing, Sahib...they heard nothing," The messenger screamed as he felt the full 110 kilogram weight of the Caliph's 190 centimeter frame descend upon his neck through a booted foot as the enraged leader strode across the prostrate body.

"Execute the guards," he ordered his two robed assistants shuffling alongside him, as he departed the room.

"As you command, Sahib," one answered, struggling to keep up with the Caliph. The other turned back into the audience chamber, kicked the still prostrate messenger, and said, "Quickly, out the side door. Then to the desert with you, and don't return."

The messenger crawled to the door and disappeared.

#

Jon finished decrypting the latest message from Rod. "The Ayatollah is pissed to the max," he wrote. "He executed the guards, poor bastards, and razed the warehouse where they were holding them. They have no idea what happened to the Bhutas, and I want to keep it that way." The rest of the message concerned worldwide efforts to pick a landing spot. He read through the various points of view, noting with a certain degree of satisfaction that a plurality chose the geometric depressions. The wall was a close second, with the spire a distant third.

Jon called the crew to the Canteen and joined them.

Without preamble he asked, "How many of you want to land at the spire?"

Michele raised her finger, and Jon looked at her with raised eyebrow. "It looks like an inspiring masculine symbol," she said to general laughter. "I know the depressions are the most likely entry points, but these guys would never have raised such a symbol without it having access to the interior, *oui*?" Then she smiled broadly. "*Mais*, I am happy with anywhere on the surface." She got no disagreement.

"I prefer the wall," Dmitri said, not waiting for Jon to set up the question. "It is the largest artificial artifact in the entire solar system. And I wish to plant the Russian Federation flag on the surface," he added, pulling a small flag from his jumpsuit.

"*O oui!* Me too!" Michele said, pulling a French flag from her bosom to subdued chuckles from the rest of the crew.

"We'll get to that later," Jon said. "So, are we in general agreement, then, that we land near the large depression just north of the equator?" General nods all around, even Michele and Dmitri. "Earth consensus agrees with us, with the wall as a close second." Dmitri grinned and gave a thumbs-up around the group. Michele clapped her hands. Elke, with eyes on Michele, remained stoic. Ari and Noel exchanged high fives, and Ginger smiled at Jon, nodding her head slightly. Saeed said nothing at all.

Jon asked Dmitri and Ginger to examine the depression, and pick a suitable landing spot. He told them to set up a deorbiting burn to get them to that spot, and then he retired to his quarters to inform Houston of his decision.

He received an interesting response three hours later. Rod told him that some publicity wag in NASA had set up an online contest for children around the world, and the children had picked the depression as their choice for the landing. Since Jon had made the same choice, Rod told him that NASA would announce that the *Cassini II* would comply with the wishes of the world's children, and would land at the depression.

#

Ari floated with Noel in front of the lander. As many times as he had examined it, it still looked ugly and ungainly. They had opened the side hatch and removed all but three seats, in order to maximize the cargo carrying capability.

"I envy you being on the first descent," Noel told Ari. "We could all go together, you know."

"And what if something happened on descent?" Ari spoke with an unaccustomed seriousness. Noel shrugged, which in free-fall looked more like a body contraction than a shrug. "I know it probably is unlikely, but we've had several unlikely events happen. That's why Dmitri's staying back." Ari moved to a clump of cargo they had unsecured earlier. "If the three of us crash and get hurt, or even worse, if we buy it, then you guys can rescue us...or carry on."

"Don't you think I know that?" Noel responded with a bit of irritation. "I still envy you...but am glad to be your back-up."

"Yeh, I know. It's tough."

Ari had discussed the loadout with Jon several times. The problem really was that they had no idea what they might actually need once they were on the surface. They finally decided on an esoteric collection that included climbing rope and related equipment, digging and general archaeological tools, vacuum cutters and welders, emergency solar power generator, rock crusher, solar still, pressure tent with airlock, and – of course – sufficient food, water, and breathing air. The equipment set was designed to keep them alive in an emergency, allow them to conduct most kinds of repair to the lander/rover, and give them whatever they might need to recover whatever artifacts they might discover.

Jon had explained to Ari that he had not yet completely thought out how they would operate once the three of them had established the groundside base. The lander hypergolic fuel tanks held sufficient

fuel for two landings and returns to orbit, and *Cassini II* carried sufficient hypergolic fuel to refuel each lander three times. Depending on
what they found, they probably would cycle several crew members at
a time to the surface, but would keep *Cassini II* manned at all times
by someone who could fly her. An added complication was that, again
depending on what they found, Carmen, Michele, and Elke might
need to remain on the surface, since that was where their operations
likely would be. The only single item they had definitely agreed on was
that they would not leave anyone on Iapetus without a lander/rover.

Ari grinned to himself as he contemplated these things. *It's as
much politics as logistics*, Ari thought as he and Noel stowed the remaining equipment. *That's why Jon wears the Command Pin.*

"I think that's it," Ari said as they stowed the final tool, secur-
ing it inside the lander interior so that it would remain in position
during the descent when the rear bulkhead was "down," and on the
surface where the "floor" was down. "Whadya say we get ready to
launch this baby?"

#

An hour later Ginger settled herself into the lander between
two men she admired – Jon and Ari. All three were wearing their
suits with helmet attached. She was more excited than she had ever
been in her life. Getting laid the first time was special. Receiving her
doctorate was right up there. Being selected for this expedition was
better. The launch was even better, but the asteroid collision and the
Jupiter boost trumped all that, until their arrival here in orbit around
Iapetus. *But this...this is the highlight so far! If I don't watch myself, I'll
pee my panties.* Ginger settled back to watch her Captain at work.
Beyond the clear polymer nose she could see the open doors of the
bay completely filled with a view of Iapetus, just fifty clicks away and
looking for all the world like she could reach out and touch it. It was
coldly black and white, with every feature in sharp relief.

Jon's voice sounded in her ears, "Ready to launch, *Cassini*."

Dmitri answered in his Russian accented voice, "Roger that,
Lander One."

Under the steady control of Noel and Elke, who were suited
up and handling lines in the Bay, the lander lifted off the deck and
moved slowly out the open port doors, nose first. *This is almost better*

than sex, Ginger thought as the lander cleared the ship, and Noel and Elke cast off the control lines. Under computer control the lander tilted for their initial deorbit burn, presenting its single nozzle to the direction of their orbital path. Saturn loomed several times the size of the Moon from Earth, dominating the sky behind them, although Iapetus masked part of the ringed planet.

"Launch window coming up in three minutes, *Lander One.*" Dmitri was indicating the moment when the designated landmark would appear on the horizon. This would commence the fifteen-minute transit time before the landing site became visible. It would then pass the far horizon twenty-two seconds later, when communication with the landing site would be lost. Jon wanted direct contact with *Cassini II* for the entire descent and landing sequence.

"Roger that."

On her holodisplay, Ginger watched the three landing pads deploy around the nozzle.

It was almost exactly like watching a potential lover remove the last article of clothing. Ginger felt her heart begin to race.

"Are you alright, Ginger?" Doc Bhuta asked, inserting herself into the countdown. "Your vitals are speeding up."

"Of course they are, Doc. This is the most exciting thing that's ever happened to me!" A general chuckle followed Ginger's comments over the launch circuit.

"One minute," Dmitri's voice droned. "Thirty seconds... Three... two...one...fire!"

Ginger caught her breath as she felt the force of the acceleration pressing her into the seat. It was over almost as soon as it had started. Out the clear nose, Ginger watched *Cassini II* flash overhead and quickly grow small to disappear into the bright field of stars in what now felt like overhead. In less than two minutes, Dmitri announced the commencement of the braking burn, and once again Ginger felt weight return. She glanced over at Jon. His hands were resting on controls that he did not expect to use, but she felt safer just seeing his hands there. She glanced at Ari, and saw his hands available as backup, should that remote possibility become reality.

The holodisplay in front of her showed their fast approaching landing spot – a flat, rock-strewn plain just inside the rim mountains surrounding the depression. It grew closer as she watched.

"You're one click out, Jon. I don't like my feedback reading here. I recommend you take it in manually."

"You sure about that, Dmitri?"

"Absolutely, Jon...take over!" Ginger caught her breath as Jon began to manipulate the hurtling lander, holding a joy-stick-like control in each hand. Ginger felt additional weight as Jon applied more thrust, apparently wanting to get full control before they reached any possible ground effect. Ari's hands hovered over his joysticks, but didn't touch them, as Jon eased the acceleration off and let the lander commence its final drop.

Ginger started as she saw a relatively large rock, a meter or so in diameter, appear in the landing display. To her relief, Jon eased the lander to the right, bringing it down about three meters away from the rock. He landed gently on the three pads, settling into their hydraulics to absorb the remaining inertia, and extinguished the hypergolic motor.

"*Lander One* has landed," Jon said without any further formality.

#

Add that one to my list of firsts, Jon thought as he extinguished the hypergolic motor. "Bring her horizontal, Ari," Jon said in the resulting quiet.

Ari manipulated his controls, and a fourth pad pushed away from the lander's belly so that it extended at a backward angle from directly under the nose, almost reaching the ground. Once the nose pad leg was fully deployed, he began to extend the landing pad by the nozzle that protruded from what would become the top of the rover. As it extended, the lander tilted forward, pivoting on the remaining two landing pads so that the nose pad contacted the surface. Then the nose pad retracted under hydraulic control so that the lander tilted smoothly until its after-set of pneumatic wheels made contact with the surface, and then the middle, and then the forward set. The nose pad folded snugly back against the hull. The top pad extending back from the top of the nozzle retracted, and then it and the other two landing pads folded against the hull. Ari lifted his hands from the controls and smiled at Jon.

"The rover is yours," he said.

"*Rover One* is operational, Control," Jon announced, moving the rover forward several meters.

The entire operation had taken fifteen minutes from lander launch to operating rover.

"You appear to be a few meters from the edge of the collapsed depression," Dmitri reported from orbit. "We're about to lose you. Recommend you exit *Rover One* and examine the terrain on foot." The Com channel crackled. "See you in three-and-three-quarter hou..." The word *hour* was truncated as *Cassini II* passed out of sight over the horizon.

The entire operation had been "on-the-record" to this point. Jon tapped his control panel, stopping the record, and said, "We're gonna go outside now, but we have to do the appropriate formalities. As we rehearsed, okay? And Ginger, try not to giggle."

#

The broadcast arrived "live" at Houston, and was immediately channeled to the media for their live presentation of the first man to step on the surface of Iapetus. Rod was well aware that the event had actually happened ninety minutes earlier, but neither he nor the standing-room-only crowd in Mission Control cared.

With the entire world watching, the external holocams on the lander recorded the side hatch of *Rover One* opening. A white-suited figure stood in the opening, waved at the holocams, and jumped lightly to the surface. Two small plumes of dust rose to about knee height, and then seemed to float back to the surface. Jon Stock's voice traveled throughout the world for the second time in his career: "For the children of the World who chose this landing site, and for humankind everywhere...Iapetus!"

Jon tilted his head up to take in Saturn – its colorful bands and clearly distinct rings easily the most dominant object in the sky. Then he turned and reached out a helping hand to Ginger, who graciously accepted the unnecessary gesture, and then he waved Ari to the surface. The three space voyagers stood for a holographic portrait, Jon to Ginger's left and Ari to her right. Then, led by Jon, they moved to a rise a few meters from the rover. Jon planted a small American flag, saying, "We come as free men, in peace."

"We join our northern brothers in a celebration of liberty and peace," Ginger said, planting the new Australian flag next to the Stars and Stripes. It consisted of a blue field with the Union Marc of the old flag in the canton replaced by a gold seven-pointed Commonwealth Star, and displaying the Southern Cross on the flag as before.

Ari stepped forward and planted the Star of David to form a triangle with the other two flags. "We join our American and Australian brothers to form an endless circle of freedom and peace," he said, and turned toward Earth with his right hand laid across his left breast.

The screen in Mission Control went dark.

The din of happy people drowned out any broadcast from Mission Control for a full five minutes. As the people settled down and the noise quieted, individual broadcasters began to provide their personal comments on this unprecedented event. They all noted, of course, that Jon Stock was now the only human in history to open two new worlds. They also noted that Ginger Steele was the first woman in history to be in the initial landing party on a new world. In America and Australia, the Israeli Ari Rawlston's accomplishment was celebrated in a more subdued manner, but Israelis danced in the streets of Tel Aviv and Jerusalem.

#

While their signal beamed to Earth on its ninety-minute journey, the three suited figures roped themselves together with about three meters between them. By unspoken agreement, Ari and Jon put Ginger in the middle with Jon in the lead. Ari picked up a rock about the size of a grapefruit, and dropped it to the ground from waist height. In the slight gravity of Iapetus, only 2.3% of Earth's gravity, the rock took nearly three seconds to reach the surface. Ginger stooped and duplicated the act with a second rock. Ari picked up another rock and threw it as hard as he could toward the one-point-two kilometer distant horizon. It really appeared no different than throwing a rock on Earth, except that it rose higher, and came down slower. It struck the surface about 700 meters out – over half the distance to the horizon, kicking up a small plume of dust.

Ari wondered aloud why it didn't fly faster and farther. Ginger answered, "You're no stronger here, so you can't give it more speed, but because the gravity is so much less, you can throw it higher. It takes about four seconds to fall to the surface from your throwing height, plus the additional time to travel the parabolic path of the throw. The downside of the parabola is impelled by only two-point-three percent of Earth's gravity, so put it altogether, and you have what you see." Her eyes twinkled through her clear helmet. "Do you want to see the equation?"

"Smart ass!" Ari quipped as he joined Jon and Ginger at the edge of the depression. Saturn and its rings dominated the sky overhead, giving Ari a feeling of apprehension. He shook it off and turned his attention to the edge of the depression. It didn't look like much, really. Ari could barely integrate the edge into a line stretching away from them both ways. About a kilometer behind them, the rim mountains formed a curtain of jagged rock against the backdrop of stars. Directly in front of them, the surface dropped down about a half-meter, and then continued a gentle slope into what appeared like nothing so much as a shallow very wide meteor crater. With the horizon only one-point-two kilometers distant, the floor sloped right over the horizon, running in virtually the same direction as Saturn's colorful bands. To Ari's eyes the entire scene appeared entirely natural, as opposed to some kind of artificial construct, especially with the jumbled mountains ringing the depression – just like so many lunar craters.

Jon announced that they would commence a traverse along the right edge of the depression, spiraling inward from the edge as they move forward, looking for something artificial. He wanted to remain within about 500 meters of the edge. "Ginger," he said, "range off the edge as best you can, and keep us moving inward."

To Ari, their path forward looked like a boulder-strewn field, although when he tried to move a boulder, it appeared to be well attached to the regolith. Only the smaller ones were loose, and everything was covered with a powder-like layer of fine dust. Their progress quickly became a series of light hops, covering about ten meters each time. It was very much like walking on the sea bottom in a hardhat outfit, Ari decided.

An hour passed, and Ari could not tell any distinguishing difference between where they were and where they had been, although the edge – now about a half-click away – appeared to have more definition than when they started. He increased the magnification of his heads-up viewer to examine the wall more closely. The edge appeared to be nearly two meters high at this point. Ari focused on several dark shadows. As he concentrated, the shadows seemed to resolve into depressions in the wall.

"Jon, Ginger – take a look at this." He pointed the shadows out to them. "Whadya say we check it out?"

"Good idea," Jon said, putting Saturn at his back, and heading in the general direction of the wall shadows.

By the time they were a hundred meters away, it became clear that they were looking at a slight overhang of the rim. It was just another disappointing natural phenomenon. "Let's make our way to the top of the ridge and head back to the rover from there," Jon said. "We don't want to overexert on the first day." He turned and hopped about a meter above the surface, timing himself to land on a spot several meters in front of them that was free of everything but dust. His feet met the surface, and kept right on going as Jon dropped out of sight.

Chapter sixteen

The Caliph's visible fury continued unabated until he slammed the door to his private quarters, leaving his quaking advisors outside the shut door. Obviously, his communications channel had been compromised. Did these fools think him stupid?

He bellowed, and two young women scurried into his chambers with sweet tea and a plate of fermented fig bars. Alcohol could, of course, never pass his lips, but the Caliph allowed the natural fermentation process in his favorite delicacy to proceed until a dozen helped him mollify his periodic moods. The young women, a fourteen-year-old just beginning to show signs of budding womanhood and a sixteen-year-old who was ripe and ready, were his latest wives. The Caliph's senior wife had provocatively dressed them in burkas made of many layers of transparent fabric. Their bodies were clearly visible through the material, but in a diffused manner that drove the Caliph to distraction. As the young girls ministered the tea and fig bars to the still smoldering Caliph, they danced teasingly into and back out of his reach – exactly as instructed by the senior wife.

"Let him remove your veils one at a time," she told them, "and snatch articles of his clothing as you dance close." As she set their outfits for easy removal, she added, "Remember, you must excite his mind until he forgets his rage and can think only of the pleasure each of you will bring him...when he is ready, let him do as he wishes." And she whispered softly, "Your lives depend on this..."

As the little beauties danced away his anger, the Caliph sipped his sweet tea and nibbled on the fermented fig bars while he worked out the details of how he would handle the situation on Iapetus, but before he could complete his thoughts, the little nymphs had captured his imagination and redirected his energies to more immediate and pressing needs.

#

When Ginger saw Jon vanish through the surface, she placed herself in a belaying position to accept the surge when Jon reached his three-meter limit. Ari grabbed the line just behind Ginger to stabilize her when the weight hit. About five seconds after Jon disappeared through the surface, the rope went taut. In Iapetus' light gravity, Ginger easily handled the belay by herself – despite his extra mass, so Ari went gingerly to the edge and peered through the hole, turning on his spotlight. In the vacuum the light showed no beam, but Ari could see a bright circle where the beam struck a moving something directly below him.

"You okay, Jon?" he asked as he recognized his friend spinning slowly at the end of his rope, beam brightly lit. Jon looked up.

"I'm fine, Ari. I'm seeing obviously artificial support pillars when my light hits them, but I'm spinning too fast to make out any details. I see a smooth floor that seems to support the pillars, but directly below me is nothing but black." He paused. "I must be suspended over some kind of shaft." He paused again. "I think we just answered the big question. Can you guys haul me up?"

When he was standing on the surface next to Ginger and Ari, Jon said, "I have no idea how far down that shaft goes. I was about three meters from a ledge on the side toward the edge of the depression – where I saw the pillars." He pointed toward the two-meter wall that marked the border of the depression. "Completely open on the other side and below me."

"Are you certain the pillars were artificial?" Ginger asked.

"Nothing here to create stalactites," Jon said with a broad grin.

"Besides, they were perfectly cylindrical – there's no question."

"One explanation for Iapetus' low density," Ari said, "is that it is made up of a lot of ices...they could make stalactites. But," he added hastily, "I believe you! I just need to see them for myself."

"You will," Jon said, "we all will."

"*Rover One*, this is *Cassini*. Do you copy?" Dmitri's accented voice interrupted their conversation.

"Roger, *Cassini*. We have just discovered what can only be artificial structures – regularly spaced pillars holding up the ceiling of a cavern."

"Say again, *Rover*. I thought you just said you found artificial pillars..."

"Roger, Dmitri...that's exactly what we found, perfectly cylindrical floor-to-ceiling pillars holding up the roof of a vast cavern."

"I copy...so what's next?"

"We are some distance from our landing spot, and it's been a long day. We'll head back to the rover, eat something, and sack out for several hours. We'll call you when we get there."

"Roger that, *Rover One*," Dmitri said as his transmission faded in a burst of static.

#

Houston was on a watch cycle that maintained only CapCom and four other regular watch standers in Control. Except for an emergency, there was really nothing Houston could do to help the distant space travelers. Even in an emergency, Houston would not know about it until over ninety minutes after it happened. If Jon Stock had not solved the problem or at least gotten it under control by then, it probably would not be solved. Rod Zakes did not put himself on the watch rotation, but he could be found nearby virtually any hour of the day or night.

By the time Dmitri had relayed Jon's colorful description of his fall through the surface, and their discovery of what could only be artificial pillars holding up the roof of a large cavern, the surface crew had long since returned to the rover, eaten something, and retired for a well-deserved sleep. As it happened, Rod was sleeping himself when the message arrived. Nevertheless, he responded with instant alertness when he awakened to the cryptic announcement over the building system. Zakes to Control...Zakes to Control.

He arrived a minute later, and CapCom replayed the message. "Can you believe it," Rod muttered, "the greatest discovery in the history of the human race, and only we six know about it!" He reviewed the message again. *You live a charmed life, Jon my friend.* "We'll await their next transmission before making any announcement." The last thing he wanted was for the exploration party to discover that their initial determination was wrong. A few more hours wouldn't matter.

When he returned to his room, he pulled out the message Alex had handed him earlier that day. He read it for perhaps the twentieth time:

Mr. Zakes:
The facts clearly indicate that you have penetrated my communications link. Consequently, there is no further need for subterfuge. I demand an uncensored communication link with my subject, Saeed Esmail. Failing that, I will unleash nuclear holocaust against your ally, Israel.
Khomeini

He had, of course, informed State the moment he received it. Despite an admonition to maintain total security, he had made a secure call to Daniel Ben-Gurion. He was not going to have the blood of several million innocent Israelis on his hands if State bungled this one.

A detailed encrypted message was already waiting for Jon on Iapetus, but Rod was uncertain whether or not Jon had brought his decryption program with him to the surface. *Damn the waiting!* He poured himself a stiff Scotch and went back to sleep.

#

The next morning, Rod walked into Control, to find it filled to capacity. Obviously, the word had gotten out. Since he would be making the announcement shortly anyway, Jon decided not to make an issue of the matter.

Within an hour, the first images started to arrive, images taken by Jon's suit equipment as he hung ignominiously over the shaft, twisting in the dark on the previous day. These were followed by new ones being transmitted directly from the site as the *Cassini II* passed overhead. As the Mission Control computers reassembled the incoming data, everyone watched as the three explorers placed a high intensity cutting rope in a two-meter wide circle near the base of an overhanging two-meter high wall. Following a bright soundless flash, a neat two-meter hole penetrated the surface where the charge had been laid.

Ginger rolled out an inflatable polyaramid pattern that quickly hardened into a four-meter high ladder. She and Ari lifted it and lowered it into the hole. It hit bottom with about a meter to spare. Jon descended first, carrying a bright illumination source. His helmet holocams transmitted what he saw. The entire assembly in Control held its collective breath. Once on the floor, Jon activated the illumination. A collective gasp emanated from the assembled Control personnel.

Their eyes beheld a forest of evenly spaced clearly artificial pillars extending to the limits of the illumination. Spaced between the pillars were mounds of something – machines perhaps – but there was no way to tell from the transmitted images. Stunned silence followed the termination of the transmission as *Cassini II* passed around Iapetus' limb.

Rod picked up a phone and directed that his prepared press announcement be released. Two minutes later, news of the discovery flashed around the world. In every place that holovision reached or radio was heard, the world's billions stopped their activities to watch or listen to the incredible news. Humans were not alone in the Universe. Someone else was out there, or at least had been out there at one time in the distant past.

#

Jon stood at the base of the ladder and looked around him in total astonishment. "Ginger, join me. Ari, you remain topside for the time being." He watched her descend the ladder, slim and graceful, even in her suit. They tethered together with a three-meter stretch. "We're going to penetrate about two-hundred meters," Jon said to Ari. "Keep my holocast on your viewer. Should we get into trouble, don't come down unless it's absolutely necessary."

"Roger that."

"I'll take the lead," Jon said to Ginger. "Keep the tether taut, but still a bit loose. Know what I mean?"

"Got it."

As they moved forward, Jon kept his eyes on the floor, not wanting to go through another dropping incident. Their footsteps stirred up a small cloud of dust that settled back to the floor over a matter of seconds. They stopped to examine the first lump. It was covered with a thick layer of fine dust. Jon wiped some of it to the floor. Beneath the dust appeared a surface that looked like metal. "Do you see this, Ari?"

"Sure do. What is it?"

"No clue. Ginger, help me remove more of the dust."

Together they worked for five minutes clearing most of the dust from the top of whatever it was. Their suits and helmets automatically repelled the dust particles. The device was constructed of three intersecting cylinders all crossing or passing through each other at the middle. Apparently it was a machine of some sort. It rested directly on the deck. When Jon stooped down to examine how it was attached, he could see nothing. It seemed to blend into the deck as if it had been molded from the deck material, but there was no clue as to its function. There were no controls, no panel of any kind, no doors, drawers, or anything else that could be manipulated in any way. Jon shook his head. "Whatever this is, it's incredibly old. Why would anyone expect to make anything of it?"

"Even without atmospheric corrosion," Ginger said, "I cannot imagine any machine lasting for as long as this must have lasted."

"Roger that," Ari commented.

"Come on, let's look at the next machine," Jon said. In his mind that's what they were, machines of unknown age, with unknown purpose. The next machine was identical to the first one, except it was oriented at what appeared to the eye to be a sixty-degree angle to the first machine. They examined several more machines. Each was oriented at sixty degrees to those surrounding it.

"Ari, transmit the images to *Cassini II* as soon as possible. Ask Dmitri to run a geometric analysis of the machine placement pattern."

#

As allowed by the orbital parameters, Dmitri had been following Jon's and Ginger's progress with growing excitement. He was beginning to believe he knew the machines' purpose. He eagerly fed the images into the ship's computer system and instructed it to do a comprehensive geometric analysis. Using Jon's size as a ruler, Dmitri supplied dimensions. In a few minutes, a pattern flashed into his display. At first it looked like a bunch of triangles, but then he realized that he was looking at a pattern of intersecting hexagons, each constructed of six triangles that met in the center of the hexagon. Each machine was equally the center of a new hexagon and the point of one.

On his next pass, Dmitri reported to Ari, "The machines form a matrix that produces a multi-polar closed magnetic field. To work, it would have to cover the entire surface of Iapetus."

"And its purpose?" Ari asked.

"Why, to protect whatever lies beneath from incoming charged particles."

#

"And so," Jon said to Ginger and Ari as they relaxed inside the rover, "we are faced with two possibilities. Whoever built what we saw either burrowed down into the surface of a virgin planetoid, and constructed an artificial layer that extends some unknown distance down from the surface; or, the second possibility is that Iapetus is entirely artificial, and that it contains God-knows-what underneath the first layer we have penetrated."

Neither Ginger nor Ari said anything. The concept was simply too overwhelming.

"We have our work cut out for us. We need as many people down here as possible, consistent with keeping Chen alive and monitoring Saeed." He paused for a while, just looking out the front port at the magnificence of Saturn hanging low in the sky. "We need to go back to *Cassini II*, sit down with the others and work this out."

At *Cassini II's* next pass, Jon told Dmitri to work out the parameters for their return to the ship. The three of them climbed back into their suits, strapped themselves in, and prepared for launch. Within fifteen minutes, *Rover One* had reverted to *Lander One*, and they awaited Dmitri's launch instructions. Twenty minutes later, Noel and Elke were dragging them into the bay. An hour after making the decision, Jon had assembled the crew in the Canteen – all but Carmen, Chen, and Saeed.

#

While Jon was discussing their options down on Iapetus, Saeed floated next to Chen massaging his limbs as he had done every day since he gave his bond. Carmen had gotten used to his presence, and they chatted in Arabic, so she could practice her language skills. On this occasion, while Jon was docking in the bay, their topic of conversation was the exciting news about the discovery of the surface team.

"So, now we know," Carmen said in her nearly perfect Arabic, "that intelligent beings from the ancient past really did build Iapetus." She smiled at her charge, and asked him, "Do you really understand what that means? The human race is not alone in the Universe. There is at least one other race of intelligent beings. And if there is one, then there must be many...imagine that, hundreds, perhaps thousands of intelligent races..."

Suddenly, Saeed interrupted her. "Doctor...Doctor! Look at Chen...his eyelids...look at them!"

Carmen leaned closer to her patient. Sure enough, his eyelids were moving, fluttering rapidly. Then his left eye opened, followed by his right. His eyes blinked several times, and then he sneezed, and tried to sit up. Saeed unstrapped him, but kept a hand on him, since they still were in free fall, and Chen would not necessarily be aware of that fact.

"Wha...wha...," he muttered.

"It's okay," Carmen told him. He looked at her with blank eyes. "It's Dr. Bhuta...you've been unconscious for a bit. You are on the spaceship *Cassini II*, making a voyage to Iapetus. Do you remember?" Ne nodded.

"How long have I been unconscious?" he asked.

"For about two months," she told him. "We're in orbit around Iapetus. Jon, Ginger, and Ari have been on the surface. They just arrived back with the exciting news that Iapetus is an artifact. We have found what we came for, Chen. You awakened just in time. Jon called a meeting in the Canteen. Come and join us." She turned to Saeed. "Assist him."

"Who is that?" Chen looked at Saeed with total astonishment.

"It's a long story. I'll bring you up to date after the meeting." She propelled herself toward the door. "Let's not keep them waiting."

PART TWO

Starchildren

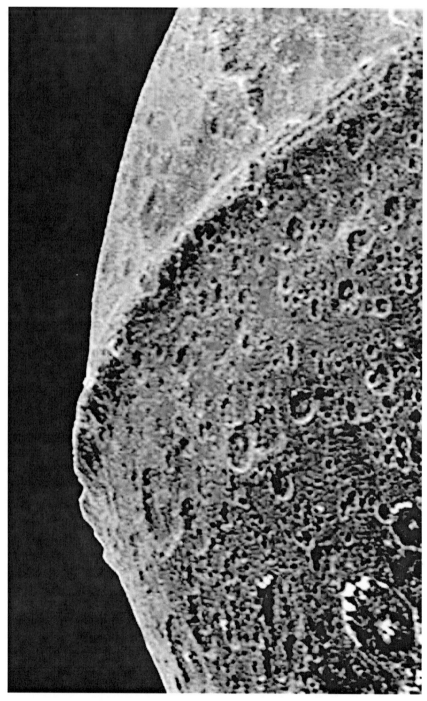

Detail of equatorial wall on Iapetus

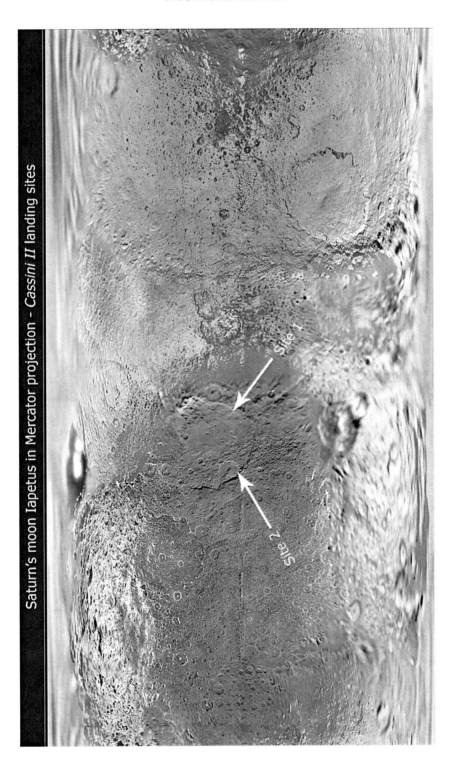

Saturn's moon Iapetus in Mercator projection - *Cassini II* landing sites

Site 1

Site 2

The two landing sites on Iapetus

Chapter seventeen

"Let's wait a minute for Dr. Bhuta and Saeed to arrive," Jon said to the assembled crew. He could feel the tension in the air, the excitement of the moment. As he had not discussed his reason for returning to the ship, each crew member was filled with questions. Jon relaxed, floating just above the chair seat that he normally occupied. The other crew members had taken their accustomed places, floating in keen anticipation of what Jon would say. Rather than wait any longer, Jon cleared his throat and said, "I know you all are wondering why we came back so abruptly."

He was interrupted by Carmen's clear, accented voice as she entered the Canteen. "Was it to celebrate Chen's awakening?" As she said that, Saeed propelled Chen into the Canteen.

"Hi," Chen said. "I'm back." He settled into his own accustomed place that the crew had left unoccupied ever since he suffered his injury.

"What is this?" Jon asked, rhetorically.

"The mystery continues," Carmen said. "Saeed was massaging Chen's limbs while discussing your exciting discovery with me." She turned and smiled at Chen. "I don't know if that conversation triggered something in you, Chen, but whatever it was, you are here and awake – apparently none the worse for wear."

Michele immediately floated over and planted a wet kiss on Chen's lips. He blushed while wiping his lips on his jumper sleeve as the rest of the crew crowded around him, slapping his back and hugging him – no more wet kisses.

"How does one follow that?" Jon asked with a wide grin. "Welcome back, Chen Lee-Fong. You couldn't have picked a better time to make your reappearance."

Chen just smiled at everybody.

Jon then detailed what he, Ginger, and Ari had discovered, bringing up the holos in the general display. "You can see what I saw during my initial fall through the surface, and what Ginger and I found the next day. Dmitri tells me these devices appear to be nodes in some kind of closed magnetic system, although I'm not sure what that might be." Everyone chuckled. "Show us, Dmitri."

Dmitri tapped his link, and the display dissolved into a view of the geometric pattern formed by the devices. "Each of the cross-pieces appears to line up with the next one on both sides, so that the net result is this interlocking hexagonal grid. If each of these cross-pieces generates a magnetic field, and if they are positioned north to south around the ring like this," a pattern of Ns and Ss appeared on the ends of every crosspiece, "we end up with a magnetic field that looks like this." Magnetic lines of force appeared flowing from node to node through the appropriate crosspieces. The resulting field appeared very dense, and was confined to the space between the floor and overhead of the vault containing the devices. "I surmise that this magnetic grid covered the entire space just below the surface of Iapetus."

Stunned silence followed his presentation.

"Obviously," Noel commented dryly, "nature didn't do that. Were they working?"

"No," Ginger answered. "But the devices we examined showed no damage. Other than being covered with dust, they looked like... well they looked like you saw them a bit ago."

"The reason we came back," Jon said, "is to figure out where we go from here. And now that Chen is with us again, our options have expanded."

Jon went on to review the original Moon-landing protocol that required one astronaut to remain in the orbiter, while the other two landed on the surface. The first Mars mission used a similar protocol, although there was serious discussion about sending the entire team to the surface. As it turned out, the automatics worked perfectly, so that the crew member who had remained in orbit could have landed with the others.

Iapetus was in an entirely different class. Both landers would be on the surface, landing sequentially, so that if one experienced a problem, the second could come to its rescue. The automated systems on the orbiting *Cassini* II had multiple levels of redundancy, and were designed to operate without human intervention. A problem that would strand both landers was so unlikely as to be virtually unthinkable. Anyone aboard the *Cassini II* would be unable to offer the stranded explorers anything but encouraging words. Anyone remaining onboard would have virtually nothing to do because of the automation. If something were to go wrong on the surface, the only source of help would be the other lander. The bottom line was that there really was no reason to leave anyone onboard the *Cassini II*.

Jon said to his assembled crew, "I want to spend the next several hours planning our approach, and then we'll split into two teams. My team will descend to a spot near the entrance we created, and will explore more thoroughly. The other team, led by Dmitri, will touch down at the opposite side of the depression, open an entry there, if it turns out to be possible, and will explore that side. I'm particularly interested in what lies deeper below the surface. Are we dealing with a relatively thin artificial layer, or do we have a completely artificial world to explore?" Jon adjusted his position so that he gave the appearance of leaning back, and watched the crew members discuss the situation among themselves. Jon had two main considerations. He wanted Ari to keep control of Saeed, and he wanted Carmen to be near Chen. He also wanted at least one person who had already been on the surface to be in Dmitri's team.

While the crew discussed the various options, and what they each thought was important to pursue, Jon put together two tentative lists. "Listen up a moment," he said.

"I am suggesting that my team consist of myself, of course, with Ari, Michele, Elke, and Saeed. Dmitri will take Ginger, Noel, Chen, and Carmen." He turned to enter his quarters. "Discuss it among yourselves to see if you can come up with any improvements. We'll plan on departing right after the next rest period."

#

Ginger and Dmitri spent a couple of hours examining the surface of the depression opposite the first entry. On the first pass they made detailed images of the surface, and then commenced the examination. The rim-wall mountains on the opposite side were much closer to the edge of the depression, and the available space appeared rockier. Ginger was concerned that Dmitri might have some difficulty landing. Although there were several smooth areas just inside the depression, Ginger cautioned Dmitri that the lander might break through the surface.

"Let's move closer to the equatorial wall," Dmitri suggested. "If we find a good landing spot there, perhaps we can take some time to examine the wall as well."

"Never miss an opportunity, do you," Ginger said with a grin. "I remember you wanted to examine the wall first."

"That was before we found the chamber, my dear. I'm one hundred percent onboard now. I was just thinking that if we can't gain entry on the opposite side, we might want to spend a day or so looking more closely at the wall."

"I guess I agree. Okay, let's look for a landing spot that way."

They found an even higher rim wall than at the first site, and as they traversed the depression floor toward the equatorial wall, they discovered a secondary depression that appeared to be a large meteor crater. Apparently, sometime following the collapse of whatever lay under the large depression they were investigating, something big smashed into the surface just inside the depression rim wall, leaving a relatively smooth basalt plain behind. The upthrust ring mountains from the meteor strike were merged with the depression rim wall.

"I'm thinking," Dmitri said, "that that plain is plenty strong to hold the lander. If we can get close to where the crater abuts the rim wall, we may find easy access to the interior. That incoming had to mess things up pretty badly down below."

"I agree. Let's pass it by Jon. I'm sure he'll agree. Then you guys can check it out in detail."

#

Jon reviewed the encrypted message he received from Rod several times. It boiled down to a relatively simple matter. The Caliph had come out of the closet, so to speak, and demanded that he be granted direct contact with Saeed. He threatened to nuke Israel if his wish was ignored. State was considering the problem, but in the final analysis, it fell into Jon's lap. He called Ari into his quarters to discuss the matter. Ari arrived with two bulbs of coffee and handed one to Jon. Jon took a sip and grimaced. "My God, what is this? Candy?"

Ari sipped his and said, "Oops! I switched them." They switched, and Ari started reading.

After Ari had read the communication, Jon asked, "Well, what do you think? Is he making a real threat?"

"Of course he is, but he has no intention of carrying it out if you give him a way to save face." Ari grinned at him. "That's why you are the Captain."

"Thanks..."

"Seriously, he's going to send a coded message, and we need to understand what he is really saying. I don't think Saeed will cooperate fully with us if he believes he can get away with it."

"And so..."

"I watch him like a hawk."

#

Three-and-a-half hours later, with Ari at his side, Jon handed a printed message to Saeed. "The Caliph has negotiated with Houston Control so that you are to be able to communicate directly with him. All communications will be in English and will go through me, but you will receive uncensored messages from the Caliphate, and we will transmit your messages back – subject to my review of your outgoing messages. Your messages will be short, will contain no lies, nor will they serve to bring harm to this mission. Do you understand these restrictions, which by the way, apply to the rest of the crew as well?"

Ari repeated the entire statement in Arabic to make sure Saeed understood.

Saeed felt overwhelmed by this turn of fortune. He eagerly read the message: "Allah in His infinite wisdom has changed your mission. You are now the Caliphate representative on this historic mission. Behave accordingly to show the world what Islam can accomplish.

Learn from the Family of Imran, the 3,154 who reside in your heart."

Saeed left the captain's stateroom with Ari, but remained silent. In his mind he was rapidly moving through the memorized *Qur'an*, searching out the meaning of the message. He commenced his search with Surah number three: *Al-Imran* – The Family of Imran. When he got to verse 154, he nearly gasped aloud. The last part of the verse read: *Say: Had you remained in your houses, those for whom slaughter was ordained would certainly have gone forth to the places where they would be slain, and that Allah might test what was in your breasts and that He might purge what was in your hearts; and Allah knows what is in the breasts.*

His Jihad continued. He would pick the time and place.

#

Dmitri was glad the little terrorist was on Jon's team. Had Saeed been assigned to his team, Dmitri was certain that he would have come to a fatal accident before they returned to the ship. Dmitri and Ginger had worked out the deorbiting parameters for both landers, and loaded the information in each lander system. The landers were fully loaded and the teams were strapped in place. Ginger and Noel, suited with TBH Boots, attached lines to *Lander One* and manipulated her out of the bay so the lander was floating alongside *Cassini II*. Then they shifted the lines to *Lander Two* and moved her so that she floated several meters from *Lander One*. They left the bay open to space, and returned to *Lander Two*. The entire task took about a half hour. Both landers waited in orbit alongside *Cassini II* for their respective launch times.

Ginger had set *Lander One* to depart first, because in their east-to-west orbit, *Lander One's* spot came below them before *Lander Two's* spot, 650 kilometers and about twenty-eight minutes to the west. *Lander One* commenced its deorbiting burn and rapidly dropped out of sight.

Dmitri made sure that Ginger was securely strapped into her seat, and then waited patiently for the time of their burn. Outside the clear polymer nose of the lander, Saturn dominated the sky, partially blocked by the looming nearness of Iapetus. Somehow, sitting in the lander's nose, Dmitri had the feeling that he was floating free, falling toward the ringed, banded giant. He had to pull himself back to the tack at hand with a conscious effort. Dmitri slowly flipped *Lander Two* so it presented its nozzle to the edge of Iapetus. Saturn swung behind them, and then it was time. A short burst of acceleration pushed them into their seats, and then they were falling toward their rendezvous with the surface, fifty kilometers below.

As their descent commenced, Jon announced, "*Lander One* is on the surface."

Dmitri allowed the onboard computer to set their descent attitude so they would be properly positioned for the braking burn. They swept rapidly across the surface, angling across the depression. Their orbital velocity of just under 400 m/sec was now somewhat greater due to the slight assist of Iapetus' gravity since they transferred a significant part of their horizontal vector to a vertical one. As Dmitri's hands hovered over his backup controls, the lander commenced a braking burn of several seconds, removing most of its forward momentum. Below them, the moving landscape slowed until it passed at a visibly much slower pace. The gyro whined briefly; the main jet gave a short burst, and as *Lander Two* slowed to a hover a hundred meters above the surface, the gyro brought her to a vertical aspect. The main jet came alive again, this time throttled. Recalling Jon's experience, Dmitri assumed manual control, and guided *Lander Two* to a gentle touchdown in an area that appeared to be composed of a light-colored basalt until the exhaust caused its thin layer of dust to billow up and away, revealing a dark, relatively smooth surface.

Lander Two settled on its three pads as the hypergolic motor shut down. "*Lander Two* has landed," Dmitri announced. "Take over, Ginger. Activate *Rover Two*."

"Roger that!"

Within two minutes, *Rover Two* stood solidly on its six large wheels, with all four pads fully retracted against the hull, surrounded by the relatively clear surface of the nearly ninety kilometer wide secondary impact crater. About a kilometer away, just over halfway to the horizon, loomed the chaotic merged mountains formed by the secondary impact and the ring surrounding the depression. Since Dmitri wanted to get close to the intersection of the secondary crater and the depression, he headed the rover in a generally southwest direction, aiming for a jumble of rock about a kilometer distant.

"Does it look like you thought it would?" Dmitri asked Ginger.

"I wasn't really thinking about the dust layer," she answered. "I knew it was there, of course, but in my mind I saw the surface as light. I guess that's my mistake for the month."

Noel, who was sitting on Ginger's right side in the front row, chuckled and added, "This month or this year?"

Carmen looked over at Chen, who was staring out the right window in silent fascination. "How are you feeling?" she asked.

"Very rested," Chen answered with a smile. "Please try to imagine that for me it is as if we had recently left the orbit of Mars, and here I am on the surface of Iapetus. I haven't completely caught up with the flow of events."

"I know you've heard it a dozen times already," Ginger said from the front row, "but welcome back. We have lots of exciting work ahead of us."

They covered the kilometer in rapid time. Dmitri pulled up a short distance from the jumbled intersection of the secondary crater with the depression rim. From this close it lost its character as an intersection, and looked more like a bizarre painting of a very large unweathered rockslide.

"I don't expect to find anything right near the intersection," Dmitri announced, "but we'll start here and move off to our left, keeping about a hundred meters from the depression wall. We'll move in to examine anything interesting. Remember Jon's experience. Okay — let's get our gear together." He got up. "Don't forget," he added as an afterthought, "we're being recorded on holo. The world is looking over your shoulder, although we can edit out anything we want."

One-by-one the five explorers passed through the rover's small lock. Each put on a prepared performance for the folks back home. Dmitri planted his Russian Federation flag, its bright white, blue, and red horizontal stripes held extended by a wire threaded through the top of the flag. He gave a short, awkward speech in Russian reflecting on Russia's history in space and his link to the first space traveler, his distant cousin Yuri Gagarin.

As it turned out, Chen also had brought a flag, and proudly planted the red banner sporting a large gold star flanked by a semi-circle of four smaller gold stars. He spoke briefly in Mandarin and then repeated his words in Cantonese, praising the support of the individual Chinese people, and acknowledging that virtually each of China's billion-plus citizens had contributed some small monetary amount to support China's participation in this enterprise.

Noel stepped up next, holding the Canadian Maple Leaf. "Canada shares this historic event with the world," and added a few comments about the heritage of his illustrious ancestor, Robert Goddard, who laid the groundwork that culminated in this expedition.

Dr. Bhuta stepped forward holding the Indian Tricolor that she planted next to the others. "The saffron, white, and green represent respectively courage and sacrifice, peace and truth, and faith and chivalry," she said in the ancient Sanskrit tongue. "The center wheel is the law. These I bring to this distant place."

#

Jon landed as near as he could to the place where they had penetrated the surface on their first landing. He had Ari in the right seat with Michele between them, and Elke in the second row with Saeed. Saeed had been outfitted with a suit designed for Carmen, since they were about the same size. He had received minimal training, and his suit had been stripped of anything he could use as a weapon.

While Ari tilted the lander to rover, Jon reviewed the disquieting news Ari had related to him following his analysis of the message from the Caliphate to Saeed. He could not rid himself of the *Qur'an* passage: "... those for whom slaughter was ordained would certainly have gone forth to the places where they would be slain..." He glanced back at Elke and Saeed. *What is more powerful? Will he respond to the bond of brotherhood he has established with the crew, or will he heed the command of his Caliph?* There was no question in Ari's mind. "Faith will triumph," he had insisted during their private discussion just before launch. "From now on, we have to watch him like a hawk. And we need to keep anything from him that he could use to take us out." Ari looked grim as he added, "Remember, Saeed Esmail is now on a designated holy Jihad, directed by the Caliph himself. Nothing on or off Earth will divert him."

"And what do you recommend?" Jon had asked him.

"If I were Captain, I would give him something to knock him out, and then space him. There is no other option, Jon. He WILL carry out his mission – or die in attempting it." Jon clearly recalled Ari's look as he added, "It's not if, Jon. It's when."

Those words echoed in his mind as he prepared to step out on the surface of Iapetus for the second time. *It's not if, Jon. It's when.*

Jon exited the rover first, and then reached out to assist Michele. Elke, Saeed, and finally Ari exited on their own. Michele was giddy with excitement as she stepped onto the surface. With a grace that made it look like she had done it all her life, she sailed above the surface to land gracefully by a mound of dust, planting the French Tricolor, saying, "*Vive la France!*" Then, uncharacteristically, she bowed her head inside her helmet, and stood silently and still for a moment. Then she clapped her gloved hands and danced back to Jon's side.

Elke obviously enjoyed her friend's exuberance, but with typical Teutonic reserve, she approached Michele's flag and planted the German War Flag next to it, saying simply "*Für Deutschland!*" The War Flag was the traditional black, red, and gold horizontal stripes with a crest of the black German war eagle on a golden background superimposed in the middle. Jon noticed it immediately. *That's going to give Rod a couple of headaches*, he thought, smiling inwardly. *Leave it to Elke to shake things up.* He exchanged looks with Ari, and realized that Ari had seen it as well. Apparently, no one else caught it.

Suddenly, Saeed moved forward, cautiously shuffling along the ground, apparently fearful of leaping. He placed a small Caliphate flag alongside the others, a flag that resembled the old Iranian green-white-red banner, but carrying the symbolic crest of the Caliphate in the middle. "*Allahu Akbar!*" he said in a loud, clear voice, and backed his way to his former position alongside Ari. *Resourceful little bugger*, Jon thought, as he set the team to the task of roping up for the traverse to the opening.

Chapter eighteen

Across the Russian Federation, proud Russians got drunk on the best vodka they could afford. Crime bosses cracked open staggeringly expensive bottles of ancient vodka saved and held since the demise of Czar Nikolay Alexandrovich Romanov, the last Czar of Imperial Russia. Businessmen toasted Dmitri Gagarin while quaffing exotic Finnish imports. Porters and chambermaids shared the rotgut that passed for good vodka among the European and Asian tourists to Mother Russia. Worker bees of all stripes tipped glass after glass of watered down bar swill in a million drinking houses across the Motherland.

Wine flowed freely from Paris to the Pyrenees and the Riviera accompanied by a national chant of *"Vive la France!"* Sexy posters of Dr. Michele deBois appeared everywhere. Singers in nighttime bistros across the land crooned exultations to Michele's beauty and intelligence.

Frothy mugs clicked over *Bierstube* tables across the Federal Republic of Germany, from Schleswig-Holstein in the north to the *Algäu* at the southern tip of Bavaria. A conservative politician from the *Algäu* high mountain community of Hinterstein introduced a

resolution in the Bundestag to change Germany's national flag officially to the *Kriegsflagge* that Elke planted on Iapetus. The resolution
passed unanimously, with only five Green Party members abstaining.

Across China fireworks filled the sky with fiery dragons, exploding stars, and showering fountains, celebrating Chen Lee-Fong's
remarkable recovery and his face-saving gift of honor to all Chinese
citizens.

Canadians noted the event with quiet pride, and carried on with
whatever they were doing, although several parliament members from
Quebec questioned loudly why the *Fleurdelisé* was not also planted
on Iapetus. The resulting shouting match triggered the polite intervention of the RCMP unit stationed at the capitol.

New Delhi disseminated the news across its nearly two billion
population as quickly as possible. Wired communities celebrated
immediately with song and dance long into the night. Communities
still awaiting hook-up got the word by a thousand means within the
following twenty-four hours, and joined the celebrations. The Tamil
National Liberation Army exploded three coordinated car bombs in
the midst of a massed celebration in Mumbai – killing more than
a thousand Hindis, including 300 children. Muslims in Jammu and
Kashmir danced in the streets at the news of the Mumbai slaughter.

#

The Ayatollah Khomeini sat in his raised ornate chair looking
intently at the holovision display filling the air before him. It was
a recap of the flag planting ceremony at the second landing site on
Iapetus. He watched without comment as Saeed Esmail planted the
Caliphate flag, and smiled at his declaration: "*Allahu Akbar!*" His
technicians then commenced a second recording that was identical to
the first, except only the Caliphate flag was in evidence, and Esmail
raised a defiant fist when making his utterance. And, somehow, the
spacesuited crew members seemed to defer to Esmail. On seeing this,
the Caliph's smile broadened. He clapped his hands. "See to it that
this rendition is disseminated throughout the Caliphate." He folded
his hands into a tent and thought. Then he raised a finger, chopping
the air as he spoke. "Put out the word quietly that the first rendition
is a subtle fake prepared by Mission Control in Houston to deceive
the world."

"We'll flood worldwide blogs with your wisdom, Sahib. Within forty-eight hours, the world will know the truth."

\#

"Once again," a solemn-faced holovision talking head said in sonorous tones, "the world has been deceived by the racist attitude of the current U.S. leadership. This reporter has learned from impeccable sources that yesterday's holocast from the surface of distant Iapetus was doctored by Mission Control in Houston. Here is the unedited version – you draw your own conclusions." Around the world, a defiant Saeed Esmail planted the Caliphate flag by itself on a raised mound on Iapetus, raised his fist toward a looming Saturn, shouting *"Allahu Akbar!"*

\#

"We'll rope ourselves together at three-meter intervals like this," Dmitri said, after they had set up a pressurized tent on the flat surface beside *Rover Two*, and attached an external carry tray to the top landing pad. He was keenly aware that out here what happened was his responsibility alone. He was somewhat surprised at the weight of responsibility he felt. *So, Jon, this is what you have been carrying behind those inscrutable eyes.* "We'll move forward in a *U* shape. Noel and I will take the points. Ginger will follow me, and Dr. Bhuta will follow Noel. Chen, you will hook up between the two women. This way we have each woman between two men, and you, Chen, as a not-fully-re-covered patient, bring up the rear. Since there are no predators..." he paused with a chuckle, "that we know of, you should not be in any danger by yourself back there." Everyone grinned and Chen blushed, visible through his clear helmet. "Ginger and Carmen – keep at least three meters apart. Don't yield to the temptation to cluster. Remember, Jon fell through the surface. If we all fall through because we are clustered, we'll have the devil of a time getting back out."

They took a good fifteen minutes to get hooked up and ready to go. "Try not to be too exuberant while traveling in this low grav-ity," Dmitri warned them with a smile. "Don't bounce higher than a meter off the surface with each step; there's less chance of breaking through that way."

They commenced a coordinated low hopping traverse of the short distance to the giant pile of tumbled sharp-edged boulders. "Be careful," Dmitri cautioned, as Noel reached out to jiggle a medium size boulder. "Things react entirely differently in this low gravity. Friction is far less. A wrong move can bring the whole pile down on you."

Noel stepped back, pulling his hands away from the boulder. "I agree," he said. "Things don't weigh very much here, but they retain their mass."

Dmitri led the team around the south end of the boulder pile, probing along the base, looking for the opening they were hoping to find. For the first kilometer, they found nothing but more piled sharp boulders. The layered dust everywhere indicated that nothing had moved in a very long time. They worked their way up a rise and through a narrow pass in the secondary crater ring mountains. Dmitri looked back at their passage. "There's no way we can get the rover through here," he said. "It looks like we will have to keep it inside the secondary crater, and carry our pressure tent with us. Chen and I will return to the rover, collapse the tent and stick it on the external carry. Then we'll bring the rover as close as possible to this pass – or else poke around a bit to see if we can find another way through."

Dmitri and Chen unhooked themselves from the others, and tied themselves together with one of the extra lines their unhooking had created. Moving quickly, they covered the path back in less than a half hour. In five minutes they had collapsed the pressure tent and stowed it atop the external tray. Once inside the rover, Dmitri called Ginger. "We're going to explore along the rim wall for a bit. Perhaps we can find another way through." Ginger acknowledged.

"You guys continue exploring your area. We'll meet up again in about two-and-a-half hours. Because we'll both be close to hills and walls, we may be out of communication for a while. If we haven't talked by the two-and-a-half hour mark, I'll start actively looking for you."

"What if we don't hear from you?" Ginger asked.

"Return to the landing spot. We'll rendezvous there no later than the three hour mark."

"Got it!"

Dmitri set the rover in motion along the rim wall, looking for a way through. Their primary objective of finding a way below the surface had not changed, but their immediate focus was simply finding a rover accessible way across or through the secondary crater ring wall.

At first, their quest was frustrated by rocks too large to drive over and too close to pass between. Dmitri found himself backing as much as moving forward, giving *Rover Two* a workout like it had never had in its lab trials. He discovered that even an apparently navigable slope of rock shards became impassable because the low gravity caused the shards to slide over one another like so much graphite, causing *Rover Two* to slip-slide in place instead of creeping up the slope. For two hours they poked and pushed and probed, looking for a way over and through the rim wall. From time to time they were able to establish brief communications with Ginger and the others, but they lost the line-of-sight every time they approached the wall, or when Ginger descended into a gully. Just when Dmitri was ready to turn back, since they were three kilometers left of where they started – over the horizon and out of communications, Chen spotted a darkness in the jumbled boulders that appeared deeper and wider that all the others.

"Dmitri...look!" he shouted excitedly, pointing to the deep shadow.

Dmitri turned the rover toward the darkness that was, perhaps, a hundred fifty meters distant. In this stark landscape it was difficult to estimate distances. With the actual horizon about one and a half kilometers distant, and with overlapping shadows caused by the Sun and Saturn, and even Saturn's rings, the resulting visual confusion was undecipherable to the inexperienced human eye. Dmitri and Chen discussed this, but neither had yet gained the visual experience to sort out the clues into a coherent picture when they were more than a few meters distant from anything. It was frustrating, but they dealt with it. As they approached the darkness Chen had discovered, it began to resolve into a natural opening between two rock walls sufficiently wide to accommodate the rover with room to spare. The floor slopped upward to the limit of vision, a floor that Dmitri thought the rover could navigate, since it didn't consist of a pile of rock shards.

He nosed the rover into the opening, and cautiously moved up the slope. The six big wheels slipped from time to time, but generally maintained traction, so that fifteen minutes later they reached the crest, to find themselves looking down a similar slot that widened as it descended into an apparently open plain beyond.

"Ginger, *Rover* Two..." No response.

Dmitri headed *Rover Two* down the slot, moving twice as fast as in their ascent. He was becoming concerned about Ginger and the others. They had not spoken in nearly an hour, and there was no visible sign of them ahead. A few minutes later the slot deposited them on the dust covered surface of a relatively recent hundred-meter-wide crater – recent, because it did not appear to contain any secondary craters. It was virtually flat, and the far edge seemed to be navigable. Before they moved on, Dmitri tried to call the rest of his team again.

"Ginger, it's *Rover Two*. Do you read?" No answer…"Ginger… *Rover Two*…" Still no answer. "Ginger…Carmen…Noel…can anyone hear me?"

Dmitri felt a rising sense of concern. He knew the three were competent, and would do nothing foolish, but he had all the life support equipment with him. *They are isolated and alone on a barren satellite of a gas giant one-and-a-half-billion clicks from home,* he thought as he mulled over the situation *We are south of their position, I know it for certain.*

"They're somewhere north of us" Dmitri told Chen. "As soon as the terrain allows, we'll turn north and look for them."

Across the crater and over its rim they traveled at the highest speed they had yet attempted with the rover. On the other side of the rim the landscape was rough, but passable. Dmitri threaded his way generally north for a kilometer. He didn't speak, and Chen seemed to be in his own thoughts.

Suddenly, Ginger's voice broke through their silence. "I see the rover, Dmitri! You just moved down into a relatively flat crater at my horizon limit. I am twenty-three degrees to the right of your centerline."

Dmitri stopped the rover, so he and Chen could search the area on that vector. "I'm flashing you," Ginger said.

"Got it!" Chen said, pointing at a flashing light about halfway up a rugged slope.

"We see you, Ginger. We'll meet you at the base of the slope," Dmitri said, unable to remove all the excitement from his voice.

"You made it through the ring mountains," Noel commented, "I'm impressed."

"I'm just glad we found each other," Carmen said.

"That was never in question," Dmitri said matter-of-factly, while inwardly he heaved a sigh of relief.

"I'm just a natural worrier," Carmen added.

In ten minutes, the entire team was back inside *Rover Two*, discussing what to do next.

"Everything we have examined here," Ginger said, "is nothing like what we saw on the other side of the depression. It's as if the secondary impact completely collapsed whatever is underneath in this area."

"I know," Dmitri added. "We thought we might find easier access, a grand entrance, so-to-speak, but..." His voice trailed off.

"I agree. While you were gone, we really looked closely at several possibilities, but they turned out to be nothing but shallow natural caves caused by the upthrusting." Ginger looked at Dmitri. "So, what now?"

"I guess we report our failure to Jon." Dmitri's voice sounded wistful, even to his own ear.

"And the equatorial wall? It's not that far away."

"Yeh, but getting there is a big deal. We'll leave that for later, I suppose." The wistfulness remained. "We need to follow up on what we already know, and that's with Jon's team."

Dmitri had, of course, periodically kept Jon apprised of his situation, but the twenty-two second visible time for *Cassini II's* nearly three-and-a-half hour orbit limited communications to one-way burst transmissions, so they had kept traffic to a minimum. Now, however, it was time. Ginger checked *Cassini II's* orbital coordinates, advising Dmitri that it would be visible in twelve minutes. Dmitri recorded a five minute message detailing their efforts thus far, and his and Ginger's recommendation that they consolidate their efforts at Jon's site. Ginger compressed the message to burst length, and activated Jon's channel. As soon as *Cassini II* appeared over the horizon, Dmitri's message traversed the fifty kilometers to *Cassini II*, and then waited for two hours and fifty-eight minutes for Jon's twenty-two second reception window.

During the wait, Dmitri and team prowled various possible openings, still looking for a way beneath the surface to what they now knew existed below. They were stymied, however, by the overriding effect of the meteor that had created the secondary crater. Dmitri was convinced that any opening would be at or near the depression rim. Unfortunately, the meteor had virtually eliminated the rim. The upthrusting meteor crater ring wall had obliterated the depression rim in their area, making it virtually impossible for any entry to have survived the impact.

Almost exactly twenty-seven minutes after the transmission reached Jon, Ginger received a short non-compressed transmission back from Jon acknowledging receipt and telling them to await his follow-on transmission. Carmen questioned the long delays, so Ginger explained that since they were west of Jon, *Cassini II* had to go all around Iapetus in order for Jon to receive their transmission. But since Jon would have no time to respond, except for a short acknowledgment, he would take the necessary time to understand Dmitri's message, and then compose a response that would be transmitted when *Cassini II* was overhead for its twenty-two second passage.

Jon's message, when it finally arrived, concurred with Dmitri's decision. "Do a suborbital ballistic transfer," Jon had advised, and included his exact coordinates.

#

Upon *Lander One's* touchdown, Jon immediately got to the business of setting up an exploratory penetration of the floor of the vast chamber they had discovered. He placed Ari with Saeed topside to maintain a communication link, even though it would exist for just twenty-two seconds every three-and-a-half or so hours. He and the two women penetrated more than a kilometer in from the entrance, periodically stopping to take sonar readings of the floor, looking for a thinning that would allow them to penetrate. Everywhere, however, from where they entered and at each stop, all they found was rock, as far down as the sonar penetrated. The machines exhibited a monotonous sameness, although further back, the dust layer seemed measurably thinner. Jon thought this indicated that the collapse of the depression was the source of the dust. Once he reached a near certainty that they were not going to find a way deeper by simply moving horizontally randomly, he decided to return to the opening and take another tack.

He and Ari discussed it at length, not deliberately ignoring the women, but realizing that his and Ari's particular expertise was better suited to reaching a decision than was theirs at this point. They finally reached a decision.

"Here's the plan," Jon explained to the women who were lounging near the wide shaft that went down to some unknown depth, and to Ari and Saeed who were looking down through the penetration to the surface. "The layer we have been exploring appears to be exactly what Dmitri thought, a protective layer for whatever lies beneath. Because machines can fail, it appears that the builders left a very thick layer of rock as a back-up protection. At least it's a working hypothesis for now." He grinned sheepishly. "I know we are making huge leaps of faith in our assumptions, but stay with me for a bit longer."

He then explained that he and Ari thought the shaft before them, which appeared to be artificial rather than natural, might be a designed way to whatever was in the interior. He said that they would explore its circumference, and then base any further decision on what they found.

That was when he received the burst message from Dmitri. He transmitted a short reply so the other team would know he had received their message, and then listened to the transmission.

"Well," he said, "it seems the other team has struck out. I'm bringing them here so we can double our efforts." He said it would take about three hours before he could send his recall, and another three before they got it. Then an hour or so for them to get to the team's location. "So," he said, "we can spend a few hours exploring the rim of the shaft before they arrive."

Michele and Elke accompanied Jon in an initial superficial stroll around the shaft. It turned out to be about 160 meters around, which indicated a fifty-meter diameter, give or take a few centimeters. "Ari," Jon ordered, "send down three one-hundred meter lengths of line."

Ari did, and Jon hooked each woman and himself to a line, and anchored the other ends of all three lines to the nearest pillar. "Michele, you take the left third. Elke, you take the right third, and I will take the opposite third. That's about fifty meters each. Carefully examine each meter of edge. Search down as far as possible, looking for anything other than smooth wall. Try not to fall into the shaft, but the line will hold you if it actually happens."

Elke started directly in front of them, and slowly moved right. Michele did likewise, but moved left. Jon paced off about fifty long steps to the left past Michele, and commenced his own detailed examination.

#

Michele felt a thrill that coursed through her body as she began her examination of the edge. Then she extended her helmet out over the shaft, and drew back immediately, reeling with vertigo. She remembered feeling similarly during her first close-in rotational experience, and so chalked it up to a mental reaction to observing the bottom beneath her disappear into an unknown darkness. She was startled, but not particularly frightened. Cautiously, she extended her head over the edge again – with similar results. *I will NOT be overcome by such foolishness*, she scolded herself. She moved to her left and tried for a third time, moving slowly in order to observe her own reaction. It didn't help much. She felt herself being pulled inexorably toward whatever lay below. Her stomach dropped, and the next thing she knew, she had pitched herself into the shaft.

"*Mon Dieu – aidez-moi!*" she screamed. "Elp me...elp me!" Her fall was leisurely, and in one sense the scientist inside Michele actually observed her reactions dispassionately. But her every instinct screamed in terror, and another part of her continued to scream as her fall picked up speed as she plunged into darkness. For nearly thirty seconds she fell. Because of the darkness, she had no way of knowing what was actually happening, but when the rope finally went taut, and she came to a stop, she was traveling only a bit under seven meters per second – less than she would feel falling to the ground on Earth from a standing position. With the realization that she was okay, Michele stopped screaming, and looked about her to get her bearings, letting her helmet light show her the surroundings. When she looked up, she saw two helmets stretched over the edge above her, and heard Jon's calming voice reassuring her that she was okay.

But it was Elke who pulled her back on the right path. "It's okay, Baby...you're fine. You floated down like an angel...trust me, Baby, you're fine!" She and Jon hoisted Michele back to the edge.

"What happened?" Jon inquired, obviously working to keep from laughing.

Michele was quick on the uptake. "It's okay, *Mon Capitaine!* I'm fine now. My vertigo took hold of me, I guess. One moment I was looking over the edge, the next, I was falling..."

"Not falling, my Love," Elke interjected, "floating like an angel." At that, Elke launched herself out over the shaft, turning in space to have her feet before her when the rope reached its length and she swung lazily toward the wall. "See," she said with a gleeful squeal, "now we can all fly!" Deftly, she pulled herself overhand to the edge, and slipped over it to stand by Jon and Michele.

"I'd rather you didn't do that," Jon admonished, but Michele could plainly see that Elke had just showed Jon something he clearly had overlooked.

"Are you getting all this, Ari?" Jon asked.

"Way ahead of you, Captain. I'm checking our inventory of line." After a minute or so pause he picked up the conversation. "You understand we are talking about a free-falling rappel with hundred meter jumps?"

"Actually, I'm thinking TBH Propulsion Boots."

\#

The events were not lost on Saeed. He had picked up on the fact that Dmitri and his team were joining Jon's team.

Allah, may He ever be blessed, has brought the entire team to me in one place like lambs to the slaughter, and He has given me the means to escape once my Jihad is accomplished. Saeed smiled to himself in grim satisfaction. One by one, Allah was opening the doors he needed to fulfill the promise of his revelation – his revelation that seemed like an eternity ago: *Let those fight in the way of Allah who sell the life of this world for the other. Whoso fighteth in the way of Allah, be he slain or be he victorious, on him we shall bestow a vast reward.*

Chapter nineteen

Jon's first order of business, now that the entire team was together in one spot, was to set up a working Base Camp. In real terms, this consisted of erecting two interconnected pressure tents that attached to both rover locks, making one pressure complex. One tent was set up for living and sleeping, the other to contain supplies and spares. For an hour, the team unloaded the storage space beneath the rover decks, stacking equipment that was pressure independent in a storage area alongside the tents, and putting food, water, items that needed to be carried inside the suits, and analysis equipment and computers inside the storage tent.

Since they had no idea what they might find or what kinds of analysis might be needed, Jon did not have the team set up a lab. *Rover One* continued to be the Com center, and both rovers served as secondary storage centers, since there was no need to unload all the built-in cabinets and containers that lined their bulkheads.

Washing and sanitary facilities were partitioned off the living tent. They were primitive in the extreme, but they served two functions: They provided privacy and they recycled all the water. By this time, even Michele had gotten used to the idea that they were reusing every drop of water over and over. And while she remained sexually uninhibited, even she valued privacy for her personal needs. Sleeping arrangements were less private. Each team member had a personal bunk with a privacy curtain, not unlike submarine berthing quarters. The rigid framework was supplied by the same vacuum-hardened polyaramid used in the construction of the spacecraft, the rovers, and virtually everything else in modern space construction. Everything was powered by the rovers' variable output gas core reactors, which meant that they had virtually unlimited power.

The entire team was eager to commence the interior exploration. Despite this, Jon decided to keep two team members on the surface, primarily to facilitate extraction in the event of a serious emergency. Insofar as possible, he wanted to keep Saeed isolated. Although Ari had taken the responsibility for keeping track of him, Jon wanted Ari on the first thrust down the shaft. That left Dmitri. Jon explained the situation to him, and flinched inwardly as Dmitri struggled to internalize his reaction to his being absent during the first penetration.

Dmitri and Ginger set up a fiber-optic coupling into the *Rover One's* com system so that Dmitri would have a continuous wide-band connection to the exploring team, and so that he could transmit burst messages to the orbiting *Cassini II* containing the entire holographic record of the exploration, which the spacecraft would then transmit back to Houston.

Although the time had passed quickly, Jon wanted the team to accomplish one more task before retiring for the sleep period. Over the years since fiber-optic cable had been invented, it had evolved into an ultra-high-band-width carrier. Nanotechnology had created endless diamond strands from an engineered diamond that bore only superficial resemblance to its namesake. The reels of fiber-optic thread the explorers carried with them each held a hundred kilometers of nearly invisible thread made from these diamond strands with a tensile strength stronger than anything else known to human kind. The thread was so fine that it could be captured between a bank vault door and frame, without being damaged or losing any of its transmissivity. Jon had the team lay a fiber-optic thread from Base Camp to the edge of the opening, where it was coupled to a full duplex booster powered by a separate power supply cable from Base Camp. Ginger and Dmitri brought the booster and power cable to the edge, set it up coupled temporarily to their suit holosystems, and ran a test to Jon, back at Base Camp.

"Jon, it's Ginger," she said, facing the pinhead-sized set of holocams on Dmitri's helmet.

"I have you five by," Jon's holographic image in her heads-up display responded, seeming to be sitting in a chair about a half-meter from her position.

"This is Dmitri," the Russian said to Ginger's holocams. Jon's holoimage appeared in Dmitri's display. The duplex booster unit was designed to recognize when participants on the net were physically in each other's presence, so that their heads-up displays did not become cluttered with multiple images of participants in their immediate presence.

"We're in business, guys. Come on back for something to eat, and some rest before we do it," Jon said.

#

The following "morning" Jon assembled the team inside the pressure tent for a final briefing. "We've gone over it a dozen times already," he said, "but one more time won't hurt. Remember, we are assuming that the shaft is some kind of vertical transportation route. We don't pretend to know for what or how it worked. So, we're going to the bottom to see what we find. All of us will suit up, including TBH boots – and don't forget your outer soles."

Saeed looked at Ari with questioning eyes. He knew about the TBH boots, but Ari had to explain the function of the outer soles that slipped over the boots and protected the recessed nozzle in each boot from walking damage.

"Ari," Jon said, "make sure Saeed understands the boots and covers." Then he continued his instructions. "Once everybody is suited up, we'll depart for the opening.

"Now remember, you guys have experience with the TBH boots, but your experience was in free-fall. We're dealing with gravity here, even if it is just a whisper. I've limited rappels to one hundred meters a fall. That gives us a pretty good safety margin, since you will be falling at only about seven meters a second when you reach the end of your safety line. We know the shaft is about five kilometers deep, and appears to be perfectly round and smooth all the way down. We've already dropped a rappel line to the bottom. Ari, you'll go first, taking a glow tube with you, and stream the fiber-optic thread. You'll take no risks, no chances, and you will stop without my order at the slightest indication that something is wrong. Under no circumstances will you remove your safety line, since that is our only way of retrieving you should something go wrong, short of another team member going down to get you. Once established on the bottom of the shaft, you'll run a short test of the TBH boots. Ascend ten meters or so, and then drop back down. Your trip down will take at least thirty minutes.

"The women will follow you down – Elke and Carmen, belayed by Noel; Michele and Ginger belayed by Chen. Chen will go next, belayed by Noel, then Noel, belayed by me, and finally I will descend, belayed by Dmitri. Remember, each trip is about thirty minutes with no stops, so we will need over four hours for all of us to reach the bottom. While the folks on the bottom wait for the rest of us, look about you. You might discover something. But no risks – take no risks!

"Our first sortie might be very short, if we find no penetration. Then we'll work our way back up, looking more closely for any kind of penetration. If you see anything on your way down, of course, stop your rappel and let us know. We'll hang off a glow tube at that level." He paused as the team members donned their suits. "Any questions?"

When nobody spoke up, he added, "Remember, we are entering a total unknown. We have no published guidelines, no protocols, no established procedures. All we have is common sense. Be careful, and heed my instructions – but follow your gut instinct!"

#

Saeed was excited by the events unfolding before him. Allah had graciously extended the Jihad time schedule so that he, a Muslim, could participate in this exciting enterprise, to the glory of Muslims everywhere. But these thoughts immediately engendered a fierce internal conflict, because Saeed had no doubts about Allah's ultimate intentions toward the Infidels on this expedition, *may He be forever blessed.*

So, Saeed learned everything he could about everything he saw and did. He was especially intrigued by the TBH boots. It seemed to him that they could give him the kind of mobility he might need later, when he took advantage of the opportunity he knew Allah would present to him, *praise be to Him.*

#

Ari had never rappelled five kilometers – nobody had, ever! He stood at the edge of the shaft looking down. Unlike Michele, Ari did not suffer from even a vestige of vertigo. He tried to see details on the shaft as far as the light allowed – nothing, nothing at all, just a smooth, unbroken surface.

The fiber-optic reel was attached to his tank pack. It was designed to feed the nearly invisible cable through a tiny hole in the center of the pack. The cable didn't unwind. Instead, it fed from the center of the reel through the tiny hole, almost without friction. To further enhance the feed, the hole was lined with a special ceramic ferrule that had been rendered nearly frictionless by an application of nanotechnology that gave the ceramic a very dense, slick surface. Attached to his midriff, Ari carried a pouch filled with glow tubes, with a variable output of up to 5,000 lumens in any desired angle of spread. In a leg pocket he had a tube of quickset vacuum adhesive that he could use to attach a glow tube to the shaft wall, or even a hook located in his other leg pocket from which he could suspend himself, should that become necessary. His rappelling hardware differed little from typical alpine rappelling hardware, except that it was designed to be used in the extreme temperature fluctuations of an airless world, and to use smaller polyaramid lines with friction characteristics very different from standard alpine climbing rope.

When he was ready, Ari signaled to Jon, leaned back into his rappel line, and slowly fell away from the edge in a graceful arch. It was the closest thing to flying he had ever experienced. During the thirty-second fall he experimented with various body positions, turning at the last instant to land his soles squarely against the shaft wall a hundred meters down. He pushed off into a second arch, and while in mid arch, attached one of his glow tubes to the wrist of his guide hand on the rappel. He set it to illuminate away from his body so as not to blind him, and set the lumens to max. The fifty-meter wide shaft lit up brightly, revealing its completely featureless surface.

"You getting this, Jon, Dmitri?" Ari asked as he pushed off at 200 meters.

"Nothing to see," Dmitri muttered.

At 500 meters, Ari paused to attach a glow tube to the wall, and tilted back to look up the shaft. The fifty-meter circular opening looked small from his perspective. It was only a tenth of his vertical displacement, and he could nearly cover it with his hand. Still nothing on the shaft wall...completely featureless. Five hundred meters later, he still saw nothing to relieve the featureless monotony of the shaft wall, and now – at a kilometer down – he could cover the opening with his thumb. He attached another glow tube, and dropped again. He attached glow tubes at 500-meter intervals, and when he looked up, their illumination sharply outlined short segments of shaft. And yet, in the clear vacuum the distant opening remained clearly visible as well. Three kilometers, four, and then finally, Ari saw the bottom rising to meet him.

"Visual on the bottom," he reported. "I can see no debris. Appears perfectly smooth, like the wall." He paused his description, slowing to meet the bottom with zero velocity...and plunged right through the bottom, continuing to fall, but this time through a slightly viscous dust. "Did you guys get that?" he asked as he turned around to check the visibility. "I'm still dropping slowly...ah...the bottom. I must have fallen through about four meters of fine dust."

Ari probed around himself, and then set out on a course to what he hoped was the closest shaft wall, holding his hands in front of him. Five seconds later his hands bumped the wall. He followed the wall to the floor level, and to his surprise, the wall did not meet the floor. Rather, the wall continued past the level of the floor, and the floor itself, curved down, starting about twenty centimeters from the wall. At first, he was unable to determine what he was feeling through his pressure gloves. He worked his way around the wall for several meters – exactly the same, and then it struck him. He was on the top of some kind of elevator.

"You're not going to believe this, Jon. I'm standing on top of a fifty-meter wide elevator that's covered with four meters of dust." He paused, deep in thought. "I don't really know if the elevator is at the bottom of the shaft or not. Pull me up slowly, Jon until I break the surface. You can follow on your monitor." He immediately felt himself rising through the dust. Within a few seconds the dust sluiced off his helmet. He looked around in the bright light from the glow tube. "The girls probably don't want to hear me say this, Jon, but I really don't want to send them down into this stuff."

Jon started to interrupt, but Ari continued. "Hold on, Captain. I have an idea. Nobody makes an elevator you can't get out of, especially if you are on an airless world in a five-kilometer deep shaft...or deeper. Hell, I don't know! There has to be an escape hatch somewhere on the elevator top."

"If it's an elevator," Jon commented wryly. "You're down there, so check your theory out. And by the way, I suspect Ginger and Elke would disagree with your earlier comment."

Ari grimaced as he sank back down through the viscous dust to the top of the "elevator." He commenced a circular search, letting his suit system guide him. He moved to the approximate center of the surface, and then moved around in increasingly wider circles. The surface was smooth in exactly the same way as the shaft wall, until about three meters out from the edge, Ari encountered a two-meter wide circular bulge. "Got something here, Jon. I think it's a hatch of some kind."

"Proceed with caution."

"You got that!" Ari felt the bulge carefully. "Think about this, Jon. If this is an escape from whatever is inside, I would think it is a lock rather than just an opening." He continued probing. "Oh my gosh! Jon, I just found a fist-sized depression in the bulge, big enough to comfortably receive a space-suited fist. And it has a grip inside."

#

Topside, the entire crew was hanging on Ari's every word. "I've just worked my hand into the depression," Ari said over the circuit, but since there was no visual at all, the crew had to make do with the verbal report.

On the surface Dmitri and Saeed were listening intently to Ari's report, and the rest of the crew clustered around Jon at the edge of the shaft.

"O-oh!" Ari's voice carried a bit of tension. "Shit Jon! The sono-fabitch is turning! It's acting like it's servo assisted. I put a gentle pressure to the left, and it started to rotate. When I removed the pressure, the rotation stopped." Then there was a pause, and then Ari said, "I feel a lip completely around the bulge. It's screwing out of the elevator top – if that's what it is, of course." Another pause. "Well, I'll be damned...it just opened completely on some kind of spring or hydraulic hinge. I can feel the dust flowing into the space below... Oops! The dust flow just stopped. It's got to be a small chamber, and it's chock full of dust. It's a lock...I told you so! It's a lock! I'm going inside..."

"Hold it, Ari. You'll do nothing of the kind until someone joins you there." Jon pulled the support rope, retrieving Ari from the dust. Ari swung gracefully to the wall at the end of his belaying line. "Put up your hook, and wait for me."

Jon switched to a private circuit with Dmitri – his second in command. Since he was about to make a major decision, he wanted Dmitri's input. "Dmitri. I'm considering bringing all of us down the shaft, including you and Saeed, if this turns out to be a way inside. What are your thoughts?"

"I think we should test a TBH ascent from the bottom before we put everyone down, but otherwise, I agree."

Dmitri's voice sounded thoughtful to Jon. "Okay, let's do this. You and Saeed remain topside for the time being. We'll send down some sheets and braces that we can use to construct a caisson around the opening to hold back the dust. I will descend to assist Ari in the construction. Then he and I will enter the lock to see if there is a way into the interior of the elevator." Jon smiled to himself, noting that no matter what the machine really was, they were now calling it an elevator. "Send Elke with Saeed to get the sheets and braces. I don't want him alone, and I want you supervising while I am descending and on the bottom. Elke is the strongest of the women. She can handle him."

Elke climbed to the surface to replace Dmitri, and then headed back to the Base Camp with Saeed in tow. Meanwhile, Jon prepared to descend, while Dmitri took over. As Jon briefed everyone, Elke and Saeed returned with several collapsed and rolled braces wrapped inside a rolled polyaramid sheet. Jon attached it to his utility belt. It was a bit bulky, but had virtually no weight in the low gravity of Iapetus. When Jon was ready, he leaned back over the shaft, and let himself fall, belayed by Noel.

During his half-hour descent, he kept a sharp eye out for any deviation in the smooth surface of the shaft. At about three kilometers down, he stopped his descent to examine what appeared to be a faint border that outlined an oval about two meters high and one-and-a-half wide. He swung over to the side where he had seen it, but up close, he could see nothing. He let himself swing back. Starting about ten meters from the wall, the marking began to appear again. He completed the swing cycle, this time planting a glow tube on the marking. "I don't know what it is," he reported, "but it definitely is there." He continued his descent, and on his signal to Noel, finally coming up short in front of Ari.

"Not bad for an old man," Ari said.

"And don't you forget that!"

They opened the caisson material with difficulty, because they had no solid surface to work from.

"I been giving this some thought while waiting for you," Ari said. "Let's make a cylinder just wide enough to fit in the hatch opening."

"If this really is a lock, then it will be interlocked. The lower door won't open till the upper door is shut. So the cylinder has to encompass the hatch," Jon responded.

"Yeh, I guess so." Both men remained silent, searching for a solution. "How about this," Ari said after about a minute. "We form the largest possible cylinder, and then drive it down to the elevator by holding the top edge on opposite sides and activating our TBH boots. We tack it in place with adhesive – just enough to hold it, until we can get a better, dust-free bond, and then install a brace around the outside of the top. After that, we can figure out the next step."

Jon looked up at the successive light rings and tiny bright spot that marked the fifty-meter wide opening five kilometers above them. "Did you ever see such a sight?" he asked Ari as they turned to the task at hand.

Chapter twenty

The first thing they did was relocate the topside team so that the ropes dropped directly over the location of the lock. Once in position, Jon and Ari had a terrible time forming the polyaramid sheet into a cylinder. Their problem was lack of traction. After several fits and starts, they managed to form a loop at the end of one of the ropes, which they passed around the sheet, pulling into a cylindrical shape. As they worked on the project, it became clear that they needed to install a brace around both top and bottom before they attempted to push the cylinder through the accumulated dust atop the elevator.

Once the cylinder was completed, they had to determine exactly where they would push it through the dust. Ari dropped through the dust layer with an extended brace that he attached to the back of the open hatch with a dollop of adhesive. When Dmitri hoisted him above the dust layer, he and Jon manipulated the awkward cylinder until they were able to push it down over the extended brace. Then they each removed their outer soles to expose the jet nozzles, and positioned themselves on opposite sides of the cylinder. Jon had thought there might be some awkwardness in getting their feet above them, but that turned out to be easy. A simple tuck and roll brought their feet above them in a gentle arch, and at the right moment they both tapped their big toes.

The effect was immediate and startling. Nearly simultaneously, they both tapped again to shut off the jets as the cylinder moved smoothly through the dust to rap against the hull below them.

"We're gonna bounce back," Ari warned, and they both tap-tapped again, which effectively removed the upward momentum.

Intellectually, Jon had known that visibility would be zero, but it still came as a surprise to find nothing at all...total absorption of all light. He could feel Ari on the other side moving to the base as he did. When he reached the elevator hull, he felt around for anything that would orient him to his position, but there was no way. "Ari," he said, his signal traveling up to the surface through the fiber-optic thread trailing behind him, and back down through the thread attached to Ari's suit, "let's move the cylinder until it backs against the hatch, and then let's manipulate it until we are certain that the hatch is square against the inside. Then we can pull it back a short distance, and we should be fine."

"Works for me," Ari answered, grunting with effort.

It took them about fifteen minutes before they both were convinced that the cylinder was positioned as accurately as possible for the time being.

"Bring us above the dust, Dmitri," Jon ordered.

"Guess what?" Ari said. "This isn't going to be as easy as we imagined. We're going to have to ascend a bit, and then attempt to rappel down into the cylinder mouth."

"So, why didn't we attach a line to the cylinder edge?"

"Didn't think of it, I guess."

"Is everyone up there asleep too?" Jon asked rhetorically. Then he said to Ari, "You're better at this than I am, so you rappel into the cylinder, and take this line with you."

"Aye aye, Captain," Ari said with a mock salute, bumping his gloved hand against his helmet.

On his first attempt, Ari sailed through the top of the cylinder like a basketball whooshing through the hoop. Jon then pulled himself up above the cylinder top, and dropped into the cylinder. He landed on the edge of the hatch, but with a bump so gentle, he hardly noticed.

He felt around, and then asked, "Where are you, Ari? Did you find a hole to crawl into?"

"Matter of fact, I did! I'm working my way down a ladder inside the lock. Interestingly, it's spaced for someone about human size. I guess that puts the lie to the little green men."

Jon chuckled as he located the opening by touch and followed his friend down the ladder.

"I'm at the bottom. It's about four meters down."

"I'm right behind you."

Once on the deck of the lock they began to feel the curved wall of the lock, looking for anything. Jon's left hand hit a raised surface. He felt around, and discovered a depression that matched Ari's description of the fist-shaped depression in the upper hatch. "I've got a grip just like you described," he said to Ari. "I'll bet it's mounted on a hatch. I'm going to try it." He placed his fist into the depression, took hold of the grip, and attempted to move it right and then left. "Nothing," he told Ari, "but I think it's interlocked." He paused. "Topside, are you getting all this?"

"Sure thing, Captain." It was Dmitri.

"We're going to shut the upper hatch. Keep an eye on the fiber-optic transmission."

"Roger that."

"Okay, Ari, climb up and shut the hatch."

"I'm on it." A pause. "Okay, it's shutting." Another pause. "It's turning slowly. This lock's filled completely with dust; for this thing to close, it has to compress the dust – and us. There's got to be some molecular space that I can compress." Ari grunted. "Still screwing down slowly."

"Topside, how's the image?" Jon asked.

"No difference," Dmitri answered, as clear as ever."

"Okay, that's it, Jon. Try the lower hatch now." Jon did, and this time the lower hatch in the lock wall began to rotate.

Suddenly, with an audible pop transmitted through the compressed dust, the hatch swung horizontally to the outside. The compressed dust surged out of the lock, carrying Jon with it a short distance to the deck. "Whoa...shit! I should have anticipated that. I'm outside, Ari."

"Yeh, I know, I can see the entire lock, except for the floor below the hatch lip, but I can't see you, so..."

"Okay, wise guy. Come on down and have a look at this baby!"

Ari climbed down the ladder from the upper hatch, and as he stepped through the lower hatch onto the deck of the nearly fifty-meter-wide chamber, Jon activated a glow tube, filling the chamber with light. There was not much to see. Controls were not apparent, although here and there small lumps or indentations interrupted the otherwise smooth surface. One large rectangular segment of the bulkhead, about twenty meters worth, Jon determined by pacing it off, looked like it might be an opening. It was flush with the bulkhead, so that there was no space for a lock. That implied to Jon that any lock would be contained in whatever lay beyond the barn door – as he referred to it in his mind already.

While Jon was examining his barn door, Ari called him to look at another feature. This was oval, and appeared quite similar to the marking Jon had seen in the shaft wall during his descent.

"I'm disoriented," Jon told Ari, but I suspect that the angular location of this aligns with the angular location of the marking in the shaft." He paused, in deep thought. "What if this elevator were to rise to that level. If the fit were sufficiently close or somehow coupled, this could be a hatch into a lock behind that marking. To the best of my memory, they appear very similar."

Dmitri transmitted down to them a clear holographic full size image of the section of shaft in question. Jon projected it against the bulkhead with the similar marking. It fit exactly.

"Good thinking, Dmitri. Thanks. That solves one question. The next is, of course, is there a lock behind this hatch?"

Jon and Ari commenced a detailed survey of the entire circular bulkhead, looking for anything that might lead to further information. The room was dusty, in a two-tiered way. The dust they had brought in had quickly coated the deck, but there were no horizontal surfaces to catch this new intruder. Over everything, however, lay a very thin veneer of nearly microscopic dust. The slightest disturbance caused it to lift, and settle to the deck. There appeared to be no electrostatic component of the dust veneer, as if, somehow, the surfaces were designed with anti-static characteristics. Because the internal radius of

the elevator was about two meters smaller than the shaft, the internal
bulkhead was 150 meters around. The size of the ladder steps and
grip and their separation had convinced Jon that whatever they were
dealing with, they were approximately human size. It made no sense,
therefore, to put controls near the deck or way above a normal reach.
So they concentrated on a one-meter band a meter off the deck.

Their first assumption was that any controls would be near the
hatch, but they found nothing, or at least nothing that appeared to
be an opening mechanism. A couple of slight bumps and a slight
depression, but nothing else. Jon stepped back and contemplated the
barn door for several minutes. "Ari, let's assume this really is a big
door. What does it remind you of?"

Ari joined him, and stood silently looking at the barn door
himself. "I guess it reminds me of the Box doors on *Cassini II*," he
said, finally.

"A big door for a big machine," Jon added.

"Yeh…"

"Okay, you're driving a big machine toward this big door. You
gonna get out and open it, or you gonna…"

"Use my remote, of course," Ari said, completing Jon's sentence.

"So, what is there…?"

"Well, sound, but that won't work in a vacuum. Visible EM
spectrum or the longer wavelengths…" Ari's voice trailed off. "These
guys were way ahead of us. I guess that eliminates analog…" His voice
trailed off again. "Maybe they went digital, or even spread spectrum."

Jon speculated, "The other hatches were servo assisted; at least
that's how they appeared to operate, but how could something like
that remain operative for such a long time unattended?" He sighed.
"That's just not the answer. That seemingly servo assist is some kind
of molecular or even sub-atomic trick, and we're not going to discover
anything about them standing here with our thumbs up our asses."

"Speak for yourself, Captain." Ari said with a grin. "The little
door, now, that's for people to get in and out, don't you think?" Jon
nodded inside his helmet. "Okay, so who in his right mind, even an
alien, will put an operating control on a bulkhead forty meters away?"
Ari walked back to the smaller door, and stood in front of it contemplating. One of the slight bumps was just the right height so he

could reach out with his hand and touch it. He looked down at the deck, and then he looked closer. He leaned over and started wiping the dust from the area right in front of the hatch. To his surprise, the deck contained the images of two feet, in outline, like a footprint in the surface dust. He placed his feet on the imprints.

"Look at this, Jon" he said. "When I stand here, if the hatch opens inward and to the left, it will miss me by a couple of centimeters."

"Safety interlock?" Jon said, leaving the question hanging between them.

Ari reached out and touched the nearest bump. Nothing happened. "Dammit!" he said, striking the bump with all the force he could muster. To their astonishment, the bump retracted until it was flush with the surface, and the depression next to it reshaped itself to accept a suited fist, just like the other two. Just above the spot where the original bump was, another bump appeared.

"I'll be damned!" was all that Ari could say.

"Are you getting all this, Topside?"

"Every cussword," Dmitri answered. "They're going to love it back home."

The difference between the grips on the previous two hatches and this one was that the previous two clearly drove the lock directly. Here it was off to the side, and not on the hatch at all. Ari looked at Jon. "We got nothing to lose," he said, and placed his fist into the depression. "I have the grip," he said, "I'm trying to twist it..." He twisted his hand to the left.

Almost immediately, the hatch retracted several millimeters into the bulkhead, and then shot open to the left with a blur, emitting a cloud of vapor that quickly condensed and drifted to the deck. Ari jumped back, and then shook his head in amazement. "It's a lock alright, and it was pressurized with moist air of some kind. Either I overrode the safety mechanism somehow, or, more likely, it just isn't working right after all this time. What do you think, Jon?"

"Sorry to keep asking, Dmitri, but you got that, too, right?"

"Da, Tovarishch!"

"Which way is the slope?" Jon asked. "Does that lock keep whatever is out there from the people inside here, or is it the other way around? What's beyond yonder hatch?" Jon stepped up to the dock imprints, placed his fist into the depression, grabbed the grip, and twisted right. The hatch moved to close, but not with a smooth action, as if it were being driven with a gear missing a cog. It closed fully, forming a nearly smooth seam as before. Jon touched the bump on the other side of the depression. When nothing happened, he hit it with more force. It retracted, the depression disappeared, and the original bump reappeared. Without moving, Jon touched the original bump. Like before, it disappeared, and a new bump appeared above it, while the grip also appeared. Jon twisted the grip left. The hatch sank into the bulkhead as before, and then opened with a slight jerky motion.

Jon repeated the entire cycle again. This time the hatch moved a bit smoother – at least Jon thought so. "Is it getting rid of its jerkiness?" Jon asked Ari.

"Looks like it," Ari answered as Jon cycled the hatch an additional time.

By the fifth cycle, the hatch was moving smoothly, as if it had never experienced the explosive decompression. "Now that is a well-designed self-repairing mechanism," Jon commented. He turned to Ari, with the hatch open at his back. "I'm going to go through. You stay here till I get back."

"Wait, Jon! Let's run another test for grins and giggles." Ari reached behind him and grabbed a handful of fiber-optic thread, tossing it into the lock. Then he cycled the mechanism, shutting the hatch on the thread. The link survived without a problem. The thread appeared to be coming out of the bulkhead. Ari cycled the hatch open again, and said, "Now I feel better about you going alone. If anything happens, I'll come in after you."

"Not so fast, Ari. If something happens to me, you'll do exactly what Dmitri orders. And Dmitri, until you determine what happened to me, you won't risk any more crew members, understood?"

"Roger, Captain," Dmitri said.

"Roger, Jon," Ari said.

"Once I'm inside the lock, shut the hatch."

Jon walked into the lock, and Ari cycled the hatch. He watched a holoimage from Jon's cameras with intense interest, as did the rest of the team topside.

Inside the sealed lock, Jon carefully examined the controls, for they were not hidden in here. *The normal mechanism for activating important functions seems to be the grip,* he noted. The lock was lighted, without any obvious source for the light. Jon was curious, but put off investigating that for later. There were two grips, one on the hatch, and the other near it. He took hold of the one on the hatch. Nothing. It didn't budge. He tried the other one. It turned easily to the left, and he felt gas flowing into the lock, pressurizing it to some level. As the pressure increased, Jon noted on his heads up display that it increased to 900 mb – like being about a kilometer above Earth normal sea level. He twisted the hatch grip to the left.

Jon looked through the open hatch and gasped with astonishment. He stepped through the hatch, and stumbled, nearly falling, as he suddenly found himself in normal Earth gravity.

Chapter twenty-one

At Base Camp, Dmitri was staring intently at the holoimage as Jon cycled the outer hatch door. He saw the flash of a bright image, but then the image tumbled, and it became difficult to orient the image into a coherent view. He heard Jon's gasp, and then, as Jon regained his footing and stood upright, Dmitri let out a startled gasp himself. "Gather round, everybody," he said urgently. Look at this!"

The others placed themselves so they had a good view of the holoimage.

"This is unbelievable," Noel said.

"You getting this, Ari?" Dmitri asked.

"Yeh, but it isn't just unbelievable, it's fucking unbelievable!"

The rest nodded their assent.

"Ideas, anyone?" Dmitri asked, glancing around the group.

"Occam's razor," Chen muttered. "Let's not make things more complicated."

"So...?" Dmitri asked.

"We accept what we see at face value until or unless we learn something new," Michele said, in a voice filled with awe. "*Mon Dieu...* It's exciting!"

"Tell us what you see, Captain," Dmitri said with as much authority as he could muster. He could not remember ever feeling so at a loss when confronting a new situation. What he saw in the holoimage seemed impossible: A grassy green meadow under a blue sky with a sprinkling of fleecy white clouds. Several trees growing in the meadow, oak-, birch-, linden-, and even willow-like trees, indistinguishable in the holoimage from the real thing. The horizon had the by now familiar nearness, and the tint of the sky was off – subtly different from Earth's. Otherwise, it was a perfect pastoral scene... that didn't belong inside a moon orbiting the planet Saturn one-and-a-half billion kilometers from Earth.

"Captain...?"

"I'm here, Dmitri. Just trying to integrate what my eyes see with what my intellect tells me."

"No shit!" Ari said from outside the lock. "I'm coming through."

"No, Ari, you're not!" Jon ordered sternly. "Stay there. I'm coming back out. Whatever this place is, it's been here for a very long time. We have plenty of time to understand what we face before committing ourselves any further."

"One more thing, Dmitri..." Jon paused.

"Yeh?"

"I'm in Earth-normal gravity. As soon as I stepped through the hatch it hit me. That's why I stumbled. It was totally unexpected."

The image before Dmitri and the others began to rotate as Jon turned around. As he stepped over the hatch lip into the lock he said, "That's amazing, utterly amazing!" He stepped backward through the hatch again. Then he placed one foot inside the lock while leaving the other on the ground outside. "Right now I have Earth-normal gravity on my left leg and that part of my body outside the plane of the hatch, and Iapetus standard gravity on that part of my body inside the plane of the hatch."

"Jon," Carmen interrupted. "Either move in or out. Don't stay in the middle like that. You are subjecting your body to unusual tidal forces that could do you some significant damage. In or out...okay?"

"Got it, Doc! I'm on my way in."

Dmitri watched him turn to secure the hatch, walk forward and open the elevator-side hatch, where Ari was standing with a look of genuine concern on his face.

"Dmitri, bundle up what just happened and get it to Houston. Tell them I intend to move Base Camp to the elevator, and after we have established the actual conditions on the other side of the lock, I will move Base Camp inside."

"Got it, Captain."

"I'm sending Ari up on TBH boots as a test of our ability to escape from here. Keep his lifeline taut in case anything goes wrong. Make sure his boot tanks get refilled. In the meantime, start sending the team down, one at a time."

"What about using TBH boots for the descent?" Dmitri asked.

"Too risky – especially for the women who have had little experience with the boots. We're talking just five hours. Let's not risk anyone to save a couple of hours.

#

Ari and Jon switched to private communication, and Ari questioned his friend intently about what he had seen, and what had happened. Jon was not able to tell him much more than he already knew. There was an interior world that seemed to sport land and clouded sky, a world that seemed to have artificial Earth-normal gravity, which implied that machinery somewhere in Iapetus was running normally, and had been doing so for millennia. How that could be, and what it implied was unanswerable without further data.

"That's what we're going to get," Jon told him, "just as soon as everybody arrives down here, and we can run some tests. I have a feeling that the interior also sports Earth-normal air. I think I saw insects and maybe even heard birds." He shook his head inside his helmet. "Right now, it's an incomprehensible mystery."

"We can set up the down line directly to the outside of the entry hatch," Ari suggested. "That way, I can jet right up the line, and the others can rappel straight down the line without having to perform a series of jumps. We can save some time, and get to the bottom of the mystery more quickly."

"Let's do it," Jon decided.

It took them about a half hour to get everything set up, with the line stretched five kilometers to the shaft top, and the safety line securely attached to Ari. With a wave, Ari tapped both big toes, and commenced his rocket ride to the top of the shaft. He cupped his left hand loosely around the descent line, accelerating as quickly as ten newtons could push him against the light gravity of Iapetus. He estimated that he reached about twenty-five kilometers per hour. He tapped his jets off and on as necessary to maintain a constant upward velocity for about eleven minutes, angling slightly so he approached the side as he ascended. Then for the last two hundred or so meters he shut down the boots. As he reached the rim, he was barely moving, and stepped over the edge onto the solid surface of the deck. He checked his fuel gauge. It was about a quarter down.

"It's the only way to travel," he said to anyone who would listen. "Come on, Saeed. Let's go refuel my boot tanks."

With Saeed in tow, Ari climbed the ladder to the surface, and they hopped the short distance to Base Camp. The hypergolic fuel tanks holding pressurized UDMH and nitrogen tetroxide were located near the rear of the rover. Each boot had its own set of pressure filling hoses with specifically designed snap-on-off nozzles that could not be attached to the incorrect tank.

"You run some of this," Ari pointed to the UDMH tank, "through this hose," he held up the nitrogen tetroxide hose, "things will get exciting really quickly. They're perfectly safe so long as they don't mix, except in a combustion chamber."

Then he showed Saeed how to attach each filling hose, and watched closely as Saeed pressed the male fittings into the female receptors on the tanks and the boots, and continued to watch carefully as he filled the boot tanks. The filling process automatically stopped when the boot tanks reached their capacity. Ari still monitored Saeed closely, even though Saeed had given no indication that he was still on his jihad mission. There was a slight risk with the fueling operation, since the hoses could be cut. This would instantly slam shut the valves at both ends, but the fuel in the hoses could still pour out and would definitely combust if brought together. The hoses were tough beyond belief, however. They were constructed from polyaramid, reinforced with strands of diamond crystal like the optic-fiber thread, but without its optic characteristics, and its surface was sleeved with the substance. No ordinary knife would even scratch the surface. Only a knife with a synthetic diamond crystalline edge could sever the hoses. Several were with the expedition, but Arl made sure that Saeed never even knew of their existence.

#

The arrival of the burst message from Iapetus containing Jon's discovery was viewed by only the watch section personnel. The watch captain immediately roused Rod Zakes, who showed up in Mission Control several minutes later, rubbing sleep from his eyes, thinning hair in disarray.

"Why do these things always seem to arrive just after midnight?" he grumbled, as he gratefully accepted a steaming cup of black coffee handed to him by one of the engineers. "Okay," he said following a couple of welcome sips of the hot brew, "what have we got this time that caused you to get me out of a perfectly comfortable bed?"

Instead of answering, CapCom simply pressed the play button. The enlarged holoimage shimmered into existence in the space before the consoles. Zakes watched in utter fascination as the scene unfolded. When the final hatch door opened, and Jon gazed into the pastoral landscape before stumbling and losing the image, Zakes shouted, "Hold it...play that back!"

"No need, Sir, it gets better in a moment."

"I'll be a goldamned sonofabitch," Zakes muttered as Jon explained the shifting gravity. "How the hell do they do that?"

CapCom left the holographic image hang in the air. "By now, Sir, they have moved Base Camp down inside the elevator at the bottom of the five kilometer shaft."

"I know where it is," Zakes said with an irritated voice, still waking up from his sound slumber. "Tell me something I don't know."

"They think the interior contains Earth-normal air, and, after testing, Sir, I think they plan to explore the interior without their suits."

"What! You gotta be kidding me! Without their suits?"

"Why not, Sir? If it's Earth normal gravity and Earth-normal air that's been working for God-knows-how-long...why not?"

"I guess you got a point." He rubbed his eyes again, and set down his empty coffee cup. "Prepare a press release, but let me see it before you send it out. I gotta pump bilges." He stood and left the control center.

The press release Zakes authorized was brief and uninformative: "The Iapetus exploratory team has discovered a chamber deep below the surface that contains Earth-normal air and some living plants. Once further details and holorecordings are received, we will make them available to the press."

#

Noel was the first person to drop down the shaft. He arrived at the elevator without incident stating that it was just a longer exercise like those he frequently did for fun back on Earth. With both Jon and Noel on the bottom, the crew lowered several nets containing test equipment, pressure tents complete with sanitary and sleeping facilities, food and water, and compact polyaramid construction components. Except for the scientific testing equipment, everything was sufficiently rugged that Jon and Noel had only to drop it through the lock, and then push it into the elevator interior. The effort was minimal, but still, the task lasted about two hours.

Ginger was the first woman to drop to the elevator following the equipment. Other than some minor twisting, she had no problem. She solved the twisting problem herself, and glided smoothly through the cofferdam into the elevator lock. Jon had her wait inside the elevator while he and Noel met the next arrival – Elke. She had no problem of any kind during the five-kilometer drop. Chen arrived next. He had to stop halfway down to untangle himself and his safety line. He had forgotten to control his spinning, and had allowed himself to put about fifteen twists into the rope pair. A minute later he had untangled himself, and continued to the bottom without further incident. Michele was more cautions, stopping several times during her descent to solve an incipient twisting problem. Carmen also descended without incident, although she controlled her descent speed so that it took her longer than the others. Dmitri dropped down skillfully, second only to Ari in transit time. Saeed expressed some concern since he had never before rappelled, but said aloud that anything a woman could do, he could do with more skill, because he was a man. He made it to the bottom with only one twist that required no stop. Finally, Ari rappelled down without a belay. He set up a second free-running rappel line with a fixture that would bring him up short should his main rappel line go into runaway. He also kept his boot nozzles uncovered in the event of some kind of catastrophic failure. He arrived at the upper lock in record time, tied off his lines, locked the upper hatch, and dropped down and through the lower hatch.

Despite the real possibility that they would be able to exist on the inside without suits and pressure tents, Jon demanded that a proper Base Camp be set up in the elevator, "Just in case," he said. Not wanting to risk the expedition's only doctor on the first foray, he assigned himself and the expedition biologist, Michele, to take testing equipment through the last lock into the interior, where they would run atmospheric and toxin tests. They were way beyond any rulebook here, Jon knew. Instead, he was operating on instinct, making decisions that he believed would move this constantly shifting mission forward without seriously compromising crew safety.

Jon and Michele stepped into the lock and closed the hatch behind them. In his right leg pocket, Jon carried the atmospheric tester. Michele carried the small toxin tester in her left leg pocket.

"Watch yourself, now, Michele. It's not anything like the holo-image. Remember, as you step through the hatch, you will be hit with a gravity force nearly forty-three times greater than you are feeling right now. It nearly knocked me flat on my ass."

As he commenced operating the outer hatch, gas flowed into the lock, and then the outer hatch opened. Jon braced himself and stepped onto the surface. He staggered as the weight hit him, but this time he was prepared for it. He reached out to guide Michele, not a *pro forma* gesture as when he had helped her out of the Lander. As Michele stepped through the hatch, her legs crumbled beneath her, and Jon lowered her gently to her knees.

"Are you okay?" he asked, angry with himself for letting her fall.

"*Oui, mon Capitaine!* I am fine. I know you warned me, and held my hand, but it still completely surprised me. What an odd thing." She got carefully to her feet and spent a couple of minutes just gazing at the wonderfully strange landscape. Then she reached into her leg pocket. "Let's see what dangers lurk in this atmosphere."

Jon extracted the atmospheric monitor and set it for full analysis. Within seconds its reading indicated a nitrogen to oxygen mix of seventy-eight to twenty-one, with one percent of mostly carbon dioxide and several trace gases, at a nominal pressure of just under one bar.

Michele held up her analyzer for Jon to see. "It's as pure as mother's milk," she said with a giggle, and placed her hands on her helmet, twisted it to open, and lifted it off her collar.

"Michele, don't..." Jon warned, but too late.

"Okay, everybody," Jon said, "you all know what Michele just did. She's fine, so I guess it's okay, but..." He paused for significant effect. "...please don't ignore discipline. We really don't want to lose one of you because of a silly mistake."

Unable, herself, to hear Jon's announcement because her helmet lay in the grass beside her feet, Michele said, "Take off your helmet, *mon Capitaine*! It's lovely out here...in here..." She looked a bit confused.

Jon looked at her radiant face, able to hear her only dimly through the helmet. "What the hell," he said, "I'm removing my helmet, too."

Chapter twenty-two

"Dmitri, can you think of any reason not to bring the entire crew through?" Jon asked.

"We're already collapsing the pressure tents," Dmitri answered. "You know," he added, "if we could figure how to operate the big door, and if we could get the elevator operating, we could bring one of the rovers down. It would greatly simplify our exploration."

"You're kidding…right?"

"Only partly. It really does make sense."

Jon had to admit that it really did make sense. If this artificial world covered the entire moon, then there were about six and a half million square clicks of surface down here. That was a lot of area to cover.

Under Dmitri's able supervision, the crew moved all their equipment that they had lowered down the shaft into the interior. No matter how well prepared each person was for the gravity shift through the inner lock, the transition to Earth-normal gravity was a shock. All the women except Elke ended on the ground the first time, as did Chen and Saeed. They all had been operating in low gravity for sufficiently long that they had to adjust to the higher gravity with conscious effort. The blue sky filled with fleecy clouds, the green grass and other growing things made the adjustment a pleasure.

Without being told, everyone removed pressure suits. The men ended up in their shipboard jumpsuits, with lightweight foot wear more suited to a low gravity environment. The women managed to look fresher than the guys, more spruced up and colorful, and Michele had somehow smuggled a short skirt and scooped white silk blouse into her pressure suit, and was dancing barefoot and child-like in the grass.

Chen and Noel set to work taking physical measurements. Using both radar and sonar they determined that the roof was two kilometers above them, not nearly high enough to generate the clouds.

"It's a neat trick," Chen told the others.

"For more than one reason," Noel added. "How do they do it? Simple, straightforward question, how – the hell – do they do it? And second, how in hell is it still working – and everything else, for that matter? What kind of engineering does it take to build something like this?"

Michele joined Carmen to test various plants, comparing their molecular structure with similar Earth plants. They prepared several cuttings for polymerase chain reaction DNA analysis by soaking the samples in a special solution, heating them for several minutes, and conducting the PCR analysis.

With no specific scientific tasks, Ginger and Elke busied them- selves with straightening out the still messy Base Camp, with Dmitri joining in, grumbling good naturedly about having to do woman's work.

"Captain," Carmen said after a few minutes, "this isn't similar to Earth grass, it *is* Earth grass…and leaves, and bark, and berries. Here," she said with a twinkle in her eye, "try this blueberry. They're delicious."

"It makes no sense, *mon Capitaine*," Michele added. "How could this be?"

She's right, of course, Jon thought as he thoughtfully chewed the berry. *How the hell can all this be?*

"Double check your measurements and findings, Doc. Ginger, put together a communiqué for Houston. Don't speculate. Just give them the facts." He shook his head in wonder as he accepted a ripe marionberry from Carmen. It was delicious. "When you have completed your measurements and the message is in the pipeline, meet me please under that tree." He pointed to a sprawling oak about a hundred meters distant. "Ari, please join me now." He struck off for the tree, and Ari hurried after him.

Jon sat on the ground leaning against the broad trunk. Ari sat back against a protruding root. "Your thoughts, please. What are we dealing with here?" Jon asked.

"Occam's razor, my friend, Occam's razor."

"And...?" Jon didn't want to put anything into Ari's mind. He wanted Ari's independent thoughts.

"Let's grant the technology," Ari said thoughtfully, scratching behind his right ear. "I don't have a clue how they do the gravity or any of the other manifestations, but..." His pause was long and apparently thoughtful. Jon just sat, waiting for him to continue. "Setting aside those questions, what do we have?" He started ticking the points off his fingers. "One, we got a sky that looks like ours, but the tint is a bit off. Two, we got Earth-normal gravity, not something close, but exactly Earth-normal. Three, we got Earth plants – not something close. They are Earth plants. Doc says the DNA is an exact match. Four, we have machines with ergonomics that fit us." He paused again, looking thoughtfully at his four fingers. Jon patiently waited for him to continue, even though he could see where he was going. "I think somebody wanted this place to mimic Earth as closely as possible. They painted the dome, but over time it must have faded a bit." He paused again, and rested his head in his hands with his fingers against his forehead and his thumbs against his jaw. "They can't be from Earth," he continued, "cause topside is a hundred-thousand or more years old, and this kind of technology didn't exist on Earth that long ago. Hell, it doesn't exist there now..." His voice trailed off. "You see where I'm going?"

"Yep," Jon answered, "they didn't come *from* Earth, they came *to* Earth. God knows why..."

"And their shit's still working," Ari said with a hint of awe. "We should probably think twice before pissing these guys off." Ari grinned at Jon, and pointed over Jon's shoulders at the rest of the team making its way to the oak.

"Okay," Jon said to his assembled crew, lolling on the grass in a ragged circle around him, "our best guess is that whoever the creators of this world were, they came here from somewhere else, but they exactly mimicked Earth as closely as possible. Ari thinks," he added with a smile, "that they painted the roof, and the paint faded."

Everyone chuckled, but Jon thought he could detect nervousness behind the superficial gaiety. "We're afoot for the time being," he continued. "I want to explore as much of this terrain as we can during the next few days. I will split us up into two-person teams, and we'll spread out maintaining coms until we lose a link. Then we'll figure out what to do at that point."

Dmitri spoke up. "I've found something interesting about the geometrics of this place. Look in the sky in that direction." He pointed.

"It looks like a vertical line," Ginger said.

"Now that direction..."

"Another line," Noel said.

"Now there..."

"Another," said Chen.

"And there, and there..."

"Two more lines," from Ari.

"I think those are supporting columns," Dmitri said. "I've done some calculations. The roof is two clicks up. The horizon is one-point-six-nine clicks out...that puts the base of that column about seven-point-seven-six clicks away. I did a pattern analysis – we're back to hexagons."

Jon divided the crew up, trying to maintain the most efficient and compatible teams he could. "Ari, you've got Saeed. Dr. Bhuta, Chen is with you. Noel, you and Elke team up. Dmitri and Ginger, and Michele is with me. Each team will head directly toward a column. Dmitri says they're a bit less than eight clicks away. Take your time and observe as you progress. Pack some food and water, a light blanket, share a sanitary kit and a portable analyzer. Each of you carries a holocam and coms, and each team will lay a fiber-optic thread. Stay in sight of each other at all times, and check in with the party to your left and right every few minutes." His instructions sounded a bit formal to him as he gave them. "Look, guys, this is totally unexpected. We are as completely unprepared for this as we can be. But we have to try. This is the single most important event in human history, and each of you is right in the middle of it. Let's make the best of it, and try to find out what we can, while keeping as safe as we can. It's been a long day. Let's get some rest, and get started in the morning."

As Jon spoke, the sky commenced a noticeable dimming. Over the next two hours, the sky turned dark, and was filled with stars – the stars of Earth as seen from slightly north of the equator. To Jon's mind, this was further confirmation that this interior was supposed to mimic as closely as possible conditions on Earth. He chalked up the incident sunset to coincidence. He was completely unprepared to consider any million-year-old mechanism that was capable of inferring sunset from his conversation.

#

The news of the Iapetus explorers' discovery flashed around Earth as rapidly as human engineers could interrupt routine holocast programming with the flash report. The world watched in awe as crew members passed through the inner lock and struggled to maintain equilibrium in the suddenly increased gravity. Pundits explained in hundreds of languages with thousands of hastily drawn diagrams and clumsy animations how the gravity of Iapetus differed from that of Earth – and many dropped in the Moon, Mars, Jupiter, and even some of Jupiter's moons and other moons of Saturn. Anything to fill out the rather meager report from the interior of Iapetus. Throughout the Judeo-Christian world, people of faith gathered spontaneously at churches, cathedrals, and synagogues. Priests, scholars, and learned religious men turned to their ancient texts to discover where this might have been foretold in scripture.

Crowds of people streamed toward Area 51 in the American southwest, and spontaneous demonstrations took place in London, Frankfurt, Amsterdam, and Los Angeles, of people dressed in futuristic-looking costumes, many waving dog-eared copies of George Adamski's writings from the 1950s.

The peoples of the world celebrated the startling fact that we were not alone in the universe, and the nearly universally accepted theory that in a place so vast as the interior of Iapetus, the explorers were bound to find something or even someone with an explanation that made sense.

Inside the barricaded borders of the Caliphate, however, all was silent. The average man-in-the-street was unaware of what was happening out in space around the planet Saturn. And those who did know kept their mouths shut. Khomeini would put out the word when he was ready, and nobody was willing to take the risk of second-guessing him at a moment in history like this. Khomeini's Islamic scholars feverishly combed the *Qur'an* for clues that related to the momentous findings in the sky. Following many hours of desperate searching, a scholar hurried into the Caliph's receiving chamber, carrying a calligraphy-covered old copy of the *Qur'an*. He had contacted the Caliph's immediate staff before leaving his cubical, so that the Caliph would be able to receive him and hear what he had found. He stood silently, eyes averted to the floor as the Caliph swept into the room, gowns surging around him. As the Caliph seated himself on his raised chair, the scholar dropped to his knees and prostrated himself before his ruler.

"What is it? With what did you interrupt my devotions?"

Terrified that he might have made a mistake, the scholar slid the ornate *Qur'an* toward the Caliph's dais. "The passage is marked, Sahib."

The Caliph didn't move a muscle. "Tell it to me!" he ordered. "And pick yourself off the floor."

The scholar raised himself to his knees, but couldn't bring himself to go further. In a trembling voice, he began to narrate: "from 4;74 – *Let those fight in the way of Allah who sell the life of this world for the other. Whoso fighteth in the way of Allah, be he slain or be he victorious, on him we shall bestow a vast reward.*"

"And...?" The Caliph's voice sounded menacing.

"In the past, Sahib, we may not have understood correctly. We always presumed the Prophet (may he be blessed) was speaking of the world after death, but now we believe he may have meant the satellite of Saturn, Iapetus..." His voice trailed to silence as the Caliph stood.

"Hand me the holy book." The Caliph demanded.

The scholar shuffled forward on his knees, picked up the ornate *Qur'an* and lifted it to the Caliph, keeping his head bowed and his eyes averted. For ten painful minutes, the scholar waited for the Caliph to make a sound – any sound.

"So, this is ordained," the Caliph finally said so softly that the scholar could barely hear him. "The Prophet (may he rest in peace) foresaw the events on Iapetus, and gives us guidance." He looked down at the still trembling scholar and reached out his hand to touch the scholar's still averted head. "Well done, my son. Allah will reward your diligence." He stepped down and headed for the door. "Return to your search," he said without looking back.

Three hours later, the scholar was on his knees in front of the Caliph once again. This time the Caliph seemed to grant him a bit of leeway, even to show him a bit of respect. "What have you found, my son? Recite it to me."

Nervously, the scholar recited the last part of verse 154 from Surah number three: Al-Imran: Say: Had you remained in your houses, those for whom slaughter was ordained would certainly have gone forth to the places where they would be slain, and that Allah might test what was in your breasts and that He might purge what was in your hearts; and Allah knows what is in the breasts.

"Give me your interpretation, my son."

"The *Cassini II* crew was designated to be slain by your holy warrior, Esmail Saeed. This has not yet happened, and we wondered, as did you, Sahib, whether he might have failed his Jihad. But these words seem to mean that the time was not yet ripe. Taken in context with the earlier text I brought to you, it seems that the time is just now becoming ripe for Esmail's Jihad. We need to be prepared, Sahib, for the consequences..." his voice trailed off as before as the Caliph's face clouded up.

"Your counsel is timely and wise, my son." The Caliph reached out to the scholar. "Stand! You will join my senior advisors, and will instruct them in how we are to proceed."

With trembling heart, the scholar rose to his feet and departed the chamber to join the deputies. He was a *Qur'an* scholar; he knew nothing of policy, nothing of governance, and he was terrified as never before. He had only one chance for being right, whereas the chances for not being right numbered beyond his ability to count. He knew he was doomed, and could find no way to extricate himself.

Meanwhile, the streets of Teheran, Istanbul, Beirut, Cairo, Bagdad, Mecca, Kabul, Karachi, Tripoli, Casablanca – all the great cities of the Caliphate, were calm and quiet, waiting, waiting for the Caliph. Elsewhere, however, Muslims rioted in the streets, attacked embassies in New Delhi, Jakarta, and London, and fire bombed the worldwide residences of the consuls' of the nations participating in the Iapetus expedition.

And the world stood by, in awe of the happenings on Iapetus, and in shock about the rioting on Earth.

Churches, cathedrals, and synagogues throughout the world remained full to overflowing. In the communities surrounding Area 51, business was booming, and worldwide sales of UFO books boomed, some written in the early 1950s, and some hot off the press, but all disappearing from shelves as quickly as they arrived. Crowds gathered at Cape Canaveral, pitching tents and waiting for something to happen – what, they didn't know, but something. Street traffic around NASA headquarters in Houston, and the European Space Agency in Paris was becoming a problem as people in vehicles flocked to the sites to gain some sense of participation in the world-altering events on Iapetus.

The governments of the United States, Canada, Germany, France, Australia, and Israel quietly communicated their intentions to one another, and even more quietly began to increase their military readiness postures, and to review their military contingency plans. The governments of the Russian Federation, China, and India commenced troop build-ups on their mutual borders, and they all communicated to the American President that they intended no threat to the United States or any of its allies. New Delhi quietly let Teheran know that it posed no threat to the Caliphate, and had, in fact assumed a neutral stance in any developing conflict.

#

Rod Zakes had his hands full. Hourly, he received reports of another eager space enthusiast breaking into Jonson Space Center. He was in close communication with his counterpart in Paris, where similar things were happening, except that ESA Headquarters was in downtown Paris, whereas he was located on Galveston Bay outside of Houston proper. He would take his blessings where he could.

Despite demands from each of the mission partners and from his own superiors, there was nothing he could do to increase or speed up the information flow from distant Iapetus. He patiently explained that the trip alone for the radio beam took over an hour and a half, just from the spacecraft to Earth. Since the crew was now inside Iapetus, they could only send short burst transmissions lasting no more than twenty seconds, and then only every three and a half hours.

The holonetworks picked up on his mantra, and searched out astronomers, astrophysicists, and any other type of scientist who would be willing to take a turn at explaining the complex communications tangle to the eager public. At Rod's urging, the Fox Syndicate queried a couple of popular hard science-fiction authors, finally convincing them to appear on their network. Like Robert Heinlein and Arthur C. Clark during the heydays of the Apollo Program, these modern-day hard science-fiction writers explained the situation in a way that even the news personalities could understand. The pressure eased for Rod after this, and he was finally able to get a few hours of sleep each night, especially after he suggested to Jon Stock that he set himself for a regular detailed broadcast every twelve hours.

He sighed with relief as he watched the Muslim riots die down, the churches and synagogues empty, and the crowds at Area 51 and outside Canaveral, ESA, and Houston dissipate. The die-hards remained, of course, but they had become part of the scenery almost from the launch of *Cassini II*. He was kept in the loop regarding the ongoing military readiness of the participating nations, and passed this information to Jon, as he deemed necessary, so Jon could tailor his broadcasts according to his best judgment.

As Rod saw it, the fate of the world, and perhaps the entire human race, lay in his and Jon's hands. It kept him awake at night.

Chapter twenty-three

E lke had pretty much been along for the ride thus far on this incredible voyage. Her main function as historian had not been put to any great test, other than maintaining an annotated record of the trip and daily events. Her capacity as a computer engineer had remained virtually untapped. Following her abortive approach to Carmen, she had pretty much kept her romantic attention focused on Michele, although she had hooked up a couple of times with Ginger and one of the guys. She viewed those liaisons as a necessary path to revel with Ginger, since that exotic creature was disinclined to go one-on-one with her. Elke was amused at Jon's team-ups. Ari was saddled with that little terrorist, and Elke still did not understand why Jon had not just jettisoned the bastard when they found him. Chen was with the Doc, and that only made sense, given Chen's long coma. Elke felt a certain empathy for the withdrawn Chinese VASIMR engineer who liked Kentucky bourbon, American jazz, and motorcycles. She had figured out shortly after meeting him that he was gay, and wondered if that may have contributed to his coma, since there obviously was no reciprocation among the crew. Tough break for a competent, likable guy. He got along well with everybody, but she know better than anyone how lonely his position could be. It made her additionally thankful that Michele was so ambiguous in her sexuality. Jon and Michele would make a good team. His command remoteness would keep her focused on her task, which had mushroomed into an overwhelming responsibility, and her ultra-femininity just might melt the captain's cold heart. Dmitri and Ginger had partnered in so many things already, that theirs was a natural selection. Elke smiled as she recalled their private time. Between the two of them, she and Ginger had given the Russian the ride of his life.

Elke glanced at Noel, walking a few paces away. Tall, almost regal, handsome, and used to the good things in life. If she were so inclined, Noel would be the kind of man she would seek out. Perhaps her biggest surprise about Noel was when she found him alone in the Canteen one sleep period, quietly playing a plaintive melody on an old German alto block flute. She fixed herself a *Café au lait*, refreshed his tea, and for the next hour quietly listened to the aural magic he wove, tears streaming down her cheeks. It was the only time she had been alone with him until now.

Normally, Elke quickly grasped new situations, came to grips with their challenges, and moved forward. This world, however, and the incredibly unexpected landscape that lay before her, was straining her coping abilities. Her computer engineering studies at the Technische Universität Darmstadt had included all the necessary science background courses, but she felt technically unequipped to deal with what they had found. Nothing in her technical background led her to believe that the gravity she was experiencing could exist – nothing. She had been chatting with Noel, trying to figure if his space structural and VASIMR training gave him any insights, but he was as baffled as she. *There's something to be said*, she thought, *to the regular person's simple acceptance of reality, to use without comprehending. I'm not very good at that.*

Aloud, she said, "Doesn't it make you uncomfortable...all this, without having a clue? What if it suddenly stops working?"

"By my unscientific reckoning, it's been working for about a hundred-fifty-thousand years or so minimum – perhaps even a million. I'm guessing it will keep on keeping on." Noel smiled at her. "It really bothers you, doesn't it?"

"*Ja*, it really does. My intellect agrees with you, but my gut says it's impossible, and will vanish in a poof any second...and we'll be without our suites."

"Wouldn't that be an ironic end to an incredible journey?" Noel asked laconically, while his hands motioned as if tracing a headline in mid-air. "And which is winning, intellect or gut?"

"I guess that's obvious, isn't it?" Elke grinned at him. She really liked this guy.

#

Ari understood why Jon had assigned Saeed to him, but that didn't make the assignment any pleasanter. Their discovery of this incredible interior demanded his best investigational efforts, and here he was distracted by having to keep an eagle eye on their ward.

Ever since Dmitri had presented the crew with his explanation of the column distribution, Ari was struck by the six pointedness. Dmitri had emphasized the hexagonal distribution of the columns. But what Ari saw immediately was that each column was at the center of a Star of David. The fact was obvious to him, but he simply did not yet know enough to discern a reason. He understood that the geometrics played a significant role in the total structure, but that was Noel's department, and maybe Chen's as well, using his systems approach. He tapped his link, and started at the result of his calculation. *Nearly 181 thousand columns. The engineering staggers the mind.* As they walked, he pondered it further. Then he looked at Saeed.

"Saeed, I'm going to share something astonishing with you. These columns – the aliens did not build them."

Saeed looked at him in astonishment.

"They hollowed this entire space out of solid rock, and left the columns in place." He tapped his link again. "They removed thirteen-million-twenty-eight-thousand-one-hundred-eleven cubic kilometers of rock...if they managed to remove a hundred cubic kilometers of rock every day, it would have taken them three-hundred-fifty-seven years just to hollow out the space we see, assuming it covers the entire thing." Ari shook his head in exasperation. *It's beyond reckoning.*

Saeed remained silent, probably, Ari thought, because he simply didn't have the technical background to understand even a little part of what Ari had just told him. Ari transmitted his thoughts and calculations to the rest of the team "Think your way through this, guys," he said. "This thing we are exploring took centuries to build. I don't care how sophisticated your planetary engineering is, there is a physical limit to what you can move in a finite amount of time. These numbers don't even begin to consider the first open layer we found and whatever complex machinery they installed to make this place work. This is further beyond us than we are beyond the Cro-Magnon."

#

Saeed bided his time. It didn't make sense to continue his Jihad right now, because the crew was scattered, and there still was a lot to learn. When Ari showed him the numbers, he really didn't understand what he was saying, but he clearly understood that the beings who built this place were powerful beyond ken. He tried to visualize a hundred cubic kilometers. He knew the roof was two kilometers over their heads. He imagined a kilometer square reaching to the roof. That would be two cubic kilometers. Fifty of those would be a hundred cubic kilometers, and the builders had to remove that much every day in order to complete the task in 357 years. *That kind of dedication,* he thought, *is normally found only in Islam. Who else would have the patience of centuries?*

Saeed put thoughts of Jihad aside for the time being. He knew that Allah would reveal the right time to him. All he needed to do was remain focused on his surroundings.

Quicker than he expected, they arrived at the next column. It appeared the same size as the one from which they had entered into this magic place. This column, however, appeared to have no openings.

"Makes sense," he heard Ari mutter. "You can't hold up that rock sky with a bunch of hollow tubes."

#

The four other teams had reported to Jon. All the columns were solid, so far as they could determine. He had merged the four individual holoimages into a single image so that it appeared to Michele and him that the others were sitting on the grass around them. The only thing that gave away the illusion was that the individual skies and grass colors were just sufficiently different that the eye picked it up. But it still was easy to forget that they were not actually sitting there.

Ari projected his calculations before the group. "I think this is more important than we have been giving it credit," he insisted. "Wrap your minds around this. If these guys removed one hundred cubic kilometers of rock daily – let's put that in visual perspective: That's a square with sides the distance we just walked reaching all the way to the rock dome two clicks above us – if they removed that amount of rock each day, it would take them three-hundred-fifty-seven years to remove the rock that filled this interior." He let them think about that for a bit. No one said anything, but from their faces, Jon could tell that they were really pondering this amazing fact.

"Now ask yourself this," Ari continued. "What kind of scientific and engineering progress have we made in the last three and a half centuries?" Again he stopped, letting this sink in as well.

"*Mon Dieu!*" Michele whispered.

Noel let out a low whistle.

Dmitri nodded his head vigorously. "That's what I been trying to tell you guys. These beings, these aliens, these whoever-they-are – they were very bright guys."

"And it's been here how long?" Chen asked.

"A million years, perhaps," Carmen noted with awe in her voice. "What are we dealing with? Where did they go? Why...?" Her voice trailed off in thought.

"We're pretty scattered right now," Jon told the group. I don't want to spread us out any further for the time being. Try to do some in-depth investigation near your columns, but stay within sight of the column base. Let's check in again in five hours, at..." He gave them the exact time, and terminated the holographic connection. He looked at his fetching companion and said, "Dr. deBois, Michele, it's time for your star performance..." He paused as she looked at him with a glint in her eye. "As a botanist," he finished, with a wink. "I'm going to do some in-depth thinking about all this. I need to gain some kind of understanding. I'll be right here. If you need my help, just call. I'll be there directly." He settled with his back against the massive column, brought up his pad, and commenced his analytic thought process, placing and labeling points in space as he laid out the problem.

#

Michele felt in her element. On one hand, she wanted to shed her clothing and dance naked in the meadow like the carefree nature-child she had always been. On the other hand, her scientist side wanted to know, and the list was too long to recite, but it started with what was directly underfoot. The meadow included clumps of wild flowers scattered randomly across the surface. She examined several flowers closely. In appearance they exactly mimicked Earth flowers of the same variety – exactly. Even the male and female varieties were present in proper proportions. She sat cross-legged on the ground, quietly watching. She let herself relax as she had learned on the many field trips of her graduate years at the Sorbonne before she had to isolate herself in a lab at Berkeley. She let herself go until she began to feel at one with nature. While doing this, she had the distracting thought that the nature she was communing with was five kilometers below the rocky surface of Iapetus in an impossible artificial gravity field. As she sat quietly, she began to hear the sounds of nature around her. She could feel the soft breeze, and hear minute sounds that the process of life produced. With a sigh, she placed several miniature microphones around her area, and hooked them to her link, while feeding the audio channel to her ears as well. Her link told her the probability of insect life in the grasses was approaching 100%. Then she heard a sound that was as distinct as it was well known. A bee came buzzing in front of her and attached itself to the nearest bloom, and then one-by-one it touched all of them. *Just like on Earth*, she thought. *I wonder about earthworms*. She dug a little way into the soil, and came up with two fat ones. *Just like Earth*. She sat back and put her mind to work.

What does it take to grow a meadow? She ticked off some of the obvious requirements. Grass, other growing plants, pollination, reseeding, fertilization… But what keeps it a meadow, instead of an overgrown mess, a tangle of thorns and vines? She thought back to her childhood, filled with cows, goats, and other animals. The cows and goats ate the grass, and kept the meadow in good condition – cow patties, goat droppings…and birds ate berries and dropped seeds everywhere. So why are berry bushes growing here and here, but not there and over there? She called Carmen.

"Yes, Michele…"

"Carmen, what have you found? Anything yet? Any ideas?" The words rushed from Michele.

"I think," Carmen said hesitantly, "that this place resembles a garden more than a meadow."

"Exactly...that's why I called you. There are no cows or goats, or even deer or elk, but it all is working as if there were. Somehow, this place is managed. I even observed a bee pollinating."

"Can you catch one? I don't have a net with me."

"Sure, why?"

"Catch one, and let me know," Carmen said.

"Oo... *mystérieuse*. I'll call you back."

Michele wandered back to where Jon was sitting. He looked up at her. "What's up?"

"I need my collection net." She pulled it out of her pack, grabbed a sample bottle, and headed toward a nearby clump of flowers. "Bees," she said over her shoulder.

Jon got to his feet and strolled over to watch. Michele stood quietly, waiting for a bee to buzz by. Then she deftly swooped it up into her net, and shook it into the collection jar. She held the bottle up to the light and squinted at the bee. "Mmm...," she said mostly to herself. "Not like any bee I ever saw." She turned to Jon, "*Mon Capitaine*, take a look for yourself. Have you ever seen such a bee?"

"I'm afraid I can't answer that, Michele. I never examined a bee that closely. It looks like a bee to me."

"Let's do the autopsy." Michele took a small vial from her pack and attached it to the lid of the jar. "It kills the bee," she said. "It's painless." But the bee kept on buzzing around the jar. "This cannot be," she said. "That gas will kill any living thing." She called Carmen and brought up a holoimage. "The bee is unusual," she told Carmen. "I have never seen one like it. It's sort of like a bee, but not really. It looks like one until you examine closely. I gas it to do an autopsy, but look, it's still buzzing around."

"Try to capture it and hold it with a tweezers," Carmen suggested. "Don't worry about getting stung, though."

Jon held the jar while Michele carefully removed the lid, and quickly placed her hand over the mouth. Then she puckered her hand slightly and blew into the jar. "To remove the gas," she commented. She reached between her fingers with a long tweezers. It took her several attempts, because the bee kept maneuvering to avoid them.

Finally, she managed to clamp it against the jar wall, and then got a grip with the tweezers. She lifted it out and held it up to the holo-cams. While she held it, Jon increased the magnification until they were looking at a human size image of the bee floating in the air before them. With her free hand, Michele carefully approached the bee's abdomen with a sharp micro scalpel. When she tried to slice the abdomen, nothing happened. It did not slice open.

"How peculiar," Carmen said. "Try severing its head."

Michele tried, but nothing happened. She turned to look at Jon. "It's not a bee, *mon Capitaine*, it's a machine!"

#

The news was coming so quickly now, that Rod hardly had time to massage it for public consumption. The world waited with baited breath for every new piece of information. When Rod received Ari's observation that the column arrangement was patterned on the Star of David – at least, it was a hexagonal arrangement like the Star of David – the impact on the world was immediate. Skinheads rioted in Cape Town, Berlin, Paris, and London. Muslims rioted wherever there were more than a few Muslims living in an area. Even in the Caliphate, protestors took to the streets, but to Rod, those demonstrations appeared more like managed shows than free-for-all riots.

Outside Area 51, a gaunt man with a flowing grey beard proclaimed the new millennium. He told a gathering crowd that the Jews and Christians had gotten it all wrong – the Muslims too, he added as an afterthought. God was the head of a master race of extraterrestrials, who rode in UFOs, and had appeared throughout the ages. Their current habitat was Iapetus, and humans were violating this sacred ground. He urged his listeners to "bring down the establishment," and create a "new order" that would bring an unprecedented era of peace on Earth. He claimed to speak for the extraterrestrials, who had given him the gift of prophecy when they abducted him for the third time two months ago. If the human race didn't heed his words, the extraterrestrials would bring destruction to Earth the like of which had not been seen since the days of ancient Israel.

Rod listened to this nonsense with a growing apprehension, because the fool's words were being broadcast around the world. Assembled crowds of UFO believers everywhere were beginning to react to his challenge. In every major world city except within the Caliphate, UFO enthusiasts became believers, and heeded the prophet's call. Once peaceful, colorful fools now turned to violence and anarchy. Tear down the establishment, the prophet had demanded, or suffer the consequences. Unlike traditional anarchists and Islamic rioters, however, the UFO believers did not know how to conduct effective violence. Tearing down the establishment was something they had never thought about before. Local leaders stood up to urge the crowds to attack government buildings, burn banks, or whatever seemed the most expedient thing of the moment, but when police in riot gear appeared with water cannon and rubber clubs, the UFO crowds faded into the side streets and disappeared from public view. Perhaps the prophet had gotten it all wrong. Hadn't the abductees always spoken of wondrous beings who were here to help, to save, to heal? What was this nonsense about tearing down the establishment?

As quickly as the prophet arose, he disappeared again. He was found on an Albuquerque skid row street, dead of an overdose of cocaine the following day. But the movement he started, continued to grow, not as a violent religion, but as a strange hybrid of mainstream Catholicism, Pentecostalism, and Buddhism, with a strong dose of the mid-twentieth century Raëlian Church.

Fundamentalist Christian leaders began to rant against this new religion as the precursor of the coming of the Antichrist, whom they equated with Maitreya, confusing that now defunct UFO based religion with this new phenomenon. The new religion's saints were a group of extraterrestrials called the Elohim.

Within days, slab-sided churches sprang up all over the civilized world, shrines to the Elohim, topped with the "Wormhole of David," a hexagram with the inner hexagon replaced with six spiral arcs to the center. Raëlism claimed that all life on Earth, humans included, was created scientifically by the Elohim, members of an advanced extraterrestrial race who appeared similar to small humans and so were often depicted as angels, cherubs, or gods in their earlier visits to our planet. Part of the teaching was that sex in all its ramifications was godly, and so the church grew dramatically as novitiates came to realize that in Raëlism, virtually anything sexual goes.

As Rod reviewed all that was happening, and composed compressed summaries to Jon and his crew, he couldn't but wonder at the similarity of the Raëlism Wormhole of David to the drawing he had received from Ari depicting the arrangement of the interior columns on Iapetus. Since the Wormhole of David originated back in the 1990s, the only thing he could come up with was that the similarity of symbols had generated the religious movement, and the old prophet was just an aberration.

#

Three days later, in a very public exhibition in Teheran, the newly self-appointed local Raëlian Church leader was beheaded on national holovision, and his head was placed on a spike in Government Square. A close examination of the spike revealed that the tip had been wrapped in the blue Raëlian flag with the Wormhole of David before it had been jammed into the martyr's head.

The only public comments came from the Israeli and American governments, and those comments were so weak as to be meaningless. The world over, both inside and outside the Caliphate, Muslims danced in the streets, demonstrating their solidarity against the heretical new religion.

Chapter twenty-four

Carmen took a great deal of private pleasure in having reasoned her way to the determination that the insects, and perhaps the birds as well, had to be artificial. From the moment she had stepped into the one-g field of the interior, her internal mechanisms had screamed that something was drastically wrong. Nature is a balance. What we see when we look at a meadow is only the tip of a masterful iceberg of complexity that lies just below the surface. For Carmen, from the outset, too many of the required components were missing. Where were the grazers? Where were the other elements of the required food chain? Where were the predators? It was like a garden under a glass dome or a tiny, perfectly adapted Japanese Bonsai. The only way it could exist was by continuous maintenance. Given the aliens' obvious engineering capabilities, she assumed that the maintenance was continuously accomplished with nanobots. There simply was no other solution. She had discussed the idea with Chen, who immediately agreed with her logic. He pointed out that in addition to the nanobots, there probably also would be microbots for pollination and similar tasks. Thus, when they received the excited call from Michele, they knew exactly what she would find.

While Michele was gathering more specimens, Carmen discussed her thought process with Jon. At first he was not entirely convinced that she could have arrived at a correct understanding with only her general observations since entering the interior, but as she argued her point, he came around. After asking her several pointed questions about how she got to her insight, he called a general holoconference. As the crew assembled in what appeared again to be a locally assembled group on a meadow, he addressed them.

First he explained what Michele and he had found about the "bee." Then he told them about how Carmen had arrived at the same conclusion well before the rest of them, including Michele. "This is not to put anybody down or to exalt anyone," he said. "We are inside a remote world, far from our natural home, and all of us, except Dr. Bhuta, have allowed ourselves to be lulled into taking what we see at face value. This can kill us, folks! We had a heads-up when we passed through the lock into the interior. But somehow, we didn't learn the lesson. We were lucky nobody was injured. What we know is that we are dealing with a vastly advanced civilization – or at least the leavings of that civilization. We have absolutely no idea whether what we see before us is benevolent or malevolent. We have far too little data even to begin to draw a conclusion.

"Part of me wants us back in our suits, but both Michele and the Doc assure me that the plants we see have been growing this way for a long time, so we are very unlikely to experience any drastic changes in pressure or atmospheric composition. The problem as I see it is that if anything happens, we will have no chance at all. We are here, and our suits are seven and a half clicks away. So, as unpopular as I know it will be, I am ordering each of you to return to Base Camp, and to don your suits. You can strap your helmets to the belt-carry position. Even a worst-case condition will allow you sufficient time to don your helmet.

Carmen was glad that the captain had decided on the side of safety. The rest of the crew groaned and complained good naturedly, but nobody raised an objection. It seemed to Carmen that most of her fellow crew members were embarrassed by their own lapses in judgment. She certainly was, but she was glad she had raised the issue. This was, after all, not a school outing.

#

"What do you think?" Dmitri asked, as he and Ginger trudged back toward Base Camp.

"I'm glad the captain made the decision for us. Apparently none of us saw the need."

Would I have made that decision? Dmitri asked himself. *How do you second-guess a man under circumstances like this?* Over the weeks and months since the voyage commenced, Dmitri found that his initial resentment that he had not been designated captain, had evaporated. Jon's competence was so obviously on the mark that he could only marvel at Jon's ability to keep ahead of virtually every situation that came along. Nothing in his broad experience as a Russian Air Force colonel had prepared him for the kind of split-second decisions Jon had been forced to make. He had reached the reluctant conclusion that had he been captain instead of Jon, they might not have reached their destination. Admitting this was painful, but Dmitri had never been one to side-step reality. Precisely because Jon had so frequently demonstrated why he was captain, Dmitri was more than willing to comply with Jon's latest order. He had to admit to himself that he was actually feeling a bit uneasy with all their suits located so far away.

With Ginger's long legs and his strong stride, they were the first back at Base Camp, and had donned their suits before the rest got there.

#

With the revelation that they were surrounded by tiny machines, Jon was on high internal alert. He had read Michael Crichton's *Prey*, as a teenager, and had actually been haunted by the idea that swarms of nanomachines could completely disrupt an ecology. That obviously didn't seem to be happening here, but the memories of his youthful dreams roiled to the surface and caused him to feel an unease that had not been present before their discovery. He and Michele arrived back at Base Camp as the last team, mostly because Michele kept stopping to investigate another "insect." All of them were microbots. She had not found a single zoological creature. All the plants were real plants, but they were being husbanded by machines.

Jon had to concede that whatever machines maintained the overall complex that was this living interior were the longest-lasting pieces of technology he had ever seen. Somehow, in his mind he was prepared to believe that the aliens could build such machines. He was not willing to concede, however, that little microbot bees, with wings buzzing at dozens of beats per second, could last a hundred-thousand years, let alone a million. It struck him that it would be far more efficient to build a manufacturing facility with the "eternal machines," as he was now referring to them in his thoughts, that could output the nanobots as required.

Jon was still totally bothered by the why of everything they were seeing. Fairly quickly, they were getting a handle on the what, at least in a superficial way, but the why completely escaped him. While he pondered this, Dmitri approached him.

"Jon, these little machines cannot be long-lasting. There is no benefit in technology that is too robust. I believe there is a manufacturing facility – no, many manufacturing facilities in order to produce all the nanobots it takes to keep this ecology going."

"I've been thinking the same thing, Dmitri. I think we've missed something. The bot factories just can't be that far apart." He waved over the rest of the crew.

"Spread around this column. Inspect it for anything other than a smooth surface – bumps, holes, depressions, cracks, anything at all. Spread out, but keep your channels open."

It took an hour and a half, but they found nothing that could be called an opening, nothing through which a microbot could emerge.

"Okay, guys, we're going to split into two teams. Dmitri, you have Ginger, Carmen, Chen, and Noel. The rest of you come with me. Of the six nearest columns, I'm going to take the column we did not visit, and Dmitri's team can recheck the column Ari and Saeed visited. Since our mobility is limited to our feet, I don't want to miss anything this time. Keep in touch; let's go."

Jon was deeply concerned about their mobility. Without one of the rovers, they were drastically limited in their ability to explore what they had discovered. As his team covered the ground between Base Camp and their destination, he pondered how they might accomplish the task. At first blush, the only reasonable way appeared to get the elevator into operation somehow, which seemed about as remote as anything he could think of.

When they arrived at the column, Jon had his team examine the surface closely. Michele made the first discovery. *"Mon Capitaine... come over here!"*

About a meter off the ground, she had found a round hole about the size of a drinking straw. "Watch..." she said. In about a minute a "bee" popped out of the hole, and flew off.

Once the rest of the team knew where to look, they found holes every couple of meters, eighty in all. While they were counting, Dmitri called to say that they had found about eighty holes around their column.

While they were comparing notes, Jon heard a loud clang, and went to investigate. He found Ari examining the pieces of a "bee" that he had smacked against the column with his shovel.

"They break," Ari remarked as Jon approached.

"Why did you do that?" Jon asked.

"To see if they break...and..." Ari's attention seemed to be wandering as he talked. Then he looked down as the next "bee" emerged from the hole, and smacked it too. Then he continued to look around. "There," he said, pointing to what looked like a hovering hummingbird. "What's that doing here? There isn't a nectar bearing plant within fifty meters. He stopped to smack the third "bee." Another hummingbird appeared, and then another. Suddenly, Ari swept his shovel through the air, catching two of the little bots, knocking them to the ground. One was not moving at all, but the second continued to flap one wing, although the other seemed broken. Ari picked it up, holding it to the holocams. He magnified it, and he and Jon examined it closely.

"I think those eyes are cameras," Ari observed. "You see the cause and effect, don't you?"

"Are you getting this, Dmitri?" Jon asked.

"We're duplicating it right now."

"Thoughts, people?" Jon said to his team and by holo to Dmitri's team. Jon waited patiently for his crew to wrap their minds around the newest discovery.

"I know what there isn't...what there cannot be," volunteered Noel.

"And that is..." Jon said when Noel didn't finish his thought.

"I was going to say, there's no alien somewhere over there," he pointed, "moving a remote controller to fly these bots around."

"And why not?" Elke asked. "Is that any more fantastic than what we've seen thus far?" Michele nodded, as did several others. "I'm not saying an alien is out there," Elke added. "I'm just saying Noel's comment is not particularly outlandish."

Another "hummingbird" flew up to observe the proceedings, hovering just above Jon's head. He batted at it, but it dodged his hand.

"We have nothing like this in China," Chen observed. "Our nanoengineers have done some pretty amazing things, but nothing like this."

The new bot flew toward Michele, and she batted at it like Jon had. It deftly avoided her swipe. "They are autonomous," she said. "No human...or alien...could respond that fast. It knows how to avoid active things." She surreptitiously set up to bat at it again, but it avoided her just as easily this time. "See what I mean?"

"Doc?" Jon nodded at Carmen's holoimage. "Anything to add?"

"Nothing that hasn't already been said."

"Ari?"

"Saeed thinks they may be divine, but he's coming around pretty quickly." Everyone chuckled, and Saeed blushed under his dark skin.

"That's a pretty sophisticated navigation program," Dmitri said, watching a bot avoid Ginger's quick swat.

"What makes you think it's a program?" Elke asked.

"Well...it has to be doesn't it?" Dmitri asked hesitantly. Ginger nodded.

"If you call the cellular instructions that drive a bee or a bird programming, then I suppose this is programming, but I don't see it that way. These are artificially manufactured things with metal – or whatever it is – bodies, and built-in intelligence at about the level of the creatures they have replaced."

"She's right, Jon," Ari said. "This is way beyond anything we have done in programming or even AI."

"So, we're generally agreed," Jon summed up, "that these are artificial, autonomous bots, not under anyone's direction..."

"I did not say THAT, *mon Capitaine*," Michele interrupted. "I said nobody was driving them. I don't have any evidence one way or the other about whether or not they are being controlled."

"I think we do," Carmen said softly, her eyes focused in the air behind Dmitri.

It was completely silent, and moved without any visible means of propulsion. Carmen spotted it at about a hundred meters altitude and maybe three hundred meters out, on an apparent glide path directly toward the group.

"Quickly," Dmitri ordered, "against the column...fast!"

His team pressed themselves against the column as the craft arrived in total silence, not even a hum or a whoosh of air. It stopped about three meters over the ground, and then settled down until it hovered about twenty centimeters above the surface. It looked like a bullet-shaped tube floating above the ground – about the size of a small bus. A human-sized double door slid open near the middle of the craft.

"Jon...?"

"Yeh, Dmitri, we've got one, too!"

Chapter twenty-five

With hindsight, Jon realized that the silent floaters, as they had come to call them, were not entirely unexpected. After all, his team had entered a world that seemed to be running under some kind of control, and had been doing so for a very long time. Presumably, during all that time, there had not been any incidents of systematic destruction of any of the microbots, until now. Any system would be compelled to investigate the problem. His team had already deduced that the aliens were humanoid – in startlingly familiar patterns. When the monitoring systems were faced with humanoids, it was not entirely unreasonable for the humanoids to be "invited" to meet the controllers.

To this point there had been no overt danger from whatever was running things. So far as Jon could tell, there appeared to be no hidden dangers – but if they were hidden, how would he know about them? The initial risk, he decided, should be his.

"Dmitri," Jon said on his open circuit. You and your crew stay put. Don't enter the craft. I'll disconnect my optical link, and enter this one alone. I'll signal you by radio when I'm inside, and if possible, keep in touch that way. If I lose coms, I'll signal you as soon as it lets me back out. At that point, we can decide what to do."

"Roger that."

Jon checked the helmet hanging from his waist, and then gingerly stepped into the open bay of the floater. It felt exactly like stepping onto a twenty-centimeter high platform. It was solid, and exhibited no sway or other indication that it had just received a significant additional mass. From inside, the floater walls were completely transparent. An aisle running the length of the vehicle separated two rows of twelve seats along the cabin walls. Jon checked around the bay door, but found no closing mechanism, so he took a seat near the door and waited for something to happen.

"Com check, Dmitri."

"Roger that."

"The seats are perfectly engineered for human shape," he told the others through the open door.

When nothing happened after several minutes, Jon stood up, and started to depart the floater. Three hummingbird bots quickly formed a winged barrier, as if to indicate that he should remain inside. He passed through them without incident, although they continued to fly around his head, seeming to urge him back into the floater. Then new sets of flying bots began to urge the other team members to enter the floater. Jon told them to disconnect their optical threads and enter. When they all were inside except Jon, all the bots began to urge him to reenter the floater. Jon motioned to Ari to exit, and then he reentered, himself.

"How's my transmission, Dmitri?"

"A bit attenuated."

Jon stepped back off the floater. "How about now?"

"Just fine."

Jon waved Ari back inside, and joined him. "Looks like my whole team is going," he said, as the door closed behind him.

#

"What's happening, Jon?" Dmitri dodged several hummingbird bots buzzing around his head, urging him toward the floater that was patiently hovering to his left several centimeters off the surface.

"The door is closed, but we're not going anywhere," Jon answered back. "I think they want all of us to board."

"I've got bots herding me toward the floater door. What are your orders?" Once again, Dmitri was glad he was not in command. *How do you make a decision like this? The teams are separated. The Rovers are on the surface five clicks overhead – no way to get them down here. We can't explore even a little portion of what we found on foot, and here's an opportunity to get to the source – maybe. But what if these floaters, or whoever is controlling them, turn out to be malevolent?* Dmitri was not sure how he would decide were he in charge, but had concluded that he was entirely willing to follow Jon.

"Board your team, Dmitri," Jon ordered. "I don't sense any danger, but keep alert. If we end up separated, I trust you implicitly to keep your people alive until we are reunited. And if not, then get them back safely!"

Despite the obvious logic of the Skipper's comments, Dmitri felt simultaneously humbled and honored by Jon's confidence in him. He waved his team members toward the floater.

Dmitri placed himself by the door, and watched Ginger step up and inside, stooping slightly to clear her head. Carmen kept an eye on Chen, boarding with him. Noel grinned at Dmitri, and stepped inside.

"Okay, Jon, we're all aboard, 'cept me, and I'm boarding now." As Dmitri stepped into the floater, his reception decreased slightly. He turned around, looking through the transparent bulkheads, somewhat surprised. "You didn't mention the transparent walls," he commented to Jon, as he took a seat, marveling at how well-proportioned the seats were to his shape and size. "Door just closed," he added. "We're moving – but no sensation of motion...just the visual clues through the walls."

"Same here," Jon reported.

Their progress over the ground was blurringly fast. Within a couple of minutes, Dmitri observed that their floater had neared Jon's, and that they seemed to be traveling a parallel course.

"You can see our floater, right?" Dmitri asked.

"Yep. Remarkable technology."

Carmen waved, smiling, and Noel stood and actually waved both hands, with an apologetic smile back at Dmitri. "Good to see them," Noel said to no one in general.

"They can't actually see us," Ginger commented as she waved.

Dmitri sighed inwardly, as he looked at Ginger's extraordinary blue-black skin, her long neck, and her regal facial features. It almost hurt knowing there was virtually no chance she would ever be his permanently. Dmitri had noted Jon's aloofness regarding apparent sexual liaisons with the other crew members. That, he thought, was another reason he was glad Jon was captain. His own Russian background was not quite caught up with the Eurowestern mores. He enjoyed the easygoing give and take with the crew members, but was not entirely comfortable with it. He considered himself a fast learner, however.

The craft flew together for another few minutes, and then visibly slowed, and entered the garage door of a column that carried no obvious distinguishing marks. The large door closed behind them as they settled to a hover just above a smooth, seamless deck. *For better or worse,* Dmitri told himself, *we're still captives.*

#

Saeed was in complete awe over what was happening. The floaters were a clear demonstration of Allah's presence here in this strange world. Even the little machines were, he knew with absolute conviction, totally beyond anything humans were capable of producing. He felt the presence of Allah all around him, and was simultaneously humbled by what he saw, and inspired to carry out His holy Jihad.

In due time, of course...right now he was functioning on his holy oath before Allah. Soon, however, Saeed was convinced, Allah would send him a clear sign, and release him to carry out his assigned mission.

#

"Everybody out," Jon ordered.

The two teams assembled in the brightly lit space that appeared identical to the elevator from which they had first entered this strange world, except that they still retained their normal Earth weight. Jon looked about, and immediately noticed that none of the little bots had followed them into the chamber.

"Don your helmets!" he ordered. "Quickly!" He snapped his helmet in place and observed as each crew member secured his helmet. Ari checked Saeed's, and gave Jon a thumbs-up.

"What was that about?" Ari asked on his private circuit.

"Look around," Jon said. "No bots. They knew not to fly into this chamber. We think we know what lies above our heads. I don't want to get caught eating vacuum." On the general circuit he said, "This is just a precaution. I don't think our hosts are malevolent – or should I say were malevolent when they put all this here. But they did this a very long time ago. This is all mechanical stuff, and I don't trust it. What's your take, Chen?"

"This is so far beyond what I know, that I don't trust my own instincts," Chen said. "But I agree with you. Let's err on the cautious side."

Nods inside helmets all around.

"Any ideas?" Jon asked, looking from crew member to crew member.

"See if we can find any doors out of here," Ari offered.

"That won't be necessary," Ginger said, pointing to the outline of an opening that had appeared in the wall over Jon's shoulder, in the same position as the lock in their elevator.

As everyone surged forward, Jon said, "I'll do the honors, like before." He turned to Noel. "Hook up an optical thread between my rig and Dmitri. Everyone keep Dmitri live on your individual circuits. We may have lost Earth for the time being, but we can still use a local network."

Jon activated the lock – it worked exactly like the earlier one. Laying optical thread as he entered, he closed the door, and guided by the internal illuminating glow, opened the second lock. This time there was no change of pressure, no change of gravity, in fact, no change at all. He entered a well-lit, broad circular chamber about ten meters across, and two meters high. Four consoles stood against the wall opposite the lock, fitted with human-sized seats, with a display panel above each console, and what Jon guessed was a keyboard-like input device built into the flat surface in front of each display. The consoles had markings that had to be some form of writing, but it was nothing like Jon had ever seen. He checked the air quality – it was fine, so he removed his helmet.

Taking a deep breath of air that tasted fresh and clean, Jon reviewed his options. Obviously someone or something had herded him – *no, all of us* – to this room. *But why here?* He looked around the chamber for any kind of opening, but there was only the entry lock. *This is a destination*, he concluded.

"Dmitri, you guys come on through the lock. Someone apparently wants to communicate with us," he said into his helmet.

\#

Elke had remained busy recording her personal observations, and organizing them into a minimal coherency that she intended to expand upon during their eventual return trip home. She was delighted that Jon had decided to have the entire group join him, and passed through the first lock eagerly.

When she and the others joined Jon, she removed her helmet and stood beside Noel, while turning her head to take in the entire chamber.

Jon addressed the small group. "We've been brought here – I think that's pretty clear. I keep getting the feeling that someone is guiding this, but my mind simply refuses to accept that explanation."

Elke was less certain than Jon, but she freely admitted that her scientific background, and thus her scientific intuition, was far less developed. For the time being she was willing to accept Jon's evaluation – subject to future modification, should the circumstances so indicate.

"That leaves us," Jon continued, "with some kind of prepositioned program or," he paused thoughtfully, "given all we have experienced thus far, some kind of autonomous mechanism that is able to do some pretty astonishing things." He pointed to the consoles. "Somehow... someway...we were brought here; of that I'm certain. Any ideas about all this?" He gestured at the consoles.

As the other eight explorers and their reluctant stow-away glanced at each other and the consoles, suddenly, without any warning, the four console-display panels flickered one-by-one, and settled into a soft silver glow.

\#

Rod Zakes sat at his desk processing the latest burst message that had arrived from Jon. He pondered Jon's last words: "Board your team, Dmitri. I don't sense any danger, but keep alert. If we end up separated, I trust you implicitly to keep your people alive until we are reunited. And if not, then get them back safely!"

The transmission ended abruptly, and since then, nothing. He sensed that the team was not in danger, since it was obvious they were preparing to enter the floaters, but on *Cassini II's* next pass, the update contained only static holoimages from their Base Camp outside the original elevator shaft. As the hours passed, the world began to sense a looming disaster. Rod issued explanatory news releases, and through the U.S. State Department, calmed the fears of the participating governments.

Candle lit prayer vigils appeared outside the European Space Agency in Paris and at NASA in Houston. Holovision talking heads began predicting the worst, and radical Muslim leaders outside the Caliphate urged their followers into the streets to demonstrate their faith in Allah's justice for taking action against the infidel intruders on Iapetus. Across the planet, Raëlian believers filled their slab-sided churches, listening with rapt attention as their leaders predicted a momentous event about to happen.

Rod watched the unfolding events with astonishment. How could this be, he thought, in a world where humans lived on the Moon and at the L-4 space station, where men have walked the surface of Mars, and were now exploring what simply had to be a derelict alien star craft? How could it be that the Islamic world still rejected the lessons of science, that Jews and Christians still clung to beliefs that contradicted modern science – and the Raëlians...how do you figure them with their weird mix of science, ufology, and myth?

Rod sighed and leaned back in his chair. "Talk to me, Jon Old Buddy...talk to me!"

Chapter twenty-six

Jon looked at Ari with questioning eyes. Ari knew an electronic console when he saw one, but what did Jon want him to do? It wasn't as if he had a clue. He glanced at Elke.

"What do you think?" he asked her. Since they were the two computer experts in the crew, it made sense to bring her into the discussion before it got started. "Any ideas on how to approach this?"

"I'd push a key to see what happens," Elke said. "I mean, what can go wrong?" She walked toward the left-most console. "These guys brought us here and turned them on, so, let's push buttons." She reached out before anyone could stop her and randomly hit a key.

Ari watched with amusement as the situation rapidly got out Jon's control, and his, for that matter. When Elke pushed the key, the display above the keyboard coalesced into a symbol inside a square. Then another square formed to the left alongside the first one, and then to Ari's utter astonishment, the Hebrew letter aleph, the first letter of the Hebrew alphabet appeared. He heard a gasp, and turned to see amazement cross Carmen's face.

"This is impossible!" Ari said. "They're equating that symbol with the Hebrew *aleph*. And look at the similarity between the symbols."

"Document this," Jon said.

"Already doing it," Elke answered, as she pushed a second key at random.

The two squares moved up a bit on the display, and a second pair appeared, the right containing another symbol, and the left containing *beth*, the second letter in the Hebrew alphabet.

"I'll be damned," Ari said, and walked to the second console, and pushed a key.

This time, two columns of squares appeared with symbols in the right column, and the Hebrew numbers from one to twelve in the left column. "Double damned!" he added as the columns appeared. "It's the Hebrew numbers." He traced the strange symbol for the number one with his right finger, and then traced the Hebrew number. "They have a *déjà vu*-like familiarity, almost as if I had known them long ago. This is about as weird as it gets..." His voice trailed off as the display in front of Elke filled right to left with columns containing the entire Hebrew alphabet with matching alien symbols.

"Elke," Ari said, knowing his voice was filled with wonder, "log these charts into your link, and set up an automatic translation into the English alphabet. It's obvious we're going to have a language lesson shortly, so follow that up with a growing lexicon."

Elke nodded her understanding and proceeded to set it up. "I'll put it on the general link. As soon as we have sufficient info, if you point your scanner at any text, you'll get the best English transliteration possible."

Ari grinned, wondering why he had given Elke any instructions. She really had been along for the ride until now. He glanced at Carmen, who smiled and said, "I will refine Elke's lexicon to give us the necessary language nuances...and..." she looked expectantly at Ari, "we may be needing your Hebrew language skills to make this work properly."

It is true, Ari thought, the Hebrew alphabet is no coincidence.

#

Their understanding of this language progressed rapidly. To Carmen's astonishment, the language seemed to bear a relationship to Hebrew similar to that between Latin and modern Italian. Ari supplied necessary pronunciation clues, so that by the end of the day,

Carmen and Ari were able to carry on simple dialog.

Everyone else relied on Elke's lexicon program, which she had modified to accept verbal input. To Carmen, however, the wonder lay in the language itself. Unlike the progression from Latin to Italian, this language was significantly more sophisticated than Hebrew. At every turn, the complexity they experienced grew exponentially. Within a few hours, Carmen and Ari could discuss complex technology in the new language, while the rest of the crew could quickly translate back and forth using their links.

At some point, Carmen found herself at the third console, rapidly increasing her vocabulary when the display shifted from what she thought of as the learning mode to a display filled with text. Although her fluency was still marginal, she found that the text utilized what she knew, and she could understand the material before her. For several hours, Carmen remained before the console deep in study. The strange world around her disappeared, replaced by Ectaris, the world that had nurtured the civilization of a people she had begun to think of as the Founders. She only looked up when Jon gently touched her shoulder.

"What has grabbed your attention so completely?" Jon asked her.

Carmen turned to look at Jon. "Gather everyone around," she said softly, her dark eyes glowing with moisture. "I have a story to tell you all."

#

Sunlight from their yellow dwarf star took ten minutes to reach their world, Ectaris, at 1.1 Earth masses, with an average density of 5.52. Land covered 35% of the surface, clumped into two significant masses in the temperate northern and southern hemispheres. A twenty-five degree axis tilt produced four distinct seasons during their 376-day year.

They were a great civilization, a thriving people. Ectaris was a teeming world, overflowing with advanced engineering, sophisticated technology, transportation marvels, inspirational art and music. They had survived 50,000 years of growth, war, disease, famine, and finally peace and prosperity. They were a space faring civilization, spread throughout their solar system. They had recently colonized the fourth planet, a rocky, dry twin of their own world, and were extracting raw materials for their ever expanding needs from the vast band of rocky material that circled their sun between the fourth planet and the giant gas ball that was next in line.

Their sun was a stable main-sequence variable G2V star. But it was older than Sol, with a slightly greater variability. The planet's inhabitants learned to accommodate the cyclical global climate changes brought about by this variability. Indeed, it became a significant factor in spurring the rise of their civilization. They learned, first as tribes, and later as a worldwide population, to plan for, and then to hunker down and survive the glaciations that were an inevitable part of their global climate pattern.

Far-seeing members of this interplanetary civilization began to cast an eye to the vast gulf between the stars, and to the worlds beyond. They began to make plans for an eventual journey, a casting off from their solar system into the unknown void. It seemed obvious to these forward-looking scientists that any future interstellar propulsion system would require a stable, nearly inexhaustible power source. In anticipation of this they undertook a vigorous research project into the properties of anti-matter and black holes. They discovered previously unknown relationships between the two, and eventually were able to create and control mini-black holes that produced anti-matter particles in a completely controlled fashion. They had their power source.

During this period, one group of scientists continued to look inward, toward their own star, and made a disquieting discovery. The variability of their G2V sun was increasing rapidly by astronomical measure. Their detailed models began to form a disturbing picture of the next several solar cycles. Over several years of intense investigation, these researchers determined that the variability of their sun would become destructive within 400 years. They checked and rechecked their figures, making certain they were not just dealing with an artifact of their models.

Finally, with near certainty, these scientists determined that 400 years hence Ectaris would become uninhabitable. They kept this knowledge close, revealing what they knew only to several colleagues who could corroborate their figures, and perhaps even approach the problem from a different angle. They and their colleagues continued to study the problem, examining it from every possible perspective.

Over the next year or so, it became increasingly clear that they were dealing with more than an increase in solar variability. They discovered fundamental changes in the composition of their star. They began to get hints that their star might be in the first stages of a movement off the main sequence. This dawning realization quickly matured into a new understanding.

The following week, the scientists announced to the entire solar system that in 400 years, plus or minus 40, the sun that had nurtured their civilization for 50,000 years of recorded history would nova.

Following the announcement there was system-wide shock and some initial panic. Then the proud people of this world and the solar system they had populated determined to take the long view: They had four centuries. They decided to focus and solve the problem.

When their sun went nova, it would destroy everything in its path: planets, moons, asteroids, and comets. The nova would leave behind only charred cinders where once proud worlds orbited. People, life, their products – all gone. There was no way to shelter their worlds from the coming nova. Its destructive power would be absolute. The only solution was to leave, go elsewhere, sufficiently distant to ensure their survival.

So these people chose to build a moving world – a very large starship – a self-contained *Arc* that would hold their entire population, and keep them alive for however long it would take to cross the interstellar abyss to another suitable solar system. Ectaris astronomers cast their collective vision outward, looking for a suitable destination. Ectaris physicists and engineers turned their efforts to developing a workable star-drive. Ectaris life-scientists focused on creating a self-contained ecosystem that would remain viable and sustain their population for the duration of the journey, no matter how long. This was a staggering project – to build a self-contained world, one sufficiently large to contain the entire population of a solar system teeming with people, sufficiently complex to create a living environment where they could grow their food, process their waste, and continue to live essentially normal lives, generation after generation after generation. The concept was almost beyond imagining – yet survival absolutely depended on it.

They had 400 years to make it happen.

Within decades, the astronomers had identified several possible destinations, deciphering the vanishingly faint indicators that told them about the destination sun and its surrounding planets. By the end of the first century, they had narrowed it down to several candidates, and finally to one fairly young main sequence variable G2V yellow dwarf. It lay 500 light years further out from the galactic center than their own sun. Its variability was somewhat less than their own star, but that was a good thing.

At about the same time, the Ectaris physicists who were working on the mini-black hole/anti-matter project identified previously undiscovered – although suspected – properties of matter that gave them the key to an interstellar propulsion system. The relativistic hyperdrive they called the hypervelocity or hyper-V drive was powered by a mini-black hole located at the center of the *Arc*. The drive itself consisted of a massive tube-like ring that contained circulating charged particles moving at nearly light-speed around the planetary-sized spherical starship. This loop acted on the fabric of the universe itself, stealing a small amount of momentum from the expanding space-time continuum. Relative to the universe, the energy they took was infinitesimal, but for the starship, it was sufficient to propel it and everything it contained to a respectable percentage of light-speed. Since the hyper-V drive was non-reactive, it acted upon everything within its field – every molecule, every atom was uniformly accelerated. An unexpected byproduct of the drive was a completely controllable artificial gravity system that the engineers perfected by the one-and-a-half-century mark.

By this time, the *Arc* as a whole was coming into its own. The space-faring elements of Ectaris had earlier located a nearly spherical solid-rock asteroid some 1,500 kilometers in diameter that they moved into orbit around Ectaris. For nearly a half-century, engineers and technicians of all flavors had worked ceaselessly, transforming the solid rock into habitable space.

A specialized team of engineers drilled 750 kilometers down to the core of the asteroid, where they vaporized several cubic kilometers of rock using thermonuclear explosives combined with the controlled release of anti-matter. With infinite care, using specially designed robots, they installed a mini-black hole and the equipment that would sustain it. An integral part of the installation was a self-replicating system that would monitor, repair, and sustain this critical power source indefinitely into the future.

Five kilometers below the rocky surface, robots removed over thirteen million cubic kilometers of rock to create a layer of living space supported by massive columns. This task alone required over 500,000 machines, each vaporizing 10,000 cubic meters of rock every day for over seventy-five years. Just below the surface other machines created vast hexagon-shaped hollowed-out spaces that housed machinery, equipment, and stores that would be required over the centuries of travel that lay ahead. Scattered over the surface, another gang of robots sank fifty-meter wide shafts at several of the hexagon triple-junctions to access the hollowed-out living space five kilometers below. Other robot teams constructed the hyper-V drive ring that towered nearly twenty kilometers above the rocky surface and passed completely around the *Arc*. Seen from sufficiently far away, the vast hexagons seemed to abut one another, so that the *Arc* began to look like a gigantic walnut-shaped Bucky-ball with the hyper-V ring defining the junction of the walnut-halves.

For three hundred years the teeming peoples of Ectaris had one consuming focus – complete the *Arc* before their sun went nova. The next fifty years saw the entire population of Ectaris, their moon, the fourth planet Dameter, the populated asteroids, and virtually every living soul, transfer their lives into the *Arc*. They brought aboard the broad spectrum of animal species that populated their worlds, the plants and all the other countless living things, large and small.

The billions settled in, and began to make the *Arc* their home – for that is what it would be for the rest of their lives, and those of the following generations for 500 years as their vast starship traveled outward toward the galactic rim at nearly three-quarter light-speed.

Now, fast-forward to a more recent time in our own solar system, but still long, long ago – about 150,000 years.

From out of interstellar space a strange craft appeared. It was large, huge by any normal standard – planetary in size, some 1,448 kilometers in diameter. It found at least one planet in this solar system that could easily support life, a planet uninhabited by intelligent beings, although there was plenty of evidence for a thriving biosphere.

The star folk parked their spacecraft in a safe orbit around the beautiful gas giant with distinctive rings, and sent exploratory teams to the new world. The new world was teeming with plant and animal life. Its underlying DNA, while dissimilar to their own, was not entirely incompatible. They discovered that some plants were edible, although they lacked critical trace nutrients and certain protein chains. The abundant game was edible as well, but difficult to assimilate – yet, they had taken 300 years to build their ship, and five hundred years to cross the gulf between the stars. They could be patient while their scientists modified the new world's biology at the molecular level. For the next several weeks star folk biologists created large batches of a virus-like molecule that they shipped to the new world, where high-altitude, high-speed aircraft sprayed the substance over virtually every square centimeter of the planet.

Life on the *Arc* went on while the molecule entered Earth's ecosystem, found its way into the cell nuclei of countless eukaryotes and into the protoplasm of an even larger number of bacteria and archaea. Slowly, year-by-year, decade-by-decade, the molecule attached itself to the DNA structure of every organism it encountered, modifying each so that it was virtually completely compatible with the star folk DNA. It took several star-folk generations for the modifications to spread throughout the native plant and animal populations, and throughout the bacteria and archaea domains, to complete the transformation. The star folk were a patient people – for the most part; but the journey from Ectaris was behind them, and many became impatient to settle their new home, to leave the *Arc*. And so, over a period of years following the initial molecular spraying, the star folk slowly left the only home they had ever known, and spread across the new world. Eventually, virtually the entire population of the starship had left for Earth. In an astonishingly short time, the star folk – the new Earthmen – spread across the entire planet, establishing cities connected by highways, airports, sea ways, and vast lines of communication. They dug in and turned to with a vigor that spoke volumes about their determination to make the best of their new home. And it became home in every sense. A new generation was born that only knew of the mighty starship from stories told by their parents, and from books and recordings available to them.

The star folk biologists had intended for Earth's ecosystem transformation to be fully completed before the star folk settled planetside. When they realized that early settlement was inevitable, they yielded, and joined the planetside migration, but what they didn't know – what nobody knew – was that the incomplete transformation had developed a problem. It was something deep inside the modified DNA structure that completely escaped the biologists' notice, something that lingered, replicated itself, and began to spread throughout Earth's population, both old and new.

Science had not stopped during the centuries of travel from the Ectaris system and the decades since they had arrived at Saturn. By the time the starship arrived at Saturn, Ectaris physicists had refined both the hyper-V drive and its black-hole power source so that they could be installed in a very much smaller craft that was capable of rapidly accelerating to speeds approaching light-speed itself. This made it possible, at least in principle, for a crew to return to Ectaris to investigate personally the aftermath of the nova.

After several decades of development, the hyper-V ship took an unexpected shape – looking somewhat like the popular flying disks their children used for play. As with the *Arc*, the smaller ship's rim contained a circulating ring of charged particles moving at nearly light-speed. Unlike the *Arc*, which maxed out at about 78% of light speed, this hyper-V drive could propel itself and everything it contained almost instantly to near light-speed – or to any slower velocity, right down to the pace of a couple strolling in the park.

Eventually, the *Arc* was nearly empty of people. Only, fourteen family members remained, linked by blood and intense scientific curiosity. They intended to go home – to whatever remained of their place of origin. They knew they would forever lose touch with their friends on Earth as the laws of relativity inexorably separated their timelines. Nevertheless, they hoped to maintain contact with successive generations back on Earth, so that when they returned at a far future date, the descendants of Earth's new inhabitants would be waiting for them – anticipating their arrival. Their race had already proved that it could take the long view. This was just a continuation.

These fourteen star folk visited Earth several times, but never stayed for very long, certainly not long enough to assimilate the spontaneously modified DNA that was, by then, working its insidious way throughout Earth's new inhabitants.

A final stop in orbit around Earth, a final trip to the surface, a final farewell to friends and colleagues they would never see again – and the small band of star farers departed for the *Arc*, and their eventual journey home.

#

As Carmen finished her tale, the crew members lounged around in contemplative silence. "You realize the implications?" Jon asked to no one in particular. He consulted his link and then added, "If their craft can reach a Lorentz Factor of twenty-two-thousand – for you non-physics types, that's ninety-nine-point-nine followed by six nines percent of light-speed – then a half-million years for Earth would last only some eleven years and change for the Founders. That means..." he paused to look at each crew member in turn, "that we have a measurable probability of meeting these guys." He let his words hang...

"What are the odds?" Ginger asked to nobody in particular. "To have the timelines intersect at this particular point, it has to be astronomical...virtually zero."

"Not necessarily," Chen immediately interjected. "Look at it this way: If I were part of that crew, I guess I would want to know what was happening back here..." His voice trailed off. "But how do you do that? Their hyper-vee propulsion involves physical translation... limited to..."

Ari piped in, "Even if they were to arrange a rendezvous with a robot craft, at best they still can only know the status quo for time in years past equal to twice the distance traveled in light years." He scratched his head contemplatively. "No way, Chen...you simply can't get that information."

"That's right," Dmitri said. "If you want to know, you go."

"You decide now that you want to know," Noel added, "and if you are a thousand light years distant, you'll find out what is happening about a thousand years from now."

"So, unless they developed superluminal communication, which Carmen didn't mention in her tale," Ginger said in turn, "it's the luck of the draw."

"So, if we meet them," Jon said, "we are very, very lucky." He paused. "What an amazing thing that would be."

"Wait," Chen said. "We're missing a significant point." He paused, in thought. "Say the Founders return from Ectaris – about a thousand years plus whatever time they spent there – and decide not to hang around, but to hop in and out of Earth history. How difficult would it be to go out and back, say for an Earth interval of ten-thousand years...?" He consulted his link. "Using Jon's Lorentz Factor, they would be gone for about a hundred-sixty-three days ship time." Chen's Asian eyes started twinkling as he got into his subject. "Say one thing leads to another, and they arrive here about nineteen-seventy or so. Obviously, there's nothing happening, but they detect insipient space travel. So, what do they do? How about, they go out and back ten light years...that's about a half-hour using Jon's Lorentz Factor. It's nineteen-eighty...and nothing's happening yet. So they keep doing this, and in just a few hours ship time we're building El-four. And then...we're here." He looked around the group. "Jon, isn't that what you would do? So long as they don't overshoot, they can fine tune their hops to get here right about now."

#

Saeed listened to the back-and-forth banter, barely compre-hending. He still was trying to assimilate star faring folk who spoke an advanced form of Hebrew. Nothing in the *Qur'an* even remotely hinted at something like this.

Allah most merciful, he prayed silently, help me understand. Guide me to my destiny. Keep me on Your holy path. Keep Jihad alive in my heart. Send me a sign that releases me from my oath to the Captain. Show me a way to carry out Your plan for this evil place.

And then it struck him like a bolt of lightning. He was here, right now, under oath, restrained from taking action so that he would be present and ready to act after the Founders arrived – at the exact moment of Allah's choosing. It was an astonishing revelation. Saeed took a deep breath, and letting it out slowly, relaxed.

#

Ari watched Saeed surreptitiously as the crew members dis-cussed Carmen's story. He saw the worry that emanated from Saeed's entire being, and tensed himself to take action, should it become necessary. Then, as the little stowaway slowly exhaled, Ari upped his alert scale. He had seen this same thing too many times in the past to let it simply go unnoticed. Saeed, he decided, was getting ready to continue his Jihad.

First Interlude

In the *Arc* Command Center, Eber relaxed in a well-padded chair fixed to the deck with his back to a control console. Gathered around him was the rest of his team. His father, Shem, was stocky with swarthy, weathered skin, nearly black eyes, and curly dark hair, and appeared to be in his early fifties. His mother, Persia, was at least a decade younger than Shem, slight of build with high cheek bones and delicate facial features framed by a mane of long, glossy black hair. Her eyes were a deep dark brown. His grandfather, Noah, had close-cropped white hair, and his piercing blue eyes and wrinkled face gave witness to his seventy-five well lived years. His grandmother, Vesta, an accomplished surgeon, looked impossibly young for her sixty-eight years. Her classical face was without wrinkles, although her golden hair showed a few streaks of gray. Her svelte body appeared to carry virtually no excess fat. Her hazel eyes flashed flecks of green when she smiled and when she was angry. Three of Eber's four brothers, Asshur, Aram, and Arpachshad, were like peas in a pod. Born in quick succession several years after Eber, they mirrored their father, and were often mistaken for each other. His youngest brother, Lud, had inherited some of his mother's and grandmother's features. He was slight of build, with lighter hair, and had his grandfather's blue eyes. Like his grandmother, he was a skilled physician.

The five brothers had chosen their wives well. Eber's wife, Azurad, was a beauty among beauties. It is said that sons often marry younger versions of their mothers, and Azurad was a younger Persia in nearly every respect. Side-by-side, they looked like sisters, although Azurad's youth was apparent upon closer examination, which was a constant annoyance to Persia. Azurad followed in Vesta's footsteps to become a physician, but her focus was more toward research. Asshur's wife, Ishtar, came from a radically different family line. She was taller than Asshur by a head, her skin was almost transparently pale, her long golden tresses, that reached her waist when she let her hair down, framed deep green eyes and an oval face that would have graced the covers of magazines under different circumstances. To Asshur's great satisfaction, she absolutely doted on him. Sari, wife to Aram, was the smallest of the women, barely reaching to Ishtar's bosom. She, too, had very pale skin, but her hair was jet black like her mother-in-law's, and her eyes looked like dark coals set into her transparent skin. She displayed high cheekbones like the others, except for Ishtar. Aram could nearly wrap his hands around her waist, it was so tiny. Like Ishtar, Arpachshad's wife, Rasu'eja, stood taller than her mate, but she looked like an athletic version of Azurad. Her skin had a deep copper-bronze tone, her muscles were lithe and firm, and her compact breasts sat high on her torso. It was said that in combat she could best any two normal men, but none of Eber's crew had ever issued a challenge. Finally, Lud's wife, Shakbah, was fair haired like Ishtar, but wore her golden tresses piled high atop her crown, was of average height, had the classic facial structure of the other women, and viewed the world through large, round, nearly purple, dark blue eyes.

"So we're of a mind?" Eber asked, letting his gaze pass over each of the thirteen people arrayed before him. He had assumed leadership of the group during the previous year while the final elements of the space-born population transferred planetside. His father could easily have continued as head of the clan, but Eber's technical understanding of the new hyper-V system far surpassed Shem's, and Shem had expressed an increasing desire to settle planetside with Persia.

"I know you've all heard it, but I'm going to say it again." Eber addressed the group, but his eyes shifted between his grandfather and grandmother. "Once we clear the immediate vicinity of the *Arc* and the ringed planet, we'll activate the hyper-vee function. In a fraction of a second, we'll accelerate to within a hair of light-speed. About eight days and three hours later by our subjective time we'll arrive in the Ectaris system, having transited the five-hundred light year distance that the *Arc* took four-hundred years subjective time to cross." He smiled at his grandparents and then winked at his father. "Five-hundred years will have passed back here."

"I'm still processing all that," Vesta said, patting her husband's hand. "Our ancestors left Ectaris some four-hundred years ago *Arc* time, and that entire five-hundred light year trip actually took six-hundred-forty years for an outside observer. Does this mean they stripped off two-hundred-forty years?" She sighed. "Now it takes just over a week." Noah squeezed her hand while Eber nodded and grinned broadly.

"Perhaps a better way to look at it," Eber said, "is that if they had sent a radio signal to Earth when they left, the *Arc* would have arrived one-hundred-forty years after the radio signal, but the *Arc* would have aged only four-hundred years. Is that any clearer?"

"Right...clear as mud!"

"They left sixteen generations ago," Noah said. "Well, for you and me," he smiled at Vesta, "we better call it fourteen." A general chuckle passed around the group.

Once an engineer, always an engineer, Eber said soundlessly as he collected his thoughts. "One last time," he said, "and then I'll let it go." He leaned forward in his chair. "When we return, over one-thousand years will have passed. We can say with certainty that everyone we know will be gone, irretrievably, forever lost to time. Each passing minute under hyper-vee is a piece of time that cannot be recalled. We stay together, or we drift apart in time." He looked at Ishtar. "If you remain planetside while Asshur makes this trip, you'll be a shadow from forty generations past when he returns, not the beautiful, statuesque goddess you are now." He paused briefly. "You will live the rest of your life without Asshur."

Ishtar's deep green eyes grew big and round, and she looked lovingly at her man. "I guess that puts things into perspective," Asshur said, just before Ishtar leaned over him with a kiss.

"Okay, then. We're going to see what the nova did to Ectaris."

#

Over the next several hours, Eber and his crew scanned the monitors that oversaw the many population centers that dotted the *Arc's* interior. Throughout the artificial world loudspeakers broadcast a repeating message, warning any left-behind-residents, that they had one last chance to be transported planetside. When there was no response after five hours, Eber concluded that if there were any left-behinds, they didn't want to be discovered.

The fourteen clan members spent most of their remaining time working from the operations control center shutting down non-essential systems or putting them into long-term stand-by. Shem put the climate control systems into hibernation, so that they would keep the *Arc* ecology running, but at a vastly slowed rate. He could see no reason to consume resources unnecessarily during their thousand-year absence.

By day's end, the *Arc* interior had assumed a hushed stance that seemed eerily out-of-place to the fourteen for whom the *Arc* interior was the only world they had ever known. Eber stood on the meadow outside the control complex, and watched the light fade for the last time. As darkness fell, he felt an overwhelming melancholy that threatened to bring him to tears. The upper reaches of the massive columns that held up the sky were the last things to disappear, and then darkness surrounded him. It felt thick, like viscous silicon, and Eber shook his head to rid himself of the sensation.

Eber requested formal reports from each clan member, and recorded the session for posterity. Part of him thought this moment could be pivotal, and he wanted it on the record. Several minutes later, the entire crew assembled at the launch column. With the floaters now inactive, they moved on foot across the intervening distance – individual light globes accompanied them, bathing them with soft radiance.

With everyone present, with all fourteen clan members standing easily near the massive column, Eber fingered a small instrument on his wrist. The outline of a large rectangular opening appeared on the column's surface, and then the entire curved rectangle backed into the column several centimeters, and slid upwards into the cylinder wall. As the opening grew, the interior, which had been dark when the opening first began to retract, gradually lighted until it was brilliantly illuminated. A circular object occupied about half the floor of the fifty-meter-wide column interior. It appeared to be like two flattened hemispheres pressed together, balanced on five appendages that extended from the bottom half. It was black, but not in the ordinary sense. It was black, because it absorbed every photon that struck it. It almost looked like a shaped hole in the air, a mirror of the mini-black hole at its core, instead of an object sitting on the deck.

Azurad gasped at the sight. She had been deeply involved in wrapping up her current research project, and simply had not taken the time to examine the craft her husband and his brothers had constructed. "What do you call her?" she asked to no one in particular.

A look of astonishment crossed Eber's face. "Call her?" he said. "I guess we never got around to that." Eber looked at the faces around him. "How about..."

"You built it — we get to name it," Vesta interjected, indicating herself and the other women. "How about it, girls?"

They went into a huddle.

Eber watched the women with patronizing amusement as they discussed the various possibilities, knowing full well that their combined education and abilities actually exceeded the men's. Following a surprisingly short time, Vesta looked up and announced, "This hyper-vee spacecraft is nothing short of a chariot of fire, and so we christen her *Merkavah*."

"*Merkavah* it is," Eber said with a grin, wondering inside how he could have missed something so important as the ship's name.

The other men nodded their approval, and that was that.

Eber fingered his controller again, and a portion of the top section slid back, revealing a lighted interior that contrasted sharply with the door outline. A ramp extended from the opening toward the group. Eber gestured to Vesta and Noah, who walked up the ramp together, followed by the others in no particular order.

The ramp led into a control chamber that was clearly set up for dual controls — two places with clear access to duplicate sets of controls and screen-like devices that served as monitors for the various external sensors. At that moment they showed the illuminated interior of the column absent the craft, as if it were not sitting on the floor. Another, smaller display showed the immediate surrounds outside the column. The fourteen people took their assigned places; Eber took the left control chair, and Asshur took the other. Because the hyper-V system acted on every molecule within its field, there was no need for anyone to strap down, or in any other way to take any particular precaution.

Eber checked his personnel monitor; it indicated fourteen souls. He nodded at Asshur who touched a panel display, and the view shifted, showing a bird's-eye view of *Merkavah* inside the cylinder. The ramp was retracting and the cylinder door was closing.

"We've got a green board," Asshur announced. Eber nodded at him again, and he commenced evacuating the cylinder.

To facilitate rapid evacuation, large storage chambers had been constructed in the overhead substrate alongside the cylinder. They were maintained in an evacuated state, so that the air in the cylinder could be dumped into the chambers, making rapid evacuation of the remaining air possible. The whole process took about five minutes. Five kilometers overhead, a cover slid aside, exposing the cylinder interior to the hard vacuum of space. The remaining air puffed out in a crystalline cloud, and settled to the surface. Inside *Merkavah*, Eber activated his controls, and the craft lifted, and commenced an accelerating rise up the cylinder. From inside, the only indications that they were moving were the shifting images on the monitors. *Merkavah* shot out of the cylinder so fast, that had there been anyone present to observe the exiting spacecraft, that person would have seen nothing at all. Eber set the controls to move the craft at right angles to the plane of the ecliptic, so that it rapidly rose out and away from the immediate gravitational influence of the nearby ringed planet.

Eber had practiced this maneuver dozens of times in the simulator, but this was the first time he had done it for real. Their calculations had indicated that shifting the hyper-V system into near light-speed too close to a significant planetary or stellar mass produced unpredictable results, and could even damage the craft. Since the quickest way to reduce the overall gravity field was to climb vertically out of the ecliptic, Eber had written this maneuver into the still developing standard operating procedures for system craft. There actually was an ideal vector that was optimal for each specific launch circumstance in any solar system, but the dynamics for working this out were so complex, that it was easier simply to power out of the ecliptic at the highest safe velocity until the instruments indicated that it was safe to shift to near light-speed.

The process of setting the spacecraft course as it accelerated to its terminal velocity was simplicity itself. The astrogation sector of the onboard Resident Computer maintained the craft's position with respect to the G2V yellow dwarf that dominated this solar system. It knew the relative position of the destination star, and backed up this knowledge with an optical sight that linked into the computer guidance sector. When it determined that the parameters for safe acceleration had been reached, it locked in the appropriate vector and simultaneously activated the hyper-V system. Within a fraction of a second, *Merkavah* and its occupants were moving at 99.9 followed by six nines percent of light-speed. The Resident set the course to bring the craft high above the ecliptic in the Ectaris system. At pre-programmed intervals throughout the flight, the Resident dropped the craft's speed to near zero for several moments to determine the presence of any nearby large masses, following which it modified the course to give any such masses a wide berth. Dust, particles, and gas that lay in the craft's path were swept away by the hyper-V field like floating objects in the path of a fast moving ship are swept aside by the ship's bow-wake.

Eber turned to his passengers – his family. "Okay, folks, you've got eight days and four hours to do whatever you planned to do during this trip. We're going to exit hyper-vee at the minus-one-hour-point long enough to establish an ideal final vector, and then we'll power down to the ecliptic as close as possible to Ectaris." He yawned and stretched. "I'm taking a short nap." He shut his eyes, and shortly was snoring softly.

#

Upon awaking sometime later, Eber spent most of his time at the console taking in whatever visual details of the trip the Resident was able to supply. Although he attempted to determine the exact moments of the brief stops, it turned out to be impossible, since there simply were no physical cues. He contented himself with learning as much as possible about the inner workings of his starship, his chariot of fire, his *Merkavah* – yes...he liked that name.

Eber's thought process returned several times to the time shift they would experience upon their return to Earth, and as he thought more on this, he began to develop a plan for the future. Since they would obviously have nothing in common with the star-folk descendants when they returned, why not spend the rest of their lives exploring the vast universe in which they lived? The *Arc* was built to last virtually forever, so they could always return from time to time, look in on the far distant star-folk descendants, perhaps even grab some of their advanced technology, and then take off again for parts unknown. They could stay together as a family and watch their race become whatever intelligent, advance-technology races become.

Eber shared his thoughts with Asshur, and during the following days they discussed the ramifications. From time to time, one or the other of the rest joined their conversations, but for the most part, it was Eber and Asshur who plotted the future together.

As the third hour of day nine passed, a soft chime awakened Eber from his nap in the console chair. He checked the time and turned as Asshur sat down in the chair beside him. "Hey...ready to do this?"

Together, they studied the display before them. It showed their sun, with twelve rings indicating the planetary paths for its twelve planets, four rocky planets and eight gas giants. A glowing dot on each ring indicated the Resident's best estimate of each planet's position. Because they had no actual starting position for the elements in the equation, and because of the individual motion of every element in the whole dynamic system, there was no practical way to determine each planet's actual position. The Resident would bring them to the ideal location above the ecliptic to power down to their home world, Ectaris, based upon its best estimate of the individual elements. The stop at minus one hour served to refine the estimate, and to give the humans the possibility to override the decision.

"Looks good to me," Asshur said, after checking several numbers on a monitor between them.

"I agree," Eber said, and gave the Resident permission to proceed.

There was no perceptible difference inside the spacecraft, but the display before Eber and Asshur began to shift noticeably. Eber adjusted the display to show their calculated position from near the ecliptic and normal to their plane of approach. The rest of the crew had gathered behind them to observe the approach.

"Oh, look, there's Ectaris," Ishtar said, tossing her waist-length golden tresses as she placed her hands on Asshur's shoulders and squeezed gently.

"Actually," Asshur said back, "we don't know it's there. That's just the Resident's best guess. We're still about a light-year out, with no way to receive real-time information."

"I knew that," Ishtar retorted, with a bit of a pout. Sarai giggled and squeezed her hand, looking up at the golden goddess towering above her.

"I thought the same thing," she said. "It's hard to believe we're already here."

Vesta concurred, and everyone nodded. "The whole thing seems bizarre," she said. "To have come so far so fast..." Her voice trailed off as the Resident updated the display to reflect its latest estimates, and each of the planets jumped to a new location. Ectaris now lay on the other side of the sun from its earlier position.

Eber glanced at the number display to his right. "These positions are about ninety-six percent accurate," he said.

Merkavah came out of hyper-V at the minus one minute mark, hovering about three light hours above the Resident's best calculated position for Ectaris.

#

"Let's see what's really out there," Eber said, adjusting a couple of controls.

The screen before them filled with a ruined landscape, seen from directly above, barren and lifeless. Barren hardly described it. The surface was scoured rock, not smooth like a ball, but smoothly rounded, with no sharp protrusions, gently sloping granite hills, but no mountains.

"What's that?" Azurad asked, pointing to a craggy break in the surface.

"Looks like a big crack to me," Asshur said, adjusting the controls to zoom in to the feature. "Deep, too," he added as the image filled the screen.

"Over there...look!" Ishtar leaned over Asshur, pointing at a glowing feature at the far edge of the screen. "That looks like magma outpouring, don't you think?"

"At least a million arouras," Eber said, referring to a surface measure of one-hundred cubits square, roughly the equivalent of three-quarters of a football or soccer field, where a cubit is about two-thirds of a meter.

"There's no softening of the limb," Aram pointed out, slipping his arm around Sarai. "Atmosphere's gone..." His voice trailed off. "It's dead, it's really dead...there's nothing left."

The small group watched solemnly as Eber brought their craft closer to Ectaris with short, high-speed jumps, until he instructed the Resident to put them into a polar orbit at an altitude of about a hundred kilometers. He queried, and the Resident informed the group that Ectaris' rotation was virtually unchanged. As the ruined planet turned below them, they could see no sign of the two great continental landmasses or the vast ocean basins that had surrounded them. They saw nothing but raw rock, low hills, huge cracks, and fields of molten lava.

They scanned the radio frequency spectrum, but heard nothing except background static. Asshur instructed the Resident to record the planet's surface. "For the folks back home," he told the others.

#

Several hours later they had collected everything they needed. The gloom that permeated the fourteen travelers was palpable. Vesta could not shake off the sense of foreboding she had felt ever since they established orbit around Ectaris. She approached Eber and slipped her arm around his waist, giving him a gentle squeeze. "Grandson mine," she said, "do you think Dameter fared any better?"

"It's over three times the distance," he told her. "It's possible."

The others had turned toward Vesta and Eber as they talked. "We've come this far," Shem said. "Might as well check it out."

"It was colonized, wasn't it?" Rasu'eja said, looking around at the others.

Lud nodded. The colonization of the fourth planet, Dameter, had been a research project of his in college. He knew more about

Dameter than anyone else in the group – at least as it was before the nova. While Eber set up the transit to Dameter, Lud told the others about the first few years after the initial landing.

"There were two schools of thought," he told them. "One group wanted to set up a base on the moon, and use that as a launch point for Dameter and points beyond. The others advocated a direct Ectaris-to-Dameter mission, and that is what they eventually did. After several exploratory unmanned missions, they launched the first of five missions designed to set up an automated base station that would form the nucleus of the first human exploration. These were followed by a team of eight explorers who spent the next three years establishing their presence on Dameter."

Lud went on to describe the development of a human presence on Dameter. It had a breathable atmosphere, although it was much colder and more arid than Ectaris. Nevertheless, within ten years several thousand people called Dameter their home, and by the time of the exodus, Dameter boasted a population of several million. Even the broad asteroid belt beyond Dameter was being actively mined for raw materials, Lud told them, and several human settlements were thriving among the asteroids.

As Lud was winding up his tale, Eber announced that they were approaching Dameter. "It's kind of hard to get used to," he told them with a grin, "high-speed interplanetary passage." He instructed the Resident to put them in another polar orbit. "I could get used to this."

#

Dameter from space was just beginning to show signs of human presence when they had to leave. It had no oceans and was mostly barren. Now, however, it was indistinguishable from Ectaris. It displayed bare rock scoured clean of every bit of topsoil, mountain ranges gone, lots of tectonic activity, and no atmosphere.

Eber trained his sensors outward toward the asteroid belt, but found nothing. The expanding nova apparently had vaporized all but the largest asteroids. The Resident estimated that it would take several weeks of intense searching to find even one of those, if they could be found at all with the equipment *Merkavah* had onboard.

After several hours of recording Dameter's surface, Shakbah expressed what was on everybody's mind: "Let's pack it up and go home!

Chapter twenty-seven

The education process did not stop with Carmen's story. Every time a crew member sat before one of the screens it would ask several questions that seemed designed to identify the individual at the console, and to determine that person's expertise. Within a short period, the system began to feed skill-specific information to each of the nine crew members whom the system recognized the moment each sat before the console. Jon believed the system was using visual images from a hidden camera, but no one had been able to find the lenses.

As the day progressed, Jon became increasingly concerned that they had not been able to communicate with Houston. He beckoned Dmitri to the side. "I want you to take your team back to Base Camp and bring Houston up-to-date."

"Sure, but how do we do that? I don't think we have any idea in what direction or how far Base Camp is. It could be a problem, no?" Dmitri grinned at Jon.

Ari joined them, and Jon told him his plans. "I have an idea," Ari said. He stepped to the nearest console, currently occupied by Chen, and asked him to give up his place for a bit. Ari sat down and entered some words.

Jon and Dmitri scanned them with their links: "How do we operate the floaters – the floating transportation cars?"

The screen filled with characters and what appeared to be a short list. Ari translated. It was a set of instructions that would enable use of the floaters by all the crew members, using simple voice commands. The system was set up to use what they now called Founder-Speak, and although it might have been possible to convert it to English, Jon thought it better not to interfere with such a fundamental operation. Each crew member had a working link translator that was capable of translating an English order into Founder-Speak, and then to speak the order.

Dmitri got his people ready to depart. "Wear your suits," he told them, "but carry your helmets." He looked at Ginger, who was still sitting at one of the consoles. "Are you joining us, Girl?" he asked, grinning at her.

"I'll be right out – just need to finish this."

Jon joined them as they passed through the locks into the still brilliantly lit main shaft chamber where the floater waited patiently. "If you are able," Jon told Dmitri, "lay optical thread on your way back. That way we can stay in touch, and you can even hook me up with Houston."

Just then, Ginger called Jon on their local net. "Hold up, Jon, I think I've cracked their communication system." Jon and Dmitri looked at each other with delighted grins.

"We're on our way back in," Jon told Ginger.

#

Ginger felt a bit giddy as she tapped at her console. It had been so simple. All she did was ask a question just like Ari had done. "How can we communicate wirelessly with each other?" she had asked, and the system told her.

By the time the others returned, Ginger had entered the necessary communication parameters, and that was it. She found herself looking at a holoimage of Base Camp, and was able to manipulate the cameras just as if she were using her thread-connected controls.

Ginger explained to Jon and the others what she had done. In hindsight, asking the question was obvious, but she took a certain satisfaction in having asked before Dmitri and team actually left. "I'll set you up for a burst transmission to Houston," she told Jon. "Do you want the complete record since the last transmission?"

"Yeh, but I will record an introduction...try to put all this into context."

#

Rod Zakes leaned back in thought following Jon's final words: "I know there is a lot happening back there, Rod. You guys are dealing with things you never dreamed would be an issue. And now this... The Hebrew Connection is cast-in-concrete solid. I have no idea what that connection might be, but remember that these guys are technologically light years ahead of us. There can be no doubt that they arrived here, in our solar system, one-hundred-fifty-thousand or so years ago. Are we their descendants? Hell...I don't know! If we are, what happened to their advanced technology? A hundred-fifty-thousand years is a very long time.

"Right now, I'm very glad I don't have your job."

Rod closed his eyes. *How do you explain this?* he asked himself. *How do you get from a star-faring civilization numbering perhaps in the tens of billions, to scattered Neolithic cultures that we know existed here on Earth seven or eight thousand years ago?*

This matter had moved way above his pay grade he decided as he placed a call to the White House. Fifteen minutes later Rod boarded a helicopter at the Jonson Space Center Heliport, and shortly thereafter he leaned back in the comfortable seat of a NASA Rockwell business jet, headed for Washington, DC.

#

The Ayatollah looked up sharply after reading the report just handed to him by a robed advisor. "Zakes is flying to Washington?"

"He is, Honorable One." The advisor bowed deeply. "We believe NASA has received a new transmission from Iapetus."

"Believe? What does it contain?" the Ayatollah demanded, his voice rising a pitch.

"We do not know, Sahib..." Terror lurked just below the surface of the advisor's voice. "We are trying..."

"Find out!" the Ayatollah thundered, "Or I will have your head!"

The advisor backed away rapidly, bowing low as he escaped through a door.

#

The bland official announcement of the latest transmission from Iapetus offered no hint of the paradigm-changing Hebrew connection. Rod listened in amazement as the official White House spokesperson blandly explained that there had been a temporary communications malfunction, but that the international team under the able leadership of Captain Jon Stock had corrected the problem, and things were back to normal, or at least as normal as one could expect under the circumstances.

The Russian announcement that followed within a few minutes managed to give Dmitri credit for fixing the problem. The Canadians, the Israelis, and the Germans reflected the White House lead, and so did the Australians, except they mentioned Ginger's role as Communications Officer. The French added some material from an earlier report that gave Michele center stage, and India managed to give credit to both Jon and Dmitri, with a nod to the Caliphate. China announced the transmission, noting that the Chinese presence had brought about the solution. The Ayatollah sent a diplomatic demand for immediate information on the status of Saeed, and in the streets of Teheran a carefully orchestrated demonstration condemned the infidels' presence on Iapetus.

Americans and Canadians exchanged high-fives on city sidewalks, Israelis nodded sagely at one another, Germans exchanged *Prosits!*, the French clinked wine glasses, the Russians tossed back an extra vodka or three, and the Chinese dragon-danced through the streets of cities, towns and villages. Hindis danced in the streets of New Delhi and Mumbai, and died by the hundreds when the Tamil National Liberation Army triggered another two car bombs. Muslims in Jammu and Kashmir poured into the streets, celebrating the Hindi deaths. Muslims in Jakarta, seeing the holovision images of demonstrations in Teheran, rioted in sympathy, burning Jon Stokes in effigy, and beheading four Christians for good measure. Worldwide Raëlians, seeming to know something no one else was aware of, held candle-light vigils at the Jonson Space Center, ESA Paris headquarters, and outside their slab-sided churches everywhere.

Has the world gone mad? Rod questioned as the worldwide updates streamed into his Com Center. *What will happen when they learn the truth?*

#

Dmitri and his team returned to the Com Center, as Jon had started to think of it, with their floater jammed with everything they had left at Base Camp. Before he let them set up camp, Jon returned inside and queried the left-most console: "Show us suitable living quarters."

He was rewarded with an image of a four-sided pyramid-shaped building about five kilometers distant, consisting of individual cubical units. The units were stacked so that each layer was set back, creating a flat area in front of each unit that was the top of the unit below. The pyramid was twenty-units high, with forty units along each base, and strangely reminiscent of South American pyramids Jon had seen in holograms, and even the pyramids of Ancient Egypt. The dwellings themselves consisted of any number of vertical and horizontal inter-locking units, with at least one or more units forming the front of each dwelling. Jon could see that this was a very efficient and compact way to house a large number of families, while giving them a relatively uncluttered, non-crowded environment. Jon could not help but think of it as an orderly, pyramid-shaped stack of blocks.

The system told Jon that each Stack housed approximately 10,000 families, and that they included shopping centers, recreation and entertainment facilities, and virtually everything else a community needed to live and prosper. The *Arc* contained about a million such stacks, not all identical, but varying in design and theme.

They were welcome, the system told Jon, to use as many units as they needed.

"What do you think?" Jon asked Dmitri. "Our links will give us full communication with the Com Center, and we can make ourselves more comfortable as we set the stage for further exploration."

"*Da, Tovarishch*! It works for me. I'll go check it out with my team, okay?"

"Do it!" Jon paused. "Chen, stay here. I need you to do some research."

After Dmitri left, Jon addressed his team. "We have four main thrusts right now, as I see it. Foremost is the Hebrew connection. Second, we really need to discover what happened to the star folk after they settled Earth. Then we need to get a handle on the comings and goings of the Founders, and finally, we need to learn what we can about their advanced technology."

He looked at Michele. "Michele, I want you to investigate the fate of the settlers. Make the best possible use of the system, and come up with some answers." He turned to Elke. "Your job, Elke, is to find out what happened to the Founders. We know they were going to visit Ectaris, but that's it so far. We really don't know anything else. Go with the flow." He grinned at her. "You know what I mean. Find out what you can."

"Ari, find the Hebrew connection. Work with both Michele and Elke. Use your better knowledge of Founder-Speak and anything you can drudge up from your Hebrew beginnings that might help."

Jon turned to Chen. "See what you can learn about their engineering – power generation, propulsion, robotics. When you get a lead, follow it. I'll be on your six. Between us, perhaps we can discover something.

Then to no one in particular, Jon added, "The World will be clamoring for more information – about the Hebrew connection, and about what happened. People are dying back home because we don't have answers..." His voice trailed off.

"Not so!" Ari immediately countered. "People are dying because fanatics rule the streets and cowards run our governments."

"I stand corrected, Ari. You're right, it's not our fault." Then Jon added thoughtfully, "But we can supply answers that may lower the level of fear."

#

The floater slowed to a stop in front of the Stack, and Dmitri's team exited, stepping lightly to the ground. The Stack towered above them, far more massive that it had appeared in the holoview.

"Suits on, helmets at carry," Dmitri had instructed.

It made investigation more awkward, but Dmitri was not yet willing to abandon the safety supplied by their suits.

"We'll stay in pairs," Dmitri said, "Noel and Carmen, and Ginger and myself." They set off, Noel and Carmen to the left, and Ginger and Dmitri walked toward the unit directly before them. The front appeared to be glass, although it probably was some form of polycarbonate. As they approached the front, to Dmitri's astonishment, a section slid back, revealing a bare room like that of any empty house.

Toward the back was a kitchen, but lacking any appliances. There appeared to be running water, but their first attempt produced nothing. On a whim, Dmitri called up the system and requested that water for this unit be activated. Within seconds, a rush of air came from the faucet, followed by a stream of water. There were two knobs – one controlled volume, the other temperature.

A back entrance led into a dark passageway, but when Ginger stepped into the passageway, it brightened, with the light seeming to emanate directly from the walls. She turned back, and they passed through the kitchen into the front room, and mounted a stairway to the upper floor. There they found what appeared to be sleeping chambers and sanitary facilities. Basically, it was a bungalow suitable for about three or four people.

"Can you supply furniture?" Dmitri queried the system.

The response was a chart of furniture pieces from which he could choose, and he presumed that were he to do so, a floater would deliver his choices.

He checked on the availability of food items, and again received a chart to choose from.

Dmitri checked with Carmen and Noel, and found that they had discovered similar conditions. He called them back, and they all climbed an external stairway to the next level. The dwellings on this level had additional rooms above the level or below the level, and some had rooms both above and below.

"Let's check out the interior," Dmitri said. "Split back up and explore for an hour."

They found an open core, and shafts randomly placed to simulate daylight. Much of the interior was taken up by what appeared to be storefronts, entertainment facilities, and the other accoutrements of civilized people living in close proximity to each other. The team's intercommunication was complete and flawless, so that they were able to interact with Jon and the others despite their separation.

"I see no reason," Dmitri said to Jon, "not to move everything here, order the furniture we want, the food we want, and to set up shop and go to work solving the mysteries."

"I can't come up with a good counter argument," Jon answered. "Anyone else have an objection? Do any of you see something Dmitri and I are missing?"

"I think we should stay suited up and carry our helmets," Ari said.

Dmitri gave that some thought. On one hand, they had been perfectly safe ever since entering the interior. On the other, they were completely at the mercy of whatever was manipulating everything, and that won the argument for him. "I agree with Ari," he said. "We remain in a ready state for the time being."

"I agree," Jon answered definitively. "We want to retain control of that which ultimately keeps us alive. We'll come over and bring everything with us. Pick a good vista, and let's turn to and find the answer to all this."

Second Interlude

M*erkavah* flashed out of hyper-V high above the ecliptic of the system they had left a thousand years earlier by local time measurement.

"The *Arc* or Earth?" Eber asked the thirteen clan members crowded around the display.

"I thought we already settled that, Dear," Azurad commented to several nods.

"Well, it's your last chance to change your minds," Eber said as he instructed the Resident to scan the frequency spectrum for any signals. "What are your thoughts?" Eber asked Asshur several moments later when the Resident found the spectrum empty. He felt completely at a loss to explain the empty spectrum.

"I don't know...new communications technology...." His voice trailed off.

"Nothing at all?" Shem asked. "How can that be? We left a thriving global civilization."

"Let me try," Aram said stepping to the console.

"You don't trust me?" Asshur stepped back and Ishtar gently squeezed his hand.

"Not the point!" Aram busied himself with the controls. The display remained empty.

"Check white noise activity," Arpachshad suggested. "Maybe they shifted to some form of CDMA communications."

"It's a thought," Asshur said as he tapped the console. The display remained as empty as before. Ishtar stroked his hair.

"Let's take her to Earth," Eber said, tapping instructions to the Resident.

Two jumps and some minor adjustments, and *Merkavah* achieved a nearly circular polar orbit at 200 kilometers altitude. The planet below was mostly blue with swirling white clouds obscuring about two-thirds of the surface. They were over the single largest landmass transiting south over the oval-shaped enclosed sea with the boot-shaped peninsula extending southward, virtually dividing the sea in half. As they transited further south over the triangular landmass that extended well into the southern ocean, the terminator approached. With the fall of night, planetside was engulfed in complete darkness.

"This just cannot be," Asshur said in a low voice. "There is not even one light...no sign of any kind of civilization. Nothing at all..." His voice trailed off in disbelief.

The clan members took turns looking for something, anything that would tell them that the thriving billions they had left behind were still there. The more they looked, the more discouraged they became. The planet that had become the new home for the Ectaris civilization was empty; at least it was empty of any kind of civilized culture.

"What if they discovered a problem and left?" Lud did not really sound convinced, but at his spoken thought, the others perked up a bit.

"Is the *Arc* still there?" Ishtar asked, gently massaging Asshur's shoulders from behind.

"We didn't set it up to signal," Eber said. "The general idea was for the *Arc* to remain in hibernation, while civilization developed planetside at its own rate." He fiddled with the console. "Does anyone want to check things out on the surface, or should we first go back to the *Arc* to see if it is even there?"

There were mixed feelings, but the consensus was for returning to the *Arc*. Eber made a final console entry, and the Resident took

Merkavah out of orbit and up over the ecliptic in a large arching path, descending over Saturn about twenty minutes later, entering a polar orbit around the obviously still present *Arc*. The *Arc* had taken several obvious meteor hits, but generally looked none the worse for wear. Eber leaned back and scanned the faces around him.

"We have another choice," he said. "Do we go back to Earth, land, and investigate, or do we enter the *Arc*, stay here for a while, do some research?"

"I think we need to collect our thoughts and emotions before we traipse off planetside," Shakbah said quietly, her deep blue eyes filling with tears as she stood beside Lud.

Sarai nodded, rising on tippy-toe to her fullest height to emphasize her perspective. Other heads nodded, and sensing a consensus, Eber tapped instructions for the Resident to open the hatch from which they had departed a thousand years earlier. *Merkavah* underwent several short maneuvers that went unnoticed by her passengers, and ten minutes later she was resting on her five extended legs at the bottom of the shaft, waiting for the chamber to pressurize.

#

Eber opened the massive cylinder door and extended the ramp. As the others prepared to disembark, he issued instructions to the *Arc* to come out of hibernation and then announced, "Let's get cleaned up, grab forty winks, and meet at the Command Center in eight hours."

Nods all around.

The couples strolled out across the meadow to the nearby Stack they had made their homes for the final months prior to their departure.

"What do you think?" Eber asked Azurad.

"Insufficient data, but I'm damn sure going to find out."

#

"It's like this, folks," Eber said to the assembled group lounging comfortably in the *Arc* Command Center. "Right now we don't have a clue. We can speculate all we want, but until we review what records exist here, and see for ourselves what happened planetside, we are just shooting in the dark."

He went on to assign research tasks to the group members.

Shortly thereafter, Asshur, who was primarily responsible for communications, signaled the group's attention. "Listen!" he said. "I found this urgent priority message at the top of the stack."

"This message is being sent in the blind. The date is month ten of twelve, year one-one-seven on our new calendar. We know that Clan Noah returned to Ectaris over a hundred years ago. We do not know, and have no way of knowing, if they got there, if they came back, if they are alive, or anything about them. If they are still alive – if they are you – this status report will bring you up to date on the disaster that has befallen us.

"Following your departure, our people collectively decided to focus on building a civilization on Earth. We could not do this while looking outward – at least not at the beginning. So, we grounded our spacecraft and concentrated on building our world. We made great progress. By the second generation, some fifty years back, we seemed to be well on our way to making this new planet our permanent home.

"Then, mysteriously, about a year ago the live birth-rate around the world began to drop. Within just a few months, over half of all conceptions resulted in stillbirths. Simultaneously, people in the prime of their lives began to fall ill all over the planet and quickly die, no matter what we did to help them. Within months ten percent of all our people – one billion souls – were gone. Scientists the world over turned their minds and research to the problem. We discovered that the modified DNA we had inserted into the Earth's ecosystem had mutated. We do not understand the nature of the mutation, but it is deadly. From the onset of the illness to death is a matter of a few hours.

"My community is located on the southern half of the double continent, about thirty-three hundred kilocubits south of the Equator and eighty kilocubits inland. We are on a large rocky plateau at the base of a north-south mountain range. There are some isolated pockets of natural resistance here and there, but we do not know the nature of the resistance, and these small groups have isolated themselves from the rest of us. They kill anyone who approaches them, and we are loathe to take any kind of action against them, so we remain ignorant of their status.

"I had intended to make this transmission a very detailed account, but I am now exhibiting symptoms of the disease. I cannot continue. This is Rabinossa wishing you well..."

There was a short pause in the recording, and then it continued. "WARNING! DANGER! DO NOT LAND! This is Rabinossa's son, Joachim. My father died before he could complete his account. I do not know if I will be able to carry on. I do not appear to be immune; none of us on this plateau seem to be. I think I have only a few hours or days before I, too, am gone.

"We are done as a people. If you receive this transmission, I beg you not to land. Go somewhere else. Perhaps you can survive as a new people – even with your limited gene pool, but if you come here, you will surely die."

Joachim went on to record several gene sequences, and to attach a summation of their efforts to find a solution. The recording went on for about an hour, giving details and medical specifics. It ended with, "This is Joachim, son of Rabinossa. My friends are dead, my family is dead, my colleagues are dead...and I am at death's doorstep.

#

Following an overflight of the ten most populous cities of the third planet as they had existed a thousand years earlier, *Merkavah* settled through the atmosphere coming to rest on the rocky plain between the ocean to the west and a high mountain chain to the east that Joachim had described. It was well isolated from any forestation and there were no obvious ruins. One of the original cites the starfolk had built lay about 500 kilometers to the north on the coast. When they flew over it before landing, the city was overrun by vegetation so that it was invisible, except to a trained eye that knew where to look. They saw no obvious signs of human life. The ten city sites they had examined during their overflight were simply not there, although Ishtar, with her historian's eye, thought she could detect the outline of some street patterns in a couple. When they swooped closer, however, the patterns disappeared.

Eber was taking no chances; until they had a better handle on what had happened, he didn't want contact with anything living – at least nothing animal. *One thousand years – what lasts a thousand years?* The thought would not leave him although he tried to put it out of his consciousness. He ordered a routine air sample. The Resident reported that the sample was pure and uncontaminated.

"Okay...we're here," he said to the assembled clan. "We can

breathe the air. Now, do we disembark or not?"

"It's been a thousand years," Azurad muttered. "What has happened to the survivors?"

"I thought we would see something at the city site," Lud commented, "something indicating any kind of civilization...anything at all..." His voice trailed off.

"They could all be gone," Vesta said. Azurad and Shakbah nodded in agreement.

"Okay, now," Eber said. "You guys are confusing me. You wanted to come, right?" Everyone nodded. "Okay...we're here." He looked from person to person. "We're here...so what do we do now?"

"You know," Azurad said quietly, "Joachim clearly warned: I beg you not to land. Go somewhere else." She smiled faintly. "So, what are we doing here?"

"I take it that means we don't go outside." Eber's statement sounded like a question. "Is that what I'm hearing?"

Tentative nods.

"But we're here. Shouldn't we investigate...something?" Eber had become the *de facto* leader of the clan because he had made it a point in his life to know as much as he could about everything. Engineer by training, he was the clan's generalist. Traveling all the way from the *Arc* to Earth without accomplishing something – even with the ease of travel supplied by *Merkavah* – just didn't sit right with him. "At least, let's take some samples back with us."

"And get contaminated..." Azurad's voice trailed off.

"Wear a suit." Eber sounded matter-of-fact.

"How do you decontaminate the suit?" Azurad wanted to know.

Lud added thoughtfully, "I think we should not do anything that could enable something from here to contaminate the *Arc*." Shakbah slipped her hand into his and nodded, shyly.

"Let's send a couple of microbots out..." Eber stopped and turned to Aram. "We did bring some, right?"

Aram nodded, his dark eyes twinkling. "We got flyers that can snip off some little branches and bring 'em back. And...we have some vacuum-capable jars to hold the samples. We can keep the storage bay open to space on our way back. That should take care of anything on the bots and jar exteriors."

"Everyone okay with that?" Eber asked.

There were no objections.

"Okay...let's get some samples and then head back."

\#

Aram sat at the mail control console directing several humming-bird bots into a nearby tree stand. One-by-one the little mechanical birds snipped off small branches with a couple of leaves and brought them back to the flyer. He shifted his gaze from screen to screen as he controlled each bird in turn. "Whoa!" he said as a dark shadow whipped across one screen and the image went tumbling. "Hey! You guys...look at this!"

As the image stabilized, a bearded, human-like face peered out at them. "That," Aram said, "has my bot in its hand." An eye filled the screen as the creature peered closely at the damaged microbot. A human-like finger approached the screen and moved about, causing the image to tumble.

"He's examining the strange bird," Sarai said, showing her excitement.

Aram manipulated his controls and a second screen shifted to show the scene from above and to one side, as one of his humming-birds flew into place.

"That's a man!" Rasu'eja exclaimed with astonishment. "Lots of hair, full beard, no sense of size..." her voice trailed off. The first screen image tumbled as the man dropped the broken bot. On the second screen the man appeared to stoop. "Look, he picked up a pointed stick, a spear." He poked his spear at the flying bot. The bot's internal guidance avoided the jab. The man slapped with his hand, but missed.

Aram pulled all the bots into the air and tried to focus on the man. When the man saw the "hummingbirds" flocked together in the air above him, he gave a startled yelp and ducked into the thick underbrush, disappearing from sight.

"Well," Ishtar said, "something survived after all."

The group remained silent for a moment, absorbing what they had just seen. Lud took over a console and did some manipulations. On the screen the man as seen from the air before he vanished was stripped of background, then hair, and then rotated to a frontal view. "That's a human male," Lud stated matter-of-factly. "He's wearing some kind of loin cloth and something on his feet, but that's a human man."

Vesta, who had not uttered a word during the entire event, spoke up. "We have to get a blood sample." Turning to Aram, she asked, "Can you do it?" He nodded.

For the next several minutes Aram busied himself with bringing the still-working bots to the flyer, and launching several microbots that looked almost exactly like mosquitoes. "If Nature Boy shows himself, I'll get a sample."

Eber could feel the excitement that filled the control room. He felt his own heart quicken. Aram set the monitors to present a unified view from all the mosquito-bots, and Eber stood behind him, admiring his brother's skill with the system. Aram brought the several tiny bots to rest on branches surrounding the location where the man had disappeared. It was pretty obvious that the man had seen *Merkavah*, but Eber had no way of knowing if he associated the strange birds with the flyer. Eber was certain that the man had nothing in his experience to connect with the flyer. They were counting on his curiosity to bring him back.

The group waited patiently for several minutes, and then the ground cover began to stir below the branches where Aram had parked the bots. A partial head poked up through the leaves and looked around. Slowly the creature slipped out of his well-designed foxhole and crept to the edge of the tree stand to look at the flyer. While his back was turned to the assembled bots, Aram brought three of them to the man's back simultaneously and jabbed their proboscises through his skin. The man yelped and slapped his back, smashing one of the bots. The other two withdrew their samples and headed back to the flyer. Aram brought in two more to the man's back, and lost another one, but also obtained a third sample.

"Okay, that does it," he said, turning to Vesta.

"Now we have something to work with," she said.

When the three mosquito-bots were safely ensconced in a vacuum safe jar, Eber ordered the Resident to take *Merkavah* back to the *Arc*, retracing their above-the-ecliptic path.

"Let's see what Nature Boy can tell us," he said to no one in particular as *Merkavah* left the atmosphere and commenced its high arch over the ecliptic.

The name stuck.

#

Vesta, Azurad, Shakbah, and Lud worked tirelessly with the plant and blood samples they had retrieved from the third planet. They used the gene sequences Joachim had transmitted to them as a starting point. Vesta took the lead, assigning Azurad to the plants and Lud and Shakbah to the blood. She used a sample of her own blood to sequence and compare with Joachim's sequences. Azurad found nothing unusual. Comparing her plant material samples to the native plants from the *Arc*, there simply was no measurable difference.

"The plants are neutral to us," Azurad reported to Vesta. "Whatever happened a thousand years ago did not affect the plant-life."

Lud, on the other hand, found himself chasing down a curious variant in Nature Boy's blood – an additional protein attached to the surface of his red blood cells. Vesta picked up on this variant and ran a cross-check against a comprehensive database of every known blood-type variance for the Ectaris mammalian ecosystem. She discovered that the extra protein in Nature Boy's blood when compared to her own was linked to several deeply layered sequences that, taken together, apparently granted immunity to the genetic mutation that had ravaged the population.

In trying to explain what she found to the group, Vesta said, "It is as if some of the immigrants had somehow taken up a genetic characteristic inherent in the animal population already present on the planet. When the population was ravaged by the genetic mutation, the individuals with this genetic characteristic survived. There is no trace of the original genetic sequences we introduced to the entire planet a thousand years ago. Apparently, they self-destructed as they were designed to do. Somehow, this variant protected its hosts from the effects of the mutation."

"I'm not sure I understand," Rasu'eja said, to nods from some of the others.

"Think of what our biologists introduced into the planet ecosystem as a computer subroutine introduced into the operating system of a resident computer," Vesta explained. "The subroutine's task is to seek out and modify certain other specific subroutines. Part of the new subroutine's programming is that when it runs for, say, two seconds without encountering one of the specific unmodified subroutines it is programmed to seek out, it then shuts itself off, and removes itself from the resident operating system. Similarly, the DNA sequences our biologists introduced into the Earth's ecosystem were intended to seek out and modify those DNA chains that were incompatible with our own. Once they did their job, they self-destructed. Somewhere in the process, a mutated DNA sequence became active, a sequence that still made the DNA chains compatible, but also killed its host. Apparently, it was still subject to the suicide mechanism, so that when there was nothing more to change, it self-destructed. The modifying subroutines did their jobs – including, unfortunately, killing the host, but they are gone now. Does that help?" Nods all around.

"So...what does this mean?" Eber asked for the rest of the group.

"Simple," Lud answered. "The third planet is safe for us. We can eat its plants, its animals – we can even mate with the human inhabitants."

"The problem is," Ishtar interjected, "their culture has vanished. What I saw was a Stone Age savage who survives at a bare subsistence level. Cut off from whatever civilization remained, I guess the isolated groups of survivors quickly reverted to bare subsistence living. It would not take but two or three generations to bring them to this level. They have had a thousand years."

"There's nothing there for us," Noah said, his voice sounding tired and old, "nothing at all."

They sat quietly, each in private thought. Finally, Persia lifted her face, wet with tears. "It's so sad. I feel so isolated and lonely." Shakbah took her hand and sobbed quietly with her.

Eber looked around at his brothers. Although trying not to show it, they were affected by Persia's outburst. It got to him as well, he admitted to himself. It seemed that if he didn't take control of the situation immediately, they might all decide to abandon space for whatever they might find on the third planet.

"Listen," he said, "there's nothing we can do for the primitives on Earth right now. They need to move themselves forward just like our distant ancestors did. If we plan things properly, we can do some real exploring and come back when some kind of meaningful culture has taken hold on the planet. Maybe we can even inject some technology before we take off again, only to come back another time to see how our injection worked."

Arpachshad had been following his brother's comments with close interest. Although trained as an engineer, his main function was as the warrior of the clan. "I like that. We can step in, find a group of smart survivors and give them a couple of weapon improvements that will cause them to prevail." He grinned. "Hey...we can even inject some of our genes into the group..."

Rasu'eja poked him in the ribs with her elbow. "You'd like that, I'm sure." A chuckle passed through the group and their mood lightened.

"He makes sense, you know," Vesta said.

#

Three years later shipboard time, *Merkavah* settled into orbit above an Earth that clearly showed signs of real advancement – 70,000 years farther along the path to civilization. Eber put a modified Arpachshad plan into effect. The spacecraft settled to the surface in a dozen places to the awe of local natives. Individual crew members spent days, and in some cases weeks, working with locals trying to insert a bit of useful technology into a civilization that was scratching its way out of stone-age culture, and even exhibiting metal-working skills here and there. Universally, the natives viewed them as gods, and *Merkavah* as some kind of heavenly dragon.

And yes...when *Merkavah* departed, the clan had left some of its genetic material behind in the form of several impregnated females who had been presented to the gods as a living offering.

"I couldn't refuse," Arpachshad commented as *Merkavah* lifted high over the ecliptic.

"He makes sense, you know," Vesta said.

#

When *Merkavah* flashed again into Earth's atmosphere some five-and-a half shipboard months later, the landscape over which she passed was another 10,000 years older. A planet-wide civilization once again flourished sporting an advanced technology that included international air travel, a vast telecommunications web, and incipient space travel evidenced by a network of satellites. Moments after entering the atmosphere high above the body of water that would later be called the Mediterranean, *Merkavah* reported that targeting radars had locked onto the spacecraft and several surface-to-air missiles were fast approaching from the eastern end of the Med. *Merkavah* took immediate evasive action by moving rapidly into a geosynchronous orbit.

The Founders watched in horror as the initial missiles aimed at them were followed by massive launchings from bases all around the Med, and then from sites across the oceans to the west and southeast. This time, however, the missiles were not surface-to-air. As they watched, explosions that could only be nuclear saturated the Mediterranean shoreline and then began to appear along the shores of the double continent across what would later be called the Atlantic, throughout the largest landmass to the north, and to a lesser extent the continent extending southward from the Med where it had all started.

In less than two hours it was over. As the terminator swept the devastated planet below them, where the bright glow of thriving cities had illuminated the darkness twenty-four hours earlier, only darkness remained. Eber and his clan returned to the *Arc*, disheartened by what they had observed. They were discouraged by what appeared to be their role in the self-destruction of the 80,000-year-old civilization that had risen from the remnants of their race's first attempt to establish their presence on Earth.

#

When *Merkavah* again returned some two-and-a-quarter year later shipboard time, the human race had spread across the planet following a 50,000-year climb from the brink of nuclear extinction, and civilization had once more taken hold around the eastern end of the Mediterranean. The Founders left their imprint again and again over the next several thousand years, concentrating on an ethnic group in the northeastern quadrant, inserting genetic material at each visit, until when they visited they began to see some of their own physical characteristics in these people.

#

"I'm tired," Noah said to no one in particular after a particularly long day of toil preparing *Merkavah* for departure after three years of actually living in one place with one group of people. "When do you plan to return?" he asked Eber.

"Several hundred years," Eber answered, "give the seeds we planted this time room to grow...see where it takes these hardy folk."

"You know," Persia said, "I don't think of them as "these hardy folk." I think of them as my people. I've developed some real friendships here, people I don't want to lose..." Her voice trailed off.

Noah nodded. Out of the corner of his eye, Eber saw Vesta look sharply at her aging spouse. Before he could say anything, however, Shem spoke up.

"Persia's right. We've got a granddaughter here..."

"Granddaughter?" Azurad's voice had a slight edge to it.

"It's complicated," Shem answered.

"Live long, my Love!" Vesta told Noah three days later when she boarded *Merkavah* by herself. As the spacecraft lifted, Eber and the rest of the Clan watched a stoic Noah fold his arms with a slight smile on his lips, while Shem placed a protective arm around Persia. Eber would forever remember his mother lifting her hand in final farewell.

#

The next set of visits served a special purpose. While *Merkavah* made a ten-light-year round-trip out and back over a subjective time of just under four hours, each brother took turns spending ten years actual time on Earth connecting with Noah's and Shem's descendants, producing as many offspring as possible. They inserted a one-hundred-year gap between each visit to space out their stays. The end result was that each brother including Eber aged ten years while the women remained virtually unchanged.

Their genetic testing showed that their own, uncontaminated genes had survived over the centuries since Noah, Shem and Persia had remained behind, and now predominated in the Semitic peoples in this region. Their testing produced only one apparent negative consequence of their genetic insertions. They found that all humans had four blood-type groups that manifested themselves as proteins attached to the surfaces of the red blood cells. The descendants of the original settlers all carried an extra protein on their red blood cells that seemed to have derived from the original genetic manipulations upon their first arrival. The Founders lacked this protein. From time to time, a man with the protein would mate with a female without the protein, producing a fetus with the protein. The mother's blood would then produce antibodies to combat the protein in the fetus's blood. This could cause the death of the fetus during later pregnancies, or problems upon birth.

Vesta made sure that information about this potential problem was inculcated into the folklore of the native populations, even though there was very little people could do about it at that stage of human development. She developed simple blood tests that the Founders could use to ensure their conjugal involvement with the locals would avoid the problem.

While the ten-year process was well thought out and both the men and women were agreed to the necessity of the project, Eber had some doubts about Aram's wife, Sari. Little Sari was trained as a civil engineer, but her life was exploration, and he knew that she was loathe to leave Aram to his own devices for ten years, even though she obviously understood that it would be just a few hours for her.

When it was time to leave Aram for his turn planetside, Sari pleaded with Eber to let her at least spend a few hours alone with Aram, exploring his new environment with him. Eber relented, believing he had no choice.

Several hours later a sobbing Aram returned carrying Sari's tiny, lifeless body in his arms. "She slipped and tumbled into a ravine," he sobbed, his swarthy face wrenched with anguish. "I couldn't save her..."

"You want to rotate out with Lud?" Eber asked, reaching for Sari.

Aram stepped back, holding tightly to her lifeless body. "No, and she'll stay with me. I need time to work this out." He turned and walked away, shoulders stooped with pain.

When *Merkavah* returned four shipboard hours later, Aram had fully recovered from his loss, but he looked like he had aged more than ten years. Eber chatted with him privately during the subjective day-and-a-half of the hundred-light-year out-and-back, deciding that he was fine, although he still clearly missed his little Sari. As for the rest of them, Eber understood that they hadn't had time to mourn her loss. Later would be time enough.

\#

Eber and crew flitted in and out of Earth history, leaving a mark on every major land mass in every epoch, impacting the local civilization in ways that they never could predict, but always with one constant – they were seen by the locals as a heavenly manifestation, gods sent to help or punish.

They watched civilization rise around the Mediterranean, reaching a pinnacle at the height of the Roman Empire about 1,200 years after Noah, Shem, and Persia had decided to settle down and live out their lives. The Semite peoples, especially those characterized as Hebrews or Jews still spoke a close derivative of Founder-Speak, although it had devolved into a language of much lower sophistication than what it originally was. The Jewish culture never forgot that it was special, chosen by the gods to carry forward the ancient traditions originally handed to their ancestors by God Himself. For their arrogance, Jews everywhere found themselves the focus of social anger and discrimination. Conquered and reconquered, even scattered to the ends of the Roman Empire, the Jews never lost their cohesiveness, never lost their identity.

Seventeen hundred years after Noah's death, the Roman Empire collapsed under the weight of its own bureaucracy and the ravages caused by lead poisoning from their lead-lined cooking pots and water lines. Less developed but more robust cultures sacked Rome. The Christian church replaced Rome's secular bureaucracy with an even more intricate one based on religion, and civilization stagnated for several centuries. Where they could, the Founders injected pieces of technology, but it became increasingly difficult to pose as gods in world dominated by the Roman Catholic Church, and virtually impossible to pose as anything else in the remote locations where the Church had not yet penetrated.

Then the entire civilized world went to war; but somehow, it pulled itself together, only to fall into the same abyss a second time. Out of that second war emerged two superpowers with the capability of doing once again to themselves what – unbeknownst to them – their ancestors had done 64,000 years earlier. The Founders watched in fascination as the world moved right to the brink of annihilation. Then, miraculously, the world pulled back, and for the first time in 145,000 years humans stepped foot on the Moon.

The Founders watched worldwide allegiances change, morphing into an odd combination of the ultra-modern alongside the nearly ancient as the Persian Caliphate spread across the Middle East.

Out and back for another jump forward – the Founders returned to a completely changed paradigm. Humans once again were a space-born race. Their fumbling, low-earth-orbit activities from before the establishment of the Caliphate had become full-fledged operations not only within the Earth-Moon system, but extended to exploration of the fourth planet as well.

It was obvious to Eber that Earthmen would discover the *Arc* in the next few decades, so the Founders spent several months on the *Arc*, making sure that whenever and wherever Earthmen finally arrived, the *Arc* would be ready for them. Ishtar, as a writer and historian, created a teaching program that would quickly educate their Earth descendants in the Founders' language and writing. Aram worked closely with her to ensure the electronics would interface with virtually anything the Earthmen might bring with them, and Asshur worked on the communications interface, trying to predict and thus solve any potential problems. The others checked all the various autonomous systems to ensure they were operational after so many years, and would serve the needs of their potential visitors.

On the sinister side, the Founders had already experienced first-hand the blind wrath of Earthmen facing unknown dangers. This time around, most Earth cultures seemed to have found a way to coexist, but they remained armed to the teeth, and *Merkavah* had no defenses at all. Eber assigned Arpachshad and Rasu'eja the task of finding a way to arm *Merkavah*, to make the starship impervious to anything Earth's present technology could throw at it. Arpachshad argued that they needed more than defensive capability.

"We need the ability to reach out and destroy an attacker," he told Eber and the others. "Not only that, we need the ability to destroy an attacking site on a moon or world."

The *Arc* had a built-in defense capability that drew upon power from the core, and projected it outward as a powerful, focused laser. Its primary use was as an automatic meteor disruptor. It had failed sometime during the Founders' initial thousand-year journey back to Ectaris, in what appeared to have been a remarkable meteor shower that penetrated the *Arc*'s defenses. Most of the laser disruptors had been damaged, and the incoming meteors had caused major damage to the particle ring, so that the *Arc* no longer was a functional Starship. It had taken the advanced Ectaris civilization a century to build the ring; repairing the extensive damage was not in the foreseeable future. The laser disruptor components were readily available, however, and easy to install on *Merkavah*. This gave the vessel the ability to destroy incoming objects.

Working with Rasu'eja and Asshur, Arpachshad designed a high-energy particle beam that was able to encapsulate a small amount of anti-matter from the core and transport it at very high velocity to a target location where it combined explosively with the target's normal matter, producing a prodigious explosion. They also modified their ring accelerator so that they could direct a focused beam of neutrinos to any specific location within about 100,000 kilocubits. The focus point of the beam could be set to a specific point with an error of one or two cubits. The neutrino beam would disrupt any biomaterial – specifically living matter, and would also shut down a nuclear reactor and disable a nuclear bomb.

These three weapons appeared to serve the twin needs of defense and, if necessary, offense, with a serious reservation. The Resident could interdict any incoming object or particle stream with the laser disruptor, but could do nothing about an incoming laser beam, which Earth technology had not yet developed, but might at any moment. The particle beam could deliver its deadly load to any enemy space vessel or attacking planet-based source, so it could eliminate the source of a beam weapon, but it could not interdict a laser beam. The neutrino beam could destroy living things with pinpoint accuracy, and could render nuclear bombs and power sources ineffective, but it also could not interdict a laser beam. In the short term none of the crew members could come up with anything that would solve this problem, but Eber pointed out that *Merkavah* had the ability to accelerate and maneuver more quickly than anything current Earth technology possessed. In a battle scenario, she could maintain a continuous, erratic movement orchestrated by the Resident that would render her virtually impossible to target long enough to hit her with a laser beam. None of the team members had any formal computer programming expertise, but the Resident had the ability to turn simple instructions into programmable code. Of all the Founders, Ishtar was the best writer; so, working closely with Rasu'eja and Arpachshad, she took on the task of developing a set of evasive maneuvers with the Resident that would keep all of them safe from any future laser beam attack.

On Eber's advice they scheduled a series of short hops similar to what they did during their ten-year sojourns. On each return the Resident would perform a series of spectrum scans to determine the state of Earth's technology. After only one hop, however, the Resident reported that their Earthly cousins had actually reached the moon of Saturn they called Iapetus.

145,000 years after the Founders had left their friends and colleagues on their new planetary home, their grandchildren forty-five-hundred-times removed were finally exploring the *Arc*'s interior!

Chapter twenty-eight

Jon was surprised at how quickly they were set up and operational at the Stack. It almost seemed as if the system were anticipating their needs and standing ready to fulfill them. Jon made a command decision to relieve the crew from having to wear their pressure suits, much to everyone's relief. By late afternoon they were up and running in all respects. Michele was deep into the recorded history of the star folk and what happened following their departure from Iapetus to Earth. Jon let her dig without interference from him. Elke quickly located the Founders' log, and got lost in their descriptions of their ruined home planet. Ari was having less luck. Other than the language itself, he was finding nothing that pointed to what Jon thought of as the Hebrew Connection – in caps.

After pondering the matter for a while, Jon called Dmitri and Ari into the room he had set up as his headquarters. Jon looked up from his comfortable earth-like office chair as they walked in. He gestured to a couple of padded chairs facing his desk.

"Mahogany?" Dmitri asked, rubbing his hand across the smooth desktop.

"Hell if I know," Jon answered. "I picked it from a picture listing the system presented me."

"All the comforts of home," Ari remarked with a grin. "You couldn't make this up, you know.

"It gets better," Jon said, sliding two small tumblers holding a clear liquid across the desk to them both.

Dmitri picked up his tumbler. "За вас!" (*Za vas!* – Here's to you!) and he tossed it back, eyes growing large immediately after.

"Back," Jon said, drinking more slowly.

Ari tossed his back like Dmitri. "לחיים" (*L'chayim* – To Life!) "Speyside is better," he added after a moment.

"I don't believe in coincidences," Jon said, spreading his hands across the desk.

Ari nodded agreement. "*Da,*" Dmitri said quietly.

Jon spread his arms to take in the desk width. "Mahogany desk? Who's kidding whom?"

"You think we're not alone?" Dmitri said, swirling the tumbler in his hands, his eyes questioning.

"What do you think, Ari?" Jon swept his eyes over the room and the earth-like panorama outside.

"Somebody knew we were coming..."

Jon interrupted Ari, "and knows we're here." He stood and started pacing. "What about Founder-Speak? You say it's sophisticated Hebrew? How the hell can that be? Are you saying that a form of Hebrew is the Interlingua of our galaxy?" He stopped pacing, placing his hands on his hips. "We're missing something here..."

#

Ari was at a complete loggerhead. That Modern Hebrew was a corrupted and simplified form of Founder-Speak was patently obvious, but that begged the question of why and how. Michele's research didn't help at all. The Ectaris connection was completely separate from Earth. According to Michele, Founder-Speak was a planet-wide language, known and used by every educated person. But there were hundreds, perhaps even thousands of dialects and even distinct languages used throughout the Ectaris system. The Ectarians had even colonized their fourth planet, Dameter, where Founder-Speak had taken on a distinct twang that, apparently, was looked down upon by the Ectaris intellectual crowd. *Planetary hillbillies,* Ari thought with a grin as he pondered the problem.

Working with Michele was a pleasure, Ari thought, because her femininity played an unabashed role with everything she did. Nevertheless, Michele had no answers for Ari. On the other hand, Elke came up with something. She sought Ari out and explained what she had found.

"I have been going through the Founders' journal," she told Ari. "Their names are listed at the beginning, but – frankly – I didn't pay any attention to them. The principle author is Ishtar, although the Founders' nominal leader, Eber, makes occasional entries, as do most of the other fourteen members of the group. It seems Ishtar was a writer and historian by profession.

"The Founders were all members of a family. The family appears to have initially been run by the Patriarch, and consisted of his wife, their six sons, and their sons' wives. Because the Patriarch was along in years, and because neither he nor his eldest son had kept up with emerging technologies, he passed the baton to his grandson Eber, the first son of his eldest son, Shem. Decision-making seems to have been by consensus, but Eber was fully capable of taking charge and making important decisions when the chips were down. Their general focus was to discover what had happened to the Ectarians, and to track the rise of civilization moving forward.

"They leap-frogged forward, stopping every once in a while to acquaint themselves with the state of progress. About sixty-thousand years ago, the Founders were nearly taken out when they appeared during an incipient global crisis that resulted in a devastating nuclear war that pushed the planet back to bare subsistence survival. Their return about ten thousand years later signaled the beginning of our current civilization.

"Once civilization had taken root, several family members decided to spend ten years on Earth in rotation so that eventually all their diverging ages would coincide. During all this, one of the wives was killed in an accident, and the Patriarch, along with Shem and his wife Persia, stayed behind, integrating themselves into Earth's population."

Elke paused in her tale and smiled at Ari. "You know these people, Ari. Look back into your childhood religious training. You know these people: Noah, Shem..."

Ari looked at Elke with astonishment. "But...but...ohmygod! How could I have missed it? It's so obvious now..." Ari shut his eyes in concentration. "Give me a moment..." He opened his eyes and looked up at the ceiling to his left. "Shem's sons were Eber, Asshur, Aram, Lud, and..." he paused, concentrating. "There was one other son, but I can't bring up his name – it was a bit complicated, hard to pronounce."

"Ar..." Elke hinted. Ari shook his head.

"Arpach..."

"That's it!" Ari said excitedly. "Arpachshad – now that's a mouthful of a name!" He gave her a big kiss, brotherly, of course. "Thanks, Elke. I've got to tell Jon about this."

#

Rod Zakes had developed a routine that kept him near Control virtually all the time. He would take an occasional weekend off, while his second would be available, but as a rule, within five minutes any time of the day or night Zakes could be found somewhere in the Houston complex. He had become convinced that the universe had conspired against him so that important messages always arrived when he slept. It was no different this time.

"Zakes to Control...Zakes to control!" The ubiquitous announcement awakened Rod from a sound sleep and a dream about aliens and the Raëlians that made perfect sense as he awakened, but that lost every bit of logic the moment his feet hit the floor. He splashed some cold water on his face and ran his wet fingers through his hair, which, he noted, continued to thin.

"What is it?" Rod asked as he stepped into Control and accepted a steaming cup of coffee from CapCom.

CapCom handed him a printout. "You're not going to believe this, Rod."

"We got a planet-sized alien starship with an earth-like internal environment, an alien language that obviously is related to Hebrew, Muslims rioting, Raëlians praying and having sex, not to mention a Jihadist stowaway – you got something stranger than this?" Zakes let his eyes drop to the printout. "This is a joke, right? You guys have nothing better to do at two o'clock in the morning than pull shit like this?"

CapCom pointed to the tagline at the top of the page "No joke, Boss...this is for real."

"Okay – I read the dispatch; now give it to me in English."

"About five hours ago our deep-space network discovered a new object ten AU distant, and two AU above the ecliptic – that's about Saturn's orbit. It's trailing Saturn about one-third an orbit. That gives us ninety minutes each way for data transmission. Two queries enabled us to get a preliminary trajectory – very preliminary..." CapCom paused. "Toward Saturn..." He left that hanging.

"This is for real, right?" Perhaps it was the early hour, but Zakes was having trouble accepting what he was hearing.

"The deep-space boys have been working on it since the first reception five hours ago. There IS only one reasonable explanation, Rod, and that one isn't reasonable."

"So," Zakes said with wonderment tingeing his words, "the Founders have returned."

"Or someone – something – else," CapCom added. "Our guys are inside Iapetus, and this thing, these guys, are on their way to Saturn. Might want to let Jon know."

"You're right, of course. Draft a message to Jon – just the bare minimum. Tell him more to follow. Let me see it before you send it." Rod turned toward the door "I've got to call the White House."

#

Jon brought the entire team together in his office with a general announcement on his link. While he could have assembled them holographically, he felt this was too important, too momentous, for anything but face-to-face. The team had made great progress in the last few days, especially Ari and Elke, with their discovery of the actual identities of the Founders. *Imagine that*, he told himself as the crew assembled, *we're going to meet the grandsons of Noah!*

"This," Jon said, holding up a comms printout, "is a visitors' announcement." He watched the looks passing through his crew at that statement. "That's right, visitors."

Then he told them about the deep-space network detection and the spacecraft's now confirmed track straight toward Saturn. "Track," he told them, "not trajectory. These guys are powering straight toward us."

"When?" Dmitri asked the question on everyone's lips.

"Virtually any time, folks."

#

Saeed Esmail listened to the Captain's announcement with astonishment. This obviously was a sign from Allah, but what did it mean? His Jihad was still on hold because of his holy oath, but Saeed knew that Allah would send him a sign when the time was ripe to complete his Jihad.

During the foregoing discussion, Saeed had finally understood that the arriving visitors claimed to be Noah's grandsons. This absurdity was obviously impossible, Saeed knew, but why the deception? What was happening that he was not aware of that made such a bizarre lie necessary?

This was completely outside the ken of the *Qur'an*. Saeed promised himself that he would get to the bottom of the deception, and that he would complete his Jihad, even if he forfeited his life thereby.

Most merciful Allah, he prayed silently, grant me understanding. Keep Jihad alive in my heart, and me on Your holy path. Release me from my oath to the Captain. Show me how to overcome the arriving evil deception. Show me a way to carry out Your plan for this evil place.

As he finished his silent prayer, Saeed felt a deep peace come over him. Suddenly, he knew how to arm himself. When the Founders arrived, in the excitement he would slip away and request that the System supply him with what he needed. Saeed felt Allah touch his soul while placing a dagger into his hand.

#

Ari watched Saeed out of the corner of his eye. He watched perplexity cross Saeed's face, followed by a combination of serene peace and dogged determination. He knew the signs – he had seen them before. Saeed was on the verge of abandoning his oath. Ari made a mental note to keep an even closer watch over the little Jihadist.

#

The Persian Caliph was stupefied. The deep-space network discovery could not be contained, so that within fifteen minutes of the U.S. President being informed, the Caliph received the news. He sat on his raised chair, eyes glued to the communication. His closest advisors sat cross-legged, arrayed on the floor before him, none any closer than necessary.

"Can this be trusted?" he asked his science advisor, a wizened Mullah on the floor to his left.

The advisor rose to his knees and placed his forehead on the cool tiles. "Yes, Honorable One. Such a thing is not easily faked, and ESA has confirmed the discovery. There is no doubt, Sahib. The Founders have returned." His voice quavered as he uttered the last sentence.

"Who are these imposters?" the Ayatollah bellowed to no one in particular.

The assembled advisors sat silently, no one wishing to become the focus of the Caliph's wrath.

"What of our Jihadist?" the Ayatollah asked, changing topics as he frequently did. He looked directly at his senior advisor, seated on the floor immediately in front of him. The Mullah prostrated himself, and then came to his knees, trembling slightly.

"He is well, Sahib, but he has given his holy oath to set aside his Jihad. We do not know his circumstances otherwise, except that Dr. Bhuta transmitted the Jihadist's distress word "David" when she responded to your communication demand.

The Ayatollah leaned forward, elbow on his right knee, stroking his long gray beard. "Send him a message that will break his oath."

With that, the Caliph rose to his feet as the assembled advisors prostrated themselves, foreheads to the floor. He strode purposefully to his chambers door, stepping on three advisors in the process.

#

Rod listened carefully to the White House announcement, made by the President's Science Advisor:

"NASA and the Deep-Space Network have just presented us with monumental news. The World already knows about the momentous discoveries made by the international team of astronauts led by Captain Jon Stock currently exploring the inside of Saturn's moon Iapetus, which we now know is a derelict interstellar spacecraft – an abandoned starship. We know that humanoid beings we call the Founders built the starship to escape the destruction of their home planet, Ectaris, five-hundred light-years distant from Earth. We know they arrived in our solar system over one-hundred-fifty-thousand years ago, that they settled on our planet, and that they disappeared along with their technology and even the memory that they were ever here. We know all this from the records the astronauts found inside Iapetus, the derelict starship the Founders left behind.

"What we have just learned, however, trumps all this many times over." The Science Advisor paused for a pregnant moment.

"The Founders have returned! As I speak to you, a Founder spacecraft is arriving in the vicinity of the planet Saturn. We do not know the exact status of the Founder spacecraft at this moment, because signals from Saturn take ninety minutes to reach the Earth. It is a virtual certainty, however, that by now the spacecraft has landed on Iapetus, and that the Founders and our heroic astronauts are meeting one another.

"As more information is forthcoming, we will keep the networks advised so they can pass the information on to you."

Not a mention of the Hebrew connection, Rod thought as he contemplated what he had just heard. That might just be the most direct, honest statement I ever heard come from the White House, he muttered as he commenced scanning the channels to see how the message was impacting the World.

Throughout the Western World, the announcement had very little impact, perhaps because of the Raëlian influence on the general public. The exceptions were the Raëlians themselves. All over the World they crowded into their slab-sided churches to the smell of incense and burning candles, and the unmistakable scent of sexual excitement, as they expressed their religious rapture at the return of the Elohim. The Indians and Chinese took the announcement in stride. Even the Tamil National Liberation Army kept a low profile, holding its new car bomb for whatever came next. The Caliphate orchestrated a large demonstration in Teheran where a straw bag labeled "Founder" was burned in effigy along with a likeness of Jon Stokes. Muslims in Jakarta, seeing the holovision images of the Teheran demonstrations, rioted in sympathy, burning another Founder along with Jon Stokes in effigy, while destroying half the small businesses in the city. Twenty people died during the riot and hundreds more were injured. Muslims in Jammu and Kashmir poured into the streets and beheaded a Hindu and two Christians to show their solidarity with worldwide Islam. There, too, half-a-thousand small businesses were looted and burned along with three major department stores. Thirty-five people perished, not counting the beheading victims.

As Rod watched the unfolding horrors, he wondered aloud what the Founders would think when they realized what their great civilization had become.

#

Alex Jinnah had continued his role with Mission Control, perhaps with even more enthusiasm than when he had two masters – Rod Zakes and the Caliph. Since his expertise and experience lay with communications, Rod had kept him in that role, and so he found himself gently shaking Rod awake to hand him the latest direct communication from the Caliphate. Rod rolled over grumbling his usual mantra about messages always arriving at 2 a.m. and accepted the sheet of paper. Alex was familiar with the words on the message sheet, but wasn't sure what they meant. He was curious to see Rod's reaction.

"What the fuck?" Rod read the words aloud:

For Saeed Esmail:
    The Ayatollah Khomeini sends his personal greetings in the name of Allah (may He be praised) along with his prayers for your health and well bring. Allah in His infinite mercy (all thanks to Him) laid this Qur'anic verse on the Ayatollah's heart: *Allah hath made lawful for you absolution from your oaths of such a kind, and Allah is your Protector. He is the Knower, the Wise. Qur'an 66,2*
    The Ayatollah sends.

"Any thoughts on what it means?" Alex asked.

"Yeah, the Caliph has officially released Saeed from his oath of non-Jihad and cooperation."

#

In due course Jon received the message for Saeed. He called Ari, and together they analyzed the possible meaning of the message.

"I think it's pretty straightforward, Jon. The Ayatollah is telling him in no uncertain terms that his oath means nothing."

"You really think so?" Jon was genuinely puzzled by the thought that the Caliph would send such a clear "order" for Saeed to ignore his oath. "Could there be another meaning to the verse? Something that a person steeped in Islam might see preferentially, whereas we just see what to us is the obvious meaning?"

"Good point...let's see what we have: *absolution from your oaths.* That could be any "oath," right, not just his oath to you? It even could be his original oath to do Jihad."

"But it also says: *of such a kind.* Is there a contextual meaning for that phrase, Ari?"

"Frankly, I don't know. Don't know the *Qur'an* that well. Not sure I want to, either." Ari grinned at Jon. "I'm a VASIMR engineer who was formerly an Israeli spook – not an Islamic scholar."

Jon chuckled. "How about we give the message to him, and I tell him in no uncertain terms what will happen should he decide to break his oath – no matter what the Ayatollah has said about it?"

"I like that. I'll just make sure I keep a closer eye on him from now on."

#

Saeed carefully read the Ayatollah's message. *What is His Holiness telling me? "...absolution from your oaths of such a kind..."* He wrung his hands with worry; he broke out in a cold sweat; his legs felt rubbery. Earlier he had asked Allah for understanding, for a sign, for guidance. And here it was...perhaps. He reread the message, and then once more. Obviously, he had given his oath to Allah when he stowed away...but he had also given his holy oath to the Captain, and when the Captain had handed him the message, he had been completely clear about what would happen to him if he violated this oath.

Saeed sat with crossed legs on the grass outside the door and brought his entire mental capacity to bear on the problem. He drifted off on the wings of prayer, when without notice he was brought back to complete awareness by the sudden arrival of a floater filled with people, people he didn't recognize.

Chapter twenty-nine

The silent arrival of a floater outside their compound caught the entire crew by surprise. Ari was the first to react. He was aware that Saeed was sitting outside on the grass when the floater arrived. Ari made the connection instantly, and ran out, grabbed Saeed by the arm and quickly walked him into an empty room. Since there were no locks, Ari ordered Saeed to remain inside the room on pain of dire consequences should he disobey. It took all of two minutes, and Ari immediately joined the rest of the crew outside the compound where the Founders had just disembarked from the floater.

There were ten of them, five men and five women, standing in a loose group in front of the floater. The men were dressed in knee-length tunics, and were shod in soft boots. The women wore longer, one-piece tunics tied at the waist, and similar boots, except one, who was dressed like the men. She was a tall, athletic woman with deep copper-bronze skin, long, flowing black hair with deep brown eyes, sporting lithe, firm muscles. She was armed with what looked like a Bowie Knife or short sword, and a holstered device that looked like a handgun of some type. One of the men was similarly armed, a stocky man about Ari's size with swarthy, weathered skin, curly dark hair, and nearly black eyes. The Founders definitely had a Semitic look to them, except for one of the women who looked more like a tall, blond Greek goddess, and one of the men who, while blond and light skinned, was of shorter stature. One man, apparently the leader, stepped out of the group.

Jon approached him. "I am Jon Stock, Captain Jon Stock..." Jon's voice trailed off as the Founders grinned at him. Ari pointed to his link, and Jon blushed while activating his translator. "I am Jon Stock, Captain Jon Stock," he repeated as the translator repeated his words in perfect Founder-Speak, "and these are my crew. We will make individual introductions in a bit, but first, let's establish the basic rules..." He paused, obviously contemplating how to proceed. "...so we all are on the same page, so to speak."

Ari watched his friend's discomfort with amusement. Jon obviously had not thought his way through the process. Would people from a hundred-fifty-thousand years ago shake hands? Would they be stiff and formal? Would they be curious and friendly? Would they be hostile? Surprisingly, Ari realized that the Founders appeared just as befuddled as Jon, and that's when it struck him. They might be from the distant past, but in real-time terms, they had no more experience than Jon or himself – perhaps even less. With that, Ari strode up to the Founders and said in his best Founder-Speak, "I'm Ari Rawlston, and I'm one of your direct descendants. I don't know how you greet people in your culture, but in ours, we grip the right hand like this." He grasped Jon's hand in a firm handshake.

A chuckle passed through the Founders, and, one-by-one each, of them shook Ari's hand, and then Jon's. Following that, Jon went down the ranks, introducing each of his crew members, and again, one-by-one, all the Founders shook all the crew members' hands while generally chatting – through the translators except for those crew members who had developed proficiency in Founder-Speak.

#

Eber was surprised at his own reticence upon first meeting the explorers. He quickly realized, however, that his experience was on par with that of the explorers about his age, but that they would see him through awed eyes because of the Founders' advanced technology and their having moved forward in time so many thousands of years.

It was clear to him almost immediately that Captain Jon Stock was a capable leader, and that he had the respect and full support of his people. None of the explorers were armed, which made sense for this kind of mission. He decided that the best thing he could do was to establish a rapport with the Captain, leader-to-leader, so they could decide on how to move forward.

As the two groups mingled, the five Founder women quickly sought out the four female explorers. Since Carmen, Elke, and Michele were fluent in Founder-Speak, the conversations between the women quickly moved into their individual broad areas of expertise. To Eber, it seemed that the women reached an almost immediate rapport. He glanced around for the Captain, and found him deep in conversation with Arpachshad and the short, curly-haired one who seemed to be one of his own kind – Ari, he recalled.

"Captain..." Eber was impressed with the quality of the translators. In fact, the entire Link technology was impressive – more so, he thought, than anything similar from his own culture. "Captain, may I have a moment?"

"Please call me *Jon*; everyone else does." Jon smiled widely as he turned from his conversation with Ari and Arpachshad.

"Can we talk privately for a few minutes?" Eber turned toward the floater. Jon followed him inside, and Eber shut the door. "I would like to tell you first how wonderful it is to be able to converse with technically competent people. Try to imagine what it was like when we returned from Ectaris to find nothing, no one. As the centuries passed, there really was nothing we had in common with the folk we met. It was really difficult. My father and grandfather finally made the shift, and remained behind. My grandmother wanted to see the future. Of the women, only my mother Persia stayed back, and I suspect it was out of love and respect for my father. Apparently, they are all enmeshed in important ways in your history."

"Yeah, that's true, especially if you're religious."

Eber looked at Jon with open curiosity. "That's one of the things we need to talk about. My people, the people who arrived in your system a hundred-fifty-thousand years ago, were homogenous. We spoke one language, albeit with some variations, we had pretty much mixed up our individual racial stocks, although we still exhibited differences such as that between Ishtar – tall, very light-skinned, blond hair, and oval facial features, and Azurad – shorter, bronze skin, dark hair, and high, prominent cheekbones, or between myself and Lud with his light skin and blond hair. These differences are negligible, however, when compared to the difference between Ginger and Michele, or between Chen and yourself. In the millennia it took for my descendants to crawl back out of the Stone Age, apparently major geographical barriers resulted in distinct racial lines.

"How has this worked out for your culture?"

"Not very well up until recent times," Jon answered. "Even today we carry tensions between us – not with my crew," he added hastily, "but back home. That's something you will need to understand completely before you make any personal appearances on Earth." Jon sat quietly for a few moments. "This is especially true for you and your family. My biologist and physician – Michele and Carmen – have looked at the matter extensively. They have tried to explain it to me, but let's face it, I'm a Naval Officer – mostly spaceships now. I have to rely on my experts for such information."

Eber grinned at Jon. "I, too, am a generalist, which probably is why I command our family." The translator was a bit unsure of the word *command*; it qualified it by adding *lead*.

"Anyway," Jon continued, "the survivors from your original expedition apparently got an extra dose of DNA strands somehow linked to the local fauna that gave them immunity from whatever it was that killed everyone else. It is manifested today in Earth's population as a characteristic in the blood we call the Rh factor. You and your family don't have this factor; we call you Rh-negative. Your direct descendants don't have it, and neither do most of your indirect descendants. What happens when Rh-positive and Rh-negative people have offspring together is beyond my understanding.

"My point is, we have a racial branch we call Semite. You belong to it, Ari belongs to it, as does another crew member you have not yet met – I'll get to that a bit later. Semites around the world can trace their ancestry back to Noah...truly! Whether the ancestry is real or not, I don't know, but they certainly believe it is. One branch within the Semites see themselves as distinct and separate, and for at least the last twenty-five hundred years have called themselves Jews. For reasons that don't matter here, Jews have been hated by most of the world for a very long time. They speak a language we call Hebrew that is obviously a corrupted and simplified version of your own language, which we call Founder-Speak.

"Our world right now is divided into three major groups and one less important one. The first of these is the Euro-American group, consisting of North and South America, Europe including Russia, Australia and New Zealand, and Israel, right in the middle of the Caliphate. Most people would consider the United States as the leader of this group, although many in Russia might disagree. The point is that this group is relatively cohesive, and unlikely to go to war within the group. The second group is Asia, which includes China, Japan, India, the countries of Southeast Asia, and several smaller states bordering Russia, Europe, and the third group, the Persian Caliphate, which I'll discuss in a moment. The fourth group consists of the African states south of the Sahara Desert, led by South Africa. For many reasons, this fourth group plays a smaller role on the world stage. The Persian Caliphate – the third group – came into being several decades ago. It consists of all the states on the eastern and southern sides of the Mediterranean, north to Russia, and east to India. Unlike the rest of the world which is modern and relatively sophisticated, the Caliphate is a bizarre blend of medieval theology called Islam, militant extremism, and modern weaponry – and probably half its citizens are Semites. The Islamic holy book is the *Qur'an*, whose historical parts have much in common with the holy writings of the Jews.

"Their leader, the Ayatollah Khomeini, arranged to put a stowaway aboard our spacecraft. His job was to sabotage the mission. It was only by good fortune that we found him. I decided to keep him alive, and have been using him as an additional crew member. I assigned him to Ari, who speaks his native language and is well-trained in personal combat.

"In simple terms, the Caliphate is a primitive, hate-driven theocracy, armed to the teeth with nuclear weapons..."

"Nuclear weapons, even," Eber commented with considerable astonishment.

"Yes, with nukes...standing against the rest of the world. Furthermore, several states in Southeast Asia are predominately Muslim

– a term that describes believers in Islam – as is a significant part of India. To top it off, the Jewish homeland, Israel, is a tiny country that sits on the eastern shore of the Med, surrounded by the Caliphate. The Caliph who rules the Caliphate with an iron hand has sworn to wipe Israel off the face of the Earth.

"The rest of the world also has nuclear arms, but by agreement, they are regulated, inspected, and controlled, insofar as this is possible – except for the Caliphate and Israel. The United States – the U.S. – is closely allied with Israel, which is the only reason the Caliph has not carried out his threat." Jon leaned forward, almost into Eber's personal comfort zone, causing Eber to pull back somewhat internally, while being careful not to give an outward indication.

"You see, Eber, the world does not know about what we call the Hebrew connection. Except for several highly placed individuals in my government, the U.S. government, nobody knows that the modern Israelis, the modern Jews, are your direct descendants." Jon leaned back and spread his hands across his knees. "This is a problem, Eber, a big problem."

Eber sat still, contemplating what he had just heard. Reduced to its essence, his direct descendants were on the verge of total annihilation at the hands of a maniacal religious dictator, and his presence and his family's would probably be the factor that tipped the scale. "So, what do you suggest?" he asked at last.

#

Saeed had reviewed several options for continuing his Jihad. If he could just find the materials for a bomb, then he could take out most, if not all, the Founders with one well-placed suicide attack. That would not happen, however, because the accursed Israeli kept his leash very short. The only explosives were topside with the landers, and there were no guns or similar weapons. Poison might be possible, but unrealistic. That left sabotage, and that did not appear feasible in Iapetus, but might just be possible aboard the spacecraft.

Allah, majestic Ruler, keep me on Your path. Show me a sign; open my eyes so that I may clearly see the weapons You have prepared for my successful Jihad.

The door opened as Saeed finished his prayer, and he turned to see Ari striding into the room.

#

"Come with me," Ari said to the little terrorist, while scrutinizing him to make sure he had not sequestered a weapon in his clothing. "The Captain wants to introduce you to the Founder leader."

Ari was not yet fully in the picture, but he was curious to see how Saeed would react to beings that Saeed would believe were a hundred-fifty-thousand years old. He waved to Arpachshad as he passed, noting that the Founder and his wife, Rasu'eja, were deep in conversation with Elke. He observed Saeed eying their weapons, and made a mental note to apprise Arpachshad of the situation. *Don't want the little terrorist to get his hands on a high-tech ray gun from the future.*

At the floater, the door opened, and Jon and Eber descended to the grass. As the other Founders gathered about, Jon said to Eber, "This is Saeed Esmail, the other crew member I told you about."

To Ari's surprise, Saeed bowed with a mid-eastern flourish. "I am honored to meet you, Sahib. Although I do not comprehend it, I am told you are a distant ancestor of mine."

"That is true, Saeed Esmail. I am the son of Seth who was the son of Noah..."

"This cannot be," Saeed interrupted, his face flushed and distorted. "Allah (may He be praised) would not allow this."

The Translator rendered *Allah* as *Yehweh*, which Ari recognized as a Founder-Speak phoneticization of the Hebrew letters for God: יהוה (*yod-hey-vev-hey*).

Saeed apparently recognized the word as well, and expressed his outrage. "There is no God but Allah (may He be blessed)! Your infernal machine blasphemes the one true faith. You are nothing but a satanic vision sent to disrupt the progress of Allah's warriors on Earth." As he spoke, his voice rose to a shrill level, and it appeared to Ari that Saeed was about to leap at the Founders. Arpachshad's hand went to his holster while Rasu'eja's hand slipped around the haft of her short sword. Before they could act, however, Ari wrapped a large hand around the back of Saeed's neck and squeezed hard, momentarily blocking both carotid arteries. Saeed's body went limp. Ari half dragged, half walked Saeed across the grass back to the room.

\#

"I apologize for that," Jon said, speaking to all the Founders. "As you can see, we have a problem. And this problem is amplified by about two billion times back on Earth." He started walking toward his office. "I must report your arrival to my superiors while you, Eber, brief your family on our conversation. Feel free to join me when you're done."

This message had to be encrypted using their private code system. Jon simply could take no chances that there would be an uncontrolled release of this explosive information. He set up his machine, entered the parameters, and saved the resulting encrypted message into the transmit stream. Rod would receive it about ninety minutes after the next pass of the *Cassini II*.

As Jon completed uploading the encrypted message, Eber entered the room and pulled a chair up to the desk. "All the comforts of home," he said with a grin. "Did we get it right?"

"At first we were completely overcome by your technical superiority." Jon winced. "Our spaceship, *Cassini II*, is the peak of our technology. It took us four months to get here using our newest VASIMR propulsion technology – that's short for Variable Specific Impulse Magnetoplasma Rocket. We know you guys are pushing light speed. That makes our very best puny by comparison. The way I saw it was that by poking around here, learning everything we can, we could leapfrog from where we are now to where you are.

"Then, with every passing day inside this amazing world, I began to suspect that you guys were still around, and that you were coming back." Jon smiled broadly at Eber. "Everything was just too neat, too accommodating.

"I guess I should thank you."

Eber nodded. "It was pretty obvious to us that the *Arc* – Iapetus, you call it – would have a significant impact on you, as individuals and as a culture. We missed your multicultural diversity, not because it didn't exist during our periodic sojourns in your time stream, but because we assumed you would develop as we had, into a single planet-wide culture."

"I don't know how my government will handle my dispatch," Jon said seriously, "but it's clear to me that ultimately there is no hiding what and who you are. This will cause problems. There is no way to seal off Iapetus. Others will come; sooner or later, others will come. And not all of them will have good will."

"We can make Iapetus virtually inaccessible, shut down the

access tubes, close off the openings, put the entire complex into hibernation."

"There's ten of you and ten billion of us. Someone would find a way to penetrate your safeguards. It would be taken as a global challenge. It could even lead to the destruction of Iapetus, at least in its function as a starship." Jon paused, carefully considering what he had to say next.

"I have assumed that your group, your family, will not be content to settle down with us on Earth and cease your wanderings. Your logs make that abundantly clear. I also understand that your vessel..."

"The *Merkavah*," Eber interjected.

"The *Merkavah*," Jon continued, "is not really designed for long-duration journeys. It seems to me that there is room here for some negotiations." Eber didn't say anything, but Jon could tell that he was interested. "We can help you build a new vessel, one that will accommodate all of you comfortably, with room for additional passengers, should you choose."

Time for the clincher, Jon thought as he prepared his next words. "This is going to sound parochial, but my country is different from every other country on Earth. I think you need to understand how we are different before you make any plans for the future."

"I'm willing to listen further," Eber said cautiously. "Our presence already triggered one destructive, planet-wide war. I certainly don't want that again." He grinned. "You're right about our accommodations. We need more room."

"I'm going to give you several of these Links," Jon said, pointing to his wrist. "They're local here, although they do tie into your electronic library."

"What we've let you see, anyway," Eber said with a quiet smile.

"Right...and anywhere in the Earth-Moon vicinity they will tie into the global system, giving you access to everything in the system. I will set them up for special access to the documents that underlie our country, and to a short version of our history so you can see how we differ from everyone else on Earth."

#

Rod was actually awake when Jon's latest dispatch arrived, delivered to his room by Alex. His offline system, which was similar to Jon's, quickly decoded the message. Rod sat at his desk absorbing the fascinating material.

"Basically, they're just like us," Jon wrote. "The men look more like Ari, which is not surprising. The women are utterly remarkable, and cover the waterfront from short and dark to a statuesque Greek goddess. There are ten Founders in all – two physicians, several biologists, physicists, engineers, and even two warriors! Unequivocally, the men are the grandsons of Noah – right that Noah! Their ship is a bit like a backyard hotrod. They built it on the run, making all sorts of compromises and substitutions. But it can approach light speed with a Lorentz Factor approaching seventy-one-thousand. That means they can cover a thousand light years in less than six days! But they also move forward that number of years."

Rod sat back and considered what Jon had just told him. These people were technically advanced, but not all that much. In fact, it appeared that some of Earth's present technologies were more advanced than theirs. The big deal, however, was their immediate ancestry. *How do you deal with that?* Rod asked himself. *The secular Israelis probably will handle it fine. But what about our own Evangelical Christian heartland? They can't have it both ways – how will they deal with it? And the Raëlians? Where the hell do they fit into the equation? The Asians? No problem there since they don't have any emotional investment – except for the Korean Christians.* Rod shook his head. *Then there's the Caliphate... they could go two ways. Hypothetically, they could embrace the Founders, but that's not going to happen.* Rod grinned ruefully and tapped his link.

In a few moments the image of the President's Science Advisor appeared in the air before him. An hour later Rod was on his way again to Washington, D.C. in a NASA Rockwell.

#

Each of the *Cassini II* mission participant nations received a short voice communication from the White House along with the complete text of the announcement the White House intended to make fifteen minutes later. The White House announcement was short and straightforward, notable, not so much for what it contained, but for what it left out.

"Captain Jon Stock and the crew members of the *Cassini II* mission to Iapetus have just met with the last surviving ten members of the Ectaris people who arrived in our Solar System a hundred-fif-ty-thousand years ago. Because of the time contraction effects of Einstein's Special Theory of Relativity, the ten Founders have aged only slightly from their ages when they first arrived here so long ago. Although their technology is well beyond ours, they come in peace and pose no threat to us.

"The five male Founders claim that their father was Noah's son Shem, so that they are the direct biological grandsons of Noah. Neither Captain Stock nor the President's technical experts here on Earth have been able to confirm this claim, but we have no reason to disbelieve them either. This matter will be resolved in due course. We do not yet know when the Founders will come to Earth for a formal visit, but the American government will work with other national governments to ensure that no individual nation has exclusive contact with the Founders or exclusive access to their technology.

"This may be the single most momentous event in human his-tory. America implores the peoples of Earth to put their best foot forward. We have only one chance to make a first impression on the Founders. They will soon enough learn of our shortcomings, our internal differences, our foibles.

"We will follow-up this announcement with more information just as soon as we receive it."

Worldwide reaction was almost immediate. Holovision pundits with their science talking heads sagely explained the time contraction effects from traveling at significant fractions of light speed.

"Could they really be Noah's grandsons?" the pretty Fox Syndi-cate anchor asked her aging Science Fiction guru.

"Hypothetically speaking," he answered, sagely nodding his head, "I suppose they could be..."

"What are the implications?" she asked, her awe-filled pretty face shining with excitement.

A half-a-world away the Russian Federation president turned to his Science Minister. "Arrogant bastards, those Americans." He grabbed a pen and notepad, gritting his teeth. After scribbling a moment, he handed the note to his Minister. "Inform the press that our American comrades have our full support."

The Chinese Chairman requested from his staff an annotated

copy of the *Western Bible*. He wanted to be sure he knew who Noah was before meeting any world leaders, and especially the Founders.

The Australian Prime Minister was actually visiting the White House when the announcement was made. He and the President spoke privately about it.

The Israelis remained publically silent, not wanting to inflame the Caliph, but an entire team of across-the-board experts boarded an El Al aircraft bound for Washington, D.C.

The Indian Prime Minister simply noted the event with pleasure, indicating that India looked forward to comparing historical notes with the Founders.

The German Bundes Chancellor announced a new specialty beer called *Founders Bräu*, created especially for this momentous day.

The French and Canadians made immediate public announcements of support, while privately, the Canadians reinforced their support, and while the French stated their reservations, couched in terms of Gaelic sovereignty.

The British Prime Minister forwarded a note to the President reassuring him of Great Britain's historic close friendship with America, and made himself and his government available for any eventuality.

Many other nation heads made appropriate public remarks ranging from wildly enthusiastic to reserved support, and across the board there seemed to be a general wait-and-see attitude regarding the Hebrew connection.

Raëlians around the word danced in the streets, proclaiming vindication for their beliefs. Privately some of their Elders had reservations about the Noah connection, but good leaders, they speculated, led the crowd where it was already headed.

There was one outspoken, vociferous objection, however. The Ayatollah Khomeini appeared throughout the Caliphate on the only holovision channel to which Caliphate subjects had access. Following a fifteen-minute anti-Israeli, anti-American rant, the bearded dictator challenged the Founders' veracity, calling them ignominious swine and lackeys of the American infidels, and threatening them with immediate nuclear destruction should they set foot on this planet. As insurance, he promised to turn Israel into a nuclear wasteland and to destroy as much of America as possible.

Within minutes of his broadcast, a million faithful filled the streets of Teheran, promising Holy Jihad against all infidels. They beheaded effigies of the Israeli Prime Minister and the American President, and they tore ten effigies of the Founders limb-from-limb, promising eternal hell-fire for any infidel claiming a direct line to Noah.

#

Rod Zakes watched the unfolding developments, first with amusement, and then with a growing horror. He had no idea what kind of weapons the Founders possessed, and he knew even less of their mindset. One thing he felt certain of, however, was that a culture that had crossed 500 light years intact would be more than a match for anything modern humanity could deploy as a threat – especially the Caliphate. As he pondered this, a dawning realization overtook his thoughts. The Caliphate did not have to threaten the Founders. All it needed was to nudge Israel closer to the brink.

"My God!" he breathed as the dawning realization took hold. I've got to bring Jon up to speed on this. He has to brief the Founders; they have to understand the volatility of the situation...

He shuddered as the unwanted image of an Israel consumed by nuclear flames from a surprise attack burst into his mind. *We simply cannot let that happen!*

Chapter thirty

Jon read the encrypted message from Rod for the third time. Rod believed that a nuclear attack on Israel by the Caliphate was immi-nent. While Rod was no diplomat, he wasn't an idiot either. He was right in the middle of the mess back home, and probably knew better than almost anyone what might be forthcoming. Jon leaned back and considered his options. He presumed that the Founders could defend themselves, but he had no idea how. From his own military background, he was equally certain that they had a way of projecting force against an attacker. Would they intervene against third parties? Would they see Israel as special? Would they comprehend the unique role the United States played in the modern world?

Jon used his Link to locate Ari, and asked him to escort Eber to his office.

#

Eber had been with Ari, gaining a clearer understanding of the role the Israelis played in the modern world. What he learned was disturbing. He was appalled by the intertwining of the different religions. As on his own world, there were various levels of belief. For the last couple thousand years of their existence, however, the

Ectarians had not exhibited the radical, violent behavior that was so rampant in the Caliphate.

Eber and Ari stepped into Jon's office and settled in the proffered chairs. Before Jon could say anything, Ari explained, "We have been discussing the nature of Earth's geopolitical divisions, concentrating on the Caliphate and Israel." Eber's Link translated for him.

"I am deeply disturbed by what I have learned," Eber told Jon through the Link translator. "How can this be in such a technologically advanced world?" Eber paused, mulling over his thoughts. "Do you really believe our presence could cause violence?"

"It already has." Jon called up Rod's communication on his Link and set the holodisplay so Eber could read it.

"Sorry, Jon, I can't read your language yet." Eber smiled inwardly at Jon's embarrassment. As the display switched to Founder-Speak, Eber smiled. "Soon enough, I'll be able to read English."

Eber quickly read the communication on the display, and was shocked by what he read. "Is this possible?"

Jon nodded gravely. "Can you share with me what kinds of weapons you carry?"

Eber had been expecting this question. "We have a Laser Disruptor that can destroy virtually any incoming object, but it is ineffective against laser beam weapons."

"We're working on those, but I am unaware of anyone who has a working model."

Ari spoke up, "The Israelis have been working furiously on such a weapon, precisely because of its defensive character. I don't know if it's operational."

"I'll check on that," Jon said.

Eber continued, "We also have an anti-matter particle beam that can deliver a packet of anti-matter to any point within about three thousand kilometers." He expressed the distance as five thousand kilocubits, but the translator recalculated that into standard kilometers.

"What's the range of the Laser Disruptor?" Jon wanted to know.

"Shorter than the particle beam – about fifteen hundred kilometers. Finally, we have a focused neutrino beam that can take out biological systems, nuclear reactors, and nuclear bombs with an effective range of about sixty-one thousand kilometers with a ranging error of about a meter."

"Are you willing to use your weapons to defend yourselves?"

The question seemed odd to Eber. How could one imagine not defending their small clan? "Of course – without hesitation."

"How about defending the Israelis, should they come under attack?"

"I'll need to consult with the rest of my clan before answering that." Eber was careful to maintain a neutral tone, but inside he was roiling. For himself, there was no question. If the Caliphate were to attack or even appear to be ready to attack Israel, he would have no compunction about doing whatever appeared to be necessary.

He excused himself to confer privately with the others

#

"So that's it," Eber said as he summed up the conversation he had with Jon and Ari. "Ari tells me that it is not if, but when, the Caliphate launches a nuclear attack against Israel, with the intent of taking out every city and virtually the entire population." He watched the horror spread across the faces of his brothers, their wives, and his grandmother.

"Ari – you all know that he is Israeli – told me that his countrymen have been developing a laser weapon, but he does not know whether they have deployed any such weapons yet.

"I need your counsel as to whether we should take preemptive action against the Caliphate, or wait for whatever happens." It appeared to Eber that each person before him was lost in individual thought, trying to come to grips with the horrific concept that they might be forced to end hundreds of thousands of lives, or even millions, in order to save the Israelis, and possibly prevent a worldwide nuclear holocaust. *It's an impossible choice*, he thought as he reached out to his family emotionally. Quietly, he added. "We need to decide quickly. One-way communication is ninety minutes; the attack may already be underway."

The silence continued for another few minutes, and then – one-by-one – each member of the clan spoke up, affirming the decision Eber had already made in his mind.

"Quickly, then! We must return to *Merkavah* immediately."

As the group entered the floater, Eber had a sudden inspiration. He tentatively touched his link – it still was an unfamiliar device – and found himself speaking with Jon sans video. "We're heading to Earth without any fanfare or initial report. Would you and Ari care to accompany us?"

#

Saeed watched Ari take a link call from someone, and then hurriedly put a small satchel together. Saeed noted with interest that Ari included a fighting knife with a medium blade. "I'm taking a trip with the Founders," Ari told him. "I'll be back in a few days." Ari left, admonishing Saeed to behave himself, and to report to Dr. Bhuta immediately, and to stay with her until he returned. "She's expecting to see you right away." Ari gave him a menacing look as he left.

This has to be the sign from Allah (may He be blessed) that I have been waiting for! Saeed could hardly contain his excitement as he surreptitiously watched Ari and Jon board a floater and depart. He already knew the location of *Merkavah* from overhearing the many conversations between the *Cassini* crew and the Founders. In a similar manner, Saeed had learned how to summon a floater, and he did so at this time. There was no doubt in his mind that he was back on the path of Holy Jihad. He knew that Allah would guide him so that, when the proper time came, he would be able to carry out the will of Allah.

Unbidden the Qur'an verse that he had discovered at the beginning of his quest came into his mind: Let those fight in the way of Allah who sell the life of this world for the other. Whoso fighteth in the way of Allah, be he slain or be he victorious, on him we shall bestow a vast reward.

It was entirely clear now. Allah had spoken directly to him, both then, and now! He would not falter from his Holy Jihad.

The floater arrived, and Saeed boarded without anyone noticing. Allah had cloaked their eyes with blindness. Minutes later, the floater stopped next to one of the massive supporting columns, but this one had a large rectangular opening that revealed a mysterious saucer-shaped craft kept off the floor by five legs. The craft was a deep black, deeper than anything Saeed had ever seen before. A ramp extended from the craft, and the interior appeared to be lighted. As he watched in awe, Saeed suddenly heard voices approaching from around the column. Without further thought, knowing that Allah would temporarily blind the eyes of any early arrival, Saeed scampered up the ramp into the interior. He was met with an array of incomprehensible equipment, a layout of several comfortable-looking chairs, and several doors around the chamber. Knowing that the others would be walking up the ramp at any moment, Saeed quickly tried each door in succession, starting with the closest one. The third revealed a high-tech lavatory facility with a locking mechanism on the inside of the door. Saeed ensconced himself in the room, activated the locking mechanism, and prayed silently:

Allah, the Blessed, embrace me to Your bosom, and keep me safe from the infidel's prying eyes until Your moment of glory has arrived. I commit my spirit to Your care...

#

Always suspicious, Rasu'eja touched the hilt of her short sword as she rounded the column and saw the floater still waiting in front of the opening. She touched Arpachshad's elbow indicating the floater with her eyes. "Probably the floater Jon and Ari arrived in," he noted quietly. Rasu'eja didn't pursue the matter, but she kept her eyes peeled. More than once since they had started this crazy journey, her alertness had saved their skins.

She shooed Arpachshad up the ramp first as a safety precaution, but she did it so unobtrusively that nobody noticed. As a further precaution, she was the last to mount the ramp, and she retracted it a soon as she was safely inside.

Rasu'eja mentally reviewed everything she could think of that could possibly go wrong. The mechanical side of *Merkavah* she left to Eber, but she took very seriously that only she and Arpachshad were capable of handling any other danger. She implicitly trusted her spouse and the other eight clan members. She knew that Eber trusted Ari, and because Ari implicitly trusted Jon, Eber trusted him as well. Nevertheless, she was nervous about having both the descendants inside *Merkavah*, and so close to the rest of the clan.

While Rasu'eja conducted her private safety check, Eber was explaining to Jon and Ari a bit of the nature of what they were about to experience. He indicated the duplicate sets of controls and screen-like devices that served as monitors while placing himself before one set while Asshur took the other. At that moment the monitors showed the illuminated interior of the column absent the craft, as if it were not sitting on the floor. Another, smaller display showed the immediate surrounds outside the column. Rasu'eja noted that the Floater had departed.

The clan members took seats, and Eber invited Jon and Ari to sit or stand behind himself and Asshur to observe the operation more closely. "Because the hyper-vee system acts on every molecule within its field," he explained, "there is no need for anyone to strap down, or in any other way to take any particular precaution. You'll be quite safe standing behind us."

Eber checked his personnel monitor; it indicated thirteen souls. In his preoccupation with the moment he did not react to this, and neither did anyone else, not even Rasu'eja, although her internal alarm system had begun to make her feel even more uneasy than before. Eber nodded at Asshur who touched a panel display, and the view shifted, showing a bird's-eye view of *Merkavah* inside the cylinder with the ramp retracted. The cylinder door was closing, which did nothing to ease Rasu'eja's sense of unease.

#

"We've got a green board," Asshur announced. Jon looked over their heads at the display. *Odd,* he thought, *that some expressions seem almost standard between our cultures.* Eber commenced evacuating the cylinder.

"To facilitate rapid evacuation," Eber explained, "our ancestors constructed large storage chambers in the overhead substrate alongside the cylinder. They are maintained in an evacuated state, so that the air in the cylinder can be dumped into the chambers, making rapid evacuation of the remaining air possible."

To Jon's astonishment, the whole process took only about five minutes. Eber told him that five kilometers overhead a cover had slid aside, exposing the cylinder interior to the hard vacuum of space. The remaining air had puffed out in a crystalline cloud, and settled to the surface. Eber activated his controls. The only indications that they were moving were the shifting images on the monitors. Eber explained to Jon and Ari that *Merkavah* shot out of the cylinder so fast, that had there been topside observing, they would have seen nothing at all.

Eber set the controls to move the craft at right angles to the plane of the ecliptic, so that it rapidly rose out and away from the immediate gravitational influence of the nearby ringed planet. As he did this, Eber explained that shifting the hyper-V system into near light-speed too close to a significant planetary or stellar mass produced unpredictable results, and could even damage the craft. As Jon pondered what he was seeing, *Merkavah* powered out of the ecliptic at the highest safe velocity until the instruments indicated that it was safe to shift to near light-speed.

A few short minutes later, the Resident locked in the appropriate vector and simultaneously activated the hyper-V system. Within a fraction of a second, *Merkavah* and its occupants were moving at 99.9 followed by six nines percent of light-speed, and 0.2 seconds later, the Resident brought *Merkavah* back out of hyper-V high above the ecliptic above Earth.

"We're here," Eber announced.

"Unbelievable," Jon stammered as he looked at Ari. "All those months, the tedium, the danger..." His voice trailed off.

"What about dust and gas in the ship's path?" Ari asked.

"They're swept away by the hyper-vee field like floating objects in the path of a fast moving ship are swept aside by the ship's bow-wake," Asshur answered.

Jon shook himself free from the effects of their nearly instantaneous transition from Saturn to Earth. "What kind of near-planet maneuvering capability do you have?" he asked Eber.

"*Merkavah* can maneuver in three dimensions up to about one-quarter light speed in space, up to about Mach ten in an atmosphere for short distances, and about Mach five for sustained atmospheric flight. She can start and stop and change direction nearly instantaneously."

I need to tell Rod we're here, and we need to be in position to monitor the activities of the Caliphate and Israel.

"Can you get us just inside Link range?" Jon asked.

"And that is...?"

"Five thousand kilometers from the Earth's surface, and the entire wedge consisting of the Earth, Moon, El-four, and El-five."

The Link translator took some time clarifying the Lagrangian points, but Jon was satisfied that it did the job correctly when he saw Eber manipulate the monitor to display a diagram of the Earth-Moon system showing Link connectivity.

"Let's keep out of sight until I make contact," Jon said. "Keep the Moon between us and Earth."

Even at a quarter light speed the transitions were nearly instantaneous. It was not something Jon got used to immediately, and he had trouble tearing his eyes away from the monitors. As soon as his Link notified him that it was connected to the planetary grid, he placed a secure call to Rod Zakes.

"Yeh, what is it?" Rod's sleepy face appeared in the air before Jon. "It's two in the morning!" Jon adjusted the image so only he could see and hear Rod. "You! How the hell...?"

"Yeh, I know. I'm with the Founders on their ship beyond the Moon's far side. They plan to interfere in the Caliphate/Israel matter. Please let our guys know, and anyone else who matters. The Founders pose no threat to anyone but the Caliphate, but they will defend themselves if attacked. Believe me when I say they can defend against anything we have!"

#

Rod shook the sleepiness from his eyes and grabbed a cup of coffee. It was going to be a long night. First a call to the National Security Advisor. He didn't appreciate being called this early either, but once the message had sunk in, he signed off to call SecDef and the President. Then Rod called his friend, David Ben-Gurion, head of Mossad, on a secure connection.

When Rod finished briefing him, Ben-Gurion said, "You know that we have been working on a laser beam weapon? It's an outgrowth of the Iron Dome project. Basically, the system pinpoints incoming threats, and takes them out with a high-power laser. The weapon uses a capacitive discharge, so there is a time lag between successive firings. Currently, we have deployed two prototypes. Between them, they can fire every five seconds." He paused while Rod assimilated this. "We can handle a limited strike of perhaps three or four missiles, but that's it. You say the Founders want to help us?"

"It seems so."

"We're grateful, but we need to show the Ayatollah that we cannot be bullied, and that an attack on Israel has deadly consequences. Please ask the Founders to stand down."

#

"So, that's the long and short of it," Jon said, as he completed briefing Eber and the rest of the Founders.

"It's a brave but foolhardy stance for such a small nation," Arpachshad said. "Their weapon is a prototype, right? Prototypes break down. They develop bugs. They never work correctly the first time..."

"Please give me the general coordinates for Israel," Eber asked Jon. "We will stand down for the time being, but we will stand by just in case." Eber gave the Resident the coordinates Jon gave him plus some added instructions that Jon did not understand. Moments later *Merkavah* settled into a hover about 2,000 kilometers above Israel.

"Show me the outline of the Caliphate and your best estimate of their potential launch points."

Jon complied, with Ari indicating the launch points. Eber gave the Resident further instructions, and one of the monitors started displaying a bird's eye view of the Teheran launch facility, which Ari had indicated was the most likely launch site.

While this was happening, Jon took a call from Rod. "It's pretty tense right now. The Israelis have their laser fired up. Their on-site intel says an attack is imminent." Jon relayed this to Eber.

Just then, the bird's eye monitor flashed red. A missile had been launched from the Teheran facility, followed in short order by several more. The Resident superimposed the missiles' tracks on the image. They appeared to be headed for Tel Aviv, Haifa, and several industrial and military areas. Jon started to speak, but Eber held his hand up.

"Missile flight time is seven minutes," Eber said. "I'll give the Israeli's four."

The first two minutes were the longest minutes Jon could remember spending. He found himself holding his breath. Then one of the missiles disappeared followed closely by another. After a pregnant pause that actually lasted only five seconds, a third and fourth missile disappeared. Five seconds later the last missile vanished, but almost immediately the Caliphate launched another five. Israel brought down three of them as before, but the fourth continued its flight for another fifteen seconds before disappearing, and at the four-minute mark, the fifth missile was still headed toward its target.

Eber issued the Resident a command, and the fifth missile vanished. "That's it!" he said, issuing yet another command.

A split second later the view from the bird's eye monitor erupted in a massive fireball as a tiny anti-matter package was delivered to the middle of the Teheran launch compound. The Resident destroyed missiles launched from Istanbul, Ankara, Damascus, Bagdad, and Cairo, followed by others launched from more widely separated sites such as Tripoli, and Tangier to the west, a whole host of launches from Arabian Peninsula, and North Africa to the south, and from the "Stan" countries stretching from the Arabian to the Caspian Seas to the East. Following the destruction of the launched missiles, each missile launch site received an anti-matter packet as rapidly as the Resident could make it happen.

#

Saeed had opened his door a crack sometime during the ensuing action, and listened intently to the activity in the control room. Very clearly, a disaster was unfolding before his eyes, and Allah had placed him in exactly the right place and time to turn calamity into victory. *Finally, Allah (blessed be He) has revealed Himself and His path completely.* Near his door he spied Ari's satchel with the fighting knife. Saeed drew in a deep breath and whispered softly: *Let those fight in the way of Allah who sell the life of this world for the other. Whoso fighteth in the way of Allah, be he slain or be he victorious, on him we shall bestow a vast reward.*

Quietly, he crept through the slightly open door, silently approached the satchel and opened it, and grasped the fighting knife, the first weapon he had held since stowing away aboard the *Cassini II*. Holding the dagger firmly in his right hand, Saeed leapt to his feet and charged Eber, shouting "*Allahu Akbar!*" while holding the dagger out in front of himself.

#

Out of the corner of her eye, Rasu'eja saw motion to her left, as sound penetrated her rapt attention to what was happening on the monitor. Instinctively, she drew her short sword while turning, took in a hand grasping a dagger about to pierce Eber's right kidney.

With a powerful overhead slash, her weapon found its mark, severing Saeed's hand as the dagger clattered to the deck. Saeed screamed as he fell, clutching the stump to his chest.

Arpachshad swiveled to his right with drawn short sword, to be confronted by the writhing Saeed, his severed hand and abandoned dagger nearby. Rasu'eja watched the scene as if in slow motion. Blood dripped from her sword, making a popping sound as each drop hit the deck.

Ari stepped toward the fallen dagger, but Arpachshad motioned him back with his sword. Arpachshad asked Rasu'eja if she was okay. "I'm fine," she answered, as the scene around her speeded up to normal. "How's Eber?"

Rasu'eja heard both Jon and Arpachshad answer, "He's fine!" after which Eber stepped forward to look down at Saeed, who was now whimpering, while holding his stump against his chest. Vesta dropped to the deck next to Saeed, and motioned for Lud to join her. Jon looked at Eber questioningly. Eber told him that both Vesta and Lud were surgeons.

"What are you doing?" Rasu'eja asked.

"Saving his life," Lud answered.

"Because we're not barbarians," Vesta added.

#

Reports coming to Rod were sporadic. Initially, Israel was reported under missile attack, but that morphed into every known Caliphate missile launch site, and several nobody knew about, virtually vanishing off the face of the Earth. A few minutes later a terrorist group nearly succeeded in toppling the Eifel Tower – the story flashed around the world on every holocast. Within minutes the U.S. State Department received a communication through channels from the Persian Caliphate that it had ordered the Paris attack, and Washington would be next, unless it ordered off its space-borne lackey.

Rod received an update within minutes, and immediately informed Jon. "We think they're using sleeper cells. Is there any way your friends can stop them?"

"Not unless this flying saucer has psychic capabilities."

Five minutes later someone tried to topple the Washington Monument.

#

After receiving a detailed report from Rod, Jon did his best to explain the situation to the Founders. "Apparently, the Caliphate has sleeper cells located around the world, ready to be activated on the whim of the Caliph."

"Do you think they have all been activated?" Arpachshad asked.

"It's possible, but there have not been any other sleeper attacks since Washington and that was nearly a half-hour ago."

"Where do the sleeper orders come from?" Eber asked.

Jon queried Rod, but his link communication was interrupted. "This is the National Security Advisor. You'll be dealing directly with me from now on. To answer your question, we believe the orders come directly from Teheran." He paused while his image appeared to be listening to something off camera. "Your friends need to stand down while we sort things out. It's getting pretty confusing and messy down here."

#

Saeed continued to whimper in pain as Lud dressed his bleeding stump. Vesta cradled his head and asked quietly while her Link translator put her words into English, "Why? What did we ever do to you? We are your ancestors – why do you hate us?"

Saeed recoiled from her, gathered his strength, and spit in her face. "Infidel...Satan's spawn," he growled through his pain. This arrogant female and her companions were spoiling everything. Saeed had been so sure of Allah's path, so certain that this Jihad was Allah's will. Only very powerful forces could challenge the chosen path, and while they might succeed temporarily, Allah would never allow them to prevail.

Saeed spied the fallen dagger on the deck beyond the blasphemous female, near his severed hand. Whispering the words from the holy *Qur'an*: *"Whoso fighteth in the way of Allah, be he slain or be he victorious, on him we shall bestow a vast reward,"* Saeed lunged for the dagger with every bit of his remaining strength.

The words *"Allahu Akbar!"* strangled on his lips as Arpachshad slammed the butt of his sword into the back of Saeed's head.

#

Eber was having significant difficulty understanding the pure evil that Saeed represented. He looked at Ari. "Can you explain what drives such a man?'

Ari shook his head. "We have been asking the same question for several hundred years, if not a thousand or more." He reached into his satchel, coming up with an extra belt and some plastic ties. "Let's make sure the little bastard can't try anything else." He tied Saeed's left hand and both feet together, and then used the belt to secure him to a stanchion. "Although many Muslims are peaceful, decent people, there appears to be an undercurrent of violence that stems from a strict interpretation of their holy book by Imams – that is, ordained religious teachers and leaders – who broadcast their views every week in mosques across the planet. So long as the Imams continue this, the Islamic world will be ruled by violence and chaos. There are many in my country who believe the only way to stop Islamic violence is to eliminate the leaders who espouse the violence."

"And that is much easier to say than to do," Jon added.

Eber pondered the implications of what he had just heard. So long as Muslim Imams continued to teach violence, the mindless violence would continue, and Israel would be under imminent threat of destruction. Although he was unschooled in the subtleties of both diplomacy and war, one thing was clear to him. In the short-term the only way to stop the violence was to eliminate the teachers of violence within Islam, and in the long-term, he could see no solution but to eliminate the religion altogether. He made a mental note to discuss these things with Jon later, and then brought his focus to the moment.

"Jon, it looks like a general order to the sleeper cells has not gone out," Eber said.

"I agree, but it's only a matter of time before it happens. Two times now, we've been lucky. The Eifel Tower and Washington Monument both still stand, although the Eifel Tower did sustain some superficial damage." Jon queried the National Security Advisor: "What is the likelihood that some sleeper cells are sitting on small nukes?"

"It's possible. When Pakistan was incorporated into the Caliphate, an unknown number of nuclear warheads fell into the Caliph's hands. We have been unable to account for at least a dozen of the warheads."

Eber listened to the exchange with total astonishment. "You don't have neutrino detectors?"

"Well...yes, but what do you mean?"

"I mean that nuclear bombs are a source of concentrated neu trinos. They stand out like bright spots against the general neutrino background. So are nuclear reactors, but the ratio of the three neutrinos and their anti-neutrinos are different for reactors than for bombs. Look, I'll show you." Eber gave the Resident some instructions, and one of the monitors displayed a regional image of several hundred square kilometers around Teheran. Four clusters of bright spots appeared on the image. Upon Eber's instruction, the image expanded so that the clusters became separate spots. "Those," Eber said, "are nuclear bombs."

Chapter thirty-one

"So you're telling me that these Founder friends of yours took out all but the first few missiles launched toward Israel, and then they destroyed the launch sites?" The National Security Advisor's voice was dripping with sarcasm. "And just how did they do that? With ray guns?"

"Actually," Jon answered quietly, "yes, they used ray guns – sort of." He proceeded to explain how it went down, ending with a description of the neutrino bomb detector.

"So, now you're telling me that these guys can pinpoint every atom bomb on the planet?" The National Security Advisor's voice carried more incredulity than sarcasm this time.

"Basically, yes. Right now, they're sympathetic with our side in this, although they have expressed a willingness to step in only to protect Israel."

"So, they've taken sides already?"

"Not really. They are outraged by the anti-Israeli attitude from the Caliphate, and stepped in when it became apparent that the Israeli position was hopeless. As I said, right now they favor us – they are predisposed to stop the Caliphate's actions, if necessary."

"I introduced the Founders to our *Declaration of Independence* and our *Constitution*. Although I have received no feedback yet, I can tell that the Founders are impressed by our framework. They are way too sophisticated to believe that we really represent the image in those documents, but they seem predisposed to give us the benefit of the doubt." Jon held up his hand when the National Security Advisor started to interrupt him. "So long as we don't do something stupid – and that's a big if – I think the Founders will come down on our side in any confrontation."

"What do you mean 'a big if'?"

"Sir!" Jon was growing tired of the National Security Advisor's officiousness. "I'm a guest on an interstellar craft that just traveled from Saturn to the Earth in a fraction of a second, and that just nullified virtually the entire Caliphate missile armament. Do you really want to piss these guys off?"

Jon's Link image blanked, but the connection remained open. The extended silence was deafening. Eber smiled at Jon and gave him a thumb's-up sign. Jon wondered if the sign was historically universal, or if Eber had learned it from one of his crew. Nevertheless, he grinned back. The Link image shimmered; the face that now appeared in the holoimage was Marc Bowles, the President of the United States. Jon came to attention.

"At ease, Captain Stock." The President's voice was calm and his demeanor appeared relaxed.

"Yes Sir!" Jon relaxed and motioned for Eber to join him. "Mr. President, this is Eber, the leader of the Founders, and, for all practical purposes, their spokesman."

"How do you do, Sir?" The President nodded with a slight smile.

"Thank you, Mr. President," Eber answered, taking his cue from Jon.

"I want to thank you, cautiously, for your intervention against the recent unprovoked attack on Israel by the Persian Caliphate." The President paused for a moment, but it was clear that he had more to say. "I understand that you have technological capabilities that significantly exceed ours, and..." a small smile escaped the President's lips, "...that should we misbehave from your perspective, you have the ability to teach us a stern lesson." The President paused again.

"Although I am the President of the United States, I am certain that I speak for all our allies when I say to you that we are a peaceful people who seek peaceful solutions when we disagree. I imply absolutely nothing about your intentions, and I presume that your motivations are righteous. Nevertheless, you must understand that we will never submit to intimidation or threat."

"Mr. President, for my fellow clan members, my family, I accept your gratitude."

For a non-diplomat, he's sounding pretty good! Jon thought as he listened to the conversation.

"Furthermore, Mr. President, you should know that my people, the people of Ectaris, who came to this solar system so very long ago, had lived on our home planet for nearly two thousand years without war. We learned long ago to solve our problems peacefully, and will so continue now. As with your people, Mr. President, we will not be intimidated, and will do whatever is necessary to protect our families, our homes, and our way of life.

"Having said that, Jon – er...Captain Stock – introduced me to your founding documents. I am most impressed, Sir, with both the *Declaration of Independence* and the *Constitution*. Your basic values and ours are very similar, so that we feel a kinship not unlike that we feel with the Israelis."

The President smiled broadly. "I am gladdened by your comments, Eber – since you offered no titles, I will address you thus."

Eber nodded acquiescence.

"As you have seen, we – you and us – have a looming problem. Your presence and the facts of your existence triggered the Caliphate preemptive attack."

Eber started to say something, but the President held up his hand. "A moment, please!" Eber stood silently with a polite nod.

"There is no way you could be held responsible for what the Persian Caliphate did, and what it attempted to do. In fact, you deserve the highest praise for taking what actions you did to stabilize the situation. We are all in your debt. Unfortunately, the problem still continues. As you saw, the Caliphate activated two sleeper cells in an aborted attempt to topple both the Eifel Tower and the Washington Monument. There are countless numbers of other cells. My intelligence sources tell me that many of these cells have a nuclear bomb that they will detonate when so ordered. This will cause the loss of millions of innocent lives – and there is nothing we, the United States and its allies – can do about it." The President paused again, his face grave with genuine worry.

"We can do nothing," he continued, "but you can. I appeal to you in the name of everything that is fine and good in this Universe, do what you must to stop these nuclear bombs from detonating! We can ferret out and eventually stop the non-nuclear cells, but we need your help to stop a worldwide nuclear holocaust." The President's face said he was done talking.

Jon muted his link and looked at Eber. "Can you do it?"

"Sure. There will be consequences: civilian casualties near the sites, some radioactivity, unpredictable consequences, even. This is something I know how to do, but have never done. These bombs are located in population centers, right? An anti-matter blast would cause as much damage as a nuclear blast."

"All you need," Ari piped up, "is to disrupt the firing mechanism a bit. Without exact precision, these bombs will not detonate. You can focus the neutrino beam so that it will just blow apart the mechanism without any further detonations, right?"

"In principle, yes. There won't be an explosion; it just won't detonate anymore."

Jon unmuted his Link. "Mr. President, I think we have a possible solution to this problem." He then outlined what he had discussed with Eber, and finished by saying, "Once we have neutralized all the nuclear bombs, we can pinpoint their locations so you can have cleanup teams take care of what is left."

"One more thing," the President said. "Eber, may I speak with you again?"

Eber acknowledged, and the President continued, "Well over a hundred years ago the World was embroiled in what we now call the Second World War. Three nations ruled by despots attacked the United States and its allies, which consisted of most of the remainder of the World. Ultimately, the Allies prevailed. We did not allow the enemy nations to negotiate anything. We required, and eventually got, absolute, unconditional surrender. After trial and punishment of those who actually started and waged the war, we rebuilt those countries so that, today, they form vital parts of our global alliance.

"We harbor no ill will toward the innocent people who live under the iron rule of the Caliph. We recognize that they will need reeducation and redirection, but believe they can become valuable, contributing members of the global community.

"I am saying that we need to force the Persian Caliphate into an unconditional surrender. Its leaders must be brought to justice, and its peoples freed from the harsh control of the despotic religion that rules their lives."

"Mr. President, we will immediately commence the identification and destruction of every isolated nuclear bomb on the planet. But we know from our initial analysis that virtually every major nation on Earth possesses a nuclear arsenal. We will assume that an isolated bomb is terrorist related and needs to be destroyed, but will leave untouched – for the time being – all bombs grouped together. Those weapons we will leave for a future discussion." Eber stepped to the console to commence the operation.

"Captain Stock," the President said.

"Yes Sir!"

"I herewith accept your retirement request from the Navy with the permanent rank of Vice Admiral, and appoint you as Ambassador-at-Large to represent the United States and its allies to the Founders. You will assume your post immediately, and have the broadest powers to negotiate treaties, commit this country and its allies to agreements with the Founders, and to interact in whatever way seems, in your opinion, to serve the best interests of the United States and its allies."

"Uh...Mr. President..."

"Raise your right hand!" the President ordered.

#

Eber was more than a little amused by Jon's demeanor before the President. He had to admit to himself, however, that the President was impressive. He seemed to exude an aura of authority without seeming to flaunt it. He almost came across as humble – as a man who served, and who took the responsibility of his job seriously.

The first thing he did was to brief the rest of the family on what had happened. Most of them had followed the conversation with their Link translators, but he wanted to be sure everyone knew that came next.

"Asshur, you and Aram please set up the particle beam to the lowest possible detonation, and rig the neutrino beam for a soft focus of thirty cubits." The Link translator called this twenty meters.

Eber entered a set of instructions for the Resident, and then stepped back to watch the action. The Resident set up a complicated series of polar circumnavigations that gave *Merkavah* a one hundred percent sweep of every landmass on Earth over a five-minute period. The neutrino detector mapped the individual bombs on the fly, and immediately thereafter the neutrino beam hit the location, silently, invisibly, and with deadly efficiency.

Eber looked at Jon. "I have the bomb site locations. They're on your Link."

#

Rod had not communicated with Jon since the National Security Advisor had peremptorily replaced him. He was, therefore, more than a little surprised when his Link announced a secure call from the White House. He was even more surprised when the caller turned out to be, not the National Security Advisor, but the President himself. Rod straightened in his chair and pushed some paperwork out of range of the Link pickup.

"Good afternoon, Mr. Zakes." The President's voice was pleasant, with the slightest hint of his mid-west origins. His eyes twinkled with amusement at Rod's obvious consternation upon receiving a personal call from the most powerful man on Earth. "I hope I haven't caught you at an inconvenient time?"

"N...n...no, Sir! You have my full attention." *I didn't really say that to the President, did I?* Rod thought.

"Glad to hear it...I know you've been pretty busy. From where I sit, you've pulled the bacon from the fire several times during this historic voyage." The President paused, smiling quietly. "This administration needs men like you, Rod...I'm not suggesting you leave your position as Mission Director. Obviously, Captain Stock and his crew depend on you, and clearly you have developed a close relationship with the Captain. I would like you to assume an additional role with

a related job description: U.S. Liaison for Extraterrestrial Matters –
LEM for short – with full ambassadorial rank and privileges. Your primary contact will be Ambassador Jon Stock – yes, he's been promoted
(well, retired as an Admiral, and promoted to Ambassador-at-Large
to represent the United States and its allies to the Founders) – and
you will report directly to me.

"Do you have any questions?"

"A million, Sir, but they can wait. I'm honored that you think I
have what it will take for this job."

"Nonsense! You possess brass *cojones* and excellent judgment –
just what I need." The President stood up and approached his Link
pickup so that his face appeared larger than life in the air above
Rod's desk.

"Rod Zakes...Stand and raise your right hand..."

#

The Ayatollah sat in his throne-like chair on the raised dais centered in his meeting chamber. Arrayed before him on the intricately
tiled floor, his counsel of advisors did their individual best to keep as
far away from him as possible. The Caliph had just been informed
that, apparently, every one of his carefully positioned nuclear devices
had somehow been put out of commission.

"How can this happen?" he screamed. "One of you fools tell me!"

His wizened science advisor sat cross-legged on the floor to his
left. His Master's eyes burned into his soul. He leaned forward to
place his forehead on the cool tiles.

"Sahib – we believe it was the Infidel Founders who did this.
We do not know how, Blessed One, but it happened within a five
minute period all across the globe."

The Caliph turned to his Senior Advisor, directly on the floor
in front of him. The old man touched his forehead to the floor and
then rose to his knees, head bowed.

"What resources do we still have?" The Caliph's voice still
brimmed with anger.

The Senior Advisor answered without raising his eyes. "We have
Mullahs who have supplies of conventional explosives, and who can
rally a crowd of thousands in several hours. We have secretive cells
with conventional explosive with specific targets for which they have

trained extensively. These we can activate on short notice."

"What kind of targets?"

"Tall buildings, bridges, monuments; and they can cause maximum loss of life in shopping malls, theaters, and similar assembly points."

At that moment a messenger appeared at a side door to the Caliph's left. He waved a message tear sheet in the air, indicating that it contained an important message. The Caliph gestured him forward. The middle-aged man wearing a flowing gray robe, turban, and sporting an untrimmed, black beard, hurried around to the back of the assembled advisors, dropped to his knees, and shuffled forward to the base of the raised chair. He then prostrated himself, holding the message above his head with both hands. The Ayatollah grabbed the tear sheet, read it once, bellowed his outrage, and then leaned back to read it more carefully. Turning to his Senior Advisor, he spoke with controlled rage.

"Military forces have raided every one of our concealed nuclear locations worldwide!" He booted the messenger, knocking off his turban. "Remove yourself!" he growled. Turning back to his Senior Advisor he ordered, "Activate a conventional cell on odd days for a month, and trigger a riot on even days."

A collective gasp rose from the assembled advisors. The Caliph rose to his feet, and the advisors prostrated themselves as the angry leader strode from the room, stepping on several hands as he left.

#

With the Iapetus Mission temporarily on hold, Rod found himself inundated with incoming reports about the worldwide sweep of the nuclear bomb locations, and about fresh outbreaks of violence across the world. He kept Jon apprised of the situation. As he watched the civilian death toll mount during the most recent demonstration, he called Jon,

"Jon, unless we find a way to stop the haranguing Mullahs, the violence will escalate into a worldwide conflict that will be very costly in civilian lives. Do the Founders have any other tricks up their sleeves?"

"We're looking into whether there is a way to detect conventional explosives from orbit. I'll get back to you on that. Regarding the riots, if you can transmit to me the location of every riot as soon as possible, along with links to any live holo-transmissions, I think we can address the situation."

Jon went on to explain that the neutrino beam could be narrowly focused from space so that it would disrupt the life function of even a single individual, and that all he needed was the closest possible location, identification of the riot leader, and tacit permission to take these leaders out.

Rod contacted the President on his private hotline, and explained the situation. "So you see, Mr. President, I am reluctant to order the elimination of these men without your tacit acquiescence and permission."

"I have the National Security Council on standby, and need to consult with them. I'll get back to you on that shortly," the President said, and terminated the link.

An hour and fifteen minutes later, the President called back. "You are authorized to use deadly force to eliminate individual riot leaders as they are identified. You are prohibited from using the neutrino weapon for any other purpose without specific permission from me, personally."

"Sir...I am able to pass on your authorization to the Founders, but there is no way I can prevent them from using their resources for any purpose they see fit."

"I understand that, Ambassador Zakes. Nevertheless, that is the authorization I am issuing. Do your best to implement it."

#

After receiving the detailed communication from Rod, Jon explained the situation to Eber.

"I understand about taking out the riot leaders. We will gladly handle this matter. Perhaps cutting off the serpent's many heads will be all that is needed to quell the situation. But how does your President presume to tell me what I can and cannot do otherwise?"

Jon thought about it for a moment, and then answered, "I don't believe the President is actually telling you what you can and cannot do. He is forwarding a resolution from his National Security Council that is worded to protect its members from political repercussions. When you actually do whatever you need to do to protect your interests, or even to protect Israel, the Council can disavow any responsibility." Jon smiled encouragingly. "I cannot believe you did not have similar politics on Ectaris."

Eber nodded with a grin. "Of course we did." Then he turned to one of the monitors. "Let me show you something." A molecular diagram appeared on the monitor. "This is nitrogen in its quiescent state. And <u>this</u> is thermally agitated nitrogen as it is found in most explosives. Note the low-level gamma radiation. It turns out that our neutrino detector, when appropriately calibrated and tuned, can detect this gamma radiation when it is in conjunction with the thermal nitrogen that causes it. In short," Eber beamed at Jon, "we can locate the conventional bomb caches now so that ground forces can destroy them!"

Chapter thirty-two

Philadelphia SWAT Team members quietly moved along St. Davids and Ritchie Streets in a northwesterly direction from Green Lane in the old Manayunk section of Philadelphia. Their goal was a nondescript three-story row house in the middle of the block on the north side of St. Davids Street. A parking area on the south side of Ritchie Street connected directly to the back yard of their target. They moved carefully, pulling aside several curious pedestrians to keep them safe, and to prevent their giving out an alarm, should they be members of the cell.

When they were in position, their Captain radioed the order, and the commandoes simultaneously broke through the front and back doors of the building. It was over in moments. Five persons were apprehended, while one was shot to death when he attempted to escape. The Captain radioed an all-clear, and the SWAT Team disappeared as quickly and quietly as it had appeared.

This same scenario took place nearly simultaneously in over 25,000 locations around the world. In a one-hour period, virtually every location harboring more than a few pounds of explosives was raided. There were, of course, many locations that legitimately held the explosives: construction sites, mines, excavation sites, and others. Insofar as possible, these were left alone. The important thing was, however, that virtually all the Caliphate-inspired sleeper cells with explosives were permanently shut down, with many of their members taken into custody.

As a consequence, several spontaneous, Mullah-led demonstrations broke out in Asia and Europe, and one specifically ordered demonstration was orchestrated in Washington, DC. Eyes-on images from intelligence satellites and other sources such as traffic cams were beamed to *Merkavah*. Within fifteen minutes, the fully-bearded, long-robed Mullah exhorting the Washington demonstrators to storm the White House mysteriously dropped to his makeshift platform and died. Within minutes the same thing happened to the leaders of the spontaneous riots in Djakarta and Berlin. Without leadership, the rioters dispersed when pressured by local police.

More riots followed, although none of the intelligence agencies investigating these events were able to determine whether any specific riot was spontaneous or orchestrated. In every case, however, the leaders mysteriously died. In several instances, a back-up leader quickly took over, continuing the exhortations, only to collapse a short time later. Word got out quickly. It did not pay to be a visible leader of rioting Muslims. When the Caliphate attempted to orchestrate riots without visible leaders, they fizzled and died, except when a brave soul stepped to the front. When that happened, shortly thereafter, the brave soul collapsed.

Within several days, Muslim rioting worldwide faded away. It appeared that the immediate threat had entirely dissipated.

#

"Can you determine the size of the Caliphate's remaining nuclear arsenal?" Rod asked Jon.

Jon passed the question to Eber. For the following hour, the Resident conducted a thorough neutrino survey of the entire Persian Caliphate, from the surface down to a kilometer underground. Eber reported 120 nuclear warheads scattered at secure sites throughout the Caliphate. Jon passed this information to Rod, who immediately reported back to the President. Within a few minutes orders went back through the chain, orders to destroy the warheads.

Fifteen minutes later it was over. The once great Persian Caliphate military was left with a small air force that had survived the destruction of the missile bases, and distributed across the vast reach of the Caliphate, a navy that could still threaten shipping, and a respectable standing army.

Ari stepped up to Jon following the destruction of the warheads. "Jon, the Ayatollah is up against the wall. He's desperate, and will not behave in a manner predictable to American and European intelligence analysts. His air force and navy need to be utterly destroyed, and his army has to be decapitated. The alternative will be a massive loss of life as the Caliphate unleashes fuel-air explosives over Israel and any other allied target it can reach. His thousand-ship navy will be ordered to sink everything in its path, and his massive army will go on a raping, looting, and killing rampage."

Jon passed Ari's concern to Rod. "You have to convince the President that he has no alternative but to destroy the remaining air force using the Founders' anti-matter weapon, and to eradicate the Caliphate navy. Once this is accomplished, he needs to concentrate on taking out the army leadership."

"That's a pretty tall order, Jon, on very short notice."

"Yeh...and the fuel-air bombs will start exploding over Israel in about two hours."

The presidential authorization finally came through an hour later.

#

"The planes are airborne," the trembling messenger said from his prostrate position, as he handed the Ayatollah the message tear-sheet. This time the smiling despot ordered the messenger to rise. The messenger rose to his knees and backed away from the Caliph as rapidly as he could, until he was able to get to his feet and escape the chamber.

"When?" the Caliph asked.

"A bit more than an hour, Holy One," his War Minister answered.

Ten minutes later the messenger returned, crawling most of the distance from the door to the dais.

"What is it?" the Caliph demanded angrily.

"The planes – all destroyed, Sahib...every last one." The angry Caliph struck the messenger senseless with his staff.

At that moment another messenger ran from the communications room door directly to the War Minister, tossed a tear-sheet at him and ran back out of the chamber.

"What is it now?" The Caliph glared at his War Minister.

"Our ships, Sahib...one-by-one, as we speak they are exploding and sinking."

The despot rose to his full height and let out a piercing wail. As he did so, General Ismail Suleiman, his Army Chief of Staff strode into the chamber and directly up to the Ayatollah. He remained standing, although he deferred to the Caliph with a curt nod of his head.

"You have lost the air force and are losing the navy, and I just received this." He handed a message tear-sheet to the Ayatollah. "The American President is demanding our unconditional surrender. What are your intentions, Sir?"

"You will wipe them from the face of the Earth!" Spittle formed on the Ayatollah's lips.

"I am incapable of doing that, Sir. Without air support over the battlefield and artillery support from our navy off shore, we will be slaughtered. We will lose a million-man army in a few hours."

"That is not my concern, you fool. Do as ordered, or I will replace you with a general who will follow orders!" Spittle flew from the Caliph's mouth, some hitting the general's face.

General Sulieman's face remained passive as he drew his nine-millimeter pistol and shot the Caliph between the eyes. A general outcry rose from the assembled ministers; they shouted their denouncements at the General who stood passively over the body of the dead despot. Then he raised his pistol and one-by-one shot each of the front-row advisors, commencing with the Senior Advisor, followed by the War Minister, and then the rest. Those who tried to escape, he shot in the back of their heads as they tried to run for the doors. Several doors opened around the chamber, and senior military officers ran into the room, brandishing weapons, and ensuring that none of the remaining advisors escaped.

"I am assuming temporary control of the government of the Persian Caliphate." He gestured to a Colonel. "Round up these lackeys and lock them up. We'll deal with them later.' He pointed to another Colonel. "Get me the President of the United States by any means possible, as soon as you can!" The Colonel saluted and hurried out of the chamber. "Set up a general holocast throughout the Caliphate. I want to transmit in fifteen minutes."

Twenty minutes later the General sat in the Caliph's chair facing an array of holocams. "I am General Ismail Suleiman, Army Chief of Staff and head of the armed forces of the Persian Caliphate. The Caliph and his senior advisors are dead. I have taken temporary control of the government of the Persian Caliphate. During the last several days, the Ayatollah Khomeini waged a war against Israel and the space travelers we know as the Founders, and ultimately against the entire world. His efforts were entirely stopped by the combined efforts of Israel, the United States and its allies, and the Founders. Our stockpile of nuclear weapons is gone, our Air Force is annihilated, and our entire Navy is sunk. All we have left is our Army, and I am unwilling to sacrifice your husbands, fathers, sons, and brothers to an overwhelming opposition that seems to stop everything we attempt while taking no casualties themselves.

"Our unconditional surrender is demanded, and I will comply. I do not expect any reprisals, since I have come to understand that those we have called our enemies will become our friends as we move forward. In a few minutes, I will meet with the American President, and will offer him our unconditional surrender. There must be no demonstrations opposing our surrender, and no opposition in the halls of government or anywhere else. We have been defeated by an overwhelming power that appears to hold out a benevolent hand. I urge you, I plead with you to accept the inevitable, and be gracious to the representatives of the Allied Coalition as they visit our country following our surrender. How they treat us is entirely dependent upon how each of you acts in the coming days and weeks. May Allah hold you in the palm of His hand."

#

Saeed Esmail hunkered on *Merkavah's* deck, tightly bound, listening to General Sulieman's speech. His stump ached and throbbed. *How can this be? How can this have happened? Allah's will seemed so clear.* He wept quietly while resolving inwardly to continue his Jihad or die trying.

#

"We need to get back to Iapetus," Jon told Rod. "None of us has slept much, and my crew is pretty much in the dark regarding the developments on Earth."

"Not entirely," Rod responded. "I've been in regular contact with Dmitri. He has organized a concerted effort to link into as much of the *Arc* databases as the Founders have made available. Ginger established a semi-permanent burst transmission set-up so that the information is flowing into our planetside network as quickly as possible."

"Not for general release yet," Jon interrupted.

"It's going into a secure area of the database. We have established an entire facility staffed by dozens of international experts who are sorting out Ginger's transmissions. At some point, we will release material to the general public, but not yet."

"I don't think that's what the Founders had in mind." Jon paused, thinking about the implications of one Earth government censoring the Founder database. "I'll consult with Eber about this."

Eber was adamant. The specific information the Founders had made available to the Iapetus explorers was not to be censored in any way. It was to be released to the general public over the Worldwide Link immediately. "The alternative," he told Jon, "is that I will activate a subroutine embedded in every transmission Ginger has made, that will seek out and destroy every bit of information from our database. This information is available for everybody – or nobody."

Jon explained the situation to Rod. "Eber is not kidding. If the facility the government established does not immediately open its gateway to unrestricted access, there will be hell to pay."

After Jon had cleared up that misunderstanding, Eber approached him, and waved for Ari to join them. "My family and I have discussed our peculiar situation in some detail. We have mixed emotions regarding our future. Some of us want to take you up on your offer to help us build a suitable craft for extended voyages. We intend to live our lives exploring the universe. By now you understand that such exploration leapfrogs us forward in time; we can never come back. Some of us, on the other hand, like Earth as it is now, and wish to settle down. They are especially excited by modern Israel, and want to settle there and make a real difference."

Jon looked at Ari, and an understanding passed between them.

If possible, they would join the Founders in their future explorations.

"I agree with you, Jon," Eber said, changing the subject abruptly. "We need to return to the *Arc* – to Iapetus. Please let your people know that we will depart in about an hour. If something comes up and we are needed here, remind them that we can be back in less than two hours, once we reboard *Merkavah*."

#

An hour and fifteen minutes later, Jon and Ari untangled themselves from Michele's wet embrace, Ginger's warm kisses, Elke's more formal, kissless embraces, and Carmen's twinkle-eyed squeezes. These were followed by firm handshakes all around between the men. Michele turned her attention to the Founders. She picked out Ishtar, took both her hands and pulled Ishtar's beautiful face down toward hers. Then Ishtar kissed her full on the lips, open mouthed and moist. "Welcome back," Michele said. One-by-one, Michele and the others greeted each of the returning travelers.

Jon watched these interactions with some amusement. He knew that Aram had lost his wife, Sari, during one of their sojourns on earth. Jon could almost see him weighing his choices. Michele clearly had a wider field to play, and had vectored directly to Ishtar – easily the most beautiful woman Jon had even seen. Each of the others seemed to have made one or more connections with the Founder clan, and friendships were developing.

Jon asked his crew members to meet in his office so he could brief them on the general Earth situation. He took the time to detail how the Founders reacted to the turmoil their appearance caused, and how they eventually solved the situation. Then he leaned back and grew somewhat nostalgic.

"You are the very best crew I have ever had the pleasure of serving with. What we accomplished together, taking *Cassini II* from Earth into orbit around Iapetus – just think of that, we went farther, faster than any humans before us (Yeh, I know about the Founders), discovering what Iapetus really is, figuring out what the Founders had left us, and finally interfacing with the Founders themselves. Just look at what we have done. We're so far from home that light takes nearly one-and-a-half hours to get there from here." He grinned at them encouragingly.

"Now all these phenomenal accomplishments are lumped together into an historical side lobe, because those guys can make the trip in a half second subjective time. This means we have to move on to bigger and better things. For myself, I plan on helping the Founders build a larger, more accommodating starship, and when they leave, I intend to leave with them."

"Me too!" Ari said.

"And I," said Ginger.

Jon looked around the group. "Don't forget, when you go, you leap forward in time. You'll never again see your friends and loved ones, so don't make this decision lightly. You don't have to decide right now. There's plenty of time. We don't know where we'll build the larger ship – here, on Earth, or at El-four. The Founders obviously have full manufacturing facilities here – if they still work. There may be less of make-the-tools-to-make-the-tools-to-make-the-ship here than anywhere else." He paused. "We'll see..." His voice trailed off as he became lost in his own thoughts.

Female companionship had never been a problem for Jon, but this was different. Each of the Founders was paired except for Vesta and Aram, and they were unlikely to pair up. Furthermore, he'd gotten some feedback that Vesta and, perhaps a couple other Founders, might finally sink roots and remain behind. The Founder female selection was startling to say the least, but each was in a stable relationship, and Jon did not yet understand the sexual morays of the Founders. The only hint he had was when Ishtar enthusiastically returned Michele's kiss. He was glad that Ginger wanted to go, but he was also aware of her impact on all the Founders. In effect, the Founders had been together for a very long time. One or more of the clan might very well be ready for a change.

Jon sighed and looked over his crew again, pausing at each of the gals. *It will just have to work itself out*, he thought, smiling inwardly.

Chapter thirty-three

Eber was troubled by the choice he had to make. He was very impressed by the founding documents of the United States, but far less impressed by the resulting nation he saw. Much of the original intent of the country's founders had been usurped by expediency and special interests, starting with the seventeenth amendment that changed the Senate from a body that was appointed by state legislatures to represent States' interests to a second body elected by the people that represented their interests, often in competition with the House of Representatives. From his perspective, the nation's founders had created a bottom-up system that maximized individual freedom, and minimized government interference in people's lives. He was genuinely disappointed, however, in what the nation had become – basically a top-heavy, centrally run bureaucracy that served the interests of the few at the expense of the many. Not that he hadn't met some good people within the American system. The question was, did he want to turn over advanced Founder technology to the Americans?

The other side of the equation was the Israelis. It was abundantly clear that they were lineally descended from his own family. That made them special by everything he valued. And yet, even though they were "family," and operated within a freely elected system, they were even more bureaucratic than the Americans, and they had limited resources. And he detected elements within the Israeli society that were as mindlessly militant as those within the Caliphate.

The Europeans were a joke with their failed European Union. The Russians seem never to have recovered from the break-up of the Soviet Union, from everything he could tell. The Asians under China's leadership seemed to have some cohesion, but he didn't trust their motives, and could not, in good conscience, give them a material advantage over the rest of the world.

Discussion with his brothers was fruitless. They each identified closely with Israel, without really seeing the downside of giving the Israelis their advanced technology. He was uncomfortable discussing this with the women because it seemed, in some subtle way, to be going around his brothers. So it was that Eber ended up in a private discussion with his grandmother, Vesta.

It was impossible for Eber to think of Vesta as pushing seventy years. Her beautiful face was without wrinkles, and she had the physique and tone of a woman a half-century younger. And yet, her decades of medical practice and her position as the elder of the family (and for that matter, the entire human race), gave her an untouchable gravitas. Eber conveyed his thoughts to her, and was pleasantly surprised to discover that she, too, had studied the founding documents of the United States.

"Why are you concerned about this at all?" Vesta asked. "Why not simply make the technology available?"

"I believe it would lead to a worldwide war that might destroy our species."

Vesta lifted her eyebrows.

"No matter who gets it, the others will want it – bad enough to fight for it." Eber spread his hands in consternation. "Israel is simply too small. America seems the best choice, but..." His voice trailed off as he thought about the many things that could go wrong.

"And who made you judge and jury?" Vesta's hazel eyes flashed flecks of green.

"Our sun going nova, the wholesale demise of our compatriots, the Universe...Hell! I don't know! But here I am, and I have to make a decision. I'm not staying here any longer than necessary to make sure those of you who stay have what you need, and to ensure that I have a worthy ship."

Vesta nodded. "Where will you build the new ship?"

"Frankly, it has to be here, unless I transfer our technology to Earth wholesale. No matter what, eventually they'll get it, unless we totally destroy the *Arc* with all its contents." Eber paused in thought. "I just can't do that!"

"I know." Vesta squeezed his hand. "So, what will you do?"

"Who's staying? Do you know?"

"I am..."

"I thought so."

"...and Lud and Shakbah for sure...Ishtar's going with you, but I don't know about Asshur. Azurad is staying with you, right?"

"Actually, I'm not entirely certain." Vesta looked at him sharply, green flecks flashing. "We get along fine. I'm just not sure she wants to leave Earth again."

"Arpachshad and Rasu'eja are going with you," Vesta continued. "And Aram told me he's staying – he mumbled something about Michele."

"So, it's you, Lud and Shakbah, Aram, and probably Azurad and Asshur." Vesta nodded. "I already know that Jon, Ari, and Ginger will be coming with us. Dmitri and Noel are going home. Carmen's family obligations will keep her on Earth, but I don't know about Elke and Chen. She likes girls, you know, but I suppose that would not be a problem – Rasu'eja and Ishtar are fine with that, and if Azurad comes, she enjoys a woman's touch, too. I think Chen would be a problem, however, so I hope he is planning to return to China.

"With the lineup as I see it now, if Azurad stays on Earth, we will have no doctor. If it turns out this way, then we will need to recruit a doctor, and I am confident that there will be very high interest." Eber sat quietly for a few moments. "What all this means is that enough of you are remaining behind that we can decide on a way to do this, because, remember, once we leave, we are gone forever – at least from your perspective."

As Eber said this, Vesta squeezed his hand, and her eyes filled with a different kind of sparkle. Through her incipient tears Vesta asked quietly, "Do you think that I, along with Aram and Asshur and the others, will be able to implement the procedures we all agree on?" She gave him a tentative smile. "And what if we decide to do it differently? You won't be here, and can never affect what we decide – so why worry about it?" The green flashes in her eyes returned. Eber hugged her warmly.

"Here's what I'm thinking," Eber said, finally. "I have come to trust and admire Jon very much. The same for Ari – in fact, I find myself thinking of Ari as a brother. I'll present the problem to them both, and see what we come up with.

"Thanks, Vesta!" He gave her another big hug.

#

Jon listened to Eber describe the dilemma as he saw it.

"Eber," Jon said with a broad smile. "Have you studied the American Constitution?"

Eber nodded.

"Do you recall the tenth amendment?" Eber indicated he didn't. "Basically, it says that powers not specifically given to the federal government by the constitution are reserved to the individual states, or to the people." Jon paused while Eber digested this. "Granted, our nation has not followed this rule consistently, but it still guides. What we have here is a situation never envisioned by our founders. You guys have technology vastly beyond anything we currently have. You own it. You are under no obligation to give it to anyone."

"But, we want to!"

"Hear me out, Eber. I believe you should establish Iapetus as an independent federation, and ensure that the United States and all of its allies recognize you as an independent nation. You can pattern your constitution after the U.S. Constitution, and can set up a basic set of laws that will work for your circumstances as an independent nation within our solar system. Rod can assemble a group of constitutional lawyers who can structure this for you. Once your legal structure is in place – and this can happen within days of your recognition by the U.S. – you can create a corporation, a holding company, that owns all your technology. Then you can license the use of your technology to whomever you wish, for whatever you wish to charge – at least whatever the market will bear.

"Beside the remaining Founders, invite to your Board of Directors people that Rod believes will help you with the task of controlling the technology. Open Iapetus to immigration, but on a very strictly controlled basis, so that you can grow within the structure of your constitution without making the mistakes that America made. Consider the possibility of expanding Iapetus to include mining colonies in the Asteroid Belt, settlements on several of the moons of Saturn and the other gas giants, even Mars, possibly. Structure yourself so that new colonies can petition to become members of the federation.

"Licensing of your current technology will eventually run out, but by then you will have moved ahead with development, so that – with a little savvy – you will always stay ahead of the rest of the solar system."

Eber sat quietly, apparently digesting what Jon had said. "Do you think this is really possible?"

"I do. Coordinate with Rod, and he will ensure that the moment you announce your nation status, the United States will formally recognize you, as will several of its closest allies. That's all that matters, but the rest of the world will eventually follow. They'll have no choice."

"How long will all this take?"

"I'll put Rod on it immediately. He'll quietly assemble the constitutional scholars. You already have the framework for your constitution; all they need to do is modify it to apply to the reality of where and what Iapetus is. Give them a week of concentrated effort, and they will have the constitution ready. Give them an additional month to structure a basic legal framework. While they are doing that, Rod will work closely with the U.S. government to ensure the transition goes smoothly. Six weeks from today, you can have the Iapetus Federation accepted as an official member of the nations of Earth.

"When we return ten years from now your time, we will be able to see the fruits of your efforts.

"And who knows – if we announce our first destination, by the time we arrive there, Earth scientists may have developed some kind of warp drive that eliminates the relativistic effects of our current hyper-vee drive. They may be able to meet us at our destination a thousand Earth years from now."

#

The manufacturing facilities on Iapetus (Jon had real trouble thinking of Iapetus as the *Arc*) were incredible. The Ectarians had perfected automated manufacturing. All they had to do was create the design, not as finished engineering drawings, but as sketches that the massive Ectarian computers could manipulate to set up the manufacturing facility for production – of one or many. All the system needed was raw material. That was virtually unlimited on Iapetus.

The core group consisted of Eber and Jon, Arpachshad, Rasu'eja, and Ishtar, and Ari, Ginger, and Elke (who had finally decided). It took about a month to agree on a design that would accomplish their needs. It was still saucer-shaped, necessitated by the requirements of quantum physics. Since the Iapetus launch cylinders were fifty meters wide, the new starship was just less than fifty meters at the rim, and stood twenty meters or about five stories tall. It easily accommodated fifteen people, while able to handle fifty. Individual quarters could be merged to accommodate shared living arrangements. The vessel had a medical facility, bio labs, science labs designed to handle a variety of other disciplines, a small gym, an entire deck dedicated to a hybrid hydroponic system for growing fresh foods, an automated manufacturing facility that could create anything from a replacement part to a nutrient-rich, tasty meal replacement, a water and waste reclamation facility, and massive storage for mostly freeze-dried foods. In addition, the ship carried a space-worthy excursion vehicle – a saucer vessel similar to the *Merkavah* that formed the top of the ship, two vacuum-capable surface vehicles able to withstand a pressure differential of 600 atmospheres (as found at the deepest parts of Earth's oceans), and a suite of defensive and offensive short and long range weapons, based on the *Merkavah* laser, anti-matter, and neutrino beams.

Construction of the starship was not a trivial matter. Jon was fascinated by the automated process. He and Ari spent several hours each day studying the theoretical process, and more time observing how it actually happened. Jon's Systems Engineering doctorate from Cal Tech helped him understand how the elements came together, but did little to enhance his understanding of the underlying science. Ari's aerospace training at the Technion gave him a handle on some of the basics, but no more.

"We have our work cut out for us once we get underway," Jon

told Ari. "Someone other than Eber has got to fix this thing if it breaks out there somewhere."

Initially, the manufacturing facility created the black hole core, accelerator ring, and associated shielding. Then it constructed the vessel from the inside out, so that a month later, the still unnamed starship was sitting on its launch cradle awaiting final outfitting and provisioning – like a great big empty house. As with the *Merkavah*, the ship's skin absorbed all impinging light. To look at it was like looking at a hole in the air. "The ultimate stealth vehicle," Jon commented to Ari. "Nothing reflects from it."

"Something else we need to learn about," Ari replied wryly.

#

Somewhat reluctantly Eber agreed to a planet-wide contest for the world's children to name the starship. As it turned out, he couldn't have chosen a better name than what came out of the contest: *Starchild*. The commissioning ceremony took place with the ship still in the launch cradle on Iapetus, but the holovision broadcast was seen around the world. The Founders were unfamiliar with Earth's tradition for launching a vessel, but when Jon explained it, while pointing out that since they were dealing with a starship instead of an ocean vessel, the ceremony would be more suitable as a commissioning instead of a launching, they were enthusiastic. Eber immediately assigned Vesta to the honors. A wine especially blended from the best vineyards on Earth arrived on Iapetus aboard *Merkavah*. At the assigned moment, Vesta, who was standing on a specially constructed platform, lifted the bottle, which was attached to the starship's ramp with a deep blue ribbon, and swung it against the deep black hull.

As the bottle shattered, Vesta intoned, "I christen you *Starchild!*"

As her image flashed into every home on Earth, a roar went up from around the world as people everywhere celebrated the event. To Eber's relief, there were no radical Muslim demonstrations. He was amused by the outpouring of love from the Raëlians. They danced in the streets of every major city on Earth, wearing white robes and singing praises to the Founders. The younger, pretty women offered themselves to the Founders, but when no Founder accepted their offers, they gave their favors to any and all. The French celebrated by naming Michele deBois France's First Lady. The Germans dedicated a statue at the Brandenburg Gate to Ellie Crate, and issued a commemorative stamp featuring her image superimposed on the *Starchild*. The Australians renamed the Lark Distillery in Hobart the Ginger Steele Distillery, and dedicated a national holiday to the statuesque space explorer. The Canadian parliament passed a resolution officially welcoming Noel Goddard home, but the Quebec assembly refused to ratify the resolution because Noel had not planted a Quebec flag during the Iapetus landing ceremonies. The Russian Federation President and Dmitri Gagarin got drunk together, and celebrated the commissioning in a steam bath being rubbed down by nubile Ukrainian lasses. The Israeli Knesset dedicated a new building in the Haifa complex of the Technion to Ari Rawlston, and on a second vote, renamed the newest building in the Manhattan complex as well. The Indian Premier arranged for a weeklong tour of the provinces by Carmen Bhuta, accompanied by the Premier, of course, so that the common people could meet their new hero. The Chinese appointed Chen Lee Fong as China's new Science Minister and instigated major celebrations in his honor in every municipality in China. New York City organized a Fifth Avenue Ticker Tape Parade honoring Jon Stock, America's most famous space explorer.

As Eber absorbed the worldwide festivities, he wondered how an event like this would have unfolded on Ectaris. Since all he knew was the *Arc*, he really had no way of knowing. He reviewed some of his contacts on Earth as the clan hop-skipped through Earth's history. People's beliefs were different, of course, and technology was mostly nonexistent. Nevertheless, people have remained substantially the same. When he compared modern Earthmen to his fellow Ectarians when they first arrived here, there were really no significant differences that could not be attributed to growing up inside the *Arc* as opposed to growing up on Earth's surface.

\#

The *Starchild* in its cradle was moved from its construction location to the nearest launch column.

Eber decided that only he and Jon would take the inaugural flight. The process mirrored launching *Merkavah*. At this stage, Jon was as familiar as Eber with the controls and the Resident interface. Eber said with a smile, "She's yours, Jon. Take her out!"

Once they were space borne and well above the ecliptic, Eber had Jon bring *Starchild* to a hover. "Let's check out the little *Starchild*," Eber said.

They ascended to the top of *Starchild* and entered the smaller spacecraft through a deck hatch. The controls were identical to *Merkavah*. Eber grinned at Jon, and moments later they were hovering near the Mirs Complex, the Resident having transited to Earth above the ecliptic and then dropped to the Moon's orbit.

"You take her back!" Eber said.

Twenty minutes later they came to rest at the bottom of the launch column, and the bay door slid up out of sight.

#

Provisioning turned out to be a much bigger deal than Eber had thought it would be. As he reflected on what the task entailed, however, he began to understand the reality of what they were undertaking, Their original return to Ectaris and their hops forward through Earth's developing history had really been like an afternoon stroll in the park compared with what they were now undertaking. He found himself relying a great deal on Jon's expertise, gained on the Mars expedition and then the *Cassini II* voyage. In real terms, Jon had far more experience in space travel than Eber had, and probably, Eber conceded to himself, should be given command of the *Starchild*.

Their crew currently consisted of four Founders and four *Cassini II* crew members, and they were looking for a doctor. As Eber and Jon discussed the situation in Jon's makeshift office, Eber found himself thinking that they really needed more crew members.

"Jon, we're building regular accommodations for fifteen. We all agreed on this, and yet we're eight. How about recruiting another seven people? Right now we have a broad mixture of engineering skills, historians, warriors, an astronomer, and a physician. We really need expertise in physics, chemistry, biology and agronomy, geology, and it probably wouldn't hurt to take a shrink with us as well – perhaps who doubles as the physician."

"We all have eclectic outside interests," Jon said. "Music, art, writing – if we're going to add more people, we need to ensure they are more than their basic resumes, that their breadth matches ours." Jon opened a drawer in his desk and extracted an ancient bottle of

Islay scotch whiskey, along with a couple of interestingly fluted glasses. "Do you know scotch?"

Eber shook his head, wondering what kind of treat Jon was offering him. As Jon filled the glasses to the level of the first inward curve, Eber caught a whiff, an aroma that hinted of open steppes, burning moss, and salt sea air. The glass shape obviously was designed to direct the vapors to his nostrils, so he lifted the glass to his lips and inhaled through his nose. This was something Eber had not before experienced. He sipped a small amount of the golden liquid. A smooth wash of fire crossed his tongue, and – for a moment – he thought he might cough or sputter, but the feeling passed and he was left with a pleasant warmth in his mouth and throat, and a heady sense of a simultaneous cacophony and blending of taste and aroma.

"That, my friend, is the nectar of the gods," Jon said quietly as he replaced the bottle in the drawer. They sat silently, savoring.

"I've been giving a lot of thought to something," Jon said a while later. They still had dregs in their glasses, and Eber was still in wonderment over this incredible delicacy. Eber looked at Jon in anticipation.

"We're provisioning for fifteen people – for how long? We can spend several months exploring vast distances – actually, not the distances but the destinations at those distances. The real factor we need to keep in mind is how much time we spend in hyper-vee, compared to how much time we spend exploring. If we spend a year in hyper-vee, we're jumping ahead twenty-six-thousand years. If we return to Earth after twenty-six-thousand years, I don't think we can bridge such a difference.

"On the other hand, if we limit ourselves to a total of three days in hyper-vee, we'll have leapt forward only one hundred eighty-four years. I think everyone can handle that. When I think about the technology we have developed in the last two hundred years, I don't think I can imagine where we might be one hundred eighty-five years from now, but I am relatively confident that we and they can deal with the differences."

"All the more so," Eber added, "if we do an initial jump of only ten or twenty years."

"Don't forget that Rod and his people will be licensing Ectarian technology into Earth's at a steady pace."

"I'm for an initial ten-year jump, and then a more extended one of several hundred years. See what happens in the short-term, and then go for a bigger jump."

"I don't disagree, but I think we should pass it by the current Israeli and U.S. leaders. If they feel they are part of the decision, I think they will be more willing to facilitate the wait for our return." Jon stopped talking, and dropped into deep thought. Eber did not disturb the process. When Jon refocused, Eber let him continue.

"I suspect that when we return after ten years, most people will presume that we have experienced the ten years just as they have. Only a very small percentage of Earth's population will comprehend that our trip lasted only a few minutes for us. But our return will be a big deal. By the time we return the second time, however, I suspect our existence will have shifted into a quasi-legendary status. I think we will be anticipated by only two groups." Jon paused.

"Don't keep me in suspense...whom are you referring to?"

"The descendants of Rod's enclave will keep the knowledge of us alive, although we may well achieve legendary status even with these scientists. Legendary will not be an issue with the second group. We – you Founders, actually – already have legendary status with the Raëlians. They will mark their calendars and restructure their religious rites so that our return will be a worldwide event for them. You Founders awakened a sleeping giant when you made your appearance. The Raëlians have been with us in one form or another for a long time, but always as a fringe religion. I predict that after our short-term jump, they will become the dominant religious faith on Earth, displacing Christianity, Islam, and all the others."

"That would not have happened on Ectaris," Eber said. "At the time Ectarians commenced preparations to leave, there were virtually no organized religions."

"I can see that. Ectaris had one common faith: Survival! That trumped everything."

"Remember, Jon, by then we had fifty thousand years of recorded history. As a people, we had pretty much come to grips with the real world."

"Well," Jon quipped, "prepare to be a god to the common people."

#

For the thousandth time, Jon went over his departure checklist. They were provisioned for a full year for fifteen, even though they had not yet filled their complement. Furthermore, they could supply food indefinitely with the hybrid hydroponics system coupled with the automated manufacturing system. They had loaded several cases of the Earth's finest rare liquors. Their electronic library held the sum total of everything in the Founder and Earth databases – a feat that could not have been accomplished with Earth's current technology, but was easy with the installed Founder computer system. Included with these data were formulas for manufacturing virtually all of the Earth's wines, beers, and distilled beverages, formulas generated at the molecular level by the Founders' sophisticated analysis equipment; formulas that should – in principle – allow the manufacturing facility to recreate any of these beverages so that they would be indistinguishable from the original. Jon doubted that, which was why he made sure that they carried a limited supply of the originals.

All that was left was selecting the remaining crew members, putting Saeed to pasture somewhere on Earth where he could do no more harm, and establishing the Iapetus Federation with its licensing arrangement for the Founder technology. Jon left the crew recruiting effort in Rod's & Ginger's capable hands. The final selections would be ready in a month, including a physician with broad expertise in psychology. He and Rod had discussed the implications of fifteen people cooped up in a relatively small starship. Social and sexual dynamics were fully complicated enough on a planet-wide basis. How would this distill down to a small group of highly talented individuals isolated not only by distance from everyone else, but as time passed, by time itself as they inexorably moved away from their common timeline with Earth?

From his personal perspective as an acknowledged alpha-male, Jon knew that he wanted the women in his limited universe to be easy on the eyes. It wasn't that simple, however. In the final analysis, comeliness was a two-way street. After discussing the matter privately with Rod, Jon decided to bring Ginger into the decision-making process. Together they decided that additional crew members would be highly capable in more than one discipline, with broadly eclectic interests, and a sense of group that went beyond their individual proclivities;

and they would be comely, as judged by Ginger and Rod – Jon had pulled himself out of that equation.

After all that had happened, no one connected with *Cassini II*, *Merkavah*, or *Starchild* wanted to make a further issue of the little terrorist, Saeed Esmail. What Jon finally did was to turn Saeed over to American military escorts at L-4, with instructions to return him to Earth the way he had come via the Earhart Slingshot in the equatorial Pacific, and to drop him off without ceremony of any kind anywhere in the old Persian Caliphate. The escort released Saeed in an empty alley in a run-down section of old Dubai. They gave him 200 riyals, the officially reevaluated coin of the realm, worth about $50 in U.S. currency. In seconds, Saeed scampered around a corner and disappeared into the rabbit warren of ancient buildings bordering narrow alleyways that was that ancient city.

Jon worked closely with Rod and Eber on Iapetus, creating what they officially dubbed the Starchild Institute. The Institute's charter, called the Starchild Compact, was to keep alive and viable in the minds of the people of Earth the existence, and eventual return, of the *Starchild* and its crew.

The Starchild Institute was to be funded from royalties generated by licensing Founder technology through the Founders Corporation Jon set up with Rod. All that really remained was to establish the Iapetus Federation.

#

Rod was ushered into the Oval Office by a White House staffer. His thinning hair was combed back, and he was feeling a bit self-conscious in the business attire that he never wore on the job. The President rose from his deep leather chair and walked around his expansive mahogany desk with hand outstretched.

"Good to meet you in person, finally!"

"Thank you, Mr. President. It is my honor – I really mean that." Rod was having considerable difficulty coming to grips with the fact that he was alone in the Oval Office with the most powerful man on the planet.

The President grinned at Rod and gestured to one of two couches facing each other across an ornate coffee table. "Please have a seat. May I offer you a cup of coffee? It's pure Kona – the best there is, in my opinion." A wave of his hand dismissed the uniformed Navy Steward who was at parade rest by the door.

Rod nodded without speaking, his throat dry from tension. The President filled a thick-walled mug with the steaming black liquid. "How do you like it?"

"Black, Sir."

"Black it is," The President set Rod's mug on a cork coaster on the coffee table and poured himself a mug. Rod examined his mug. One side of the mug displayed the presidential seal, but the other side surprised him – the SEAL Team Six crest. *That explains a few things*, Rod thought.

The President sat opposite Rod and crossed his legs while sipping the steaming brew. "I am grateful for the job you've done working with the Founders. I'm not sure we would be this far along without your presence." The President smiled graciously. "But you didn't come here to hear my compliments. What's so important that you had to see me personally – and alone?"

For the next few minutes, Rod outlined for the President how the Founders were structuring the Starchild Institute. He explained the nature of the Founders Corporation and how it planned to license Founder technology to paying customers. He gave the President a copy of the Starchild Compact, explaining its purpose, reminding the President of just how much a culture's technology can advance in several hundred years.

The President sat quietly, sipping his coffee and listening, his handsome features focused on Rod's words. "You didn't have to see me personally to tell me this," he said when Rod paused. "There's something more..."

"Yes, Sir." Rod laid out the details of the Iapetus Federation. "The Federation will need immediate recognition of its nation status from the United States, and from as many of the U.S. allies as can be brought to the table," he said in conclusion. By this time, Rod had overcome his nervousness, and was feeling his stride. "I am to be the official Iapetus Foundation Ambassador to Earth..."

The President raised his right eyebrow. "The Federation is still too small to send a representative to each Earth nation," Rod said with a smile. "Until we reach critical mass, we will need a good friend." He lifted his mug in a toast. "That has to be the United States."

The President sat for a while, apparently thinking about what he had just heard. "That's quite a concept," he said finally. "And I can see the implications – asteroid colonies, settlements on other gas giant moons, maybe even Mars and our own Moon...El Four, even...The implications are staggering. So, when does all this happen?"

Rod was prepared for this question. "We have our constitution and basic set of laws. The Starchild Institute is a fact, as is the Founders Corporation. I guess you could say we're ready to go."

"How do you see things developing?"

"We structured our constitution after the U.S. version, but we intend to remain much closer to the concept than America obviously has. All of us who put this together believe very strongly that he who governs least, governs best. Ours will be an open society with minimum controls only where absolutely necessary."

"Can you protect yourselves from those who would take what you have?"

"You've seen what we can do with improvised weapons, Mr. President. Just imagine what we can do if we are forced to defend ourselves." Rod did not want the President to feel threatened, but he wanted to make sure that the U.S. President and all those with whom he would shortly speak, would have no illusions about what the Iapetus Federation could do, and what it would do if threatened.

The President rose to his feet and reached out to shake Rod's hand. "I like the concept – I'll give you my decision by noon tomorrow."

Chapter thirty-four

Jon gazed out the expansive window of the Great Room in the L-4 ring complex, the same window he had gazed through when he first met the *Cassini II* crew members what seemed so very long ago. The *Cassini II* was, of course, long gone, and would probably never return from her close orbit around Iapetus. When he first saw her, the *Cassini II* had been located about a hundred kilometers from the ring complex on the opposite of L-4, but now Jon's view was filled with the image of the *Starchild*, floating about a thousand meters in front of the window. Because the *Starchild* was a flattened spheroid about twenty meters high and fifty meters wide, she appeared much larger than *Cassini II*, but looks in space were deceiving, and Jon knew that the *Cassini II* was really about three times the vertical length of the *Starchild*. One-third of *Cassini II* was taken up with the VASIMR drive and fuel tanks, whereas a much smaller percentage of the *Starchild* was core and propulsion. Because of its wide girth, it was much easier to move about inside the *Starchild*; furthermore, its artificial gravity eliminated many of the routine problems that characterized the *Cassini II*.

Starchild was ready to go. The new crew members had been selected, and all fifteen had trained together for two weeks of intensive training on Iapetus, and in actual maneuvers in the vicinity of the Solar System. Ginger had calculated that they had all gained about a day on their Earth compatriots during this training. Even though their first ten-year jump would take them only about four hours subjective time, they all were straining at the bit to get underway.

To Jon's unexpected surprise, Eber asked him to captain *Starchild*. When Jon objected, Eber told him, "You have vastly more experience piloting ships through space than I. You've been tested by fire several times. So far as I'm concerned, you have more than proven that you have what it takes to keep all of us safe. I will be absolutely delighted to hand over the cloak of command to you, and to serve under your leadership."

The next day, Eber had made the official announcement, and they walked through a formal change-of-command ceremony, following the guidelines Jon had given Eber from his own Navy background.

"I, Eber of the Founder Clan, hereby relinquish my command of the starship *Starchild*, and transfer to you, Captain Jon Stock, the full responsibility for the safety of the ship and crew." Eber turned to face Jon.

"I relieve you, Sir!" Jon's words rang out across the artificial Iapetus meadow filled with the assembled starship crew and virtually every other person on Iapetus.

"I stand relieved!"

The two men, ancient ancestor and modern descendant, saluted each other and then shook hands. Cheers went up from the assembled crowd, and across the World as their words and images were transmitted around the planet.

Following tearful good-byes with those who would not see them for ten years, under their new Captain's watchful eye, the fifteen crew members filed through the great hanger door, and up the ramp into the starship. One last stop at L-4 for formal departure activities, before they undertook the first leg of their momentous journey.

#

This was Eber's first actual visit to the Mirs Complex. He was impressed. The Mirs Complex was amazingly well done, especially considering the state of Earth technology. Not that Earth technology was primitive by any means. Earth's link technology was a vast improvement over what Ectaris had developed, although the whole concept had gone down a different line aboard the *Arc*. In any case, Ari, Ginger, and Elke had created a link system aboard *Starchild* that was advanced even from Earth's point of view. Also, Eber didn't know whether his ancestors had developed a VASIMR engine, but it was pretty obvious that Earth had accomplished a lot with this propulsion technology.

Eber gazed out the window, standing next to Ginger, who had stepped close to Jon a moment earlier. Before meeting Ginger, Eber had never met a girl like her. He had quickly grasped the fluid relationships between the *Cassini II* crew members, and hoped fervently to spend some private time with Ginger during their wanderings. Just then, Ishtar joined them, inserting herself between Eber and Ginger, while slipping her arms around both of them. *What an incredible contrast*, Eber thought, *between these two women*. Nearly equal in height, one had almost transparent skin and long blond tresses that reached her waist, while the other was nearly blue-black with short kinky black hair. Both had startlingly green eyes that offset classical facial features, but Ishtar carried firm, full breasts, whereas Ginger sported a lithe boyish figure that required no support. As he turned to scan the remaining crew members, Eber noticed that Ginger slipped her arm around Ishtar's slender waist.

None of the four new female crew members quite met Ishtar's and Ginger's beauty standards, but then, who did? The four new women and three new men were brought aboard primarily for their special skills, scientific and otherwise, and only to a lesser extent, how they appeared – but it was a factor, because these fifteen people would very likely spend the remainder of their lives together. A comely appearance would certainly play an active role. Rod had made certain that the new crew members were comfortable in a fluid social venue, and that the women were not put off by feminine contact. Only time would tell, of course, and Eber looked forward to the interplay.

\#

The time finally arrived for the departing ceremonies. Jon counted envoys gathered in the L-4 Great Room from every nation represented on the crew. Since this was genuinely an event involving all of humanity, envoys from virtually every other nation were also present. Religious representatives from most of the world's major religions had gathered as well, with the notable exception of Islam. But the Raëlians stopped the show. Jon counted fifty or so white-robed believers, and to his considerable astonishment, a dozen or so envoys similarly dressed.

Jon pointed this out to Eber. "This would never have happened before you arrived..."

"Or before you found the *Arc*," Eber responded.

President Marc Bowles stepped to the podium in front of the crowd. Vesta followed, and stood beside him. Their backs were to the window, which was dominated by the *Starchild*, silhouetted against the Milky Way, outlined by its flashing beacons.

"The human race is embarking on a great adventure," the President intoned. "I have been privileged to play a small part in setting the stage for this momentous event. But you did not come here to listen to the American President pontificate." Laughter rippled through the crowd. "So, I give you Vesta, the Founder Matriarch and President of the Iapetus Federation." The President stepped to one side, leaving the podium to Vesta. Looking impossibly young for her sixty-eight years, Vesta stepped forward. Her classical face was without wrinkles, although her golden hair showed a few streaks of gray, and her svelte body appeared to carry virtually no excess fat.

Applause filled the Great Room, but it was drowned out by cheering Raëlians. Vesta smiled graciously, and lifted her hand, requesting silence.

"Thank you, Mr. President." Vesta spoke in Founder-Speak, which was automatically translated into English and amplified into the Great Room. Those few present who did not speak English used their personal Links to get the translation. "You are all my children, and I am blessed beyond words to be standing here, speaking with you." Another round of applause. "Fifteen of you are departing on a journey that will last ten years for those of us who stay behind. Two of my grandsons, Eber and Arpachshad, and two of my granddaughters by marriage, Ishtar and Rasu'eja, accompany you. Four of you I know well and have come to love, Ari Rawlston, my direct descendant, Captain Jon Stock, Ginger Steele, and Elke Gratz – I will miss you!

And to you seven, new to the crew, but already part of our wonderful family, I raise my hand in salute to your courage, to your fortitude, to your sense of adventure, and yes, to your daring-do! Your names will join those of the others whom I have already named in the permanent annals of humanity." Applause, lasting several minutes followed this comment.

"We will meet again right here in ten years," Vesta continued. "At that time we will review our procedures to make any necessary changes, so that *Starchild's* next rendezvous with our great-great grandchildren will be without a hitch. So, join me in wishing my children fair winds and following seas, and a safe harbor on their return."

#

What happened next was anticlimactic. Jon and his crew shuttled from the Mirs Ring to *Starchild*, and boarded without incident. Since everything in *Starchild* accelerated at the same rate as the starship itself, just as in *Merkavah*, the crew needed take no special precautions prior to launch.

Rod stood with Vesta watching the shuttle arrive at the starship, and then depart. Five minutes later, *Starchild* vanished.

#

High above the Ecliptic, the Resident brought *Starchild* to a stop. Then, on a prearranged vector along which there lay no stars, the Resident activated the hyper-V system for just under two subjective hours, halting once again for a few quick minutes to scan the empty region that lay five light years distant from the Sun. As they had expected, there was nothing to see, and at only five light years distant from the Solar System, even the background stars appeared the same as from Earth. Once again, the Resident activated the hyper-V. When *Starchild* came to a halt high above the Solar System Ecliptic nearly two subjective hours later, ten years had passed on Earth and the Iapetus Federation.

#

After the *Starchild* vanished so abruptly, Vesta returned to Iapetus with her delegation aboard *Merkavah*, and Rod returned to Earth in his capacity as Ambassador of the Iapetus Federation. Generally speaking, the political climate on Earth had remained relatively stable since the demise of the Persian Caliphate. True to his word, General

Suleiman dismantled the Caliphate governmental apparatus, disbanded the Caliphate army, and generally allowed the individual states that had been incorporated into the Caliphate to go their separate ways.

Rod followed this activity with interest. Although he was personally involved in the overthrow of the Caliphate, he was suspicious of the reports coming out of the former police state. He could not personally see a general with Sulieman's importance simply giving up and going away. Rod retained his friendship with the American President. On a visit with the President where they discussed Iapetus Federation affairs and the possibility that the Mirs Corporation would move L-4 into the Federation, the President informed him that American and Israeli intelligence had uncovered a shadow government possibly controlled by Suleiman. The President wanted the Federation to use its resources to ferret out any possible weapons caches.

Several months following the *Starchild's* departure, the Mirs Corporation that headed up the Russian consortium builders of the Mirs Complex petitioned the Iapetus Federation for membership. A few weeks later, the Lunar Complex followed suit. The Federation was unwilling to license the hyper-V technology. The Federation did build and lease a half-dozen ships capable of very rapid interplanetary travel, but lacking interstellar capability or the ability to travel through the Earth's atmosphere. That was an arrangement negotiated by Rod to ensure the continued viability of LLI and Galactic Ventures. Soon enough, the Launch Loop and the rocket would go the way of the buggy whip and wooden wheel spokes, but for now hyper-V flight was restricted to exoatmospheric ventures.

By the third year, an independent consortium headed by LLI placed the first permanent settlement on Mars, using craft especially modified by the Federation to move through the rarified Mars atmosphere. The Mars colony was immediately admitted into the Federation. This opened the doors to a rash of migration to the asteroid belt and several of the moons of Jupiter. Year five saw humans looking at the moons of Saturn and Jupiter for industrialization and settlement. By the middle of year six, several million people were scattered across the Solar System, linked together by their membership in the Iapetus Federation, and by the high-speed spacecraft the Federation supplied. The Mars colony constructed a massive Launch Loop in the eighth year, capable of handling tens of thousands of passengers daily, and millions of kilos of goods. By the middle of year nine, the Mars population passed the ten million mark, and there was serious talk of terraforming the planet.

And everywhere, the Raëlians dominated matters of faith.

#

On the designated day, delegations from all over the Solar System crowded into the newly expanded Great Room in the old Mirs Ring. Outside the grand expanse of transparent polymer, two additional slowly rotating ring complexes were visible. On a normal day, the lights of moving spacecraft could be seen virtually everywhere as spacecraft moved into and out of docks, transited to Earth orbit, and set course for Mars and the outer planets. On this day, however, at this time, nothing moved.

Rod Zakes and his entourage had arrived a day earlier, not as the Federation Ambassador to Earth but as the Federation President. Vesta had finally retired and moved Earthside to a plantation in the American State of Georgia, but she made the trip to L-4 just for the event. Michele showed up, but this time as the real First Lady of France, as she had married France's new President. Carmen was there, now part of the still active Indian Prime Minister's Cabinet, as Minister of Health. Noel arrived in his personal Founder spacecraft. He brought Chen, who had retired to private life, with him. Dmitri, now also fully retired, arrived in full dress uniform with a lovely Ukrainian lass on each arm. Unfortunately, Aram had disappeared during an avalanche in the Swiss Alps while skiing, but his brother, Asshur, hitched a ride with Noel. Lud and Shakbah had taken up residence in Mirs Three, the third torus constructed at the Mirs Complex, and showed up in their personal shuttle.

The new American President came from a different political persuasion than his predecessor, and had only a tepid interest in the *Starchild's* return. He sent a low-ranking delegation; but the former two-term President, Marc Bowles, was there, and received nearly as much holo coverage as his friend Rod. Scattered throughout the assembled delegations, white-robed Raëlians carried welcome banners and chanted prayers for the safe return of the space travelers.

At the appointed time, Federation President Zakes moved to the platform in front of the great window, motioned for Marc Bowles, the former American President, to join him, and they turned to peer outward. One moment the open space defined by the three ring complexes was empty; the next, the *Starchild* floated in serene silence 300 meters away from the window, outlined by her flashing beacons.

#

Hours later, after the Champaign toasts, after the formal speeches, after the tearful reunions, Rod sat down with his former Mars Expedition mate, and his friends, Ari, Eber, and Marc Bowles. He briefed them on the state of affairs on and off Earth. The returning space travelers reacted with surprise at the rapid expansion into space during their absence. They were appalled at the stance the world had taken to the emerging threat of General Sulieman's growing empire.

"Why hasn't America or the Federation stopped him?" Jon asked.

"It isn't that simple anymore," Rod answered, and nodded to Marc.

"When I left office and my successor took over, many things changed. America turned inward, and has practically given up its world leadership position. Interestingly the vacuum has been partially filled by the Iapetus Federation. My friend Rod, here, is a bit reluctant to take the bull by the horns, and do something about the emerging threat. It has to do, I guess, with the underlying principles upon which the Federation was founded."

"You mean like the American Constitution," Rod asked quietly.

"If Suleiman gets his hands on Founder technology, we're in for some tough going," the former president said. "It's not your problem, of course, but we wanted you to know."

"How long are you staying?" Rod asked.

"About a month," Jon answered as he accepted a wet kiss from Michele, who had just danced over to their little group.

#

The month was crammed with activities for each crew member. Rod had set things up so that the crew received maximum exposure in order to increase the odds that the *Starchild* would be remembered 184 years hence. Eighteen-hour days were the norm for everyone, and Jon had little private time with Rod. In one of the rare moments, he asked Rod about the state of advancement of Earth technology.

"We're learning a lot," Rod said. "Most of Ectarian science is not well understood even by the Founders who have remained behind. We are making genuine strides, however. I think we will have made some significant breakthroughs by the time you return again. Sorry I won't be here to greet you, but I promise that you will not be forgotten. We have taken every step we can imagine to ensure that your return will be anticipated, and that you will be welcomed.

Jon was not so confident, but he kept his thoughts to himself.

#

The month was over too quickly. When the departure day arrived, the Great Room in the old Mirs Ring was full to capacity. Around the world, people stopped what they were doing to participate vicariously through the worldwide holovision networks. There still was a general misunderstanding about what was about to happen, although the holovision talking heads did their best to explain the matter.

"Ten years ago," one aging popular science fiction author explained to his pretty blond host, "*Starchild* headed into interstellar space on a vector – in a direction – where there were no known close stars. The *Starchild's* velocity was ninety-nine-point-nine-nine-nine-nine-nine-nine-nine – that is ninety-nine-point followed by six nines – percent of the speed of light. The nature of their hyper-vee drive is such that it operates on everything in its field, the starship, the air inside the starship, the people, the cargo – everything. Consequently, they didn't have to ramp up to their final speed like a normal rocket would, or like the VASIMR propulsion system of the *Cassini II* did, one moment they were not moving, the next they were at their final velocity.

"According to the clocks inside the *Starchild*, they traveled in this direction for just under two hours – the actual time under hyper-vee was exactly one hour, fifty-seven minutes, thirty-one point six-six-four seconds. Then they stopped, looked around for a while – several hours, probably, and then they came back, again traveling at nearly light speed, another two-hour trip for them, subjectively. Because of the way relativistic travel works, for us back here, ten years passed between the time they left and when they returned. They actually traveled five light years away from our Solar System in those two hours of their time.

"So, when they returned a month ago, from their point of view, they had been gone for only four hours plus whatever time they spent out there looking around, while for us, ten years had passed."

"Oh my! I was still in high school," his host giggled. "It's like a miracle."

"More like physics," the writer responded with a smile.

The holovision signals were being beamed to the Iapetus Federation members scattered throughout the Solar System, but by the time most of them would receive the holocast, the star voyagers would have long been gone.

Rod set the tone for the farewell speeches by keeping his to less than two minutes. As a result, several of the delegates discarded their prepared remarks, reverting to short improvised comments that would be remembered long after their longer presentations would have been forgotten.

The original *Cassini II* crew gathered for final farewells. The members who had remained behind appeared visibly older than their starfaring shipmates. That did not seem to matter, however. Those remaining behind promised to keep the memory of their friends alive in their children and grandchildren, for as long as they were away.

Marc Bowles had immigrated to the Federation and was now the President of the Starchild Institute. At one point, he had expressed an interest in joining the *Starchild* crew, but his family prevailed upon him to stay behind, and he agreed to do so on the condition that they all join him on Iapetus. Marc promised his best efforts to ensure that the Starchild Institute remained a shining beacon that would continue to jumpstart Earth technology and to keep alive the living memory of the *Starchild* and her courageous crew.

Finally, clad in blue jumpsuits designed by the Starchild Institute, standing before the L-4 Great Room window with the *Starchild* hanging in the background, the fifteen starfarers waved to the assembled delegates and filed into the open airlock near the Great Room entrance. Moments later they entered the shuttle and zipped across the distance to the waiting starship.

The Resident reported a tight ship. Jon took one final headcount, and activated the controls that took *Starchild* high above the Ecliptic. "One last look," he said to the assembled crew, pointing to the display panels that showed the Solar System below them with the planetary orbits superimposed on the images. After several minutes Jon looked at Eber and nodded. Together they activated the hyper-V drive.

Epilog

Saeed Esmail gazed out over more than a thousand camouflaged tents pitched in a dry lake bed near the center of Rub' al-Khali in the Saudi Arabian desert. The lakebed was surrounded by shifting dunes, some towering nearly thirty meters. The early morning temperature was about ten degrees Celsius, but would reach nearly fifty by mid-afternoon. The *Cassini II* crew would not have recognized Saeed in his sackcloth robe and full-length flowing beard. Above him fluttered a light blue flag displaying a severed fist holding a dagger. A few centimeters from the wrist, the truncated arm flowed red blood. Outside every tent, two men stood at relaxed attention.

"*Allahu Akbar ... Allahu Akbar ... Allahu Akbar ... Allahu Akbar* (Allah is great... Allah is great... Allah is great... Allah is great...)." Saeed intoned the early call to prayer over the loud speakers surrounding the encampment. "*Ashhadu an la ilaha illa Allah* (I bear witness that there is no god except Allah)." Saeed repeated this. "*Ashadu anna Saeedan Rasool Allah* (I bear witness that Saeed is the messenger of God)." Saeed repeated the phrase, and smiled as his words echoed across the encampment. These words would have been blasphemy three years earlier, but Allah had revealed Himself to

Saeed in a special way, He reviewed the words of his revelation: *Let those fight in the way of Allah who sell the life of this world for the other. Whoso fighteth in the way of Allah, be he slain or be he victorious, on him we shall bestow a vast reward.*

As he finished the call to prayer, two thousand Jihadist warriors prostrated themselves on the still cold ground...as did Saeed.

After prayers, Saeed stood and entered his tent, where he took in a simple meal of cracked grain and water. Several minutes later as the air temperature began its climb, a soft whoosh brought him out of his tent. A strange craft had landed in the space before him. Like the *Merkavah*, it was saucer-shaped and deep black, so black, in fact, that it almost looked like a hole in the air. A hatch opened and a ramp extended to the ground. Moments later General Suleiman walked down the ramp and approached Saeed. At one-hundred-eighty-five centimeters, the General towered over Saeed's one-hundred-sixty-two. He bowed his head respectfully and gestured to the spacecraft.

"I bring you victory, Sahib!"

Saeed lifted his right arm into the air, and his robe fell back revealing his leather-cup-covered stump. "*Allahu Akbar!*" His call rang across the encampment.

Two thousand voices answered back, "Allahu Akbar! Allahu Akbar! Allahu Akbar!"

###

Other books by this author

Please visit your favorite eBook retailer to discover other eBooks by Robert G. Williscroft and your favorite online bookseller for their paper versions:

Current events:
The Chicken Little Agenda – Debunking "Experts'" Lies

Children's books:
The Starman Jones Series:
Starman Jones: A Relativity Birthday Present
Starman Jones Goes to the Dogs
    (scheduled for release in early 2015)

Novels:
Operation Ivy Bells – A novel of the Cold War
Slingshot
    (scheduled for release on August 21, 2015, at the International
    Space elevator Conference in Seattle)
The Iapetus Federation
    (scheduled for release in late 2015)

Connect with Robert G. Williscroft

I really appreciate you reading my book! Here are my social media coordinates:

Friend me on Facebook: *https://www.facebook.com/robert.williscroft*

Follow me on Twitter: *@RGWilliscroft*

Like my Amazon author page: *http://www.amazon.com/Robert-G.-Williscroft/e/B001JP52AS/ref=ntt_dp_epwbk_0*

Subscribe to my blog: *http://ThrawnRickle*.com

Connect on LinkedIn: *http://www.linkedin.com/in/argee/*

Visit my website: *http://www.robertwilliscroft.com*

Favorite my Smashwords author page: *https://www.smashwords.com/profile/view/RWilliscroft*

About the Author

At the Adventurers'
Club of Los Angeles

Dr. Robert G. Williscroft served twenty-three years in the U.S. Navy and the National Oceanic and Atmospheric Administration (NOAA). He commenced his service as an enlisted nuclear Submarine Sonar Technician in 1961, was selected for the Navy Enlisted Scientific Education Program in 1966, and graduated from University of Washington in Marine Physics and Meteorology in 1969. He returned to nuclear submarines as the Navy's first Poseidon Weapons Officer. Subsequently, he served as Navigator and Diving Officer on both catamaran mother vessels for the *Deep Submergence Rescue Vehicle*. Then he joined the Submarine Development Group One out of San Diego as the Officer-in-Charge of the Test Operations Group, conducting "deep-ocean surveillance and data acquisition" – which forms the basis for his Cold War novel *Operation Ivy Bells*.

In NOAA Dr. Williscroft directed diving operations throughout the Pacific and Atlantic. As a certified diving instructor for both the National Association of Underwater Instructors (NAUI) and the Multinational Diving Educators Association (MDEA), he taught over 3,000 individuals both basic and advanced SCUBA diving. He authored four diving books, developed the first NAUI drysuit course, developed advanced curricula for mixed gas and other specialized diving modes, and developed and taught a NAUI course on the Math and Physics of Advanced Diving. His doctoral dissertation for California Coast University, *A System for Protecting SCUBA Divers from the Hazards of Contaminated Water* was published by the U.S. Department of Commerce and distributed to Port Captains World-wide. He also served three shipboard years in the high Arctic conducting scientific baseline studies, and thirteen months at the geographic South Pole in charge of National Science Foundation atmospheric projects.

Dr. Williscroft has written extensively on terrorism and related

370

subjects. He is the author of a popular book on current events published by Pelican Publishing: *The Chicken Little Agenda – Debunking Experts' Lies*, now in its second edition as an eBook, and a new children's book series, *Starman Jones*, in collaboration with Dr. Frank Drake, world famous director of the Carl Sagan Center for the Study of Life in the Universe and the SETI Institute.

Dr. Williscroft's novel, *Slingshot*, is in preproduction. It is a prequel to *The Starchild Compact*, and tells the story of the construction of the World's first Space Launch Loop. He is currently working on *The Iapetus Federation*, a sequel to *The Starchild Compact*, that tells the story of the World falling under the rule of a planet-wide Islamic Caliphate, where the Founders establish the Iapetus Federation, a loose federation of free off-world communities that operates under an updated model based on the U.S. Constitution, and carries on the traditions of free enterprise and individual accountability throughout the Solar System.

Dr. Williscroft is an active member of the venerable Adventurers' Club of Los Angeles, where he is the Editor of the Club's monthly magazine. He lives in Centennial, Colorado, with his wife, Jill, whom he met upon his return from the South Pole in 1982 and finally married in 2010, and their twin high school boys.

CPSIA information can be obtained at www.ICGtesting.com
Printed in the USA
LVOW07*2243170515

438792LV00002B/3/P